24f you have any specific questions out how to protect yourself, you 1 7n always ask."

1 do, I will," she said, not sure she meant it. He s giving off all the vibes of a man who was spicious of her motives as it was. The last thing e needed to do was pique his curiosity.

o, I'll see you this afternoon in the intermediate c urse?" Mike glanced at her, his expression su esting he wasn't sure she'd say yes.

But he wanted her to say yes, she realized. The question was, why?

 s," she said finally. "I'll be there."

 an you stick around for the rest of the class?"

 get to be the damsel in distress?"

 He shook his head slowly. "The one thing I'm pretty sure you've never been, Charlie, is the amsel in distress."

THE GIRL WHO CRIED MURDER

BY
PAULA GRAVES

First Published in Great Britain 2016
By Mills & Boon, an imprint of HarperCollins*Publishers*
1 London Bridge Street, London, SE1 9GF

© 2016 Paula Graves

ISBN: 978-0-263-91922-6

46-1116

Our policy is to use papers that are natural, renewable and recyclable products and made from wood grown in sustainable forests. The logging and manufacturing processes conform to the legal environmental regulations of the country of origin.

Printed and bound in Spain
by CPI, Barcelona

Paula Graves, an Alabama native, wrote her first book at the age of six. A voracious reader, Paula loves books that pair tantalizing mystery with compelling romance. When she's not reading or writing, she works as a creative director for a Birmingham advertising agency and spends time with her family and friends. Paula invites readers to visit her website, www.paulagraves.com.

For Jenn and her mad brainstorming skills.

Chapter One

Mike Strong scanned the gymnasium for trouble, as he did every time he walked into a room. Fifteen years in the Marine Corps, in war zones from Africa to Central Asia, had taught him the wisdom of being alert and being prepared. All that training hadn't gone out the window when he'd left the Marines for life as a security consultant.

Especially at a company like Campbell Cove Security Services, where preparation for any threat was the company's mission statement.

The new 6:00 a.m. class was amateur hour—otherwise unschooled civilians coming in for an hour of self-defense and situational awareness training before heading off to their jobs at the factory or the grocery store or the local burger joint. In all likelihood, none of them would ever have to draw on their training in any meaningful way.

But all it took was once.

His later classes were more advanced, designed to give law enforcement officers and others with previous defense training new tactics to deal with the ever more complicated task of defending the US homeland. He'd come into this job thinking those classes would be more challenging.

But if the newest arrival was any indication, he might have been wrong about that.

She was tall, red-haired, pretty in a girl-next-door sort of way. Pert nose, a scattering of freckles in her pale complexion, big hazel-green eyes darting around the room with the same "looking for trouble" alertness he'd displayed a moment earlier. Beneath her loose-fitting T-shirt and snug-fitting yoga pants, she appeared lean and toned. A hint of coltish energy vibrated through her as she began a series of muscle stretches while her eyes continued their scan of the room.

What was she afraid of? And why did she expect to find it here?

Trying to ignore his sudden surge of adrenaline, he started with roll call, putting names to faces. There were only twelve students in the early-morning class, eight men and four women. The redhead, Charlie Winters, was the youngest of the group. The fittest, too.

Most of the others appeared to be fairly average citizens—slightly overweight, on the soft side both mentally and physically. Nice, good-hearted, but spoiled by living in a prosperous, free country where, until recent years, the idea of being the target of ruthless, fanatical predators had seemed as likely as winning the lottery.

"Welcome to Campbell Cove Academy's Basics of Self-Defense class," he said aloud, quieting down the murmurs of conversation in the group. "Let's get started."

He followed Charlie Winters's earlier example and took the group through a series of stretching exercises. "I want you to get in the habit of doing these exercises every day when you get up," he told them. "Because you won't have time to do it when danger arises."

"How will stretching help us if some guy blows himself up in front of us?" one of the men grumbled as he winced his way through a set of triceps stretches. Mike searched his memory and came up with the name to go with the face. Clyde Morris.

"It won't, Clyde," he answered bluntly. "But it might help give you the strength and mobility to get the hell out of Dodge before your terrorist can trigger the detonator."

He didn't miss the quirk of Charlie Winters's eyebrows.

Did she disagree? Or did she have an agenda here that had nothing to do with preparing for terrorist threats?

Nothing wrong with that. There were plenty of reasons in a free society for a person to be ready for action.

But he found himself watching Charlie closely as they finished their stretches and he settled them on the mats scattered around the gymnasium floor. "Here's the thing you need to know about defending yourselves. Nothing I teach you here is a guarantee that you'll come out of a confrontation alive. So the first rule of self-defense is to avoid confrontations."

"That's heroic," Clyde Morris muttered.

"This class isn't about making heroes out of you. It's about keeping you alive so you can report trouble to people who have the training and weapons to deal with the situation. And then return home alive and well to the people who love you."

He let his gaze wander back to Charlie Winters's face as he spoke. Her gaze held his until the last sentence, when her brow furrowed and her lips took a slight downward quirk as she lowered her gaze to her lap, where her restless fingers twined and released, then twined again.

Hmm, he thought, but he didn't let his curiosity distract him further.

"I guess I should take a step backward here," he said. "Because there's actually something that comes before avoiding confrontation, and that's staying alert. Show of hands—how many of you have cell phones?"

Every person raised a hand.

"How many of you check your cell phone while walking down the street or entering a building? What about when you're riding in an elevator?"

All the hands went up again.

"That's what I'm talking about," he said. "How can you be alert to your surroundings if your face is buried in your phone?"

The hands crept down, the students exchanging sheepish looks.

"Look, we're fortunate to live in the time we do. Technology can be a priceless tool in a crisis. Photographs and videos of incidents can be invaluable to investigators. Cell phones can bring help even when you're trapped and isolated. You can download apps that turn your phone into a flashlight. Your phone's signal can be used to find you when you're lost."

"Thank goodness. I was afraid you were going to tell us we had to lose our iPhones," one of the students joked.

"No, but I *am* suggesting you start thinking of it as a tool in your arsenal rather than a toy to distract and entertain you."

Again, he couldn't seem to stop his gaze from sliding toward Charlie's face. She met his gaze with solemn eyes, but her expression gave nothing else away. Still, he had a feeling that most of what he was telling the class were things she already knew.

So what was she doing here, taking this class?

Swallowing his frustration, he pushed to his feet and retrieved the rolling chalkboard he'd borrowed from one of the other instructors. "So, revised rule one—stay alert." He jotted the words on the board. "And now, let's talk about avoiding confrontations."

MIKE DISMISSED CLASS at seven. One or two students lingered, asking questions about some of the points he'd covered in class or what points he'd be covering in their class two days later. He answered succinctly, hiding his impatience. But it was with relief that the last student left and he hurried to his small office off the gymnasium. It was little more than a ten-by-ten box, but it had a desk, a phone and a window looking out on the parking lot.

He caught sight of Charlie Winters walking across the wet parking lot. She'd donned a well-worn leather jacket over her T-shirt and baggy sweatpants over her yoga pants, but there was no way to miss her dark red hair dancing in the cold wind blowing down the mountain or the coltish energy propelling her rapidly across the parking lot.

She stopped behind a small blue Toyota that had seen better days. But she didn't get into the car immediately. First, she walked all the way around the vehicle, examining the tires, peering through the windows, even dropping to the ground on her back and looking beneath the chassis.

Finally, she seemed to be satisfied by whatever she saw—or didn't see—and pushed back to her feet, dusting herself off before she got in the Toyota and started the engine.

As she drove away, Mike turned from the window, picked up the phone on the desk and punched in Maddox Heller's number. Heller answered on the second ring.

"It's Strong," Mike said. "You said to let you know if I had any concerns about the new class."

"And you do?"

He thought about it for a moment. "*Concern* may be too strong a word. At this point, I'd call it…curiosity."

"Close enough," Heller said. "So, you want a background check on someone?"

"Yes," Mike said after another moment of thought. "I do."

CHARLIE KEPT AN eye on the rearview mirror as she drove home as fast as she dared. She'd like to get a shower before her early-morning phone conference, and she was already going to be cutting it close. Could she really keep this up two days a week, given her boss's delight in scheduling early meetings?

Besides, after this morning's class, she wasn't even sure it was worth her time. All that stretching and they didn't do anything but go over the basic tenets of self-defense. On a chalkboard. Hell, she'd already covered those basics with a one-hour search of the internet. She didn't need an academic journey through the philosophy of protecting oneself.

She needed practical tools, damn it. Now. And she didn't want to spend the next few weeks twiddling her thumbs until Mr. Big Buff Badass deigned to detach himself from his chalkboard and teach them something they could actually use.

Channeling her frustration into her foot on the accelerator, she made it back to her little rental house on Sycamore Road with almost a half hour to spare. As had become habit, she waited at the front door for a few seconds, just listening.

There was a faint thump coming from inside, but she had two cats. Thumps didn't exactly come as a surprise.

Taking a deep breath, she tried the door. Still locked. That was a good sign, wasn't it?

She unlocked the door and entered as quietly as she could, standing just inside the door and listening again.

There was a soft *prrrrup* sound as His Highness, her slightly cross-eyed Siamese rescue cat, slinked into the living room to greet her. He gave her a quizzical look before rubbing his body against her legs.

"Did you hold down the fort for me like I asked?" She bent to scratch his ears, still looking around for any sign of intrusion. But everything was exactly as she'd left it, as far as she could tell.

Maybe she was being paranoid. She couldn't actually prove that someone had been following her, could she?

There hadn't been a particular incident, just a slowly growing sense that she was being watched. But even that sensation had coincided with the first of the dreams, which meant maybe she was imagining it.

That could be possible, couldn't it?

She went from room to room, checking for any sign of an intruder. In her office, her other cat, Nellie, watched warily from her perch atop the bookshelf by her desk. If there had been an intruder, the nervous tortoiseshell cat would still be hidden under Charlie's bed. So, nobody had been in the house since she left that morning.

Beginning to relax, she took a quick shower and changed the litter box before she settled at her computer and joined the office conference call.

Because she worked for a government contractor, Ordnance Solutions, most of her conference calls consisted of a whole lot of officious blather and only a few nuggets of important information. This call was no different. But she wrote down those notes with admirable conscientiousness, if she did say so herself, especially with His Highness sitting on her desk and methodically knocking every loose piece of office equipment onto the floor.

She hammered out the project her bosses had given her during the conference call, a page-one revision of the latest operational protocols for disposal of obsolete ordnance from a recent spate of military base closures. Most of the changes had come after a close reading by the company's technical experts. Charlie was used to working her way through multiple revisions, especially if the experts couldn't come to an agreement on specific protocols.

Which happened several times a project.

Nellie, the cockeyed tortie, ventured into her office and hopped onto the chair next to her desk. She let Charlie give her a couple of ear scratches before contorting into a knot to start cleaning herself.

"Am I going crazy, Nellie?" Charlie asked.

Nellie angled one green eye at her before returning to her wash.

The problem was, Charlie didn't have a sounding board. Her family was a disaster—her father had died in a mining accident nearly twenty years ago, and her mother had moved to Arkansas with her latest husband a couple of years back. Two brothers in jail, two up in South Dakota trying to take advantage of the shale oil boom while it lasted, and her only sister had moved to California, where she was dancing at a club in Encino while waiting for her big break.

None of them were really bad people, not even the two in jail. But none of them understood Charlie and her dreams. Never had, never would.

And they sure as hell wouldn't understand why she had suddenly decided to dig up decade-old bones.

And as for friends? Well, she'd turned self-imposed isolation into an art form.

She attached the revised ordnance disposal protocols

to an email and sent it off to her supervisor, then checked her email for any other assignments that might have come through while she was working on the changes. The inbox was empty of anything besides unsolicited advertisements. She dumped those messages into the trash folder.

Then she opened her word processor program and took a deep breath.

It was now or never. If she was going to give up on the quest, this was the time. Before she made another trip to Campbell Cove Security Services and spent another dime on listening to Mr. Big Buff Badass lecture her on the importance of looking both ways before she crossed the street.

Pinching her lower lip between her teeth, she opened a new file, the cursor blinking on the blank page.

Settling her trembling hands on the keyboard, she began to type.

Two days before Christmas, nearly ten years ago, my friend Alice Bearden died. The police said it was an accident. Her parents believe the same. She had been drinking that night, cocktails aptly named Trouble Makers. Strawberries and cucumbers muddled and shaken with vodka, a French aperitif called Bonal, lime juice and simple syrup. I looked up the recipe on the internet later.

I drank light beer. Just the one, as far as I remember. And that's the problem. For a long time, those three sips of beer were all I remembered about the night Alice died.

Then, a few weeks ago, the nightmares started.

I tried to ignore them. I tried to tell myself that they were just symptoms of the stress I've been under working this new job.

But that doesn't explain some of the images I see in my head when I close my eyes to sleep. It doesn't explain why I hear Alice whispering in my ear while the world is black around me.

"I'm sorry, Charlie," she whispers. "But I have to do the rest of this by myself."

What did she mean? What was she doing?

It was supposed to be a girls' night out, a chance to let down our hair before our last semester of high school sent us on a headlong hurdle toward college and responsibility. She was Ivy League bound. I'd earned a scholarship to James Mercer College, ten minutes from home.

I guess, in a way, it was also supposed to be the beginning of our big goodbye. We swore we'd keep in touch. But we all know how best intentions go.

I should have known Alice was up to something. She always was. She'd lived a charmed life—beautiful, sweet, the apple of her very wealthy daddy's eye. She was heading for Harvard, had her life planned out. Harvard for undergrad, Yale Law, then an exciting career in the FBI.

She wanted to be a detective. And for a golden girl like Alice Bearden, the local police force would never do.

She had been full of anticipation that night. Almost jittery with it. We'd chosen a place where nobody knew who we were. We tried out the fake IDs Alice had procured from somewhere—"Don't ask, Charlie," she'd said with that infectious grin that could make me lose my head and follow her into all sorts of scrapes.

For a brief, exciting moment, I felt as if my life was finally going to start.

And then, nothing. No thoughts. Almost no memories. Just that whisper of Alice's voice in my ear, and the haunting sensation that there was something I knew about that night that I just couldn't remember.

I tried to talk to Mr. Bearden a few days ago. I called his office, left my name, told him it was about Alice.

He never called me back.

But the very next day, I had a strong sensation of being watched.

MIKE WRAPPED UP his third training session of the day, this time an internal refresher course for new recruits to the agency, around five that afternoon. He headed for the showers, washed off the day's sweat and changed into jeans and a long-sleeved polo. Civvies, he thought with a quirk of his lips that wasn't quite a smile. Because the thought of being a civilian again wasn't exactly a cause for rejoicing.

He'd planned on a career in the Marine Corps. Put in thirty or forty years or more, climbing the ranks, then retire while he was still young enough to enjoy it.

Things hadn't gone the way he planned.

There was a message light on his office phone. Maddox Heller's deep drawl on his voice mail. "Stop by my office on your way out. I may have something for you."

He crossed the breezeway between the gym and the main office building, shivering as the frigid wind bit at every exposed inch of his skin. He'd experienced much colder temperatures, but there was something about the damp mountain air that chilled a man to the bone.

Heller was on the phone when Mike stuck his head into the office. Heller waved him in, gesturing toward one of the two chairs that sat in front of his desk.

Mike sat, enjoying the comforting warmth of the place. And not just the heat pouring through the vents. There was a personal warmth in the space, despite its masculine simplicity. A scattering of photos that took up most of the empty surfaces in the office, from Heller's broad walnut desk to the low credenza against the wall. Family photos of Heller's pretty wife, Iris, and his two ridiculously cute kids, Daisy and Jacob.

Even leathernecks could be tamed, it seemed.

Maddox hung up the phone and shot Mike a look of apology. "Sorry. Daisy won a spelling bee today and had to spell all the words for me."

Mike smiled. "How far the mighty warrior has fallen."

Heller just grinned as he picked up a folder lying in front of him. "One day it'll be you, and then you'll figure it out yourself."

"Figure out what?" he asked, taking the folder Heller handed him.

"That family just makes you stronger." Heller nodded at the folder. "Take a look at what our background check division came up with."

"That was quick." Mike opened the folder. Staring up at him was an eight-by-ten glossy photo of a dark-haired young woman. Teenager, he amended after a closer look. Sophisticated looking, but definitely young. She didn't look familiar. "This isn't the woman from my class."

"I know. Her name was Alice Bearden."

Mike looked up sharply. "Was?"

"She died about ten years ago. Two days before Christmas in a hit-and-run accident. The driver was never found."

Mike grimaced. So young. And so close to Christmas. "Bearden," he said. "Any relation to that Bearden guy whose face is plastered on every other billboard from here to Paducah?"

"Craig Bearden. Candidate for US Senate." Heller nodded toward the folder in Mike's lap. "Keep reading."

Mike flipped through the rest of the documents in the file. They were mostly printouts of online newspaper articles about the accident and a few stories about Craig Bearden's run for the Senate. "Bearden turned his daughter's death into a political platform. Charming."

"His eighteen-year-old daughter obtained a fake ID so she could purchase alcohol in a bar. The bartender may have been fooled by the fake ID, but that doesn't excuse him from serving so much alcohol she was apparently too drunk to walk straight. And maybe her inebriation was what led her to wander into the street in front of a moving vehicle, but whoever hit her didn't stop to call for help."

"And he's now crusading against what exactly?"

"All of the above? The bartender was never charged, and the bar apparently still exists today, so I guess if he sued, he lost. Maybe this is his way of feeling he got some sort of justice for his daughter."

Mike looked at the photo of Alice Bearden again. A tragedy that her life was snuffed out, certainly. But he hadn't asked Heller to look into Alice Bearden's background.

"What does this have to do with Charlie Winters?" he asked.

"Read the final page."

Mike scanned the last page. It was earliest of the articles on the accident, he realized. The dateline was December 26, three days after the accident. He scanned the article, stopping short at the fourth paragraph.

Miss Bearden was last seen at the Headhunter Bar on Middleburg Road close to midnight, accompanied by another teenager, Charlotte Winters of Bagwell.

"Charlie Winters was with Alice when she died?"

"That seems to be the big question," Heller answered. "Nobody seems to know what happened between the time they left the bar and when Alice's body was found in the middle of the road a couple of hours later."

Mike's gaze narrowed. "Charlie refused to talk?"

"Worse," Heller answered. "I talked to the lead investigator interviewed in the article. He's still with the county sheriff's department and remembers the case well. According to him, Charlotte Winters claims to have no memory of leaving the bar at all. As far as she's concerned, almost the whole night is one big blank."

"And what does he think?"

"He thinks Charlie Winters might have gotten away with murder."

Chapter Two

Making four copies was overkill, wasn't it?

Charlie looked at the flash drive buried at the bottom of the gym bag's inner pocket. Were four copies a sign of paranoia?

"I wonder if Mike is married." The voice was female, conspiratorial and close by.

Charlie looked up to find one of her fellow students applying lipstick using a small compact mirror. Midthirties, decent shape, softly pretty. Kim, Charlie thought, matching the name from Monday's roll call to the face. She'd tried to memorize all the names and faces from the class. Partly as a game to relieve her boredom, but partly because the knowledge might come in handy someday.

Like during the zombie apocalypse?

Oh man. She *was* paranoid, wasn't she?

"I didn't expect him to be so hot," Kim said, punctuating the statement with the snap of her compact closing. "I didn't see a ring."

"Maybe he doesn't like to wear it when he's engaging in self-defense activities." Charlie grimaced at her lame response. Kim was clearly trying to be friendly, seeking to engage Charlie with a topic they might both find intriguing. And her response was to cut her off at the knees?

"Maybe." Kim's smile faded. "Probably. A guy that good-looking is either married by this age or gay."

"Or commitment-phobic," Charlie added.

"Honey, that can sometimes be a feature, not a bug." Kim finger-combed her honey-blond hair and smiled. "You ready?"

"Sure." Charlie walked with Kim out of the locker room into the gymnasium, where about half the number of their Monday classmates were already waiting. Today, the gymnasium floor was covered nearly wall-to-wall with padded floor mats. Apparently they were going to do more than just take notes today.

Thank goodness.

Mike Strong stood against the front wall, flipping through papers secured on a clipboard, his brow furrowed with concentration. The light slanting in from the east-facing windows bathed him in golden warmth.

Beside Charlie, Kim released a gusty sigh. "Lord have mercy."

Mike put the clipboard on the floor beside him and looked up at the students gathering in front of him. His gaze settled on Charlie for a moment, and he smiled at her. To her surprise, her stomach turned an unexpected flip.

"Oh, wow," Kim murmured. "Probably not gay, then."

"This is crazy," Charlie muttered, as much to herself as to Kim.

Mike checked his watch, the movement flexing his biceps and sending her stomach on another tumble. "It's time to get started. Everybody remember the stretches?"

Charlie's heart was beating far more quickly than her exertion level warranted. She forced herself to keep her gaze averted from Mike Strong's lean body and focused instead on maximizing the flex of her muscles.

But when she looked up again, Mike was walking slowly through the small clump of students, observing their efforts. He stopped in front of her and crouched, his voice lowering to a rumble. "You've done this before."

"High school gym," she answered, trying not to meet his gaze.

"Not college?"

Her gaze flicked up despite her intentions. "College, too. Core requirement."

His lips curved. "So I hear."

"You didn't have phys ed classes in college?"

"I went straight from high school to Parris Island," he said with a smile. "Lots and lots of phys ed, you could say."

She dropped her gaze again, but it was too late. Now she was picturing him in fatigues, out in the hot South Carolina sun, sweat gleaming on his sculpted muscles and darkening the front of his olive drab T-shirt...

When she risked another peek, he'd moved on, walking from student to student, offering suggestions to improve their stretches. She let go of her breath, realizing her exhalation sounded suspiciously like the gusty sigh Kim had released earlier as they entered the gym.

"All right," Mike said a few minutes later, "I'm going to pair you up and we're going to talk about some of the basic escape moves. This really shouldn't be the first thing we do, but I can tell by the low attendance today that maybe you want a little less talk and a lot more action."

A few laughs greeted Mike's words, along with a few murmurs of agreement. Then everybody fell silent, watching with interest as Mike paired them up.

He left Charlie for last. There was nobody left to pair

up with, she realized with a flutter of dismay. It was fifth-grade kickball all over again.

"You're with me," Mike said bluntly, nodding toward the front of the pack. She followed him with reluctance, revising her earlier thought. It wasn't kickball. It was Public Speaking 101, and it was Charlie's turn at the front of the class.

Heat flooded her cheeks, no doubt turning her pale skin bright red. Her hands trembled so hard she shoved them in the pockets of her sweatpants and tried not to meet the gaze of anyone else in the gym.

"If you've read any books or watched any movies or TV shows, you've probably heard of the vulnerable spots on an assailant and some of the ways to target them. Knee to the groin. Foot to the instep or the knee. Fingers to the eyes or heel of the hand to the cartilage of the nose." There were soft groans at the images those words invoked. "Those are all vulnerable targets on an attacker, true. But how easy is it for a small person to do damage to a larger person, even targeting those areas? That's what we're going to experiment with today."

Charlie realized he'd paired people up by size, small with large. At the moment, most of the larger people in the pairings were looking around with alarm.

Mike nodded toward the side of the room, where a man stood in the doorway next to what looked like a large laundry bin. "This is Eric Brannon. He's a doctor. I thought y'all might want him to stick around for this."

Eric grinned. Charlie's classmates didn't.

"He's also got some equipment to hand out."

Eric reached into the bin and pulled out something that looked like a cross between a life jacket and a catcher's chest guard. He handed it to the man standing closest to him and continued through the other students, passing out padding to the larger of each pair.

Eric stopped before giving anything to Mike. Charlie looked up at the instructor, one eyebrow arched.

Mike grinned back at her, then turned to the class. "We're going to start with the first thing you need to know how to deal with—someone grabbing you."

Without warning, he reached out and wrapped his arm around Charlie's shoulders, pulling her back hard against his chest.

She gasped, caught entirely flat-footed, and began struggling on instinct. His grip tightened and he lifted her off her feet.

Her vision seemed to darken around the edges, sight becoming a single pinpoint of light as anger fought with panic.

Damn it, Charlie. Do something!

She was back in a darkened alley outside the Head-hunter Bar. The world was tilted and spinning, like she was stuck on a merry-go-round twirling at an impossible rate of speed. She couldn't breathe. Couldn't think.

She kicked her heel backward, hitting his shin with a glancing blow that didn't even elicit a grunt. His grip tightened. Clawing at his rock-hard arms with her fingers had no effect at all. She stamped her heel down on his foot, but his boots were hard and her foot glanced off, which was probably the only thing that saved her from a broken foot of her own.

I'm sorry, Charlie, but I have to do the rest of this by myself. Alice's whispered words rang in her ears, clarity in a world of insanity.

She stopped struggling, and the grip on her shoulders loosened. The world seeped back in brilliant light and color, and panic won over anger. She dropped her whole weight downward, slipping from his grip, and rolled as hard as she could into his knee. The move sent Mike sprawling to the mat, and Charlie scrambled to her feet and ran for the door, her whole body rattling with the need to escape at all costs.

Eric Brannon caught her arm, pulling her to a jerky halt. She was about to fight when she realized he was smiling at her.

She made herself stop running. It was just a class. Just a game, really.

No dark alley. No woozy world. No whispers in her ear.

"Nice job," Eric murmured, his blue eyes bright with amusement.

She looked at Mike, who was back on his feet. Unlike Eric, he wasn't smiling. Instead, he was watching her with a knowing wariness that made her stomach twist. After a moment, however, his expression cleared and he motioned her over. "That was actually a pretty good example of one of the things we're going to talk about today," he said as she walked with reluctance to his side. "What Charlie did was to use deception to change her circumstances. The more she struggled, the tighter I held her. When she seemed to give up, to stop struggling, I loosened my grip. It's a natural response—assailants can tire of the struggle as well, even if they're considerably stronger and larger than their targets."

Charlie slanted him a skeptical look. He didn't look as if he'd tired at all. She was pretty sure he could have held her in check a whole lot longer than he had.

He met her gaze, his smile seemingly warm. But he was smiling only with his mouth. His green eyes were narrowed and still wary.

"The other thing she did is what I'd like to address

today," he added. "As soon as she was in the position to do so, Charlie bowled me over. She used her full weight to catch me off balance and send me to the ground. And yet I outweigh her by at least eighty pounds. Probably more. Which goes to show, even if your assailant is larger than you, you have more leverage than you think."

Charlie wrapped her arms around her, feeling exposed and vulnerable. She edged back toward the wall as Mike Strong walked the rest of the students through an attacker's vulnerable points and how to strike back at those areas more effectively.

"Put your weight into everything you do. If you can hurt them, you're that much closer to knocking them down and getting away. Now, I want the bigger partners to suit up and play the part of the attacker. Smaller partners, go after the pressure points. For now, avoid the nose and face. What I want you to practice is putting your full weight into everything you do. Turn your body into a weapon."

The rest of the group got started. There was a lot of noise, most of it self-conscious laughter. Charlie watched the others for a moment, until she felt Mike's gaze on her.

She looked at him. He was studying her as if she were some scientific experiment on display. Her cheeks, which had finally started to cool off, went hot again.

She half expected him to ask her what the hell had happened when he grabbed her. Surely he'd seen that her panic had been real.

But when he spoke, he asked, "Have you had any self-defense training before?"

"I was a skinny freckled redhead in public school," she answered, going for levity. "I had twelve years of self-defense training."

He smiled faintly. "Formal training?"

"I've read a lot. Watched a lot of videos on the 'net."

"So you've done the mental work. Just not the physical."

"Something like that."

"I have an intermediate class that meets Tuesday and Thursday afternoons at four. Do you think you could make that class?"

He thought she should go into an intermediate class? Why? She hadn't exactly covered herself in glory so far.

"I have a flexible work schedule," she said finally, wondering just what an intermediate self-defense class would entail. "But I'm really just a beginner," she added quickly. "I just got lucky earlier."

"That wasn't luck. That was your instincts kicking in. You've internalized the lessons in your head. Now your body needs to learn how to do the things your brain has already processed. But there's no need for you to start from the beginning when you'd be learning a lot more in an advanced class."

Charlie narrowed her eyes, not sure she trusted Mike Strong's motives for wanting to move her out of the beginner class. She'd seen the wariness in his eyes earlier. And even now, there was a hint of tension in his jaw when he spoke, as if he was trying to hide his real thoughts.

"You think I could keep up?" she asked.

"I think so. If you feel differently after a class or two, you can always come back to this class."

"And is self-defense the only thing you learn in the intermediate class?" she asked before she thought the question through.

His brow creased. "What else would you be looking to learn?"

She cleared her throat. "I just meant—there's more

to protecting yourself than just being able to get out of physical situations, isn't there?"

Mike looked at her for a long moment, then jerked his attention away, his gaze shifting across the gymnasium, as if he'd just remembered that he was supposed to be supervising the class. "Darryl, the padding doesn't mean you can be a brute. This is our first time out. Try not to break Melanie's neck, how about it?"

Charlie watched the rest of the class giggle and grunt their way through the exercises while Mike went through the group, offering suggestions and gentle correction. Right about now, she'd give anything to be one of them, one of the group instead of standing here like a flagpole in the middle of the desert, visible from every direction.

Mike finally wandered back to where she stood. "The intermediate class is mainly about physical self-defense," he finally answered in response to her earlier question. "But if you have any specific questions about how to protect yourself, you can always ask."

"If I do, I will," she said, not sure she meant it. He was giving off all the vibes of a man who was suspicious of her motives, and considering her little freak-out a few minutes ago, she couldn't really blame him.

The last thing she needed to do was pique his curiosity.

"So, I'll see you tomorrow afternoon in the intermediate course?" Mike glanced at her, his expression suggesting he wasn't sure she'd say yes.

But he wanted her to say yes, she realized.

The question was, why?

"Yes," she said finally. "I'll be there."

"Can you stick around for the rest of the class?"

The twinkle in his eyes gave her pause, but she made herself smile. "Should I say no?"

He laughed. "There are still a few moves I need to show the class. And since you're here…"

"I get to be the damsel in distress?"

He shook his head slowly. "The one thing I'm pretty sure you've never been, Charlie, is the damsel in distress."

"So, what do you think?"

Mike turned his head away from the window, dragging his gaze from Charlie's little blue Toyota. She hadn't emerged from the gymnasium yet; when he'd left, she'd been talking to a couple of the other students.

He met Maddox Heller's gaze. "I don't know. She's hard to read."

"In what way?"

He thought about her reaction to being called to the front of the class that morning. "She can be shy. And then turn around and be assertive. But there was something that happened today—I'm not sure how to describe it."

"Give it a shot."

"I was demonstrating how quickly an assailant could strike. Partly as an example, but also because I wanted to know how she'd react. I expected her to fight."

"And she didn't?"

"No, she fought. But there was something about the way she did it. It was as if she was somewhere else. Seeing something else."

Heller's expression was thoughtful. "Post-traumatic stress?"

"Maybe. She was able to keep herself together enough to escape my grasp, though. And she did it pretty well. Bowled me over."

"There wasn't a lot in the background check other than what I told you. The sheriff's department never liked her story that she could remember nothing. But I don't know if that's because of who she is. Or, more to the point, who her family is."

"Who are they?"

"The Winters, according to my source with the local law, are one of those families that just spell trouble. Two of her brothers are in jail. Daddy died in a mining accident when they were young, and apparently Mama tried and failed to replace him with a series of men who all brought their own brand of trouble to the family."

"Does Charlie have a record?"

"Nothing as an adult. If she had any record as a juvenile, it's sealed."

"I've moved her up to my intermediate class," Mike said. "The beginner class will just bore her. She might quit."

"And you don't want that?"

He didn't. "Something strange is going on with that woman. I don't know what yet. But I think it's in our interests to find out what it is."

He turned back to the window. Charlie was out there now, unlocking the driver's door of the Toyota. She slid behind the steering wheel and pulled out of the parking lot, heading onto Poplar Road.

Mike's gaze started to follow the car up the road, but something in the parking space she'd just vacated snagged his attention. There was a wet spot on the pavement beneath where the Toyota had been parked.

Right about the place where her brake line should be.

He muttered a curse and strode past Heller, already running as he hit the exit. He skidded to a stop at the empty parking place and crouched to look at the fluid on the ground.

Definitely brake fluid.

He gazed at the road, spotting the Corolla just as it started the climb up the mountain.

Without a pause for thought, he pulled his keys from his pocket and sprinted toward his truck.

THE TOYOTA HAD to be on its last legs. Fifteen years old, well-used before she'd ever bought it, the little blue Corolla had put up with a lot in the five years since she'd bought it with cash from a small used car lot over in Mercerville. The heating and air were starting to falter— never good in the dead of winter or the dog days of summer. And as she crested the mountain and started down the other side, she realized her brakes felt unresponsive, spongy beneath her foot.

That was not good.

She dropped the Corolla to a lower gear, and the vehicle's speed slowed, but only a little. She thought about putting it in Neutral, but in the back of her mind, she had a fuzzy memory that doing so wasn't the answer.

Damn. Why hadn't she read that road safety brochure her insurance company had sent out last month?

Fortunately, there wasn't much in the way of traffic on the two-lane road, but she was fast approaching a four-way stop at the bottom of the hill. There were a handful of cars clustered at the intersection, far enough away now that they looked more like specks than vehicles.

But that was changing quickly.

She dropped to an even lower gear and gave her brakes a few quick, desperate pumps. They were entirely unresponsive now.

Don't panic don't panic don't panic...

The roar of an engine approaching behind her took her eyes off the road to check the rearview mirror. There was a large pickup truck coming up fast behind her. Suddenly, it swung left, around her, and whipped into the lane in front of her.

What the hell was that idiot doing?

The truck slowed as it moved in front of her, and on instinct, she stamped on her useless brakes. The front of her car bumped hard into the back bumper of the truck, bounced and hit a second time. A third time, then a fourth, each bounce less jarring until her front bumper settled against the back of the truck.

The pickup slowed to a stop, bringing her Corolla to a stop, as well. She turned on her hazard lights and put her car in Park, setting the parking brake to make sure it didn't move any farther downhill.

The driver's door of the pickup opened, and a tall, lean-muscled figure got out and turned to face her with a grim smile.

Mike Strong.

What the hell was going on?

Chapter Three

"The brake line's been cut." Bill Hardy, the mechanic at Mercerville Motors, who'd taken a look at the Corolla's brake system, showed Charlie the laceration in the line.

Charlie stared at it in horrified fascination, trying not to relive those scary moments as she'd struggled to bring her car under control on the downhill stretch of Poplar Road. If Mike Strong hadn't pulled his driving trick to bring her car to a stop—

Don't think about it.

"How could that have happened?" she asked Bill.

"Well, maybe you could have kicked up a sharp rock or a piece of metal in the road," Bill said doubtfully.

"But you don't think so?"

"Honestly, if I didn't know better, I'd think this was a deliberate cut." He gave her a sidelong look. "You haven't made any enemies lately, have you, Charlie?"

Had she?

She glanced toward the tiny waiting area, where Mike Strong sat in one of the steel-and-plastic chairs pushed up against the wall across from the vending machine. She'd told him he needn't wait for her, but he'd insisted. And given that he'd more or less saved her life this morning, she could hardly quibble.

"No, no new enemies," she said.

Except, she supposed, whoever had killed Alice.

She turned her head to look at Mike again and found him standing in the open doorway between the waiting area and the garage. "Any news?"

"Brake line's cut," Bill said shortly before Charlie could stop him.

Mike's eyebrows came together over his nose. "On purpose?"

"Hard to say with certainty, but it's possible." Bill looked at Charlie. "What do you want me to do? You've got a little body work needs doing on the front now, and the brake line needs replacing—"

"Can I have the damaged brake line?" Mike asked.

Charlie frowned at him. "Why?"

Mike's green eyes met hers. "Evidence."

Bill's brown eyes darted from Charlie's face to Mike's and back again. "Should I call the cops?"

"No," Charlie and Mike said in unison.

"Okay, then." Bill licked his lips, looking confused.

"Fix the body damage and replace the brake line," Charlie said. "And preserve the brake line in case we need to let someone examine it to establish whether or not the cut was intentional."

"Will do," Bill said with a nod. "Listen, it's probably going to take me a few days to get this done. You gonna have a way to get around?"

"I'll figure out something." Charlie nibbled her lip, wondering if she could make do with her bike for a few days. She didn't have any meetings scheduled at work for the next couple of weeks, so she didn't have to worry about a commute. There was a small grocery store a half mile from her house, so she and the cats wouldn't starve. Even Campbell Cove Academy was within a mile's ride. It would be good exercise.

"I can give you a ride home, at least," Mike said.

"Thanks."

"What *are* you going to do for wheels?" Mike asked as they walked to his truck.

"I have a bike."

He slanted a look at her as he unlocked the passenger door of the truck. "What if it rains?"

There was no what-if; rain fell practically every week in the mountains, and often multiple days a week. She hadn't really thought about rain, but that was what raincoats were for, right? "I'll deal."

He waited for her to fasten her seat belt before he started the engine. The dashboard clock read 11:35 and, to her chagrin, her stomach gave a little growl in response. Breakfast had been a long time ago.

"I could go for an early lunch," he murmured, sounding amused. "You wanna come?"

She looked at him through the corner of her eye, trying to assess his motives. "To lunch? With you?"

His sunglasses had mirror lenses, so she couldn't be sure his smile made it all the way to his eyes. "I suppose we could sit apart, if you like. Though that seems like a waste of a table."

Mayfair Diner was little more than a hole-in-the-wall, one of three storefronts that filled the one-story brick building on the corner of Mayfair Lane and Sycamore Road. Charlie ate there often, since her house was just a short drive down Sycamore. By now, everybody who worked there knew her by name and called out greetings when they entered.

"What's good here?" Mike asked as they headed for the counter.

"Depends on how much weight you want to gain."

He smiled at her blunt answer and looked up at the big menu board. "How are the omelets?"

"I like them," she answered with a little shrug. "The cheese-and-bacon ones are particularly good."

"I bet."

The counter waitress, a plump, pretty woman in her forties named Jean, smiled as she approached to take their order. "Hey, Charlie, what can I get for you and your friend today?"

"I'll have a grilled cheese with chips and a pickle, and iced coffee with cream and sugar," Charlie said.

"And you, hon?" Jean looked at Mike, her voice instantly flirtatious.

"I'll have a veggie omelet and a small fresh fruit cup," he ordered. "And water to drink."

Disgustingly healthy, Charlie thought. Would explain his smokin'-hot body, though.

"Find yourself a seat, and I'll send someone out with your orders in a few minutes," Jean said with one last flirtatious smile at Mike before she turned to clip their orders to the chef's order wheel.

Charlie and Mike settled in a corner booth. He took the bench seat that faced the door, she noticed. Always on the lookout for trouble?

An uncomfortable silence lingered between them for a moment before Mike broke it in a gravelly murmur. "You didn't seem that surprised when the guy at the garage thought your brake line had been cut."

She looked up sharply. "What's that supposed to mean?"

He shrugged. "If someone told me my brake line had been cut…"

"You'd start with your self-defense class roster?" She

flashed him a cheeky grin to hide her own sense of unease with his question.

He grinned back. "Probably."

What she didn't want to admit, even to herself, was that there might be someone out there who wanted her dead. For most of her life she'd been fairly invisible, by design. Her ne'er-do-well brothers had brought more than their share of ignominy to the family name. Better not to draw any attention at all than the kind her brothers had managed to elicit.

A smiling teenage girl came over with their orders on a large tray, saving Charlie from having to find something else to say to break the silence. The girl eyed Mike with starstruck shyness, giggling a little as he smiled his thanks. Charlie wasn't sure the girl even realized there was a second person at the table.

"Does that happen often?" she asked, taking a sip of her iced coffee.

Mike looked up from his plate. "Does what happen?"

Charlie nodded toward the waitress who was still darting quick looks toward their table as she talked with another server. "Googly-eyed females growing tongue-tied in your presence."

He frowned. "Never noticed."

Of course he hadn't. She changed the subject back to the topic of the hour. "How on earth did you even notice that brake fluid in the parking lot?"

"I happened to be looking out the window when you drove away. There was a big puddle of fluid underneath the car, so I thought I should check it out. When I realized it was brake fluid—"

"You hopped in your truck and raced to my rescue?"

"Seemed like the thing to do."

"When you first whipped around in front of me, I

thought you were a maniac." She shook her head. "That was kind of a crazy thing to do."

"Blame the academy. Crisis driving is one of the things we're trained to do, you know."

"Does the Campbell Cove Academy teach those skills to civilians, too?"

"Only to professional security personnel at the moment," he said with a shake of his head. "It's an intense and expensive course, and most civilians won't have any need to learn the skills."

"Not sure I agree with that," she said wryly.

He leaned a little closer, lowering his voice. "You really have no idea who might have tampered with your car?"

"Why would I?"

"You just started taking a self-defense course, and now your vehicle is sabotaged. I have to wonder if there's a correlation."

She pretended not to understand. "You think someone messed with my car because I'm taking a self-defense course?"

He frowned. "Don't be obtuse. I'm asking if the reason you're taking a self-defense course has anything to do with why someone might tamper with your brakes. Have you been threatened? A stalker or a disgruntled ex?"

"Nobody's threatened me."

He sat back, studying her through narrowed eyes. "I'm not sure you can say that with a straight face after today. Assuming your mechanic is right about how the brake line was cut."

"I don't know who would want to hurt me," she said firmly.

That was the problem, wasn't it? She didn't know who would want to hurt her any more than she knew who would have hurt Alice. But someone had. She was more convinced of that fact than ever.

"Okay," Mike said after a long silence. "But I think you should be careful anyway. Maybe this morning was a warning shot."

"I'm planning to be careful."

"You still planning on trying to get around by bike?"

"Or on foot. I work from home, and most of the places I go on any given day I can reach by walking."

"Not sure that's a good idea."

"It's not like my track record in a car is exactly stellar after this morning," she joked.

He didn't smile. "Are you going to be at my class tomorrow afternoon?"

She shook her head. "The academy is a little too far away for a bike ride. Maybe I can pick up the class the next time you offer it."

"You'll have your car back soon. I can give you a ride to the class until then. Just be ready about a half hour early and I'll swing by to pick you up."

She narrowed her eyes. "Why? Why would you do that?"

"Because I think you need it. It's not like it's a big problem for me to give you a ride."

She nibbled her lower lip, considering his offer. He was right about one thing—she'd like to know how to protect herself in a pinch. Wasn't that why she'd picked up the self-defense class in the first place?

But Mike Strong was taking a peculiar amount of personal interest in her well-being, and she had a feeling it wasn't a matter of altruism. He had seemed suspicious of her the very first class, hadn't he?

A new thought occurred to her. Could Mike have been the person who'd tampered with her brakes?

"What is it?" he asked, looking suddenly concerned.

She schooled her own features, trying to hide her doubts. "Nothing. I was just remembering this morning. Can't seem to shake it."

"That's natural," he assured her with an easy smile. "That had to be a pretty terrifying few minutes."

"Definitely." She forced a smile. "And you're right. I should be back in my car in a week, so there's no real reason not to try to keep up with the self-defense courses."

His concerned expression had cleared completely, now that he'd gotten his way. "So I'll pick you up about thirty minutes before class starts? I like to get there early and do some prep work, if that's okay."

"That's fine," she assured him, smiling again. "Do I need to bring anything besides me and my sparkling personality?"

He grinned. "That should be all you need. We'll supply the rest."

At her insistence, Mike let her pay for lunch. But he insisted on coming into her house with her instead of just dropping her off.

"You didn't think someone was going to cut your brake line, either," he argued when she told him he was being paranoid. "I'd like to be sure you're not about to walk in on an intruder alone."

Grimacing, Charlie gave in, hoping she hadn't left the place in too much of a mess that morning. Fortunately, neither of her cats had pulled one of their insane stunts, such as trailing toilet paper around the house or dumping over all the potted plants.

The house was silent and still when they entered. No sign of intruders. And thanks to Mike's presence, no sign of the cats, either, save for His Highness's well-worn catnip mouse sitting in the middle of the living room floor.

"You have a pet?" Mike asked, picking up the toy.

"Two. Cats. Currently in hiding, since you're here."

He gave a nod of understanding.

A quick walk-through seemed to satisfy his need to play protector, and Charlie walked him to the door. "Thanks for your help this morning."

"I'm glad I was able to help." He looked up and down the street behind him, as if he expected trouble. But the street was as quiet and normal as the house. "See you tomorrow afternoon?"

"Yes. Thanks."

"Lock the door behind me." He started down the porch steps and crossed to his truck, turning as he reached the vehicle. "Lock the door, Charlie," he repeated, nodding toward her.

She closed the door and engaged the lock as he asked.

But as the sound of the truck's engine faded to silence, she realized she didn't feel any safer.

MIKE PULLED OFF the road onto the gravel-paved scenic overlook and got out of the truck, pacing with restless energy to the steel railing that kept visitors from stepping off the edge of the bluff. He curled his fists around the top rail, ignoring the burn of the cold steel against his bare palms. If anything, the discomfort helped him focus his scattered thoughts.

Lunch with Charlie Winters hadn't gone the way he'd expected. He'd figured her obvious shakiness after the near disaster with her car might have made her drop her guard. He could use her rattled state to coax a few secrets out of her, and then he'd have a better idea what her real agenda might be.

Instead, not only had she managed to keep all her secrets, he was now convinced she was hiding even more than he'd suspected.

And instead of probing her story, trying to break through her wall of protection, he'd just sat back and listened. Because he liked to hear her talk. He liked the soft twang of her Kentucky accent, the way her lips quirked when she shot him a quizzical smile. He liked the twinkle in her eyes when he said something she found amusing. He liked the way she smelled—clean and crisp, like a garden kissed by the morning sun.

And the fact that he could come up with a description as ridiculous as "a garden kissed by the morning sun" was why he felt as if he'd just walked into a booby trap and all that was left for him to do was curl up in a ball and wait for the explosion.

He took several deep breaths and gazed across the hazy blue mountains that stretched out for miles before the first sign of a town showed up in the distance. Maybe he was just making too much of the way Charlie was making him feel. It had been a while since he'd really let himself think about a woman as anything other than a fellow soldier or one of the faceless, nameless civilians his orders had required him to protect from the enemy.

After his career as a Marine had ended and he'd entered the civilian force, it had taken a while just to get back into the swing of a life that didn't include gunfire, explosions and endless miles of dirt and sand. He hadn't wanted to look within the walls of the academy for a woman to share his bed and he'd been so focused on his job that he hadn't really looked outside the academy walls, either.

What he needed was a real date. A woman, a nice dinner, maybe some dancing or a movie. Ease into a love life again. No strings, no pressure. No bright hazel eyes making his stomach feel as if it were turning inside out.

Maybe Heller's wife had a friend he could meet. Weren't women always trying to fix up their husbands' single friends?

He pulled out his phone to record a reminder to feel Iris Heller out about her single friends the next time he ran into her, but he saw there was a "missed call" message. It was from someone named Randall Feeney.

For a moment, he thought it must have been a wrong number. Then he remembered the phone call he'd made before he'd set out on his search for Charlie Winters. He took a chance and called Feeney back.

"Randall Feeney," a man answered. In the background, Mike heard the low hum of voices and the ringing of phones—the sounds of a busy office.

"Mr. Feeney, this is Mike Strong from Campbell Cove Security Services. You just called my cell phone."

"Right, because you called the campaign office wanting to talk to someone about Alice Bearden." The man's voice lowered a notch. "May I ask the reason for your interest?"

Mike had already prepared his answer, but he'd really hoped to talk to Craig Bearden himself. "I'd rather discuss it with Mr. Bearden."

"That's not going to happen," Feeney said firmly. "However, I'm Mr. Bearden's executive aide and a long-time friend of the family. If you have any questions about Alice or the tragedy of her death, I may be able to help you. But I'd prefer to meet in person. Can you be at the campaign headquarters in Mercerville tomorrow afternoon? Say, around three?"

"I'm sorry, I'll be busy then. What about later today? Maybe around six?"

There was a brief pause before Feeney agreed. "Six is doable. I'll meet you here at the campaign headquarters. Do you know where that is?"

"I do." He'd looked up the address before he'd made the first call.

"I have to admit, however, I'm a little puzzled why someone from your company would have any interest in what happened to Alice," Feeney added, sounding wary.

"It may have some bearing on a case we're helping to investigate," Mike said, keeping his tone noncommittal. "I'll know more when we speak."

"Very well, then. See you at six." Feeney hung up without any further goodbye.

Mike pocketed his phone, feeling a little less rattled than before, now that he had a mission. He'd go talk to Randall Feeney, hear the story of Alice Bearden's death from someone who, as Feeney had proclaimed, was close to the family. If anyone would know what role Charlie Winters might have had in the death of Alice, it would be Craig Bearden's personal assistant.

Maybe Feeney could shed some much-needed light on what Charlie Winters really wanted from her self-defense classes at Campbell Cove Academy.

Then Mike could put the confounding woman out of his head for good.

Chapter Four

If there was one thing Charlie was good at, it was making lists. Grocery lists, to-do lists, Christmas lists—she found satisfaction in writing down things that needed to be addressed and marking them off when she'd tackled and conquered them.

Today's list was a to-do list of sorts, though marking off the items would take more than just a few hours of concentration and dedication.

First item on the list was already underway, at least. Learn the basics of self-defense. Couldn't really mark it off yet, since she was only two classes into her lessons. But maybe if she agreed to Mike Strong's offer to join his intermediate class, she'd reach that particular goal more quickly.

On the other hand, what if he turned out to be a problem? He was already giving her strange looks, as if he knew her reason for taking a self-defense class wasn't as simple as the fact that she lived alone and wanted to be able to protect herself.

Was there something else on the list she could start to tackle before she was finished with her self-defense classes?

The second item was a possibility: make another attempt to talk to Mr. Bearden. Alice's father.

She knew there wasn't any chance of talking to Alice's mother, Diana. The woman hadn't been able to look at Charlie at the funeral, even though she'd always been kind to Charlie before Alice's death.

To be honest, Charlie hadn't been that eager to face Diana Bearden, either. Fair or not, Charlie had always felt a great deal of guilt for what had happened to Alice, too.

But maybe she could handle Craig Bearden. Assuming she could get the man to talk to her after all this time. It had been years since she'd seen Craig Bearden, if you didn't count the signs and billboards that had cropped up all over eastern Kentucky since he'd announced his run for the US Senate. And even if they'd been closer, how easy would it be to get any face time with a political candidate?

Besides, they hadn't exactly parted company as friends. He'd never said the words aloud, but Charlie believed he'd blamed her for Alice's accident. Most people had. After all, Charlie was one of the Winters from Bagwell. The wrongest of the wrong sides of the tracks.

And her childhood talent for elaborate story fabrication hadn't exactly helped her case, had it? *That Charlotte Winters never met a truth she couldn't gussy up.*

Mr. Bearden hadn't wanted to listen when she'd told him she thought Alice had met up with someone else that night at the bar. Facing the tragic death of his eighteen-year-old daughter had been horrific enough.

He'd never been willing to contemplate the idea that what happened to his little girl might not have been an accident.

Charlotte hadn't wanted to believe it, either. It was one bald truth she'd had no desire to doctor up and make more interesting.

But after a while, the nightmares had started. It had

taken a while to realize the fragmented scenes of fear and confusion were actually memories that had been buried somewhere in her subconscious.

That night at the Headhunter Bar, three sips of light beer were all Charlie could remember for years. After that, nothing. No memories. No sensations or sounds or smells. Nothing but a terrifying blank.

Until the dreams had started.

She didn't imagine she could have gotten drunk that night, because she had never been much of a drinker. Thanks to her two jailbird brothers, she'd taken her first taste of alcohol at the age of twelve. The hard stuff, hard enough to turn her off alcohol for years. When she hit high school, she'd occasionally drunk a beer when she was with other people—peer pressure, she guessed— but she had no taste for it, and she certainly wouldn't have drunk enough to get so wasted that she'd black out.

But the alternative had been far more horrifying to contemplate, so she hadn't. She'd gone along with the accepted story—two teenage girls buy fake IDs and go drinking. One passed out and the other wandered drunkenly into the path of a car and died of her injuries. Alice's blood alcohol level had been elevated—.09, which was over the legal limit to be considered impaired.

But had she been impaired enough to walk in front of a car without trying to escape?

The police had used a breathalyzer on Charlie when they'd shown up to ask questions about Alice's death, but several hours had already passed since she'd awakened, half-frozen and disoriented, in her backyard.

Charlie rubbed her forehead, feeling the first grind of a tension headache building behind her eyes. She drew a line through goal number two—speaking to Craig Bearden—and rewrote the goal several steps down the page. It was way too early to talk to Alice's father about her death, especially now that he had made increasing penalties for both serving alcohol to minors and reckless driving laws a significant part of his political platform.

Besides, she'd called him not that long ago, without getting any response. Well, unless you counted brake tampering. And did she really think Craig Bearden would do something like that?

Nellie looked up with alarm when Charlie scraped her chair back quickly, bumping up against the bookcase where she perched. His Highness merely blinked at her, uninterested, from his sunny spot on the windowsill.

"Mama needs to get out of here," Charlie told them, going as far as to grab her jacket before she realized she couldn't leave. Beyond the work she still had to complete before quitting time this afternoon, she no longer had a car at her disposal. And the bike wasn't exactly a safe alternative, was it?

An image flashed through her head. Alice lying dead on the road, her body battered and broken from the collision with a car. Blood seeping from her head, thick, dark and shiny on the pavement.

She sat down abruptly, her limbs suddenly shaky. Why was that image of Alice's broken body in her mind in the first place? She hadn't been there when Alice died.

Had she?

MIKE REACHED THE Craig Bearden for Senate headquarters in Mercerville with only a few minutes to spare, but he used every one of those extra minutes trying to get his mind off those terrifying moments when he'd thought he wasn't going to catch up to Charlie Winters before her runaway car slammed into the line of vehicles waiting at the four-way stop.

It had been close. Too close. And strangely, the time that had passed between their close call and now only seemed to intensify his memories of those heart-racing seconds.

Catching up, then passing her to get in front. Trying to time his slowdown—not too sudden, or the impact of her car against his might have injured her. But if he hadn't slowed down soon enough, they might have run out of pavement between them and the cars on the road ahead.

It had been a nerve-racking few minutes, and he was in no hurry to repeat the experience anytime soon.

The clock on his dashboard clicked over to 5:59. He made the effort to shake off the unsettling memories. Put on his game face.

It was showtime.

Bearden's campaign office was a storefront with wide plate glass windows and a glass door, all imprinted with Bearden for Senate in big red letters. The place was still bustling with staff and volunteers, including an energetic young woman in jeans wearing a large round Bearden for Senate button on her sweater. "Bearden for Senate. Would you like to sign up to volunteer?"

"Actually, I'm here to see Randall Feeney. Is he here?"

The girl looked sheepish. "Oh no, I'm sorry. You're Mr. Strong, aren't you? Mr. Feeney was called away unexpectedly and I was supposed to call you to ask if he could reschedule for another day, but it just got so busy."

Mike suppressed his irritation and pulled his wallet out of his back pocket. He withdrew a card and handed it to the woman. "Please see that Mr. Feeney gets this card. He can call and reschedule when his calendar is less crowded."

"Will do," the girl said brightly. "Sure you don't want to volunteer to work for the campaign?"

"Yeah, I'm not very political." He'd been in the Marine Corps long enough to avoid politics like the plague. It just got in the way of doing his duty. He supposed now that he was a civilian again, it was time to start thinking about his civic responsibilities.

But not today.

He returned to his truck, wondering if Feeney would bother to get back to him. Probably not.

Mike would just have to follow up later.

He called Heller and told him about Feeney's no-show. "The girl at campaign headquarters said he was called away, but I have to wonder if that wasn't just an excuse to blow off the appointment."

"Maybe Feeney agreed to meet with you before he had a chance to talk to Craig Bearden."

"And then Bearden told him to cancel?"

"Politicians are careful to control the message," Heller said. "He may want to know more about you before his people answer your questions."

"I left my card. It'll tell him my name and who I work for."

"That might make it less likely he'll talk to you, not more," Heller warned. "What are you doing next?"

"I'm not going to quit, if that's what you're asking." Mike had a feeling Heller—and maybe Quinn and Cameron, too—had been testing him with this impromptu investigation at first. He suspected they hadn't been all that interested in finding out why Charlie Winters had decided to take his self-defense class. They were more interested in seeing how well Mike was able to investigate Charlie and her motives.

But that had been before someone had cut Charlie's brakes.

"By the way, Strong, Cameron wants a word with you

tomorrow after your afternoon class. Can you drop by her office around five?"

"I'll be there." He ended the call and opened the calendar app to jot down the details of his appointment with Rebecca Cameron. Heller was an old friend from the Marine Corps, and Alexander Quinn, the wily spymaster who had been a legend during his time in the CIA, had crossed Mike's path from time to time during his tours of duty. But Cameron, a former diplomat, was a virtual stranger. She'd been an assistant to the American ambassador in Kaziristan during Mike's two years in that war-troubled country. But he'd met her only once, briefly, under difficult circumstances.

Why did she want to talk to him now? Was it something to do with what happened to Charlie?

THURSDAY AFTERNOON WAS cold and rainy, the mild warm snap of the first part of the week long gone. Forecasters were even talking about sleet and snow flurries for the weekend, driving out the last of Charlie's doubts about the wisdom of catching a ride with Mike to Campbell Cove Academy.

He arrived a half hour early, as promised. She thwarted any chivalrous instinct he might have had about getting out of the truck in the downpour by racing out the door the minute she heard the truck. Darting through the rain, she hauled herself into the passenger seat and turned to him with a laugh. "I now officially think catching a ride with you was a great idea."

He smiled back at her. "I thought you might."

"So, mind giving me a sneak preview of what we'll be doing in class today?" She shook the rain out of her hair and buckled in.

"The first part of the class won't be any different from

what we've been doing in the beginner's class. Stretching is stretching."

"But afterward?"

He just smiled. "You'll see."

Even though Mike was able to find a parking place close to the gym entrance, they still were mostly drenched by the time they burst through the doors. Charlie ran her fingers through her wet hair, attempting to tame the curls trying to burst out all over. She could tell by Mike's amused glance that it was a lost cause.

"You can wait in the gym if you like. I've got a little paperwork to tackle in my office and a couple of phone calls to make before class. It would only bore you."

"That's fine." She gave a little wave as he walked out the side door of the gymnasium, quelling the urge to follow him.

She had done most of her stretching exercises by the time some of her other classmates started to drift into the gym. They greeted her with nods in the normal way of strangers thrown together by circumstance and, as she didn't encourage any further conversation, most settled in a few feet away on the floor mats to follow her lead and do their stretches.

By five minutes until class time, seven other students had entered, almost all of them male. She was also pretty sure most if not all of them were cops or some sort of law enforcement officers. Nobody survived life in her neck of the Kentucky woods without developing the ability to pick out a police officer in a crowd.

As she pushed to her feet, the door from outside opened, and one more student entered the gym, stopping in the doorway to survey the room, as if he expected trouble to break out any second.

His gaze locked with Charlie's, and she swallowed a groan.

Of all the people to run into here at the Campbell Cove Academy...

The newcomer was tall and well built, with broad shoulders and a lean waist that hadn't gained any padding since the last time Charlie had seen him almost ten years ago. His gray eyes were hard but sharp, like chips of flint, and his lips curved in a thin smile as he approached the mat where she stood.

"Well, if it isn't Charlotte Winters."

She hid her dismay with a smart-alecky grin in return. "Well, if it isn't Deputy Trask."

Archer Trask's smile widened, without a hint of humor making it anywhere near his eyes. "Have you woken up wasted in your backyard lately?"

Across the gym, the side door opened and Mike Strong walked through, his pace full of energy and purpose. His hair had dried during the time he'd spent in his office. In fact, he looked far more unruffled and put together than she felt at the moment.

Charlie turned away from Trask and moved closer to the other cops in the room. At least none of them looked familiar.

"Five more minutes," Mike called, taking his place at the front of the gym. He gave a little wave of his hand, and the rest of the class continued their stretching exercises.

Charlie continued with her stretches as well, hoping Archer Trask would go somewhere else and leave her alone.

In that, she was disappointed.

"So, how'd you end up here?" Trask's voice was deceptively casual.

"Here as in Campbell Cove?"

"No, here as in a self-defense course. Picked up a stalker or something?"

Charlie slanted a look at him, wondering for a moment if he'd heard about what happened to her car the previous day. "Only you, apparently."

"I heard you had a car accident yesterday."

So he *had* heard. "Is that the sort of thing people in your department investigate, Deputy Trask?"

"Not drinking *that* early, were you?"

She shot him a glare. "Go to hell."

"Something wrong here?"

At the sound of Mike's voice, both Charlie and Trask took a step back.

"Not a thing," Trask said, wandering away.

Mike moved closer to Charlie. "You look angry."

"I'm fine."

"Do you and Archer know each other?"

"Not really. Not in years." She made herself calm down. Getting into a fight with Archer Trask after all this time was the absolute *worst* thing she could do if she was serious about finding the truth about Alice's death. He'd been one of the first cops on the scene. She might end up needing his corroboration sooner or later.

Mike lowered his voice. "Has he been bothering you before today?"

She looked up sharply, realizing what he was asking. "No. No, of course not. Deputy Trask is just— No. This has nothing to do with what happened to my car. I promise you."

"You don't know who tampered with your car. How can you be so sure who it wasn't?"

"Trask is a cop. I'm a Winters. Around here, that's like oil and water."

Mike didn't appear appeased, but he gave a brief nod and turned to the rest of the class. "Okay, let's get started."

CHARLIE WAS QUIET on the drive back to her house, a stewing sort of silence that made Mike uneasy. She had managed to pull herself together after her run-in with Archer Trask, doing a creditable job of holding her own in the advanced self-defense class. She had a gangly, slightly awkward way of moving that reminded Mike of a long-legged puppy trying to figure out how to run, but what she lacked in pure grace she made up for in fierce intensity. She fought like a person who'd faced trouble before and would do anything to survive.

He broke the silence as they took the turn onto Sycamore Road. "You want to tell me about your history with Deputy Trask?"

She sent a glare angling his way. "No."

"Might make you feel better."

She laughed. "Trust me. It wouldn't."

He let it go. He had Archer Trask's contact information. If he wanted to know more about the deputy's relationship with Charlie, he could go to the source. "You did well today. Hung tough. Good job."

The look she gave him made him wonder if the concept of praise was foreign to her. "Thanks."

He pulled up at the curb in front of her house. "You want me to go inside with you?"

She shook her head. "No, I'm sure that's not necessary. Thanks for the ride. Hopefully, I'll have my car back by the next session."

She slipped out of the truck without saying anything further, loping up the flagstone walkway to her front porch. He waited, not wanting to leave until she was safely inside.

But she stopped with her hand on the doorknob, her body straightening suddenly. She turned to look at him. Even from several yards away, he saw the alarm in her expression.

He slid out of the truck and hurried up the walkway toward her. "What's wrong?"

She met him at the bottom of the steps, her eyes wide and scared. "I locked my door this afternoon before I left. Didn't I? You were here. You saw me do it, didn't you?"

He nodded.

"Well, it's not locked now."

He put his hand on her arm. "Wait here."

But she tagged along, right behind him, as he climbed the porch steps and approached the door.

She'd already touched the doorknob, so the likelihood that an intruder's prints were still intact was a long shot. But Mike used the hem of his T-shirt to turn the knob anyway, trying not to smudge anything.

He braced himself for the possibility of a blitz attack as he pushed the door open. His pistol was locked in the glove box of the truck. Too late to go back and get it now.

He stepped inside and swept the room, military style. There was no sign of an intruder still hanging around the living room.

But his handiwork was everywhere.

"Oh, my God." Behind him, Charlie's voice shook as she got a good look at the devastation.

Furniture was ripped apart and overturned. Picture frames had been smashed to the floor, scattering shards of glass across the hardwood. Porcelain knickknacks had been crunched to dust underfoot, mixing with clouds of fiberfill from the ripped-up sofa cushions. A wood rocking chair lay on its side near the hearth, its rockers now perpendicular, the wood snapped almost in two.

"Who would do this?" Charlie moaned.

"You should go back outside," Mike said as he caught sight of something dark and wet amid the clumps of fiberfill. Something that looked like…

"Is that blood?" Charlie asked.

"I don't know—maybe?"

"Oh, God!" She rushed past him before he could stop her, disappearing into the back of the house.

He followed. "Charlie, wait!"

As he reached a room near the back of the house, Charlie's voice rose in a wordless wail.

He skidded to a stop in the open doorway, his heart in his throat.

Charlie knelt on the floor in front of a Siamese cat lying on its side, blood darkening his smoky fur.

Chapter Five

Charlie couldn't breathe. Her pulse hammered in her ears, deafening her, as she reached down to touch His Highness's dark fur. "Hizzy."

The cat's blue eyes opened, his head lifting at the sound of her voice. His blue eyes blinked slowly, his breath coming in little pants.

"Oh, baby, you're alive." Tamping down her panic, she made herself breathe, running her fingers over his body. The tremble in her fingers started to dissipate as she found the source of the blood. "He's got a wound in his shoulder. It's deep. But he's still alive." She looked at Mike over her shoulder.

He stared back at her, his brow furrowed and his eyes dark with an emotion she couldn't quite read.

"There are a couple of cat carriers in the mudroom at the back of the house," she told him. "Just to the left of the kitchen. Find those for me. And there should be dry towels in the bathroom. I'll need a couple of those, too."

She checked her watch. Almost six. But the staff at her vet's office didn't leave until six thirty, and she could call ahead, let them know there was an emergency case on the way.

"Nellie?" she called gently, hoping her nervous girl

had stayed true to form and hidden somewhere the moment she realized there was a stranger in the house.

A plaintive mewling noise came from under the bed. Charlie scooted a few feet across the floor to the bed and looked underneath. Nellie's green eyes stared back at her, wide and afraid. "Are you okay, baby? Come out and let me take a look."

At the sound of Mike's footsteps coming down the hall, she called out, "Wait out there a minute."

Nellie froze, but Charlie made another coaxing sound. The tortoiseshell cat slinked from under the bed and rubbed her head against Charlie's shoulder.

Charlie gave the cat a quick check. She seemed uninjured. Charlie dropped her chin to her chest, trembling with relief.

"Charlie, can I come in yet?" Mike's soft voice sent Nellie scurrying back under the bed.

Charlie didn't try to coax her back out. "Yeah. Did you find the carriers?"

He entered the room, holding a towel and the two plastic carriers. "Why two of these?"

"I have a second cat, but she's okay. She's hiding under the bed." Charlie took the towel from Mike and gently wrapped it around Hizzy's bloodstained body, wincing as the cat uttered a low yowl of pain. "It's okay, sweetie. We're going to get you some help."

Mike crouched by her and set the carrier on the floor. "What can I do?"

"Open the carrier door and hold it until I can get him inside."

Mike did as she asked, and she eased His Highness into the portable cage, trying not to let panic take over again, despite how scary she found it that the cat wasn't fighting her at all. Usually, getting His Highness into the carrier was a battle of wills.

She snapped the door shut. "I hate leaving Nellie here, in case someone comes back."

"I've called someone from the agency to guard your house while we're gone."

She looked up at him, surprised. "Someone from your agency?"

"Yeah. Technically, this is a crime scene. You should call it in to the cops."

Her knee-jerk reaction was to shake her head no.

"Charlie, someone cut your brakes yesterday. Today, they trashed your house and injured your cat. Call the police."

"There's no time. We need to get Hizzy to the vet. In fact, I need to call ahead to make sure the doctor stays around." As Mike picked up the carrier, she led the way, pulling her phone from her pocket. She dialed the number, holding her breath until someone answered. As she and Mike hurried for the truck, she summarized the situation for the vet clinic assistant, who assured her the doctor would be waiting.

"Eric Brannon is on his way here." Mike buckled up and started the truck. "You need to call the police."

She sighed, aware he was right. "It's not an emergency, so I don't want to call 911."

"I have Deputy Trask's phone number in my phone," Mike murmured.

She looked at him. "No."

"So there *is* some bad blood between you two."

She waved toward the right when they reached the four-way stop. "The vet clinic is a half mile down this road, on the left."

In her lap, cradled by the carrier, His Highness had

stopped his heavy panting, giving her a moment's panic. But when she looked into the carrier's metal grid door, Hizzy blinked back at her. His breathing had returned to something approaching normal, she realized, starting to feel a little more hopeful.

The doctor himself, Pete Terrell, greeted them at the door. He was a thick-set, bearded man in jeans and a blue plaid flannel shirt under a white coat, with a friendly, competent manner that made Charlie feel instantly better about His Highness's chances of survival.

"I'll wait out here and check to see what's going on with Eric," Mike said, pulling out his cell phone. "Is it okay if I call the cops, as well?"

Charlie's gaze flicked between him and the vet. "Yes. But not Trask."

She followed Dr. Terrell into the exam room and set the carrier on the table. "I found him on the floor. He was bleeding from his upper left torso, around his shoulder. There seems to be a deep laceration there, but I didn't see any other wounds."

"All right, big fella. Let's take a look." Dr. Terrell gently eased the cat from the carrier and unfolded the towel holding him still. Blood had seeped into the terry cloth of the towel, but not a lot, she was heartened to see.

She held His Highness by his back legs, but the cat wasn't kicking up his usual fuss. He seemed to know he was in need of help and didn't try to fight.

A scrubs-clad veterinary assistant came into the room. She nodded at Charlie and took her place with His Highness so Charlie could step back and observe.

"We've got a laceration in the vicinity of the left scapula," the doctor murmured. "Deep. To the bone. Margins are clean and uniform. I'd say it's a knife wound. Smooth blade."

Charlie pressed her hands to her face, feeling sick at the thought.

"It isn't that wide. Looks like a stab rather than a slash." The doctor looked up at her. "What happened?"

"I don't know," she admitted. "I got home from an appointment and my place was trashed. Furniture ripped up, things shattered and crushed. And then I saw blood and followed the trail to Hizzy."

"He's a lucky cat. It looks as if the blade hit the scapula and bounced off before it hit any internal organs. I'm going to want X-rays to be sure."

"Of course."

A half hour later, the doctor had stitched Hizzy up and transferred him to a cage, hooked up to an IV drip. "To replenish the fluids he lost from bleeding," Dr. Terrell explained. "We'll want to keep him overnight for observation, but I think he'll be okay. Barring any unexpected complications, you can probably take him home tomorrow."

Charlie blinked back tears of relief. "Are you sure?"

"He was a little shocky when he came in, but his vitals have stabilized nicely. He's young and otherwise healthy, and you got him here quickly." Dr. Terrell patted her shoulder. "How about Nellie? I take it she wasn't injured?"

"She's fine. Scared and hiding, but fine."

"I hope you find out who did this." Dr. Terrell's smiling demeanor slipped. "You know, it's possible His Highness in there scratched whoever stabbed him. I could clip his claw tips and save them for you. Might be some DNA on them."

She stared at him, unable to stop a wobbly smile. "DNA on a cat's claws. I never even thought of that."

She returned to the vet clinic waiting room to find

Mike sitting on one of the benches, scrolling through his phone. He looked up quickly, his brow furrowed when he realized she wasn't holding the cat carrier. "What happened?" he asked, his tone cautious.

"He's going to be okay, but they want to keep him overnight for observation. You know, pump some fluid into him, keep him lightly sedated for pain. The doctor said I'll probably be able to take him home tomorrow."

Mike's worried expression cleared. "That's great news. You ready to go, then?"

She glanced back toward the hall that led to the overnight cages. "As ready as I'll ever be."

In the truck, Mike told her there were policemen at the house waiting for her. "I mentioned what happened with your brakes yesterday."

She grimaced. "I wish you hadn't done that."

"I figured you'd say that."

"So you told them anyway, knowing I'd object?"

He glanced at her. "This is serious. The brake line alone could have been an accident. But a break-in and the intentional injury to your cat—"

"Dr. Terrell thinks Hizzy might have scratched the person who stabbed him."

"Can they clip his claws for DNA?"

Charlie gave a small huff of grim laughter. "Yeah. It's already in the works."

"Brannon waited outside your house for the cops. We agreed it was smart to leave the scene as it was for the police."

"It was a break-in. Cops barely blink at break-ins."

"It was a break-in with injury."

She stared at him. "Injury to a cat. That's not exactly going to warrant a task force around here. The cops have enough real crimes to investigate—drug trafficking, murder, fraud…"

"The cops can do whatever they're going to do. But I'm treating this like the threat it was obviously meant to be."

Something in Mike's tone sent a little quiver up her spine. "What do you mean?"

"If the police won't take your safety seriously, I will."

She stared at him for a moment, struggling for a response. "Why would you do that?"

"Because protecting people is what I do."

"For pay. And I can't pay you anything. I don't make that kind of money."

"I'm not asking for pay."

"You do realize that makes no sense, don't you?"

They had reached Charlie's house. A single Campbell Cove Police Department cruiser sat parked in the driveway, while a silver sedan sat at the curb. "That's Eric's car," Mike said, nodding at the sedan.

Brannon was still on the porch. He stood and walked down the flagstone path to greet them. "Officer Bentley is photographing the destruction in your house," he told Charlie. "He'll want you to take a look around when he's done, to see if anything has been stolen."

Her laptop, she thought with a sudden rush of panic. In the chaos of dealing with Hizzy's injury, she'd forgotten all about her computer. Beyond all her work files— absolutely vital for her job—there were the files she'd started to compile of her research into what had happened the night Alice died.

All of those files were backed up to a cloud archive, so she wouldn't lose anything. And the security on her laptop was top-notch. It wouldn't be easy to crack her passwords.

But if the wrong person got his hands on those research files about Alice, they'd know how much she knew.

And how much she didn't.

She entered the house, trying to control her rising panic. Ignoring the sounds of the police officer moving around in her kitchen at the back of the house, she hurried into her bedroom.

The laptop was where she'd left it.

With a sigh of relief, she dropped into the desk chair and opened the lid. The machine flickered to life, the lock screen greeting her.

She typed in the password to unlock the system and started scrolling through her files, checking to see if there was any sign of an intrusion.

Everything seemed to be the way she'd left it. As far as she could tell, no one had accessed her Alice Bearden files since she'd last had them open the day before.

"This is still a crime scene, Charlie." The twangy drawl that made her whirl around belonged to a barrel-chested cop with a weathered face and a crooked smile.

"Officer Everett." Charlie stood up. "I know. I just— I work from this computer, and if someone had gotten in her and messed things up—"

Bob Everett's smile widened. "Lord, look at you, girl. All growed up. How's your mama?"

Bob had always been a little sweet on Charlie's mother, she remembered. They'd been schoolmates years earlier, and apparently Bob had never quite lost his soft spot for Marlene.

"She's doing pretty good these days," Charlie said. It was mostly true. Marlene had been married to her new husband for almost four years. "She's in Arkansas now. With her new husband."

"Yeah." Bob's expression fell.

She changed the subject to put him out of his misery. "I guess you want to know if anything's been stolen."

"Well, I've been taking a good look around. Everything's an unholy mess, but the kind of stuff you figure a burglar's gonna take seems to all be here. Your TV, your stereo system, your computer. The TV and stereo are all busted up, but they're still here."

But they hadn't done anything to her computer, she thought. Maybe because they wanted to access the files within?

But why hadn't they just stolen the laptop while they had the chance?

"Is the destruction throughout the house?" she asked.

"Looks like they stopped here. Didn't see nothing out of place in the kitchen or the mudroom, and the next room down doesn't look like it's been touched, either."

The only damage in the bedroom was Hizzy's blood on the hardwood floor. They hadn't done the sort of destruction here they'd done in the front of the house.

"Maybe someone interrupted them?"

Charlie and Bob both looked up at the sound of Mike's voice. He stood in the bedroom doorway, his broad shoulders filling the space.

"Who are you?" Bob asked.

"Mike Strong. I'm a friend of Charlie's."

Bob looked from Charlie to Mike and back, his expression skeptical. "Well, Mr. Strong, I guess it's possible the intruders got interrupted. I'll talk to the neighbors and see if anyone saw or heard anything. But I don't know there's much more I can do here. I could call in a crew to do fingerprints, Charlie, but I gotta be honest. If they didn't steal anything, and you don't reckon they did, what you're lookin' at here is plain ol' vandalism.

You'd be better off callin' your insurance company and lettin' them handle the claim."

Charlie looked at Mike. He sighed and looked away.

"I appreciate your comin' by, Officer Everett." She walked with him to the door.

Bob turned in the doorway, his expression darkening. "I heard they hurt one of your cats. I hope the little fella's gonna be okay."

"Doc Terrell seems to think so."

"Good to hear. You let me know if anything else happens, you hear?"

"Thanks. I will. And I meant what I said about Mama. I bet she'd love you to drop by and say hello."

Bob smiled at her again, looking ridiculously pleased. "I'll do that."

She watched him go, swallowing a sigh.

"You were right. The cops aren't going to be able to protect you." Mike's voice was close behind her.

She turned to look at him. "I know. I'll get better locks. Maybe splurge on a security system. I just never thought I'd need one here."

"You can't stay here alone. Especially without a car."

"I'll be fine. I don't think they'll be coming back so soon."

He put his hands on her shoulders, his grip somehow both gentle and firm. "Charlie, look at this place." He turned her until she faced the chaos that the intruder had made of her once-tidy living room. The sight of her stereo system lying shattered on the floor brought tears stinging to her eyes. She'd bought the system on her twenty-first birthday, after saving up every penny she could during her four years of college. It had been the first thing to ever truly belong only to her, and she'd spent the past eight years enjoying the thing, even as it aged and, in the eyes of a lot of people, grew obsolete.

She blinked back the tears. "I saw it before."

"This isn't just vandalism. This is terrorism."

She twisted her head to look at him. "Terrorism?"

"Terrorism is more than just bombs in Baghdad or Jerusalem, Charlie. It can be graffiti painted on the wall of a black man's home or a Jewish man's shop. It can be stalkers sending threatening notes to their prey. This—" He waved his hand at the mess. "This is meant to terrorize you."

"Well, it won't work," she said firmly.

"Good. But you can't just declare it won't work and then go on with your life the way it is."

"If I change my life, doesn't that mean the terrorists win?" She meant the question to be flip and breezy, but to her own surprise, it came out angry.

He reached up and brushed away a lock of hair that had flopped into her face. His fingertips brushed down her cheek before he dropped his hand to his side. "I'm not asking you to change your life. I'm just offering to watch your back."

"Why?" The sensation of his touch lingered on her skin. She tried to ignore it, struggling to focus.

"Because I hate terrorists," he said simply.

"Oh."

"I'll stay here tonight."

No. That was a bad idea.

Wasn't it?

"There's no sofa left," she said, her voice faint.

"I'll sleep on the floor in the spare room. I've got a rucksack in my truck's lockbox that has some camping gear."

"I can't pay you," she reminded him.

"This is a freebie." His lopsided smile made her heart flip in response. "I'll go talk to Eric and then I'll be right back. We can tackle some of this mess tonight if you like, or we can wait until morning."

Oh, what the hell, she thought. She could certainly use his help cleaning up the place. And if he wanted to spend the night on her hardwood floor, roughing it, who was she to say no?

The truth was, she'd feel a lot safer with him here.

She sighed. "I'd be stupid to say no, wouldn't I?"

"And stupid," he said softly, "is something you're not."

She watched him go, thinking with every step he took that she should call him back, change her mind. Tell him to go home. She'd be fine. She didn't need him watching her back.

But somehow, he was out the door before she opened her mouth.

Releasing a shaky breath, she looked around the living room, taking in the malicious destruction, and couldn't muster up any regret for having agreed that he could stay the night.

The last thing she wanted right now was to be alone.

Chapter Six

"She's playing it tough and stoic, but I know she's got to be scared." Mike glanced toward the front door of Charlie's house, remembering the look on her face when she'd seen the blood on the floor. "Brake tampering yesterday, and now this."

"And she doesn't have any idea who could be behind either of these attacks?" Eric's breath fogged in the cold night air.

"She says not. I'm not sure I believe her."

"You're staying with her tonight?"

"Yeah, unless she changes her mind and kicks me out."

"And if she does?"

"I'll stay in my truck and watch the place from there."

Eric nodded slowly, not saying anything for a moment. Finally, he looked up at Mike, his blue eyes gleaming in the faint moonlight peeking through the scudding clouds overhead. "You really do think she's in trouble, don't you?"

"I do." Mike rubbed his chin, his beard stubble scraping against his palm. "There's something in her past—I can't really talk about it, but it's reason to worry."

"Something she did?"

"Maybe. I don't know. Something she was involved

in, a long time ago. Someone died, and I don't know how exactly she was involved, but it's a place to start looking."

"Did the intruders take anything?"

"Charlie says no."

"So they just made that awful mess for the hell of it?"

"Or maybe as a warning," Mike said.

Eric pressed his lips into a tight line. "Stabbed the cat for the same reason?"

"Maybe. Or maybe the cat got in the way. Wrong place at the wrong time."

"Hissing and spitting, getting in the way…"

"Right."

Eric's voice dipped a notch. "Do the bosses know you're getting involved in Charlie's mess?"

"Sort of." Mike hadn't really talked to Heller about anything that had happened since the tampered brakes incident. His boss was probably expecting to hear something from him soon. "I'll give Heller a call. Catch him up on everything."

But not tonight. He couldn't risk Heller telling him to back off and let Charlie handle things alone.

He didn't want to defy a direct order.

"You want me to stick around awhile?" Eric asked. "I could help with the cleanup."

Mike thought about it. "I think she's going to be uncomfortable enough with me there. You go on home. If anything comes up, I have your number."

Eric clapped him on the shoulder. "Okay. Take care. Tell Charlie I'm sorry about the mess, and I hope her cat's going to be okay."

When Mike entered the house, he found Charlie already hard at work cleaning up the mess. She had a broom and a long-handled dustpan in her hands, sweeping up the shattered bits of her belongings and dumping them into a large trash can lined with a plastic bin liner.

"How can I help?" he asked.

She looked up at him, her hazel eyes dark with anger, and for a second, he feared she was going to throw him out. But finally, she thrust the dustpan at him. "I'll sweep. You dump."

He took the dustpan and helped her sweep up the mess. When the worst of the small pieces had been thrown away, they started tackling the bigger pieces of detritus—the ruined sofa cushions, the mangled bits of electronics. They worked that way for another hour, in silent concert, until the living room had been cleared of most of the chaos.

"Good thing someone scared them off," Charlie muttered as she retrieved the dustpan from him. "Or we might have been at this all night."

"Why don't you go on to bed?" he suggested. "I can lock up."

"Fat lot of good that lock did me today," she muttered, slanting an accusing glare at the door.

"We'll put in a new lock tomorrow. And if you're serious about a security system, that's one of the things we offer at Campbell Cove Security Services."

She turned her glare on him. "So all this solicitude is a sales pitch?"

"No, of course not—"

She gave his arm a light punch and grinned. "Just kidding."

He couldn't muster up a smile in return. "You *are* taking this stuff seriously, aren't you, Charlie?"

Her smile faded. "Yeah, I'm taking it seriously. I just don't know why it's happening."

"Are you sure about that?"

Her eyes narrowed. "Believe me, if I knew who was doing this, I'd find a way to stop it myself."

He moved away from her, crossing to the remains of a rocker they'd stacked next to the door. He'd told her not to throw it out until he'd had a chance to look at it more closely. He crouched next to it now, examining the damage. "It's just— It seems such a coincidence that you start taking a self-defense class and suddenly you're facing two threatening incidents."

"Coincidence. Luck. Whatever you want to call it." She didn't sound terribly convincing.

He quelled the urge to look at her and kept his focus on the rocking chair instead. The pieces weren't broken, he realized with a closer look. The legs were pulled out of their sockets and the rockers twisted out of place, but none of the individual pieces had been damaged. He could put everything back together with a little wood glue and elbow grease. "Okay. Whatever you say."

"You make it sound as if you think I'm lying."

He stood and turned slowly to face her. "I think I can fix that rocker, no problem."

Her lips thinned with annoyance, and she took a couple of belligerent steps toward him. "You *do* think I'm lying. Don't you?"

"Yeah. I do. But it's your business. I could do a better job of helping you protect yourself if you'd level with me, but that's entirely up to you. I'll do what I can. The rest is up to you."

Her nostrils flared, and he could tell she was furious, but he had a feeling she was angrier with herself than with him.

"I'm going to bed," she said bluntly and walked out of the room.

He watched her go, wondering how long it would take her to realize she couldn't face her trouble alone.

ALICE'S SMILE WAS ELECTRIC, her straight white teeth gleaming in the bluish tint of the bar's low light. "Relax, Charlie. Nobody here knows us. And it's just beer, right?"

Her stomach was already cramping with anxiety. If her mother found out what she'd been doing, she'd freak completely. Charlie was supposed to be the sane one in the family. These days, with Vernon and Jamie up in Blackburn Prison, and the other two boys barely keeping their noses clean, Mama depended on Charlie to be the one she didn't have to worry about.

And here she was, three years under the legal drinking age, at one of the seediest bars in eastern Kentucky, nursing a light beer and hoping like hell nobody she knew walked into the place.

"Isn't this place great?" Alice sipped her Trouble Maker through a long black straw, her blue eyes shimmering with excitement. "This is a big night, Charlie. Bigger than you know."

"Why?" Charlie asked.

Alice's gaze flitted around the room, never settling anywhere, though for a moment, when her lips curved around the straw, Charlie thought Alice might have spotted someone she knew. But when Charlie twisted around to see what Alice was looking at, all she saw was a stuffy-looking man in a shirt and tie, drinking something gold in a tumbler with ice. Whiskey of some sort. Probably bourbon.

"Do you know that guy?" Charlie asked.

Alice shook her head and took another sip of her cocktail. "Drink your beer, Charlie. It's just beer."

Charlie took a sip of the beer, grimaced at the bitter, yeasty taste and wished she'd gone for something like red wine instead. At least it would have been sweet. And classy.

Instead, she was sitting here in her short ill-fitting dress, drinking a low-rent beer like the low-rent little redneck she was.

Alice had flitted away, her womanly curves selling the lie that she was over twenty-one. Red was her color, and she was wearing the hell out of the body-skimming little red dress with the tiny spaghetti straps and the hem that stopped several inches above her knees. Her tawny blond hair was scooped up into a messy ponytail, with lots of wavy golden tendrils dancing around her face and neck as she walked.

The room was starting to feel close and hot, and her stomach was rumbling a little. Maybe she should have eaten something before coming here, but she'd been too nervous and jittery to swallow even a bite of the sandwich she'd made before leaving the house.

She should relax. Try to have fun.

She took a third sip of the beer. It didn't taste any better than the first two sips. The rumbling in her stomach continued, accompanied by a cold sweat breaking out on her forehead.

The room closed in on her. The lights seemed to dance before her eyes in rhythm with the bass beat of the music blaring from the music speakers. She pushed away from the bar, leaving the beer where it sat. She wasn't going to drink any more of it, especially not the way her stomach felt.

There was an outdoor patio. She could see other bar patrons out there, enjoying the unseasonably mild night. She slipped her leather jacket on, gave her skirt a quick downward tug and weaved her way through the crowd.

The air outside was colder than she'd expected, but she didn't mind. In fact, the chilly night air seemed to clear her foggy brain for a moment.

But then the dizzy sensation returned, along with a sudden, bone-deep weariness. She found an empty table near the edge of the porch and sat, pressing her hands to her eyes.

"There she is." The voice was male. Distant. Sort of familiar, though Charlie couldn't place it.

"How much longer?" That whisper was female, and for a confused moment, Charlie was sure it was Alice's voice.

"Soon, I think," the male voice answered, closer now.

Charlie put her head on the table, closing her eyes against the whirl of color and light assaulting her brain.

Then it all went away. For what felt like a long time.

The darkness ebbed slowly, replaced by a muddy yellow glow just beyond her closed eyelids. Something hard, cold and damp lay beneath Charlie's cheek. It smelled of gasoline and grime, and as she tried to move her head, grit stung against her skin.

She stopped trying to move and concentrated instead on opening her eyes. Her eyelids felt leaded, hard to lift. She forced them open anyway.

The light came from streetlamps. Without moving her head, she couldn't see the lamps themselves, but the circular glow that spilled onto the pavement suggested the light source.

Something lay in the street a few feet away from her. Red and pale white. Crumpled. Still. The tawny waves spilled out around her head, streaked with blood. One blue eye was open and staring.

Alice. Oh, God, Alice!

The world seemed to narrow to a pinpoint, until all she could see in the blackness was that one blue eye.

Then it disappeared into an endless black void.

Charlie fought against the darkness, but she couldn't seem to move. Couldn't push air past her vocal cords to make a sound.

She wanted to scream her fear and anguish. Cry out for help. Beg for someone to find them and save them from whatever had happened.

But she couldn't.

Hands caught her arms and gave her a shake, and she heard a voice in the blackness.

"Charlie!"

CHARLIE JERKED AWAKE, her breath rising on a keening gasp. For a moment, she felt as if she was still trapped in the darkness, but after a panicked few seconds, the dim light from outside the house filtered through the curtains and into her sightless eyes, and she realized she was in her own bed, in the small house on Sycamore Road.

And the strong hands clutching her shoulders belonged to the broad-shouldered man sitting on the bed beside her.

"Charlie?" He sounded wary.

She realized her hands were bunched into fists in front of her, pushing against Mike's hard chest. His hard, bare chest.

She dropped them to her lap. "Sorry. I must have been dreaming."

"You called out a name," he said quietly.

"I did?" She shook her head, not sure she wanted to remember whatever images fluttered elusively at the edge of her mind.

"You called out the name Alice," he said. "Does that mean anything to you?"

"Yes."

He waited a moment, perhaps expecting her to continue. When she didn't, he added, "You sounded scared."

The image from the dream had stuck with her, vivid in a way dreams rarely were once she awoke. She could see Alice lying crumpled in the wet street, her hair splayed around her head. She could see the blood staining Alice's tawny hair and the blank stare of her one visible eye.

She'd never remembered seeing Alice before. The voices, the jumble of words and phrases that had played games with her mind, yes. But the sight of Alice, lying dead in the road—that image was new.

Was it a memory? Or was it her vibrant imagination bringing Alice's death to life for her?

She didn't know. She only knew that something wasn't right. She had taken three sips of light beer and her head had started to swim. She wasn't much of a drinker, but she knew that it would take a lot more than three sips of beer to make the world turn upside down the way it had.

And no way would it have made the rest of the night a blank until she woke in her own backyard just before dawn the next morning.

"What are you thinking?" Mike asked.

She shook her head, not ready to share her thoughts with someone she'd just met. Not until she'd had a chance to try to piece everything she was starting to remember together into a more coherent pattern.

The last thing she needed to do was give people ammunition to dismiss her stories as typical Charlie Winters's confabulation.

"I was just trying to remember my dream," she said. That answer was true, wasn't it? If not quite complete.

"And did you?"

"Bits and pieces." She pressed her hands to her face. Her elbow brushed against Mike's arm, reminding her again just how close he was sitting to her.

And how little clothing he was wearing.

"What time is it?" she asked. She didn't have an alarm clock. She'd always lived by her own internal clock, somehow able to wake up in time to do whatever she needed to do.

"A little after three."

"And you heard me calling out from the living room?" That was where he'd bedded down for the night.

He shifted, running one hand through his short-cropped hair. "I moved the sleeping bag to the hall. Outside your door."

"Why?"

"Because I wasn't sure I could beat an intruder to your room if they entered through the back door."

"Oh." Clearly, he was taking the possibility of a threat against her life seriously. "I wish I could offer you a sofa to sleep on instead. Sleeping on a hard floor can't be fun."

His soft laugh was a warm, low grumble in the darkness. "Beats the hell out of sleeping on an Afghanistan mountainside in winter."

She jumped at the chance to change the subject. "How long were you in Afghanistan?"

"A couple of years. I went to Afghanistan first, then Iraq. Then Kaziristan for a few years."

"Then where?"

His tone grew suddenly cautious. "Then I retired and came back to the States."

"How long ago was that?"

"A couple of years. I worked security here and there

for a little over a year before one of my bosses called to see if I was interested in working for him at Campbell Cove Academy. He was looking for instructors and thought I'd be good for the job."

"You seem pretty good at it," she said. "Not that I have a lot of experience with self-defense instructors."

"I'm just sharing some of the things I learned in boot camp. Geared toward civilians, of course."

"Yeah, no rifles or bayonets in our training."

"Well, not at the intermediate level, no."

Her eyes must have better adjusted to the dark, because she could see the pale white gleam of his teeth in the dark, suggesting he'd spoken the last words with a smile.

"Why did the security company choose little Campbell Cove, Kentucky, as their home base?" she asked, starting to enjoy the warm intimacy of the moonlit conversation.

"Not sure," he admitted. "I think maybe one of the owners is from this area. I know they liked the seclusion of the property. It's not easy to get to if you don't live right in the area. And we're in a place where we can see trouble coming well ahead of time."

She nodded, only half listening to his words. Instead, she was drinking in his voice, a gravelly rumble of masculinity that somehow made this dark bedroom feel like the safest place on earth.

"I like it here," he added. "It reminds me of home."

"And where's home?" she asked, feeling half-drunk from his nearness.

"North Carolina."

"Whereabouts?"

"I lived a little ways east of Cherokee, in the Smokies. A town called Black Rock."

"Evocative."

"Yeah?"

She closed her eyes, breathing deeply. In the warmth that flowed between them, she could smell a faint piney scent coming from him. It reminded her of long, hot summers playing in the mountain woodlands as a child, as perfect a memory as she had.

"I can picture the place. It's small. Surrounded by the woods and mountains. There's probably a little creek running through the town, and a little stretch of downtown you can drive through in about a minute. Am I close?"

"Yeah, pretty close," he admitted. "You sure you've never been there?"

"Yes." She opened her eyes. He was looking at her, his gaze intense, as if he could read her expression in the dark. "I'm just from a place a lot like that. Bagwell, Kentucky. Population six hundred and holding."

"I think I've been through there. It's on the way to Pineville, right?"

"Yeah."

Silence fell between them then, thick with exquisite tension. Attraction, she realized. Unsurprising on her part—he was talk, dark and lean, with the sort of powerful body that women bought magazines to drool over. His face looked as if it had been chiseled by a master sculptor, and that voice was made for seduction.

What threw her off balance, however, was the attraction she felt radiating from Mike. Attraction for her.

So not what she expected.

"You should try to go back to sleep," he said, rising from the bed and edging toward the door.

She felt his sudden absence keenly, as if a cold breeze had just washed over her. "Okay."

"Sweet dreams this time, okay?"

"I'll try," she said, grimacing a little at the smitten sound of her own voice. "You, too."

"'Night." He slipped from the room and closed the door.

Charlie laid her head back on her pillows and stared at the ceiling, about as far from sleep as she'd ever been.

Chapter Seven

"It had definitely been cut. Our forensics guys are trying to figure out what kind of blade made it."

Mike opened the refrigerator door and peered inside. Thank goodness the intruders hadn't made it as far as the kitchen. The carton of eggs stored in the door compartment was still intact. "Even if you do," he said into the phone, "we'd have to find a weapon before we could make a match, wouldn't we?"

"Probably," Maddox Heller admitted. "But maybe we can narrow down the type of blade. Then you can ask Charlie Winters if the description rings any bells."

"Yeah," he said, not adding that he couldn't be sure Charlie would tell him if she did find the description familiar. She was clearly keeping secrets from him, if her nightmare the night before was any indication.

"I take it there weren't any further problems last night?"

"No, it was quiet as a church." He'd already made a circuit of the house, indoors and out, to be sure there had been no further attempted incursions into Charlie's house. He supposed his big F-150 pickup parked in the driveway might have been enough to discourage the intruders from trying again.

He was curious, however, why they had stopped their

destruction halfway through the house. The vandalism had obviously been meant as a warning of some sort. Had they figured one room's worth of destruction was enough? Or had something scared them off?

"I don't suppose the police bothered to ask the neighbors anything about the break-in," he said.

"I have a friend on the force. I can ask."

"Thanks. I'd appreciate that."

"By the way, Cameron still wants to see you."

He jerked upright, nearly hitting his head on the edge of the freezer door. "Oh, damn. I was supposed to meet with her yesterday afternoon."

"I told her what happened. She understood. But she says she still needs to see you, today if possible."

Footsteps padded softly down the hall toward the kitchen. "I'll call her and set something up," he said. "Gotta go."

He didn't wait for Heller to respond, pocketing his phone and turning to look at Charlie as she entered the kitchen.

She was still wearing the thermal pajamas she'd put on last night after showering before bed, the hem of the top scrunched up enough that he got a glimpse of flat stomach and the glint of a small silver belly ring. Her short hair was a spiky, bed-headed mess, and her hazel-green eyes drooped with weariness. "Coffee," she groaned.

He picked up the mug he'd set out for her, a dark green mug with the words *First Coffee, Then Coherence* on the front, and poured her a cup of the coffee he'd just brewed. "How do you like it?"

"Hot and now." She took the cup and swallowed a gulp, grimacing as it went down. But she took another gulp and leaned against the counter, looking at him beneath sleepy eyelids. "How long have you been up?"

He glanced at his watch. Seven thirty. "About an hour or so. Did I wake you?"

"No, my internal clock did that." She took another drink of the coffee. "No new intrusions, I take it?"

"Not that I saw." He turned back to the fridge. "Are you a breakfast-eater?"

"Yes, please. Are you cooking?" Her expression perked up. "Tell me you're cooking."

"I'm cooking, if you can settle for scrambled eggs."

"I'd settle for dry cereal, so eggs sound great." She poured a second cup of coffee, this time adding a packet of sweetener and a spoonful of the hazelnut creamer that sat in a plastic container next to the coffeepot. She fetched a spoon from a drawer and stirred the coffee as she crossed to the small table next to the kitchen window. Morning sunlight filtered through the pale blue curtains, bathing her pale face with a rosy glow.

"What time do you have to go to work?" Mike asked.

"Well, I usually like to be at the computer by eight thirty, since that's when the on-site staff shows up."

Mike frowned. "You work from home?"

She cocked her head. "I told you I had a flexible work schedule."

"Yeah, but I didn't connect that to working at home."

She set the coffee cup in front of her. "You seem… dismayed?"

"Well, I was thinking there'd be safety in numbers if you were going to an office somewhere." He carried three eggs to the stove and looked for a frying pan. "Where's the skillet?"

"Over the stove."

He found the pan and set it on the stove eye, setting the heat to medium high. "Do you use the laptop in your bedroom for work, or do you have a different computer?"

"I use the laptop," she answered, grabbing her cup and walking over to stand beside him. "You're really worried about my being here alone, aren't you?"

"Aren't you?"

She seemed to give the question some thought. "I wasn't. I figured these people don't want to risk getting caught, so they wouldn't attack me in my own home."

"But they were willing to kill you in your car."

"Or maybe they figured I'd think there was something wrong with the brakes before it became dangerous. If I hadn't been traveling on that particular road heading down a mountain, I wouldn't have had nearly as much trouble stopping my car, even without the brakes."

Heat radiated from the pan on the stove eye in front of him. He poured a dollop of oil into the pan and it sizzled immediately. He forced himself to concentrate on cooking for a few moments, until he was ready to spoon the fluffy yellow scrambled eggs onto the two plates Charlie had retrieved from a nearby cabinet.

She'd also put a couple of pieces of bread in the toaster. They popped up as he was spooning the eggs onto the plates. "Butter?"

"Sure," he answered. He'd hauled and tugged enough debris the night before while cleaning up Charlie's living room to allow himself the indulgence.

Over breakfast, he picked up the dropped thread of conversation. "I don't think you can assume the tampering with your brakes was just an attempt to frighten you."

"You're a very comforting man," she said drily.

"I'm serious, Charlie. Someone went to pretty drastic measures to put you in danger. And what happened in this house yesterday afternoon may have been just a warning, but it was a pretty brutal one."

"I'm taking it seriously." She put down her fork. "Believe me."

"I'm not crazy about leaving you here alone today." Mike poked at his eggs, not nearly as hungry now as he'd been a few minutes earlier. "Is there any way you could work from another location? Since you work on a laptop anyway."

"I could," she said with a slight nod, picking up her fork. She tried a bite of eggs. "Pretty good."

"Thanks."

"But there aren't any trendy little internet cafés anywhere around here," she added with a sigh. "And if I go over to Mercerville to the office, they may decide they like having me around there all the time."

"And that would be bad?"

"Very." She stuck out her chin. "One of the reasons I took this particular job was that I could work from home and keep flexible hours."

"Then come to my office."

She shook her head. "I can't leave this place. I can't. I have one traumatized cat still hiding under my bed and another I have to pick up from the vet today who's probably going to have to have one of those plastic cones around his head for the next few days. I can't leave them here alone, and I can't take them with me to your office."

"Then you can take them to my place."

His words fell like a bomb in the middle of the room. Charlie stared at him as if he'd lost his mind, and his own gut clenched as if he'd just taken a sucker punch.

"That is…an unexpected offer," Charlie said finally into the deafening silence.

"Yeah." He picked up his fork and poked at his eggs, now growing cold. "Kind of surprised myself with it, too."

"I won't hold you to it."

He dropped his fork. "I'm not saying it's a bad idea, Charlie."

"Moving into your place with my two special-needs cats isn't a bad idea?" Her expression oozed skepticism.

"No, listen," he said, starting to warm to the idea. "My place has good locks and a state-of-the-art security system. I have two bedrooms, which means I wouldn't have to sleep on the floor. Cable TV, Wi-Fi, central heat and air—"

"Are you trying to sell me on the idea or on a time-share?"

He smiled. "It could work, Charlie. I live close to the office, so if there was any kind of trouble, I could be there in minutes. It's right near the center of town in Mercerville, easy walking distance from a couple of eating places and shops. And I like cats."

"Even crazy ones?"

"Crazy is my favorite breed," he said. Of people as well as cats.

She sighed, her head cocking to one side as she considered it. "Cats can be messy. And temperamental."

"I grew up with cats. I'm not new at it."

"I can also be messy and temperamental."

"I'll cope." Was he really sitting here trying to talk her into invading his bachelor territory? After nearly ten years in the Marine Corps, living alone had turned out to be an unexpected pleasure. Not having to account to anyone else for what music he listened to, what television shows or movies he watched, how late he stayed up or how early he rose—why was he suddenly so eager to bring this unpredictable redhead and her two cats into his domain?

"Okay," she said.

"Okay," he echoed with a nod, wondering what the hell he'd just gotten himself into.

CHARLIE PULLED THE rolling chair closer to the wide oak desk where her laptop computer sat, trying to settle in. It wasn't that the chair itself was uncomfortable. It was the very opposite, a large, ergonomically built manager's chair with plush leather upholstery and caster wheels that moved as smoothly as a hot knife through butter.

No, the problem was the unfamiliarity of the setting and her own growing uneasiness at how quickly she'd allowed Mike to talk her into moving herself and the cats into his house.

What she needed, she realized, was a best friend. Someone like Alice, who'd understood her and could give her sound advice. The problem was, after Alice died, Charlie hadn't tried to find a new best friend. Best friends meant opening yourself up to loss and pain, and she'd had about all she could take of that, thank you very much.

She didn't need other people. She was a strong, independent woman, damn it.

She didn't need a protector.

So what the hell was she doing ensconced in a strange man's house, locked in and safeguarded by a state-of-the-art security system?

A plaintive meow beside her interrupted her fretful musings. His Highness gazed up at her with baleful blue eyes, his dark face framed by a plastic Elizabethan collar the vet had provided to keep him from licking his shoulder stitches.

"I'm sorry, Hizzy. We all have our crosses to bear."

"Everything okay?"

Mike's voice behind her made her jump and sent

Hizzy shooting under the desk, his collar slapping against the wood and sending him sprawling at her feet. Charlie picked up the cat and whirled the chair around to look at Mike, who shot her an apologetic look.

"Yeah, peachy," she answered drily.

"Sorry about that. I'm heading to the office—I have a meeting this afternoon. You sure you're good here by myself?"

"Of course. I'll be fine."

"Help yourself to anything in the fridge. Don't worry about answering the phone—the answering service will get it. If I need to reach you, I'll call your cell phone."

"Yes, Mom."

He grinned. "I'll be back soon. I can grab something on my way home for dinner if you like. There's a nice pizza place near the office—you like pepperoni?"

"Doesn't everyone?"

"I'll call if my plans change. Lock up behind me. And set the perimeter alarm."

She set the cat on the floor and followed him to the living room. "I'll be fine, Mike. This place is a fortress."

"Okay. Call if you need anything."

"Go." She nodded toward the door. After he left, she dutifully locked the door behind her and checked the security system box to make sure the perimeter alarms were set.

Then she returned to the cozy office, where Hizzy sat impatiently in the desk chair, gazing at her through slightly crossed eyes.

"If I take off the collar, do you swear you won't chew your stitches?"

He uttered a mournful meow.

With a sigh, she pulled the edges of the collar apart,

releasing him from the plastic cone. He immediately started licking his shoulder.

"If you chew those stitches, the cone goes back on," she warned and set him on the floor by the chair.

She'd gotten behind on some of her work projects while she was dealing with the problems with her car and the vandalism of her house, so she buckled down to handling those tasks, checking every few minutes to make sure Hizzy hadn't started picking at his stitches.

An hour later, she had worked her way through the three most time-sensitive documents on her to-do list and was about to tackle the fourth when a loud trilling noise sent a shudder of surprise skating down her back.

The phone trilled a second time. It sat in a base on the right side of the desk, next to the crook-necked lamp. The phone display lit up with a phone number and a name.

Craig Bearden for Senate.

Charlie stared at the number, first with confusion, then with a flood of dismay. Why was Craig Bearden's campaign office calling Mike Strong?

Maybe it's a campaign call, Charlie. Stop being so suspicious.

Only one way to be sure. She picked up the phone. "Hello?"

"Is Mike Strong available?" The voice on the other line sounded vaguely familiar. It wasn't Craig Bearden, however. Bearden's voice was a rich, sonorous baritone. The tenor voice on the line spoke in clipped tones, with only a hint of a Kentucky accent.

"Mr. Strong isn't in. May I take a message?"

"This is Randall Feeney. I'd like to reschedule our appointment and apologize for missing our meeting two days ago."

Charlie's stomach sank. Now she knew why the voice

sounded familiar. Randall Feeney had been Craig Bearden's chief aide since his early days on the county commission, back when Alice had still been alive.

She cleared her throat. "I'm sorry. I don't know his schedule. May I have him call you back?"

There was a brief pause on the other end of the line. "I'll call him back later," Feeney said. He hung up without saying goodbye.

Charlie set the phone back on the base and slumped in her chair, her mind racing. So, Mike had made an appointment with Randall Feeney, just a couple of days after Charlie showed up in his self-defense class.

Was that a coincidence?

She didn't think so.

She opened her purse and pulled her phone from the inside pocket, pulling up her list of contacts. She'd had five different phones since Alice's death, but she had always put Alice's number in her contact list on the new phone, as if that one small gesture would keep Alice alive for her somehow.

Had the Beardens changed their number? Would someone answer if she pressed Send?

Her finger trembled over the phone screen for a long moment. Then she set the phone on the desk in front of her, releasing a long, shaky breath.

She wasn't ready to deal with the Beardens yet. So if she wanted to know why Mike Strong had contacted Craig Bearden's campaign office, she'd just have to ask him herself.

She picked up her phone, shoved it in her pocket and grabbed the jacket hanging on the back of the chair.

And she had to do it as soon as possible, before she lost her nerve.

Chapter Eight

Rebecca Cameron was a formidable woman. Not just because she was sleekly beautiful and graceful, a woman of impeccable manners and dazzling intellect. But she was a woman who'd come from humble beginnings, an African American girl raised by a steel worker and a kindergarten teacher in the deepest South, who'd risen above discrimination and oppression with dignity and determination to become one of the most well-respected diplomats in the Foreign Service.

With her steely will, she had faced down the most aggressively domineering men in the halls of power and won her battles with a smile. And it was with that same core of iron she greeted Mike with a cool smile and waved him into the seat in front of her desk.

"So," she said with no preamble, "why have you contacted the Craig Bearden campaign office?"

Mike tried not to fidget like a kid in the principal's office. "I was doing a background check."

The arch of Cameron's perfect eyebrows rose a notch. "I wasn't aware your job description included investigations."

"Technically, it doesn't," Mike admitted, holding her gaze with a little steely determination of his own. "But one of my self-defense students pinged my radar—"

"And you thought you'd look into his background?"

"Her," he corrected. "And I discussed it with Maddox Heller first."

"Ah." She sat back, relaxing a little. Her long fingers steepled over her flat stomach as she held his gaze thoughtfully. She was a musician, he remembered. A violinist. Those long fingers had plucked strings in concert halls across the globe.

Her continuing silence started to make him nervous again. "Is that why you wanted to see me?"

"Not entirely. But the other matter can wait for now. I'm rather more interested in your impromptu investigation. Why did you contact Mr. Bearden?"

"If I may ask, how did you learn that I did?"

"Mr. Bearden, his wife and I have mutual friends. We've met several times in the past, and when one of my employees made contact with his campaign, he wanted to know why."

"I see. What did you tell him?"

She smiled. "I told him you were doing a background check on someone looking for work with one of our clients."

"And did that appease him?"

"He wanted to know who we were vetting."

"And you didn't know."

Cameron's expression made clear how little she enjoyed being asked a question she couldn't answer. "I told him you were working under a different division and I would contact you directly for the information." She sat forward again, closing the distance between them until he felt the intensity of her focus. "Which I am now doing."

"Her name is Charlotte Winters. I asked Maddox Heller to do a preliminary background check on her—

confirm her name, address, that sort of thing. He discovered she was a person of interest in a murder."

Cameron's eyes narrowed. "Whose?"

Mike could tell from her tone that she already suspected the truth. "Alice Bearden's."

"I see." Cameron released a slow breath. "Is she still?"

"If she is, she's never been charged."

"What do you think of her?"

The memory of Charlie's quirky smile flitted through his mind, along with her fresh soap-and-water scent. He pictured her long limbs, her coltish gait, her husky drawl and her raspy laugh, and he tried to imagine her hitting Alice Bearden with a car and driving away without trying to help her.

"I don't think she could have done it," he said aloud before he could stop himself.

"But you're still looking into her past?"

"There have been a couple of new developments." He told Cameron about the car tampering and the break-in at Charlie's house. "Her cat was injured in the vandalism attack. If Charlie had been home, she might have been the one who was hurt."

"And this has something to do with Alice Bearden's death?" Cameron's voice was tight with doubt.

"I don't know," he admitted. "It seems unlikely that something that happened so long ago would suddenly put her life in danger now. Nothing's changed in the case, as far as I've been able to tell." Although, he hadn't contacted the police to see if there might have been a new development, had he? There was a Mercerville cop in his intermediate self-defense course, Archer Trask.

The same cop he'd seen locked up in a tense conversation with Charlie just yesterday.

"What are you thinking?" Cameron asked.

"I'm thinking I need to ask a few more questions. Which is why I tried to talk to Craig Bearden or at least someone who works for him."

"I told Craig he should speak to you. I'm sure you'll be hearing from him or someone in his campaign soon."

"Good."

"What about the woman—Ms. Winters? Does she have a safe place to stay until her home has been better secured?"

To his mortification, Mike felt heat rise up his neck. Was he blushing? He hadn't blushed since third grade. But he knew better than to lie to one of his bosses. All three of them—Cameron, Heller and the third partner, Alexander Quinn—had a long history of uncovering secrets people wanted to keep hidden.

"She's staying at my place," he said.

Cameron's gaze was expressionless and she said nothing, letting his last words ring in the silence between them.

"I have a spare room and a good security system. I'm close enough to reach her quickly if she needs my help."

"That's rather…altruistic of you."

"I can also keep an eye on her," he added, trying not to sound defensive. "If she's done something to invite danger into her life, I'll be in a good position to figure out what it is."

"Makes sense," Cameron said in a tone that suggested it did no such thing. "Perhaps, given your proximity now, you should ask her a few questions about herself. Get the information straight from the source."

Well. Didn't he feel stupid now. "You're right. I should."

Cameron pushed her chair back and stood. "I may ask you for your help with a project in a week or two, but for now, I think you should follow your instincts about Charlie Winters. If she is using our academy for questionable reasons, we need to know so that we can put a stop to it. And if she's genuinely in trouble, well, putting a stop to trouble is one of our prime directives, isn't it?"

Mike stood as well, aware he was being dismissed. "I'll keep Heller informed of what I find out."

"Do that." Cameron walked him to the door. "And do take care."

He left her office and took a left toward the gymnasium. While he was here, he might as well put a little time in with the weights. He hadn't had a chance to work out since Charlie Winters had crashed his life, and working out helped him clear the clutter from his mind and think.

He had a lot to think about.

But he didn't make it to the weight room. A door opened down the hall, a door from outside, letting in a gust of wind and rain. A tall, long-limbed silhouette filled the rectangle of light before the door closed behind it, plunging the end of the corridor into darkness again.

The dark figure moved toward him, into the dim light shed by the recessed lights in the ceiling. It was Charlie, drenched from head to foot, her red hair dark and curling, and her sweater and jeans plastered to her body, revealing unexpected curves that her loose-fitting clothing usually concealed.

"What the hell are you doing here?" he blurted, taking in her bedraggled appearance. "Did you walk here in the rain?"

Her hazel eyes were wide and dark in her pale face, and she was shivering. "You had a phone call. I took a message."

Even through chattering teeth, she conveyed an unmistakable tone of anger. He took an instinctive step back from her, out of her reach.

"Yeah? It was important enough to risk your life and health to walk a mile in a cold rain to get here? Wouldn't a phone call have been more logical?"

Her eyes flashed irritation at him. "Are you mocking me?"

He shook his head quickly. "I'm just trying to understand why you're here."

"I'm here," she said tightly, her teeth still clacking together as she spoke, "because the person who called was a man named Randall Feeney."

Oh. "You answered my phone?"

"Is that a problem?"

"You could have let the voice mail pick up." He tried to sound nonchalant, but he didn't seem to be succeeding, if the thunderclouds in her expression were anything to go by.

"I might have, but the name was familiar. And insatiable curiosity is one of my worst flaws." Her hair was dripping rainwater down her face in rivulets; she pushed the soaked curls back away from her face and ran her palms over her damp cheeks. "Why did you want a meeting with Randall Feeney?"

"Listen, I'll be glad to talk to you about this. But you're dripping all over the hall. You have to be freezing." He put his hand on her arm, felt the icy chill of her wet sweater and shivered himself. "Let's get you into some dry clothes, how about it? Before you become hypothermic."

She pulled her arm away from his grasp. "Don't handle me, okay? Just tell me the truth. Are you investigating me or something?"

"Why would you think that?"

"Because you've taken an unusual interest in my well-being all of a sudden. Coming to my rescue, standing guard over me and now moving me into your house, where you can keep an eye on me. Am I a suspect?"

"I don't know," he admitted. "I just know that you didn't join my self-defense course out of the blue, for no reason. You had an agenda. You pinged my danger radar the very first day."

"Is that why you put me in your intermediate course?"

"No, I told you the truth about why I switched you to the new class. But I can't help but wonder at the coincidence of your starting a self-defense class just a couple of days before your car's brakes were tampered with and your house was trashed by an intruder."

She stared back at him wordlessly for a moment. Then her gaze dropped, and she lifted shaky hands to her head again, shoving her fingers through her damp hair. "I'm freezing."

"I know. Let's find you something to change into."

THE SWEATSHIRT AND jersey-knit workout pants borrowed from one of Mike's female colleagues were a little short for Charlie's long limbs, but they were dry and blessedly warm. She huddled in a shivering knot in the chair in front of Mike's desk and watched him dig through a battered military-green footlocker until he found what he was looking for—an olive drab blanket that looked as if it had seen a few rough tours of duty.

"Sit forward," he said gruffly. She did as he said, and he wrapped the blanket around her shoulders. "It's warmer than it looks."

She pulled the blanket more closely around her as he took his seat behind the desk. "Thanks."

"Warmer?"

She nodded.

"Ready to tell me why you walked all the way here in the rain?"

"I told you."

"You found out I was trying to make a meeting with someone from Craig Bearden's campaign." His eyes narrowed. "But you didn't explain why that was alarming enough to make you come dashing over here in the middle of a storm."

"Why did you contact Randall Feeney?"

He didn't answer immediately. Instead, he leaned back in his chair and looked at her with an uncomfortably direct gaze, as if taking her measure. The silence unspooling between them had become uncomfortable before he finally spoke. "You set off my radar in class."

"I know. You told me that."

"I asked one of my associates here to look into your background."

She stared at him. "You did a background check on me?"

"I needed to know if you had an ulterior motive for joining my class. What we do here at Campbell Cove Academy is important work. We're training people to protect themselves, their families and their communities in the case of a terrorist attack or some other mass-casualty event. Or to prevent those events, if possible."

"I know your company's mission statement." She waved one hand with impatience. "You actually saw me as a potential threat?"

"I have to assume everyone is a potential threat," he answered with equal exasperation. "I have to run all the scenarios in my head and make sure I'm not letting an enemy through the gates."

"Which you thought I was."

"I thought you might be, so I had someone check your background."

"And that led you to Craig Bearden." She wiped a drop of rainwater away from her forehead, wishing she'd asked for a towel to dry her hair.

"You were with Alice Bearden the night she was killed. The police considered you a person of interest for a long time."

"I wasn't driving the car that hit Alice."

"So what happened that night?"

She looked at him through narrowed eyes. "Didn't your background check give you all the details?"

"Not everything. Not the things you could tell me."

She tucked her knees up to her chest and pulled her cold, bare toes beneath the soft cotton of the olive drab blanket. "Why does it matter now? It was so long ago."

"Ten years, right?"

She nodded. "Give or take a few months."

He rose and came around the desk to stand in front of her. "Did it have anything to do with your decision to take a self-defense course?"

How could she answer his question without revealing just how much of a hidden agenda she really had? She hadn't told anyone in her life about her decision to take a new look at Alice's death because everybody, including Alice's parents, considered her death a closed chapter. She'd died in a hit-and-run accident. Period. Someone had gotten away with vehicular homicide, but it wasn't as if her death had been premeditated, was it?

Except Charlie was starting to think maybe it had been premeditated. Or, at the very least, her death wasn't nearly as cut-and-dried as the police reports had finally concluded.

Charlie's memories were incomplete. But fragments

had begun to emerge in her dreams recently, revealing enough mysteries and unanswered questions to pique her lifelong curiosity.

Charlie needed the questions answered. The mysteries solved.

But could Mike Strong understand that need? And if he did, would he really be willing to help her find those answers?

"Just say it, Charlie." He crouched in front of her chair, his voice low and soft, a seduction. Not just a physical temptation, though she was already resigned to her physical attraction to him. It was the emotional attraction she felt, the all-too-enticing desire to pile all her fears and troubles on his extrawide shoulders and let him handle things for a while, that left her feeling upended and unsettled.

She told herself she couldn't let herself surrender. She'd survived the harsh world of her childhood by never depending on anyone else for anything.

Could she really start now?

But she hadn't exactly done a great job of going it alone, had she?

He touched her hand where it clutched the blanket. "You want to tell me, but you're afraid."

She met his gaze, remaining silent.

"Do you remember something new?" When she didn't answer, he added, "Someone seems to think you do."

He was right. And she was foolish to think this time she could handle things alone. She had to trust someone.

Maybe it could be Mike.

"Tell me, Charlie." His growly whisper sent a shiver through her. "Someone tried to kill you. They trashed your house. They're not playing games. They're serious."

"I know." If she let herself think about it, the memory

of pressing her foot on the brake pedal and feeling no response at all could send panic rocketing through her again. "I just don't know why."

"Are you sure?"

"Mike, I don't remember most of the night Alice died."

"Why? Were you drunk?"

"I shouldn't have been. I've never been much of a drinker. I grew up with drinkers, and all alcohol ever did for them was raise their levels of stupidity to legendary heights." She shook her head. "I wouldn't have drunk enough to pass out. I just wouldn't have."

"So why don't you remember?"

He was too close, the heat of his body too intense. She pushed back her chair and rose, wrapping the blanket tightly around her as she crossed to the window. Outside, the day was drenched and gloomy, drizzle pebbling the window to render the view of the parking lot misty and dreamlike.

"I think maybe I was drugged."

She'd never said the words out loud before, never let herself consider the ramifications. But it was the one thing that made sense of what little she could remember of that night.

"Were you—" Mike's voice was unexpectedly close behind her.

"No," she said quickly, turning to face him. In a bar situation, a dose of Rohypnol or GHB—gamma hydroxybutyric acid—was usually the precursor of sexual assault. Charlie hadn't felt as if she'd been assaulted in any way when she woke cold and damp in her backyard early the next morning after her night out with Alice.

Well, her head had been fuzzy and throbbing, and her memory was a wide vista of nothingness, but her clothes were all in place and she didn't have any of the morning-after sensations she associated with sex. "I don't think I was raped. I think I was…removed from the situation."

He cocked his head. "Meaning?"

"I think Alice went to the Headhunter in hopes of running into someone else. She took me along so she didn't spend the whole night fending off pickup artists."

"Did you tell the cops your theory?"

"I wasn't sure. By the time I had a chance to think anything through, the story was already set in the news. Bar sells alcohol to underage teens. One of them dies in a hit-and-run accident outside the bar. The grieving father vows to honor his daughter's memory by working to close the gaps in the law that allow those things to happen." She shook her head. "Nobody wanted to hear an alternative theory."

"I do," Mike said gently.

"So do I," she said. "But the problem is, I still don't have one. At least, not one I can prove."

Mike lifted his hands to her cheeks, his palms warm against her cold cheeks. His thumbs brushed lightly across her cheeks, smearing moisture, and she realized she had been crying.

"Then let's find some proof," he said.

"How? It was ten years ago."

"We do what a cop would do," he said with a gruff firmness that gave her an idea what he must have been like as a Marine. "Tomorrow night, we'll start at the scene of the crime."

Chapter Nine

Charlie hadn't expected to sleep much on her first night at Mike's place. Besides the strange bed and the strange man in the room across the hall, she'd also had to contend with a grumpy Siamese cat in a plastic cone collar and a scaredy-cat tortoiseshell cat who jumped at every strange noise.

But the walk in the rain and the stress of the afternoon as she and Mike mapped out their plan for a trip to the Headhunter Bar on Saturday night had apparently wrung out all of the adrenaline left in her body, and she slept all night, waking only when Hizzy plopped onto her chest and butted her with the sharp edge of his plastic cone.

"Ow!" she complained, pushing him gently away. "You're a menace with that thing."

There was a knock on the door and Mike's muffled voice from the other side. "Are you up?"

"Getting there," she called, rolling to a sitting position on the edge of the bed. "Give me a few minutes."

"Breakfast is almost ready."

Breakfast, she discovered when she finished dressing and headed into the kitchen, was again scrambled eggs and toast, plus hot coffee that hit the spot. While they were eating, Hizzy wandered into the kitchen, bumping his cone against the door frame on the way to her side.

"How much longer does he have to wear the cone of shame?" Mike asked.

"The vet said I could take it off for a few hours at a time as long as I could keep an eye on him and make sure he doesn't chew his stitches." She bent and offered Hizzy a bite of eggs. "This reminds me, I need to go back home and get the extra bag of cat food I left in the mudroom. This morning I used up the last of the food I brought with me."

"I'll swing by and get it for you," Mike offered. "I've got to head that way to meet with Randall Feeney."

Charlie stopped with her coffee cup halfway to her mouth. "He got back to you?"

"I called him back. While you were in the shower yesterday afternoon." Mike bent and held out a piece of egg for Hizzy. The cat sniffed at it and finally nibbled the food from Mike's fingers.

"And you didn't tell me?"

"You were tired and stressed. I thought it could wait for this morning."

"What are you going to say to him?"

Mike wiped his hands on a paper towel. "That I was doing a background check on you."

"What if he asks you why?"

"I'll tell him it's routine for anyone who attends any of our classes."

Charlie shook her head. "Don't tell him I'm taking classes at the academy."

"Why not?"

"I just don't want him to know," she said, not certain why she felt that way.

Mike gave her a curious look, but he just nodded. "I'll say it's for a potential employer, then."

"That's good."

"Speaking of employers, did everything go okay yesterday? Your computer setup working like it's supposed to?"

"Everything was fine. I managed to get all caught up, so I won't need to do any mop-up over the weekend."

"Great, because we have plans this evening."

The thought of their excursion into Mercerville's seedy side made Charlie's breakfast settle in a queasy lump at the pit of her stomach. "Right."

He reached across the table. "If you don't want to do this, say so. I'll figure out something else."

The temptation to back out of their plan was unexpectedly potent. But she'd never be able to look herself in the mirror if she chickened out. "No. We're going. I need to see if I can remember anything else."

He gave her an odd look. "Anything else? Have you remembered something already?"

She hadn't told him about the dreams. She wasn't all that sure she thought they were real memories herself. Dreams could be deceiving.

But her behavior would suggest she'd already made up her mind. If she didn't believe those dream-memories had meaning, she wouldn't be dredging up the most horrific night of her life, would she?

"Charlie?"

"I've been having dreams," she said.

STILL PONDERING THE things Charlie had told him, Mike pulled his truck into the driveway of Charlie's house and sat there for a moment, the engine idling, while he took a look around the neighborhood from the safety of the cab. Yesterday's rain had given way to watery sunshine brightening inch by inch as morning crept toward midday.

Despite the improved weather, the other houses in the neighborhood were still and silent. No children played in the winter-brown yards. No home owners raked away the last of the autumn leaves.

People must keep to themselves in this area, Mike thought. He'd talked to the Campbell Cove police officer who'd come to Charlie's house the day the intruder trashed the place. Officer Bentley had canvassed the neighborhood to see if anyone had spotted the intruders. No one had seen anything, although the nearest neighbor had arrived home early from work the day of the vandalism. Bentley had theorized that the sound of the neighbor coming home at an unexpected time might have sent the vandals running before they finished the job.

What Bentley hadn't said was how the vandals would have known what time the neighbors usually came home in the first place. It suggested a level of surveillance that didn't seem likely for a random intruder.

Someone was afraid of what Charlie was starting to remember. That was the only possible reason for the things happening to her now.

Charlie told him that she'd tried contacting Craig Bearden a few weeks ago, after the dreams started. She'd left a message, telling him she wanted to talk to him about Alice's death. She'd even mentioned the memories she was starting to recover, hoping he'd be interested enough to call her back and help her figure out what had really happened that night.

Could someone at the campaign office have intercepted the message? Or had Craig received it himself and mentioned it to the wrong person?

For that matter, could Craig Bearden himself have been involved in what had happened to his daughter?

Pondering the possibilities, Mike walked up the path

to Charlie's porch. The key Charlie had given him opened the front door. He made a mental note to call a locksmith to change the front dead bolt, though he wasn't sure it would make a difference. Whoever had wrecked Charlie's house a couple of days ago had gotten in without forcing the lock. Either they'd had access to Charlie's keys or they knew how to beat a lock.

He'd talk her into spending the money on a decent alarm system, too. Campbell Cove Security Services worked with a good outfit who would do the work for her at a reasonable price.

The living room looked depressingly bare, now that he and Charlie had moved the worst of the destruction to the alley behind her house. He could pack most of the bigger pieces into the bed of his truck and carry them to the dump outside town, he thought. Then maybe the trash collection truck could take the rest.

The desolation made the house seem colder than it should have been on that mild December day. It was lifeless without its vibrant inhabitant and her two cat companions.

He paused halfway down the hall, drawn toward the bedroom and the quilt-covered bed where he and Charlie had sat two nights before, talking about themselves in hushed tones in the dark.

He ran his hands over the intricate pattern of the bedcover, noting the hand stitching and the faded patches that suggested the quilt had been handmade years ago. A family heirloom? A thrift store treasure?

There was so much he didn't know about her, and normally such a thought didn't bother him. He was a results-oriented sort of guy. Get in, get the job done, get out. He didn't bother too much about personalities and avoided thinking about emotions and motivations, except to make sure they didn't come between him and his goal.

But Charlie made him want to know more. Sometimes, meeting her gaze, he sensed there was a whole other world beneath the reflective mountain-pool eyes, a place of mysteries and wonders he wanted to investigate. How much was she still keeping secret from him? What was she hiding, and why?

He tugged the quilt from the bed and folded it into a neat square. It would fit nicely on his spare bed, he thought, and it would make her feel a little more at home. Maybe help her relax her guard and share a few of her secrets with him.

He set the blanket on the kitchen table and took a step into the mudroom.

There was a flash of movement. He had the impression of something black and red moving toward him in a rush, then pain exploded in the side of his head, sending him reeling hard into the door frame. Agony bloomed like a noxious cloud, filling his stunned brain with a blinding mist the color of dried blood. For a moment, he could hear nothing, feel nothing but throbbing pain filling his head. Then sensations returned in a flash of light and noise. Sunlight pierced the mudroom window and into his brain like a dagger. He heard a door open and slam shut behind him, the sound like a hammer blow.

He pushed himself away from the wall, wincing at the thudding ache that had replaced the fuzzy sensation in his brain. Staggering to the back door to look through the four-paned window, he scanned the backyard. Behind her house, the woods encroached on the lawn, casting a shadowy gloom over the vista. At first, he saw nothing but the faint sway of the winter-bare tree limbs rattled by the light breeze. But movement caught his eye, and he spotted a man dressed in dark green camouflage zigzagging through the underbrush several yards from the house.

He opened the door and headed toward the fleeing figure, but his feet didn't want to cooperate with each other. He tripped over the uneven ground, staggering sideways. He caught himself before he fell to the ground, but by the time he regained his balance, he could no longer see the man in camouflage. He watched the woods for several moments, trying to reacquire his target, but he quickly realized the effort was futile. The intruder had gotten too large a head start, and Mike's brain was too fuzzy from the knock on the head for him to make up any ground, even if he'd managed to catch sight of the fleeing man.

He lifted his hand to the side of his head and felt the sticky heat of blood oozing from a tender spot on the side of his forehead. He reentered the house and looked around the mudroom, wondering what had hit him. There was a dented can of stewed tomatoes lying on the floor beside an otherwise neat row of canned goods on a set of shelves against the inner wall of the mudroom. Up on the top shelf, packed inside a large plastic bin with a lid, there was a large unopened bag of cat food.

He reached up to bring down the bin, grimacing at the pain shooting through his head. He thought better of taking the bag of food out of the plastic bin—if Charlie had stored it there, she must have had a good reason why—and just carried the bin into the kitchen and set it on the table next to the quilt.

Then he grabbed a few paper towels and carried them with him into the bathroom to take a look at the damage the intruder had done.

The cut on the side of his head was evenly curved, confirming his suspicious that he'd been coldcocked with the can of tomatoes. Fortunately, the can had caught him on the side of his forehead, where the thicker bone had protected his brain from the blow. A few inches lower, the thin bone of his temples might not have sustained the hit nearly as well.

There was a surprising amount of blood for so small and shallow a wound, but head wounds tended to bleed a lot. Mike had sustained worse injuries in his time in the Marine Corps. He mopped up the mess and pressed against the tender spot to stop the bleeding, then took a closer look.

The skin was already turning blue around the wound, and it would probably only get worse as the day went on, but the split in the skin wasn't deep enough to require stitches at least. He found a couple of adhesive bandage strips in the medicine cabinet and covered the cut. With the wound hidden from view by the bandages, he almost looked back to normal.

Well, except for the blood staining the left side of his shirt. But his jacket should cover the stains for the drive home.

But he wasn't quite ready to leave yet. Someone had come back to Charlie's house looking for something.

What had he been looking for?

"WHAT DO YOU THINK, Nellie? Should we take off the cone of shame and see if Hizzy can behave?" Charlie scratched behind Nellie's brindle-colored ears and looked at His Highness sitting in front of her, blue eyes staring back at her with haughty disdain.

He had finally stopped bumping into everything with the small plastic cone fastened around his head, but he was clearly unhappy with its continuing presence.

The wound on his shoulder wouldn't be easy for him

to reach, even if he twisted his head as far as it would turn, she decided. "Come here, Hizzy. Let's get that thing off you."

The cat eyed her warily for a moment before he slowly slinked across the floor to her and let her pet his head. She unfastened the plastic cone collar and eased it from his neck. Immediately, he started to groom himself.

She watched to make sure he didn't start chewing his stitches, but he seemed more interested in washing his paws and his face.

The trill of her cell phone ringing made her nerves jangle and sent both of the cats skittering away to stare at her from opposite corners of the room. She pulled the phone from the pocket of her jeans. Mike's number. "Hello?"

"Everything going okay there?" He sounded a little strange, she thought, his voice a little thick.

"Everything's fine. Did you find the cat food okay?"

"Yeah. You want me to bring the box it's in, too?"

"If you don't want the cats to rip into the cat food bag and leave food scattered all over your house, yes."

"Ah. That's why it's in the box."

"I thought you had cats before."

"It's been a while. Since I was a kid. I didn't bother with where to store the cat food back then."

"You sound strange. Everything okay?"

"Yeah."

She didn't find his tone convincing. "Did something happen?"

There was a long pause, then he sighed. "There was someone in the house when I got here."

"My God." She tightened her grip on the phone. "Did you see him?"

"Only at a distance. He caught me off guard and got away. I didn't get a good look."

"Caught you off guard? Are you okay?"

"I'm fine. I'll tell you all about it when I get home. But while I'm still here—do you have any idea what the intruder might have been looking for?"

"No," she said without hesitation. If she possessed anything that might prove dangerous to anyone else in the world, it was locked inside her brain, unreachable even by her.

"Then what was he here for?"

To stop her, she thought. To keep her from ever remembering what happened that night in Mercerville.

"I think maybe he was there to kill me," she said.

Suddenly, from somewhere down the hall, she heard a loud electronic beep. Over the phone, Mike uttered a soft profanity.

"What is that?" she asked, pushing to her feet to follow the sound.

As she reached the source and saw the electronic monitor with one light blinking bright red in time with the beeping noise, Mike said, his voice tight with dismay, "It's the perimeter alarm. Someone's moving around outside the house."

The nerves the beeping noise had set jangling were rattling hard now, making her shake as she tightened her grasp on the phone before it fell from her trembling fingers. "What should I do? Will the system notify the cops?"

"No. It can be set off by an animal crossing the sensor beam. I don't have it set for automatic notification."

"Should I call the cops?"

"I'm a lot closer. I'll be there before your call gets forwarded to the right people. Just hang tight. I'm heading out now." Over the phone, she heard a symphony of disparate sounds—Mike's rapid breathing, a few strange, rattling thuds and then a door slamming shut. A few thumps and bangs later, she heard the sound of the truck engine roaring to life. "Stay on the phone with me, Charlie. Whatever you do, don't put down the phone."

He was scaring her now. "Shouldn't I go see who's at the door?"

"No," he said quickly, "don't go near the door."

"I could look through the security lens—"

"The door may be steel reinforced, but the windows aren't bullet resistant. You could be targeted. Stay away from doors and windows. Where are you now?"

"In the hall by the alarm keypad."

"Stay right there. I'll be home in minutes."

She heard three hard rapping noises coming from down the hall. "I think someone is knocking on the door."

"Don't answer it, Charlie."

"Not moving," she assured him.

Two more knocks rattled the door. "What if it's someone looking for you?"

"They'll just have to try back later," he answered. "Charlie, I know you're as curious as a kitten—"

"I'm not stupid," she snapped back. "Trust me. I'm not moving from this hall until you get here."

"Good." Mike fell silent, apparently concentrating on driving. From the sound of the truck's engine, he was driving way too fast for the narrow mountain roads between her house and his, but she had a feeling he was a good enough driver to handle it.

In fact, she was certain he was one hell of a man to have in her corner no matter what the situation. She took comfort from the knowledge that he was on the way and would be here soon. It was almost enough to calm her jangling nerves.

Until she heard the scrape of metal on metal coming from the front of the house.

Chapter Ten

There was a soft gasp on Charlie's end of the phone, and then all Mike could hear was rapid breathing.

"Charlie?" He tapped the Bluetooth earpiece. "Are you still there?"

"Someone's coming in the door!" Her voice was a panicky hiss of breath. "Oh, my God—"

"Go to my bedroom and lock the door behind you. There's a table by the bed—drag it in front of the door. Then go to my closet and get inside."

"Okay." He heard the soft thud of her footsteps as she hurried down the hallway and into his bedroom, then the scrape of the bedside table moving. A moment later, she spoke again. "I'm in the closet. There's no way to lock the door."

"I know. I just wanted you in the closet because that's where I keep my weapons."

There was a brief pause, then she whispered, "Oh."

"Do you know anything about handguns or rifles?"

"I've shot guns before," she said softly. "But it was a long time ago."

"I don't think they've changed that much since then. Can you see anything in the closet?"

"No," she whispered.

"There's a light switch just inside the door."

He heard a muted click and a huff of breath from Charlie. "That's better."

"See the gun safe now?"

"The big safe with a keypad?"

"That's the one." He gave her the number combination and waited for her to punch it in.

"It's not working," she said, her voice rising with alarm.

He knew the sound of panic when he heard it. "Stop, Charlie. Stop a second and just take a couple of deep breaths, okay? In and out." He breathed with her, even though his own body was so pumped with adrenaline, he felt as if ants were crawling all over him. "In and out."

He was only a couple of blocks away. Another block and he'd have his own preparations to worry about. His Glock 19 was loaded and snug in a hip holster, so he could go in hot. But he still needed to be prepared mentally as well as tactically, especially with a civilian in danger.

"Try it again," he said, pulling to a quick stop at the corner stop sign. He could almost see his house from here. Just a few more yards...

"It's open," she breathed. Then she sucked in a swift breath. "Good grief, how many people do you plan to shoot?"

His lips curved, trying to picture his gun cabinet from her point of view. He owned several pistols, a shotgun and a rifle with a sniper scope. He'd hoped he'd never have to use any of them, but life in a free country came with costs.

"Do any of them look familiar?"

She was quiet a second. "My brother had a Mossberg shotgun. I know how to load it, and from there, it's pretty much point and shoot."

"Okay. Load it. But don't shoot it unless your life is absolutely in danger, understand? I don't want to get shot when I get there."

"I'll sit right here and try not to shoot anyone," she muttered.

"I'm nearly there." He could see his house now. There was a dark blue sedan parked in the driveway. He didn't recognize it. He didn't see anyone in the vehicle or standing on his porch, so apparently the driver had somehow made it past his dead bolt and entered the house.

He drove past, parked on the street two houses down and used the neighbors' yards and houses to provide cover as he headed for the back of his house. He could still hear Charlie's soft, rapid breathing in the Bluetooth earpiece. "I'm on my way, Charlie. Can you hear anything outside the closet?"

"I think maybe footsteps. I'm not sure."

"Nobody's tried to get in the bedroom?"

"No."

"Great. Hang tight. I'm hanging up now so I can concentrate, okay?"

"Okay." She didn't sound as if she meant it.

"It's almost over. I promise. The next thing you'll hear is me coming in the back door."

"You gonna bust in, SWAT-style?" she asked.

"You like the sound of that, do you?" He kept his voice light.

"Sounds kind of sexy," she admitted, her own voice a little less shaky. "Once things are under control, I won't complain if you take off your shirt and smolder at me a little bit."

He couldn't hold back a grin. "You read too many books, Charlie."

"One can never read too many books." She sounded

considerably calmer now. Clearly, a little flirtation was Charlie's version of relaxation.

"Talk to you soon." He disconnected the call, pulled off the Bluetooth headset and shoved it in his pocket.

He was at the back door now. He stuck the key in the lock, taking care to turn it as quietly as possible, glad that he'd oiled the door hinges recently. The back door swung open with little noise, and he stepped into the kitchen and swept the room with his pistol.

Clear.

He heard a soft scraping noise coming from the front room. A chair leg moving across the floor?

Silently, he crept up the hall, leading with the Glock. He paused just clear of the doorway into the living room and listened. He heard breathing now. Quiet. Calm. If the intruder was nervous about breaking into Mike's house, he showed no outward sign of it.

Edging forward, Mike peeked around the door frame and caught sight of the intruder. Tall, rawboned, with wavy blond hair cut short, poking at the wood in the fireplace, trying to coax the flickering flames to life.

He dropped the pistol to his side. "Mom?"

Amelia Strong gave a start, whirling to face him, the fire poker she held brandished like a weapon. "Michael, you scared the stuffing out of me!"

He stared at her in confusion, his adrenaline rush subsiding. "What are you doing here?"

She flashed him a sheepish grin and threw her arms out to the sides. "Surprise!"

He frowned. "Surprise?"

She put the fire poker back in the stand beside the anemic fire in his hearth. "Your birthday tomorrow? You didn't call to make plans for celebrating..."

"So you decided to drive up here and take it into your

own hands." He put his pistol in the holster and gave her a swift hug. "I'm sorry. I should have called and told you things had gotten crazy busy around here."

She was staring at his head. "What did you do to yourself?"

He lifted his fingers to the bandages. "It's nothing."

"My God, is that blood on your face?"

"Mom, I promise you I'm fine."

"You've been bleeding. And now that I look at you, you're looking a little sweaty and pale."

"Maybe because I thought there was a burglar in my house," he grumbled. "When I gave you that key, it was supposed to be for emergencies only. Remember?"

"A forgotten birthday is an emergency."

"Mom, hold on a second, okay?" He put his hand up to keep her where she was, then hurried down the hallway to his bedroom. He knocked on the door. "Charlie, it's Mike. Everything's fine. You can unlock the door for me now. And leave the shotgun in the closet."

He heard the closet door open and footsteps from the other side of the door. The bedside table scraped out of the way and Charlie opened the door, looking up at him with wide eyes.

Then she launched herself at him, her long arms wrapping around his neck as she buried her face in his neck.

"Whoa, there." He enfolded her in his embrace, breathing deeply of the clean smell he now associated with her alone. "Everything's okay. It was just a false alarm."

She pulled her head back. "You mean nobody was here? I swear I heard someone coming in. And just a minute ago, I thought I heard voices."

"Michael?" His mother's voice sounded uncertain.

Mike and Charlie both turned to look at her.

"I'm sorry. Did I interrupt something?" Amelia asked.

Mike took a deep breath and turned to look at Charlie. "Charlie, meet your intruder. My mom."

"SO, OF COURSE, since I hadn't heard from him in over a week, I thought he was probably too busy to come visit me for his birthday, so I asked Lauren to watch the shop for me a few days while I went to visit my handsome son." Amelia Strong flashed Charlie a smile that had "I want grandchildren and I want them now" written all over it. "So, Michael, where have you been hiding Charlie?"

"In the closet," Charlie quipped with a nervous laugh.

"Charlie is a client," Mike said carefully. "She's dealing with an unknown stalker. She's staying here a few days so I can keep an eye on her."

"And she brought her cat?" Amelia arched one sandy eyebrow at His Highness, who had settled next to her on the sofa and was watching her with crossed blue eyes.

"Cats," Charlie corrected. "Although Nellie hasn't ventured out from under the bed that much since I got here, so it's almost like there's only one cat. Except for the two food bowls." She shut up, aware she was starting to babble, something she often did when she met strangers.

She could almost see Amelia Strong striking Charlie's name from her list of potential grandchild producers with a big red marker.

She shot Mike a helpless look, her gaze snagging once again on the bandage strips stuck to the side of his head. He'd shrugged off her earlier question about it, but from her viewpoint from the armchair beside him, she caught a glimpse of drying blood on the patch of shirt she could see beneath his jacket. The fire had finally reached full blaze, driving out all the chill of the day, so she knew he had to be growing warm beneath the jacket. But he still hadn't taken it off.

What was he hiding?

"Mom, I wish you'd called ahead. I could have told you the spare room was already taken."

"Don't worry about that," she said, smiling at Charlie again. "I've already made a call to that nice bed-and-breakfast in Campbell Cove. You know, the one near your office? They said there's a room available and I can have it for three nights. So we're set, then, aren't we?"

Mike smiled at his mother, but Charlie didn't buy his cheery demeanor. Amelia didn't, either, it seemed, for her expression fell.

"I'm sorry. I should have called. I just—" She twisted her hands in frustration. "I thought I'd see more of you after you left the Marine Corps. I was counting on it."

Mike glanced at Charlie. She gave a slight nod toward his mother.

He got up and crouched in front of his mother, taking her hands. "I'm sorry. I've been so busy trying to get used to being a civilian again that I've forgotten some of the perks of not wearing a uniform anymore. I should have called you. Made plans for my birthday. And Christmas."

"You missed Thanksgiving, too," she murmured.

"But I did call."

She touched his face. "Yes, you did."

"We'll do something while you're here. Maybe drive up to Lexington and see the holiday lights?"

"Oh, and there are some lovely Christmas shops up there, too. I can pick up some new ornaments for the tree." Amelia clapped her hands. "And Charlie will come with us, right?"

"Oh, I don't think—" Charlie began.

"Absolutely," Mike said, giving her a pleading look. "Charlie's from around here, as a matter of fact. She can probably tell you all the best places to go shopping while you're in town."

"I'm not much of a shopper," she muttered.

"Don't worry about that. I'll do all the shopping." Amelia's smile was infectious. "Tomorrow, yes? I'll take my things to the B and B and rest for tonight. It's a long drive from Black Rock."

"That's a great idea, actually. Charlie and I have something we have to do tonight." Mike pushed to his feet as his mother rose, already heading for her suitcases by the door. He grabbed them for her, glancing over his shoulder at Charlie. "But I'll call you in the morning and we'll all go do something fun tomorrow. Okay?"

"It's a plan!" Amelia smiled up at him, then looked at Charlie, who had trailed along behind them because she didn't know what else to do. "It's been lovely to meet you, Charlie," she said as Mike headed out to the car with her bags. She lowered her voice. "Get that jacket off him. I think you'll find there's blood on his shirt. He's going to act as if it's no big deal, but make him let you see what he's hiding under those bandages."

The cheery good humor, Charlie realized, hid a quick and serious mind.

"Already on it," she told Amelia.

Amelia reached out and took her hand. "I like you, Charlie Winters. Mike must like you, too, to go to such lengths to protect you."

"It's his job."

"Right." Amelia squeezed Charlie's hand and headed after her son.

Mike was back in a few minutes, carrying the box with the cat food. He had also brought the quilt from her bed, she saw with surprise. "I thought you might want a little piece of home. Besides the cats, I mean."

To her surprise, tears pricked her eyes. She blinked them away. "Thank you. That was very thoughtful."

He set the box on the coffee table. "I'm sorry about all that. With my mom, I mean. She should have called first."

"Don't worry about it. A little adrenaline rush in the middle of the day gets the blood pumping." Now that the scare was over, she mostly meant it. Most of her days were spent editing technical manuals and directives for handling military demolition ordnance, which sounded a lot more exciting than it was.

"My father died not long before I left the Marines, and with my brother working in England—he's a news producer for a cable network's European bureaus—"

"Your mom just misses you?" Charlie finished for him.

"Yeah." He tugged at his jacket collar absently. "You want me to take that box into the spare room?"

"In a minute." She crossed until she stood close enough to see the first purplish hint of bruising on the side of his forehead. "But first, you want to show me that gash on your head?"

He touched the bandages with his fingertips. "Just a cut."

"Trip on something?"

He dropped his hand. "You remember that intruder in your house?"

"He did this?" She reached up and tugged the collar of his jacket aside, revealing an alarming number of bloody blotches on the front of his shirt. "Did you have a fight with him?"

"No. He hit me right off. After that, it was all catch-up. Which clearly I didn't do."

She tugged down the zipper of his jacket. "Are you hurt anywhere but your head?"

He shrugged off his jacket, his expression a valiant attempt at playing it cool. "It's just a little cut on my head. No big deal. I didn't lose consciousness or anything."

"And that's your criteria for whether or not an injury is serious?" She tugged at the edge of the lower bandage, wincing as it tugged against his wound and made him suck in a quick breath. With the first of the bandages gone, she saw a nasty, curved gash in the thin skin of his forehead. "Oh, Mike. That looks terrible. What did he hit you with?"

"A can of tomatoes, I think." Mike caught her hand as she started to lift the second bandage. "I can do it."

He pulled off the remaining bandage. The wound was about two inches long and curved like the edge of a metal can, suggesting Mike was right about what had hit him. The skin around the cuts was starting to turn an ugly shade of purple.

"Maybe you should see a doctor," she said.

"No need. I'm not concussed and the wound isn't deep enough to require stitches. I'll just give it a good wash and put something on it, mercurochrome or antibiotic ointment or something."

"Come into the kitchen. Let me get a better look at it."

His eyes narrowed. "Is this where I'm supposed to take off my shirt and smolder at you?"

"Yes." She caught his hand and tugged him with her down the hall to the kitchen. Pointing toward one of the kitchen chairs, she asked, "Where do you keep the first aid kit."

"Shh. I'm smoldering here."

"You can't smolder with your shirt on. Is the first aid kit in the bathroom?"

"In the top drawer of the sink cabinet," he said with an exaggerated sigh. "Can't we just skip right to the kissing it all better part?"

She leaned toward him, closing the distance between them until she felt his breath on her lips. Catching his stubbly chin in her fingers, she made him look at her, almost instantly regretting it. He was, quite simply, a pretty, pretty man. And all she had to do was lean forward a notch and her lips would be on his.

It took all her strength to pull her head back and say, "No."

She turned on her heel and hurried away to the bathroom, her heart pounding like a drum. She found the kit right away, but she took a moment to calm her rattled nerves.

It was just a game. A way of putting the tension of the intruder false alarm out of their minds and finding something to laugh about. That was all.

Wasn't it?

When she returned to the kitchen with the first aid kit, she found Mike at the table, tugging off his shirt to reveal the lean, toned body of an infantry Marine.

She stopped midway to the table and let out a quick breath.

"Can you tell if I have a wound back here?" he asked, his head twisted toward his back. "When I got hit by the can, I slammed into the door frame, and there's a really sore spot on this shoulder." He turned his back to her, revealing another spectacular set of muscles, along with a linear bruise from the top of his shoulder to the bottom of his rib cage.

"Just a bruise," she said, "but a pretty big one. Sure you didn't crack a rib, too?"

"No, I've had cracked ribs before. Not something you

can have without knowing it." He turned back to face her. "I can treat my head wound myself."

"I can see it better," she murmured, not willing to give up the chance to touch him, complication-free. "You think we should call the police about what happened?"

"So they could do what?"

"Take fingerprints?"

"The guy was wearing gloves." Mike's brow creased suddenly, the movement apparently pulling at the cut on his forehead, for he winced immediately afterward. "I didn't remember that until just now."

She opened the first aid kit, pulled out an antiseptic wipe packet and tore it open. "Do you remember anything else?"

"There was a scar. On the inside of his wrist. It looked kind of like a half-moon. Just below his thumb pad, I think."

"That's a lot to suddenly remember." There was no good way to get close to his injured head without stepping between his legs. But she could put aside her attraction to him long enough to nurse his injury, couldn't she? Of course she could.

He watched her approach, his green eyes smoldering as promised. He spread his legs open, daring her to come closer. "Come on, Charlie. You're the one who wanted to play nurse. Chickening out?"

She lifted her chin a notch. "Not on your life."

With a deep breath, she crossed the room and settled her hips between his thighs, forcing herself to concentrate on his oozing head wound. "Fair warning. This is probably going to hurt."

"Not if you do it right," he whispered.

Chapter Eleven

Mike cocked his head to the side to give her a better angle, slanting his gaze to hold hers. She stared back at him, her eyes shimmering like a mirror pool, hiding her thoughts. She was nothing less than a tantalizing mystery, begging to be solved.

And he wanted to be the one who uncovered all her deepest, darkest secrets, one by one.

"Come on, Charlie," he said, his voice barely above a whisper. "You can do this."

She let out a slow breath, bathing his cheek with warmth. With a gentle touch, she applied the antiseptic wipe to the open cut, wincing in sympathy at his hiss of pain. "Sorry."

"What do you think? Will I live?"

She finished cleaning the rest of the blood from the wound and took a closer look. "It's not too deep. I think you're right about not needing stitches. I guess you're probably up-to-date on your tetanus shot, since you were in the military."

"Yep," he drawled, intentionally smoldering at her again.

She cleared her throat. "Are you sure you didn't lose consciousness?"

"I saw stars, but I didn't really black out."

"Because you're remembering things you didn't remember before."

"Just that thing about the gloves. And the guy's scar."

She started to back away from him, but her feet tangled up with each other, and she started to fall backward.

Mike grabbed her, tugging her back between his legs again. He settled his hands over her hips, his thumbs drawing circles over her hip bones. "I've got you."

This was crazy. *He* was crazy.

But she felt so good beneath his hands, all interesting angles and surprising softness. She was beautiful like a mountain spring, calmly pretty on the surface but full of surprises beneath, cool currents and warm eddies, with lots of hidden dangers and delights. He wondered if she could see that beauty in herself when she looked in the mirror. He hoped she did.

She gazed back at him, her expression shifting from emotion to emotion, too fast for him to read them as they flashed across her mobile features.

So he asked. "What are you thinking?"

For a long moment, she was silent. He lifted one hand to take the hand she still had pressed against his shoulder to keep her balance, sliding his thumb over her palm.

"I was…" Her voice cracked, making him smile with satisfaction. Whatever else she was thinking, apparently she wasn't as immune to seduction as her cool exterior might suggest.

She started again. "I was wondering if there was anything else you could remember about the guy. Since you saw his wrist, could you tell if he was white or Hispanic or African American?"

"White," he said, still not letting her hand go. He held it out in front of him, his thumb slowly tracing over the angles of her knuckles. "I'd say he's probably relatively young. No older than forty or so. Or else he's in amazing shape for a man that age. He was fast getting away."

"Height? Weight?" She kept dropping her gaze to his hand, watching his fingers join his thumb in the slow exploration of her fingers.

"About as tall as I am. Maybe an inch or two shorter. A little heavier, though not much."

Her breathing had quickened, and her hazel eyes had darkened, as if reflecting storm clouds. He was getting to her. Breaking down her reserves, touching a place of pure want inside her.

The problem was, he was breaking down his own walls, the ones he'd learned to build over the years, designed to keep the rest of the world at a safe distance. A life of war had destroyed his faith in a whole lot of humanity. Even now, working at Campbell Cove Security Services, he had no illusions about his job. He wasn't a savior. He couldn't protect the innocent. There weren't many innocents left anyway. After the things he'd seen, he was pretty sure this world was doomed to be swallowed by its own darkness, sooner or later.

He was just holding back the night as long as he could.

He felt her other hand slide gently across his jaw, tugging his chin up until he had to look at her. Her gaze was intense, inescapable. He felt as if she had reached inside his head and started to rifle around, searching the scattered contents for some meaning or illumination.

"What are *you* thinking?" she asked in a raspy drawl.

He curled his hand behind her neck and pulled her closer. "How much I want to kiss you," he said, before he slanted his mouth over hers.

Something inside him let go as she curled her fingers around his shoulders and leaned into his embrace, her softer curves fitting snug against the harder edges of his own body.

Oh, hadn't he known she'd feel like this? Lush and hard and utterly right.

When he felt her tongue brush across his lips, he was lost. He opened himself to her kiss, deepened the caress until his heart was beating against his ribs like a caged animal, wild to be free. She let her hands roam up his neck to tangle in his hair, taking control with a thrilling show of confidence.

And when his cell phone started buzzing on the table beside them, it was Charlie who dragged her mouth away from his and took a step back, breaking the magic.

"Get it," she said hoarsely, moving several steps away.

He checked the display and sighed. "Hi, Mom," he answered.

"I just wanted to let you know I'm all settled in at the B and B."

"Good." He checked his watch and saw, to his dismay, that it was almost two o'clock. He was supposed to have met with Randall Feeney at two. In the chaos of the blitz attack at Charlie's place, and the false alarm of his mother's unexpected arrival, he'd forgotten all about it. "Mom, I've got to make a work call. Can I call you back later?"

"Of course. Talk to you soon."

"You were supposed to go see Randall Feeney," Charlie said after he'd hung up the phone. "What time?"

"About five minutes from now."

She tugged down her shirt, which he'd managed to displace during their kiss, and gave him a cool look. "Better get on the move. I know where to hide if the perimeter alarm goes off again."

He didn't want to go see Randall Feeney. He wanted

to pull Charlie back into his arms and finish what they'd started.

But she had put up all her walls again, and maybe he'd do well to shore up his own, also. No matter how attracted he was to Charlie, he'd be a fool to forget the hidden dangers beneath her mirror surface.

And depending on what Randall Feeney had to say today, he just might learn a few things about Charlie he wasn't going to like.

WHEN MIKE STRONG laid on the smolder, he was downright lethal.

Charlie leaned her head back against the side of the guest room bed and looked at Nellie, who had ventured out from under the bed after Mike left and was sitting in front of Charlie, gazing back at her with solemn green eyes.

"He's a handful, Nels. A big, hunky handful."

Nearby, His Highness had curled into a ball and lay halfway between waking and slumber, his blue eyes blinking slowly at her.

"Don't judge me," she muttered. "A few hours ago, you had a cone on your head."

She definitely needed to cultivate a few human friends, she thought. Back during their teen years, she'd had Alice to share all her relationship troubles with, but Alice was gone. Had been gone for almost ten years now, and Charlie had never even tried to find a new best friend to whom she could tell her secrets.

Losing Alice had hurt too much for her to ever want to get that close to anyone else again.

Funny thing was, Charlie had always suspected that she was a lot more open with her thoughts and feelings with Alice than Alice ever had been with her. Alice had been far more worldly than Charlie, perhaps a result of growing up with money and social position, going to expensive adventure and learning camps in far-off places every summer while Charlie had been stuck in Bagwell, babysitting her cousin's brats for a little spending money and trying to steer clear of her brothers' latest crime sprees.

What was Randall Feeney going to tell Mike about her? she wondered. She couldn't imagine he'd have much good to say. The Beardens had been kind enough to her, from their safe position of social acceptability and comfortable wealth. Charitable, even.

No, Charlie thought with a shake of her head. That wasn't really fair, was it? Craig Bearden and his wife, Diana, had been genuinely kind and accepting of her.

At least, while Alice was alive.

But afterward...

Afterward, a lot of things had changed.

As for Randall Feeney, Charlie doubted he'd given much thought to her one way or another. He was Bearden's right-hand man, had been since Bearden had taken over the family law practice after his father's death. Feeney had been a young law clerk, and he'd become fast friends with Craig Bearden and even Diana, according to Alice.

She hadn't liked Feeney that much, Charlie remembered. Sometimes called him a toady, but Alice could be like that sometimes. Sharp-tongued when someone rubbed her the wrong way.

Feeney had apparently rubbed her the wrong way, though she hadn't really talked about him that much that Charlie could recall. Most of their conversations had been about the guys they'd crushed on in high school.

Alice had been the one who'd insisted on going to the

public schools, headstrong from childhood. And as it had suited her father's political career to be seen as a man of the people rather than another rich fat cat, he'd agreed, though he might have come to regret that decision after Alice had become fast friends with a girl like Charlie.

Charlie pushed to her feet, the sudden movement sending Nellie scrambling for the space under the bed. She left the bedroom and headed into Mike's office, where her laptop was still plugged in, and checked her work email in hopes of a new project to tackle. But apparently nobody else wanted to work that weekend. All she found were a few spam emails and a couple of digests from one of the writing lists she subscribed to.

One of the messages was headed "What am I waiting for?" It was another member's rant at herself for putting off starting a new book. She'd received a rejection from an agent a few days before on a book that she'd sent just about everywhere in search of representation or publication. Now she was finding it hard to start something new rather than dwelling on her recent failures.

Which was still better than what Charlie was doing, which was avoiding starting anything at all.

For as long as she could remember, she had been a storyteller. Sometimes the stories had been crafted to stay out of trouble or to make her not-very-perfect life a little more palatable. Sometimes, her imagination just ran away with her, turning the ordinary into the fanciful because it entertained her and made her feel hopeful about the world.

But what she hadn't done in a long, long time was write a story down. Not since her college English teacher had told her she'd be smarter to focus on technical writing, where she'd be much more likely to find employment.

And she'd followed the advice, with good results. For the past six years, she'd managed to become a damn good technical writer.

But there were still stories running around in her brain, screaming to be heard.

When was she going to give them voice?

"What am I waiting for?" she murmured, staring at the laptop screen.

She switched programs, opening her word processor. The most recent file, besides the work-related documents, was titled "Alice."

She opened the Alice file and read the first line.

Two days before Christmas, nearly ten years ago, my friend Alice Bearden died.

She read the rest of the way through what she'd written, then she lifted her hands to the keyboard and continued.

Since that time, someone tampered with my brakes. Someone broke into my house and left a vivid message of destruction. A warning, perhaps, of what might happen if I keep trying to remember what happened the night of Alice's death?

Or is there someone else who might have a reason to want me dead?

Charlie sat back from the keyboard and stared at what she'd just written. She had a vivid imagination, it was true. But even she couldn't buy that she had some nameless, faceless tormentor out there, determined to terrorize her for no apparent reason.

Whatever was happening to her had to be about

Alice's death. She wasn't high enough in the hierarchy at Ordnance Solutions to show up on the radar of anyone who might want to do harm to the company. She had very few friends or even acquaintances these days, much less enemies who would find her important enough to terrorize.

Everything went back to Alice and that night.

She erased the final line of her document, replacing it with a new sentence.

The only way to find out why someone has targeted me now is to return to the night Alice died. The memories of that night can't be gone completely. I'm remembering things now that, while I can't prove they're real, feel right to me. They make sense. They have a familiarity that tells me they're true.

So that's why tonight I'm going back to the place it all began.

The Headhunter Bar.

IT WASN'T RANDALL FEENEY who met Mike at the front door of the campaign office but the man himself, Craig Bearden. He looked remarkably like his head shots on the billboards and signs Mike had seen around Kentucky, from the white-toothed smile to the perfectly styled brown hair with just a touch of silver on the sideburns. His blue-eyed gaze was direct, and his handshake when he welcomed Mike into the office was dry-palmed and firm.

"I'm sorry you've gotten the runaround, Mr. Strong. May I call you Mike?"

"Certainly." Mike followed the man into a smaller office and discovered they were not alone. A tall, slim woman with tawny hair and sharp blue eyes was sitting on a small sofa in the corner of the room. She gave a nod as Mike entered.

"Mike, this is my wife, Diana. Diana, this is Mike Strong. He works at that new security agency in Campbell Cove."

"It's nice to meet you," Diana said, extending one long-fingered hand.

Mike shook her hand, then sat where Bearden indicated while the other man closed the door, shutting out the chatter of the busy campaign office.

"Mike, as you can imagine, Diana and I have had to deal with all sorts of people over the years interested in an emotional postmortem of my daughter's death. Some people can be vultures, I've learned, so I tend to be very cautious about whom I agree to talk to." Bearden took his seat behind his desk and folded his hands on the blotter in front of him. "But Becky Cameron assured me you're not one of those people and said I should hear you out. So. Talk."

"I was expecting to meet with Randall Feeney," Mike began. "I wasn't expecting to speak directly with you and your wife."

"Does it matter?"

Of course it mattered. With Feeney, anything Mike asked wouldn't be a potential land mine the way it would be with Alice Bearden's parents. "I don't want to resurrect sad memories."

"They're not dead," Bearden said bluntly. "Grief doesn't die. It remains with you until *you* die."

"I'm sorry. Of course."

Diana Bearden waved her hand impatiently. "Don't feel you have to censor yourself. Ask what you want to know."

"Charlotte Winters is one of my students at Campbell

Cove Academy." Mike watched Craig for any change of expression.

He was rewarded with a slight narrowing of Bearden's eyes. "Interesting. What kind of course?"

"Self-defense."

Diana Bearden's eyebrows lifted. "Charlotte Winters is quite able to take care of herself."

"She has good self-protective instincts," Mike said carefully.

"What about Charlotte directed you to me?" Bearden sounded curious. "Did she mention me to you?"

"No. We do background checks on students. To be certain their motives for taking part in our classes are what they say they are." That wasn't the truth, exactly—most of the students underwent a cursory check upon registration to make sure they didn't have outstanding warrants, but the kind of check he'd had Heller run on Charlie was out of the ordinary.

But the Beardens didn't need to know that.

"And our daughter's name came up." Bearden nodded slowly. "Alice and Charlotte were close. Perhaps too close."

"What do you mean?"

"Charlotte and our daughter came from different worlds," Diana said bluntly. "Perhaps that sounds elitist, but it doesn't make it untrue."

"Charlie was from a poor family."

"Not just poor," Craig said. "Unstable in a lot of ways. No father. A poorly educated mother with six small children to raise after his death. The children ran wild most of the time. There were discipline problems, especially with the two older boys. I suppose you know her two oldest brothers are in prison?"

"She said something about that, yes."

"That world was a world our daughter knew little about."

"Until she met Charlie?"

"Charlotte was different. I will grant you that. Unpolished, but very smart. She liked to please, and she wasn't afraid of working hard to get the things she wanted."

"I'm sensing a 'but' here," Mike murmured.

"Charlotte had a somewhat adversarial relationship with the truth."

Diana Bearden made a soft huffing sound, but when Mike glanced her way, her expression was unchanged.

Mike's stomach tightened. "She lies, you mean?"

"Not lies, exactly. *Augmentation* might be a somewhat better term," Craig suggested. "Charlotte starts with a kernel of truth, but she always seemed to find a way to make her reality bigger and better than it really was. For instance, her father didn't just die in a mining accident. He died saving a dozen other men."

"Did he?"

Bearden looked surprised by the question. "If he did, nobody ever spoke of it but Charlotte."

"Understandable, that she'd want to believe her father died a hero."

"Of course. But understanding a lie doesn't make it true."

"Charlie was with your daughter the night she died."

Bearden's lips tightened. "Yes."

"Do you blame her for it?"

Bearden didn't answer right away. The ache in the pit of Mike's stomach started to grow before the man finally spoke. "The person who ran over our daughter is to blame. The police assured me there was absolutely no evidence that Charlotte was that person. For one thing,

I don't believe Charlotte had access to a vehicle at that time in her life."

"But if she had, do you think she was capable of leaving your daughter on the street to die?"

Again, Bearden's pause went on too long. "Do you?" he asked finally.

"I haven't known her long," Mike hedged.

"My gut instinct is no," Bearden admitted. "Charlotte might have been a fabulist, and she sometimes led Alice into situations that weren't good for either of them. But I never doubted her affection for our daughter. I don't think Charlotte would have left Alice to die."

The tension in Mike's gut started to ease. "I understand Charlie doesn't remember very much about your daughter's death."

"It seems the girls went out drinking at a bar in Mercerville." Diana Bearden clasped her hands more tightly in front of her. "They told us they were going to a movie that night."

"Not an uncommon thing for high school seniors to do, I suppose?"

"Not uncommon," Bearden agreed. "We just expected better judgment from our daughter. No matter what Charlotte wanted to do that night."

From what little Charlie had told him, it had seemed the idea to go to the bar had been Alice's, not Charlie's. But the Beardens had known the girl Charlie had been then. They'd also known their own daughter. Could Charlie be lying about what had really happened that night?

Or was she remembering only what she could allow herself to remember?

"I'm not sure we've given you the information you were looking for," Bearden murmured.

"You've both been helpful," Mike disagreed, though

Bearden was right about one thing—they definitely weren't giving Mike the answers he was hoping for. They were just adding to the stack of unanswered questions piling up around the night of Alice's death.

And the more questions that arose, the more Charlie seemed to be in danger.

Bearden rose, as if he sensed this was the perfect time to bring the meeting to an end. "I've told Becky Cameron that we'll be happy to answer any of your questions in the future. I hope Diana and I haven't wasted your time today."

"On the contrary. I appreciate your time. I know this is a busy time for the two of you."

Diana remained seated on the sofa while Bearden walked Mike out to the sidewalk in front of the campaign office. He offered his hand.

Mike shook it. "Thank you."

"Charlotte wasn't a bad girl. And she's had almost ten years to grow up. I hear she's working as a technical writer for Ordnance Solutions."

So, Mike thought, Bearden had taken pains to keep up with his daughter's old friend. Interesting.

"Age and experience have a way of smoothing out the rough edges of a person's life," Mike agreed.

Bearden's expression darkened. "Alice never had that chance to grow."

Mike didn't know how to respond, so he just nodded and walked down the sidewalk to his truck, pulling out his phone as he slid inside the cab.

Charlie answered on the second ring. "How did it go?"

"It was interesting," he said vaguely.

"That's...unhelpful."

"Well, how about something I hope *will* help?"

"What's that?"

He put the keys in the ignition. "Put on your dancing shoes, darlin'. We're definitely going to the Headhunter Bar tonight."

Chapter Twelve

The Headhunter Bar hadn't changed in a decade. There were still kitschy fake shrunken heads hanging from the wall and a cheesy attempt at a tiki bar ambience complete with a straw-covered awning over the bar in the center of the room.

In contrast, the music was all Southern-fried classic rock—Lynyrd Skynyrd, the Allman Brothers, Marshall Tucker Band, the Doobie Brothers—blaring from large speakers in each corner of the room.

The sense of walking straight into the past sent goose bumps scattering across Charlie's skin. She paused in the entryway, trying to reorient herself to the world she'd left outside the bar, where she was a grown woman who had made a life for herself and not a nervous teenager with a fake ID burning a guilty hole in her pocket.

"Whose idea was it to come here that night?" Mike's voice barely carried over the driving beat of Lynyrd Skynyrd's "Gimme Three Steps," but it made her jump.

Mike put his hand on her arm, his fingers circling her wrist and holding it lightly. The look in his eyes was somewhere between sadness and understanding.

"Alice's. Everything was always Alice's idea."

"And you did everything she suggested?"

Charlie shook her head. "Not everything. I had a well-honed instinct for survival. I knew there were things a rich girl could get away with that a poor kid from Bagwell never would."

"Illegal things?"

"Nothing terrible." Charlie nodded toward an empty table in the far side of the bar, far enough away from the speakers that they should be able to hear each other over the music.

Twining his fingers with hers, Mike led the way through the rough-looking Saturday-night crowd and pulled out her chair for her.

"You were saying, nothing terrible?" Mike sat across from her and leaned over the table to hear her better.

"Alice fancied herself a girl detective. Like Veronica Mars or something. She was always trying to solve things. I used to tease her that her life was too easy if she had to go looking for trouble to get into." She shook her head. "Finding trouble in Mercer County doesn't take much effort, you know?"

"Was she looking for trouble that night?"

"She was looking for something. She just never told me what." The déjà vu sensation was starting to get to her, making her head swim. Or maybe it was the loud music. Or the nearness of Mike Strong and his chiseled features and smoldering green eyes.

"Let's dance, okay?" She pushed up from her chair and headed for the dance floor, not waiting for him. The song had changed to a Little Texas ballad, slow enough for even Charlie, with her lack of dancing skills, to handle.

Mike caught up and wrapped one strong arm around her waist, drawing her close. "What are you afraid of?" he asked, his voice a rumble in her ear.

"This place," she said.

"What about it? The memories?"

She nodded, her forehead rubbing against his chin, the stubble of his beard rasping against the sensitive skin. "This place hasn't changed a bit. It's like walking into the past, and I didn't know how much that would affect me."

"I've got your back, you know. I'm not going to let anything happen to you tonight."

Oh, she wanted to believe him. Wanted to think that someone might actually be on her side for once.

The way Alice hadn't been. Not that night.

I'm sorry, Charlie. But I have to do the rest of this by myself.

"Alice came here for a reason, but she didn't tell me what it was. And she made sure I didn't know anything else about what she had planned."

"Made sure?" Mike repeated.

Charlie drew her head back and looked up at Mike, voicing the thought that had been creeping around the back of her mind since she first remembered Alice saying those words that night. "I think it was Alice who drugged my drink."

Mike was silent for a long time. The physical ease she was beginning to feel with him faded, and she started to tense up again, studying his face for signs that he thought she was crazy.

"Why would she do that?" He asked the question as if there could be a plausible answer. She started to relax again.

"I told you I've been having dreams about that night, right?"

He nodded.

"In one of the dreams, Alice said something odd. I clearly remember her saying 'I'm sorry, but I have to do the rest of this by myself.'"

His brow furrowed. "The rest of what?"

"I don't know!" Her voice rose in frustration. She lowered it quickly, not wanting to draw attention. "I told you she thought of herself as Veronica Mars, always looking for a mystery."

"You think she found one that killed her?"

"Yes. But I don't know what! She might have been my best friend, but I'm not sure I was hers."

"Was there someone else she might have confided in?" Mike asked.

"That's not really what I mean." The song was ending, but the temptation to stay in Mike's arms had a distracting effect. She couldn't seem to gather her thoughts to explain the kind of relationship she and Alice had shared.

Mike took her arm and steered her back to the table they'd vacated. A waitress came over from a nearby table. "What can I get you?"

"I'll take a ginger ale," Mike said. He looked at Charlie. "What's your poison?"

If she'd come here to relive that night, she should probably order another light beer. "Whatever light beer you have in a bottle."

The waitress jotted down the orders. "Want a menu?"

"Charlie?" Mike asked. She shook her head and he said, "Nothing, thanks," to the waitress.

After she left, he reached across the table and touched Charlie's hand. "You look ready to jump out of your skin."

She tried to shake off her nerves. "I'm sorry. I just— I haven't been back here since Alice died. I thought it would have changed a lot more than it has."

"You don't have to do this tonight if you're not ready." He hadn't released her hand, and the warmth of his fingers curled around hers had a settling effect on her, as if his strength were passing through his fingers into her own. "We can do this later. Or not at all."

"I've spent the past couple of days trying to think of anything else that might make someone want to hurt me." She turned her hand until her palm pressed against his. "And there's nothing else. My job can't be it. I don't have a boyfriend or a stalker ex."

"If what happened to Alice is what's behind the attacks on you, why now? It's been nearly ten years. Why would someone decide it's time to go after you now?"

"I think it's because I've started to remember things."

"Has something happened that would trigger your memories?" His thumb had begun tracing circles across the skin of her wrist. The caress somehow managed to be both soothing and electrifying at the same time.

"I found a note from Alice a couple of weeks ago. It was stuck in an old Dickens novel I hadn't read since high school. I was having trouble sleeping, so I thought Dickens ought to do the trick," she added with a rueful smile. "It's so funny. Alice wasn't much of a note writer. She preferred phone or text or face-to-face communication. But she slipped a note into my book the day before she died, between classes. We were so close to graduating. Our lives were about to really begin."

"What did the note say?" Mike's voice had a gentle, coaxing tone, as if he understood how difficult it was for her to talk about her friendship with Alice and the night that led to her death. He was offering a kindness nobody else ever had, she realized. Certainly not the Beardens. Or her schoolmates, who'd never understood why pretty, popular Alice had taken one of those Winters kids under her wing. Not even Charlie's mother or her siblings, who had never felt comfortable with her running around with a Bearden. *Our people and her people just don't fit*, her mother had warned her, with genuine concern. *Nothing good will come of it.*

Maybe her mother had been right.

"It was our Christmas holiday," Charlie said, tightening her grip on Mike's hand. "School would start in a week, and then it would be a hard slog to graduation, with just spring break between us and the big bad world of adulthood. So Alice wrote me a note suggesting we needed to get a sneak peek at being grown-ups. The note told me to meet her outside her house at seven that night, and to be sure to dress to party."

"Are you sure it was from Alice?"

"I told you, she slipped the note in my book herself. Besides, she met me at the right place and time, as the note asked."

"I guess what I'm really asking is, are you sure the idea to come here was originally hers?"

"Oh." She thought about it. "I think it must have been."

"If she was going to drug you and ditch you, why invite you at all?"

"I don't know. For the longest time, I thought maybe she had been drugged, too, although nobody ever said so, not even when the police questioned me."

"They didn't think maybe you were drugged, too?"

She shook her head. "You'd have to understand where I came from. What my family was like. We were poor. Both my parents drank too much, and when they were drunk, they had a way of finding trouble. My two oldest brothers were mean drunks. In and out of jail all the time before they finally committed crimes they couldn't wriggle out of. When a Winters kid ends up passed out in the backyard and can't remember anything, it's not exactly a novel situation."

"But you didn't make a habit of that, did you?"

"No." She sighed. "But I think the cops always figured it was just a matter of time."

"They should have dug deeper." Mike sounded angry.

She gave his hand another squeeze. "Maybe they should have. But I get why they didn't."

"Take me through that night. Do you think you could walk me through what you remember? Where did you go when you entered the bar?"

She looked at the door, trying to recapture that moment in time. "The music was loud, just as it is now. Southern rock. A little country." She smiled a nervous smile at the memory, just as she had that night when they walked through the door. "Alice was wearing a short dress and a leather jacket with cowboy boots. Red snakeskin. All eyes turned to her. As always."

"Are you sure they weren't looking at you?"

She met Mike's eyes, relished the appreciation she saw there. "No, trust me. They were looking at Alice. I hadn't known how to dress, so I asked my brother. He told me to wear jeans and a sweater and I'd be fine. I think it was his way of trying to keep me out of too much trouble."

"I've seen you in a sweater," he murmured. "You're nothing but trouble in a sweater."

She flashed a smile. "Sweet talker."

"Did anyone approach y'all?"

Her smile faded. "Bees to honey. But Alice just swatted them all away. I just wandered along in her wake."

"Where did you sit?"

She nodded toward an empty table in the back of the room, close to the restrooms. "Right there, by that window in the back. She wanted to sit with her back to the wall, I guess so she could see the whole bar. I wondered at the time if she was looking for someone."

Mike nodded toward the table. "Go sit where you were that night. I'll let the waitress know we changed tables."

Charlie grabbed her purse and took a seat at the table in the back, shivering a little as snippets of memory flashed back to her. Alice's tawny hair had been pulled up in a messy ponytail at the crown of her head, wavy tendrils spilling over her cheeks and neck. She'd favored cat-eye makeup, with exaggerated liner that made her blue eyes look large and mysterious. She'd been smiling that evening. A lot. The kind of smile that said "I've got a secret and wouldn't you like to know?"

Charlie hadn't tried to coax her to spill the beans. By then, she'd known Alice well enough to realize that she couldn't be wheedled into anything she didn't want to do. Alice would tell her what was going on when she was good and ready.

And maybe she would have, if she hadn't been killed.

"Here we go." Mike's voice jarred her from the past. He set their drinks on the table in front of her and took the seat opposite. Immediately his eyes narrowed. "You look a little spooked."

"Alice was keeping a secret."

"Did she tell you that?"

"She didn't have to. It was written all over her face." Charlie looked at the small bottle of beer in front of her. Her stomach rebelled at the thought of taking a drink, but her throat was parched. She eyed Mike's ginger ale with envy before she forced herself to take a small sip of the beer. It was as bitter and unappetizing as she'd feared. She swallowed the sip quickly and pushed the bottle away.

"And you have no idea what that secret was?"

She shook her head. "I remember thinking that Alice

would tell me when she was good and ready. But the evening never got that far."

"How do you think Alice drugged you?"

"She must have done it while I was in the bathroom. She stayed behind with our purses and the drinks."

"I thought women always went to the bathroom together." He smiled.

She managed a weak smile in return. "We do. In fact, I remember being a little surprised Alice didn't offer to go with me."

"And that was the only time she was alone with your drink?"

Charlie nodded. "I hadn't even taken a sip yet."

"And you don't remember anything after the first few sips of beer?"

She poked her fingernail at the coaster under her beer. "I had a dream the other night. Just a snippet of an image in time. I was lying on the ground, my cheek against the concrete. And across the street from me, Alice was lying there, too. In the street. One of her eyes was open but I knew she wasn't seeing anything." Charlie closed her eyes, but the image from her dream lingered in the darkness beneath her eyelids. She shuddered.

"You saw her when she was dead."

Charlie snapped her eyes open. "I must have. It seems so vivid now, like I was really there. But how?"

Mike drank half his drink before he spoke again. "When you woke up in your backyard, what did you do?"

"Sneaked back inside and crawled under my blankets. I was half frozen to death. I was lucky the weather didn't turn bitter that night, but it was December. Believe me, it was cold enough."

He frowned. "You were out in the elements for how long?"

"It had to be a few hours."

"Amazing you didn't have hypothermia."

"I was close. But where I woke was in a sheltered place. Under a juniper bush in the backyard. I guess maybe it was enough to shelter me from the worst of the cold."

"Still." Mike's frown deepened, carving lines in his face. "Whoever dumped you there couldn't have known you'd wake up before you lost too much of your body heat."

"You're saying whoever dumped me in my yard didn't care if I died."

"Or maybe thought you *would* die."

She wrapped her arms around herself, fighting off a shiver. "Whoever it was must have been surprised when I showed up alive."

"What did you think when you woke up with no memory of the previous night?"

"I was scared, obviously. And, to be honest, I was pretty embarrassed, too. I was supposed to be the Winters kid who didn't get drunk and pass out in the backyard."

"You didn't wonder how you got there?"

"Of course I wondered. I thought Alice must have delivered me home but forgotten to make sure I made it all the way inside. So I hurried inside, got into my pajamas and settled down in bed so I'd be there when Mama came to wake me up."

"Nobody was surprised when you didn't show up until morning?"

"No. I told Mama I'd be out late and not to wait up. She took me at my word." She rubbed her forehead, where a headache was starting to form. "I was the only kid in the family who never gave her any trouble. Well, not that kind of trouble, anyway."

The expression on his face suggested she'd piqued his curiosity. "What kind of trouble *did* you get into?"

"Little stuff. Lying, mostly. Harmless little lies to make my life seem better than it was. Lying so my teachers wouldn't know that my mom had been out all night drinking and hadn't had time to wash my jeans. I'd make up some kind of wild story about how I'd fallen in the mud that morning walking to the bus stop and hadn't had time to change before the bus came. Or make up some exotic ailment that kept me from showing up for school on days when Mama had to go out and couldn't take my little brother with her."

"What lie did you tell the morning after Alice's death?" Mike asked quietly, not sounding surprised by anything she was telling him. Did he already know about her reputation as a story fabricator?

"I told my mother that Alice and I had given each other makeovers, then fell asleep watching a movie."

"And she believed you?"

"Yes. I didn't lie to her. I mostly just lied about her."

She braced herself for the pity she feared she'd see in his eyes, but he merely nodded. "When did you find out what happened to Alice?"

"Around lunchtime. Someone from the high school started making calls to all the students because they were going to be setting up grief counselors on Monday and wanted us to know they'd be available." She smiled without mirth. "My mother was very surprised to learn that Alice had been killed in a hit-and-run when she was supposedly home in bed, tired out from a night of movie watching."

Mike took a sip of his ginger ale. "Did you tell her the truth?"

"I had to." Despite all the memories that had gone missing from that night, the images of the following day were vivid in her mind. She tugged at the collar of her shirt, starting to feel increasingly claustrophobic. "Could we get out of here? I really need to get out of here."

"Of course." Mike downed the rest of his ginger ale in one long gulp, then stood and pulled money from his wallet. He dropped a twenty on the table and helped her into her jacket. "You want to go home or do you want to look around outside, see if anything triggers your memories?"

She nodded toward the window next to the table. "See that alley out there? It leads down to Peavine Road. That's where Alice was found. I thought maybe if I went there, it might trigger more of that memory I had of seeing her body."

"Then let's go." He led her to the door, his hand settling against the base of her spine. There was a comforting heat in his touch, a hint of possessiveness, of staking his claim.

Or maybe that was the way it felt because that was how she was starting to think of him.

Her Mike. The stand-up guy who put himself on the line to protect her. Who looked at her with barely veiled desire in his green eyes. Whose fingers played lightly against her spine, sending shivers of answering desire through her body, despite her simmering tension.

She led the way to the alley, trying to focus her mind on the reason they'd come here in the first place. The narrow strip of gravel road was dark after the neon glow of the bar's front facade, forcing her to pick her way carefully through the broken glass and cigarette butts that littered the alley. Deep shadows, cast by the trees that grew haphazardly on the edge of the empty lot across the alley, shifted and writhed across the pathway.

It was quiet out here, too, the only sound the rattling tree limbs overhead, the muted bass line throbbing from inside the Headhunter Bar and the sound of their own breathing, quickening as they walked.

She found her gaze moving toward the empty lot. It hadn't been empty that night, she remembered. There had been a building there. One story. Cinder block. Looking closely, she could just see the remains of a foundation, almost hidden by the high grass.

They were nearing the end of the alley, where it fed into Peavine Road, when Mike's hand clutched suddenly at the back of her jacket. His weight toppled into her, pushing her down toward the ground. She landed hard on her shoulder and rolled until she lay with her cheek against the gritty dirt. Muddy yellow light bled onto Peavine Road from the streetlamp on the corner, and for a shuddering moment, she fully expected to see Alice's body lying broken and bleeding on the blacktop in front of her.

But the street remained empty. And the groaning sound that filled the silence came not from her own throat but from somewhere behind her. She rolled up to a sitting position, looking for the source of the noise.

She spotted Mike, lying in the gravel behind her. His eyes were open, but he seemed to have trouble focusing them.

She crawled to his side, ignoring the pain of gravel biting into her palms and knees. "Mike, are you okay?"

Suddenly, his eyes rolled back into his head and his eyelids closed.

Chapter Thirteen

"No, Mike. Please don't do this to me!" Terrified, Charlie pressed her fingers to Mike's carotid artery and, with shivering relief, felt his pulse. But it seemed slow to her. His breathing, as well. And he didn't respond when she gave his shoulder a shake and said his name again.

She pulled her phone from her purse and dialed 911, trying not to panic. He'd been hit on the head earlier in the day. Had he sustained a closed head injury he hadn't realized?

Damn it, the phone wasn't ringing. She looked at her phone display and saw, to her dismay, that her battery was nearly dead.

"No no no! Mike?" She patted his cheeks. "Mike, wake up. Talk to me, please!"

His eyes opened briefly, and for a second, she thought he could see her. His mouth opened, a word escaping his lips on a whisper.

"Drug," he said. Then his eyes fell shut again.

Drug? What the hell? Had he taken something?

Had someone given him something, maybe spiked his drink in the bar? But why?

Look around you, Charlie, a voice murmured in the back of her mind. *You're all alone. Defenseless. No one could hear you if you screamed, not over that noise in the bar.*

And Mike wasn't able to save her this time.

The night air seemed to chill by several degrees, making her shiver uncontrollably. She reached into Mike's pocket in search of his phone, but it wasn't in either of his front pockets. She started to roll him over but stopped herself, realizing he might have injured his spine when he fell. If she moved him now, it could make his injuries worse.

But she needed a damn phone! If he was wrong, if his head injury was worse than he'd thought, there could be blood filling his brain and killing him right now.

"I've got to go find help, but I'll be right back," she told him, reaching out to brush his hair away from his forehead. "I promise."

She pushed to her feet and started walking unsteadily on the gravel path back to the bar's well-lit facade. But before she made it halfway, a shadow moved across the rectangle of light slanting across the end of the alley.

It was a man. He was dressed in dark clothes, barely perceptible in the gloom. Dark jeans, a long-sleeved top that seemed to have a hood. His features wouldn't have been easy to make out in the low light as it was, but the shadows from the hood rendered his face nothing but a black oval, devoid of all light.

He didn't speak. Didn't call out to ask if everything was okay. He just stood there, silent and terrifying.

Then he took a step toward her. Then another.

She backpedaled, almost losing her balance as her feet skidded across the loose gravel. She turned and ran, fighting the urge to try to grab Mike's body and drag him along behind her.

She couldn't help Mike by getting hurt herself. She

needed to get back to the crowded bar, where there would be safety in numbers, and get some of the patrons to help her.

Reaching the end of the alley, she twisted to her left to head up the side street to the front of the bar. But the second she rounded the corner, she ran headlong into a solid obstacle.

Hands grabbed at her arms, holding her still when she tried to jerk away. Panic was scrambling her brains, but she somehow remembered to use her weight to her advantage. Dropping her shoulder, she rammed into her captor, hitting him somewhere between his stomach and his upper thighs. He expelled air with a pained growl, twisting aside, a move that sent her sprawling to the pavement.

For a moment, she felt as if she were trapped in one of her dreams about Alice's death, the one where she was lying on the pavement, looking across the road to where Alice lay bloody and dead.

But there was no Alice tonight. Only the pained panting of the man whose clutches she'd just escaped.

She scrambled up from where she'd fallen and started to run. But a hand snaked out and grabbed her elbow, jerking her backward again.

As she started to struggle again, a familiar voice gasped, "For God's sake, Charlie, stop it. It's me."

She stopped fighting and stared up into the flint-gray eyes of Deputy Archer Trask.

"What are you doing?" she asked, her voice rising. "Why are you here?"

"I could ask you the same question. Imagine my surprise when I spotted you and Mike Strong walking into the Headhunter Bar. Not exactly a place I ever thought you'd visit again, under the circumstances—"

"Mike!" she said, panic starting to wane enough for

her brain to start functioning again. "You've got to help me, Trask. Mike's in the alley. He's passed out—I don't know why. He got hit on the head earlier today, but he said he never lost consciousness, and he hasn't been acting strange, so I don't know if it's that or if maybe someone spiked his drink. Wait!" she added as he started to move toward the alley. "There was someone else in the alley. He didn't say anything, didn't ask if Mike was okay. I think— I think he was following us. Do you have your gun?"

Trask pulled a pistol from inside his jacket. "Stay here."

"Be careful!"

She pressed her back against the side wall of the bar, feeling the thud of the music throbbing through the brick behind her. Her heart was tripping along at light speed, making her feel light-headed and queasy.

A moment later, she heard Trask call her name. "It's clear," he called.

She hurried back into the alley to find Trask crouched beside Mike's body, the beam from a small flashlight illuminating part of the scene. "Is he still breathing?" she asked.

"Seems to be. His pulse is pretty slow, though." Trask flashed the light around the alley. "I didn't see anyone when I got here."

"He was there, Trask. I didn't make him up."

Trask looked up at her. "I didn't say you did. He might have heard the commotion we were making and run the other way. Do you think he was after you or Mike?"

"I don't know. Maybe me. Or maybe I read the whole thing wrong. I'm a little on edge, and when the guy didn't say anything at all..."

On the ground at her feet, Mike's head rolled from side

to side, as if he were trying to shake off the effect of the drug and return to consciousness. He mumbled something that sounded like her name, then fell still again.

"My phone battery's dead. We need to call 911."

Trask pulled out his phone. "I'll call it in. Don't move. I have more questions."

Of course he would, she thought. She knew he'd never really been happy with the official story about what happened to Alice. Trask had always thought it was a little too convenient that Charlie said she couldn't remember anything that happened that night after her first few sips of beer.

Trask returned to where she crouched beside Mike, stroking his hair. "Paramedics are on the way."

"Thank you."

"What about you? You feeling woozy or anything? How much did you drink?"

"One sip of beer. I'm fine. I think maybe the idea was to get Mike out of the way so I'd be vulnerable."

"To who?"

"That's the question." She rubbed her forehead, where a dull ache had formed above her eyes. "I don't know. That's why we came here, to see if I could piece anything together."

"Piece what together?" Trask asked, his tone wary.

She made herself meet his flinty gaze. "What really happened the night Alice died."

AMELIA STRONG PACED the waiting room floor, her pale face creased with worry. Charlie watched her for a few seconds, swamped with guilt, before Archer Trask walked back into the waiting room with two cups of coffee, drawing her attention away from Mike's mother.

Trask gave Amelia one of the cups, then brought the

other to the chair where Charlie sat. He took the seat next to her, inclining his head when she thanked him.

"Still nothing from the doctors?"

She shook her head. "I think they were taking him for a CT scan first, to be sure it's not a closed head injury. They're also going to do a tox screen to rule out the usual drugs, but I don't think they'll find anything."

"I asked them to do a urine test for GHB," Archer said quietly.

She looked up at him. "So you *do* think he was drugged."

"I want to rule it in or out," Trask said carefully.

"I think I was drugged the night Alice died."

Trask's eyes narrowed a notch.

"I remember almost nothing from that night. I took three sips of beer that I remember, and then the night is mostly a blank until I woke up in my backyard."

"Mostly?" Trask turned toward her. "You remember something?"

She wished now that she'd never told Trask what she and Mike had been doing at the Headhunter Bar. She should have known he'd immediately think the worst of her, put the most damning possible spin on what she had been doing.

"Is this an interrogation?" she muttered.

"No, I just—" Trask cut off whatever he'd been going to say when a thin black man in green scrubs entered the waiting room and headed for Amelia Strong.

"Mrs. Strong?" the doctor asked as Amelia stopped pacing and turned to watch his approach with anxiety-filled eyes. "I'm Dr. LeBow. I've been treating your son."

"Is he going to be okay?" Amelia asked, reaching her hand toward Charlie.

Charlie caught Amelia's hand and gave it a squeeze.

Trask moved up to stand on her other side. She quelled a grimace.

"The good news is, the CT scan didn't show any sort of brain injury, and the cut on his forehead seems to have caused only minor bruising and minimal swelling." Dr. LeBow's deep voice was calm and reassuring. "The tox screen came back negative, but the urine test Deputy Trask requested came back positive for gamma hydroxy-butyric acid. It was probably ingested shortly before he lost consciousness."

"So how do you treat something like that?" Amelia asked.

"For a GHB overdose, we primarily offer supportive care—he's breathing on his own, but if his respirations dip to a critical point, we can intubate and breathe for him until the drug is out of his system."

Charlie's heart squeezed at the thought of Mike on life support, all because he was trying to help her. "Do you think you'll have to do that?"

"At this point, no. He's already starting to show signs of waking, so we'll continue to monitor his vitals. He's fit and, from what you've told us and we've observed, in good health. He has an excellent chance of full recovery with no lingering effects." He lowered his voice, even though there were no other people in the waiting room at the moment. "Has this ever happened to Mr. Strong before? Is he a recreational drug user?"

"No," Amelia snapped. "Of course not."

"He wasn't using drugs tonight," Charlie said firmly. "I was with him from about five o'clock on, and the only time he left my sight was tonight at the bar, when he picked up our drinks from the waitress. He was drinking ginger ale. I believe someone spiked it."

Dr. LeBow looked mildly skeptical. "I see."

"It can't be the first time you've treated someone who was roofied," Charlie said, not quite able to hide her annoyance.

"No, but the victim is usually female." Dr. LeBow glanced at Trask. "I'm going to have to get back to my other patients. We're moving Mr. Strong to ICU until we're satisfied that he's awake and able to maintain his respiration and blood pressure without intervention. The waiting room for ICU is on the fourth floor. Let the nurse know you're there and she'll let you visit him for a short time."

Amelia followed the doctor out of the room. As Charlie started to follow, Trask caught her arm.

"What?" she snapped.

"We weren't finished talking yet. You know you won't get to see him right away, so what does it hurt to hear me out?" He nodded toward the seats they'd recently vacated. "I promise, I'll go upstairs with you when we're done and make sure you're allowed to see him if you'll stay here and finish answering my questions. Deal?"

She sighed, frustrated and anxious. She knew he was right, even if she didn't want to admit it. She wasn't family. In most people's eyes, she'd barely qualify as a friend. Archer might be her best hope of getting to see Mike again tonight at all.

And maybe it was time to bring Archer Trask in on what she was beginning to suspect about Alice's death. Her murder had been his first case as an investigator. If he had lingering doubts her death was anything but a hit-and-run accident, then he had almost as much incentive as Charlie had to get to the truth.

She sat in the waiting room chair and folded her hands on top of her knees, waiting for him to sit, as well.

He pulled one of the chairs around to face her and

took his seat. "What have you remembered about that night, Charlie?"

Slowly, carefully, she told him about her dreams. "I know you're thinking they're just dreams. My imagination running ahead of me. But I think they're real."

"So you were there on the street that night that Alice was killed."

"I think so. And I think the reason I can't remember much of that night is that I was drugged, just like Mike was tonight."

Trask's eyes narrowed. "Who drugged you?"

This, she knew, was the part that would be hard for anyone else to believe. But she had to say it.

"I think it was Alice."

Trask stared at her for a moment. "Why would you think that?"

"I had a memory of hearing Alice talk to me when I was barely awake. She said, 'I'm sorry, but I have to do the rest of this by myself.'"

"Do you know what she meant?"

She shook her head. "But she was being really mysterious about something. She did that, sometimes. Went all Trixie Belden on me."

"Trixie Belden?"

"Books Alice and I read when we were kids. Trixie Belden, girl detective. Or maybe Alice was emulating Veronica Mars or something. She just liked to solve puzzles. Sometimes, she stuck her nose where it didn't belong, and the people at school would get mad at her." Charlie smiled grimly. "They couldn't stay mad, though. Alice had a way about her."

"Yeah, that's the picture I got of her, too."

Charlie looked at Trask through narrowed eyes, feeling as if she might be getting her first real glimpse of the man behind the badge. He hadn't been that much older than her and Alice when he caught the hit-and-run case. Midtwenties at most. Which put him in his midthirties now, around the same age as Mike. Funny how much older he'd seemed ten years ago.

"You never thought it was just a hit-and-run, either, did you?" she asked.

He held her gaze a moment without speaking. Then he looked down at his hands, which twisted together almost nervously between his parted knees. "No. I didn't."

"I thought you suspected me. Am I right?"

"You were a person of interest," he admitted. "Of course. You were there with her that night. You disappeared. You claimed you couldn't remember anything that happened and you couldn't account for your whereabouts between eight that night and four the following morning."

"When you put it that way…" she murmured.

"You didn't exactly cooperate."

"When you're a Winters, it doesn't pay to cooperate with the police." She tried out a wry smile.

He answered it with a quirk of his lips. "Fair enough."

"Do you believe me about that person I saw in the alley tonight?" she asked, a little afraid of how he'd answer.

"Yeah, I believe you."

"Even without seeing him?"

"I sent an officer to ask around the bar after we left," he said. "I gave him your description of the man you saw. The clothing, the build, the general impression that he was young and fit. Three people at the bar remembered seeing a man in a hoodie come in not long after you and Mike. One of the officers is watching the bar's surveillance video to see if he can spot the guy."

"I didn't even think about security video." She rubbed her gritty eyes. "I didn't think about anything but what was happening to Mike. I wish I'd never gotten him involved in all this."

"If I know anything about Mike Strong, I doubt you could have stopped him from getting involved if it was something he wanted to do." Trask sighed, frustration beginning to show in his sharp eyes. "Don't you think it's weird that you were drugged in this bar ten years ago, and now you're there again and your buddy Mike gets slipped a mickey?"

"Yes. And what if it's connected?"

Trask's eyes narrowed. "You said Alice drugged you."

"Yeah, I think she did. Her father had warned her and me both about date rape drugs before he let Alice go to any parties. And as curious as Alice was, I can easily see her finding out where to get her hands on GHB or something like that if she thought it would be helpful to whatever she was investigating."

"Investigating," he said skeptically.

"Trixie Belden, remember?" She looked at Trask. "Can't we talk about this later? I really need to see Mike. I need to see for myself that he's getting better."

Trask's expression softened and he rose to his feet. "So let's go see what we can do."

Chapter Fourteen

Mike could hear a steady cadence of beeps and the occasional sound of voices in quiet conversation in the distance. The ringing of a phone. A voice over what sounded like an intercom. A medicinal tang filled his nose when he breathed, giving him a vague sense of unease.

Something was wrong. He couldn't seem to open his eyes. He couldn't move. He knew he wasn't where he was supposed to be, but he didn't know where he was.

"Mike?" Her voice sliced through the haze in his brain, and he latched onto it like a lifeline.

Charlie.

"Can you hear me, Mike?" She sounded worried. Afraid. That wasn't the way Charlie was supposed to sound. Charlie was snappy comebacks and whistling in the dark.

"I need you to wake up, Mike. Please. I need to know you're going to be okay."

For you, Charlie, he thought, *I'll crawl through glass.*

His eyelids felt like lead weights, but he made himself open them. The world spun a few times before coming to a stop, and he finally got a look at his surroundings.

Hospital. ICU, maybe. Lots of monitors, lots of annoying beeps. There was a nasal cannula pouring oxygen into his nose and a blood pressure cuff folded around his right arm. A clip on his finger measured his blood oxygen level.

And standing next to him, her face pale but her hair a shock of color in the otherwise drab room, was Charlie Winters, gazing at him with a quivering smile on her lips.

"Hey," he said, his voice coming out raspy.

"Hey." Her smile widened, and it was as if the sun had come out to dazzle him. "Do you know where you are?"

"Either the worst hotel room in the world or the hospital. What happened?"

Her smile faded. "You don't remember anything, do you?"

"No." He grimaced, lifting his hand to his head, which had started to ache behind his eyes. His fingers touched a bandage on the side of his head.

Right. The assailant in Charlie's house.

When had that happened? It seemed like just a few minutes ago, but he'd been able to go home, hadn't he? He'd gone home because Charlie needed him.

Hadn't he? But why had she needed him?

"Was my head injury worse than I thought?" He was starting to worry now. Why couldn't he remember anything? He tried to think past the run-in with the man at Charlie's, but everything seemed to be a blank.

"No." Charlie took his hand in hers. Her fingers were cold, but her grip was tight. "Do you remember anything about last night?"

"Last night?" He frowned. "What time is it?"

"It's about three thirty in the morning. You're in the hospital."

"I don't understand."

"We went to the Headhunter Bar. Do you remember anything about that?"

That's right. They had planned to go to the bar that

evening. He'd gone to see Randall Feeney and ended up talking to Craig Bearden.

But what had happened after that?

"What happened to me, Charlie?"

"The best I can tell, someone drugged your drink at the bar."

"At the Headhunter?"

Her thumb was doing all kinds of distracting things to the inside of his wrist. He had to exert a lot of mental effort in order to focus on what she was saying. "We ordered drinks. You had a ginger ale. I had a beer. You drank the whole glass of ginger ale pretty quickly, which is probably why it hit you so fast and hard."

"Did I pass out in the bar?" It was stupid to feel embarrassed by the idea, since he'd done nothing wrong. But still, he didn't like the idea of face-planting in front of a bunch of strangers.

"No, you fell down outside. We were going to see if the road where Alice died would jog my memory."

"Did it?"

"We didn't get that far." She bent closer, near enough that her clean, crisp scent managed to mask even the sharpest of medicinal smells in the hospital room. He breathed her in, let the heady scent of her fill his lungs. "Mike, I'm so sorry. I'm sorry I ever got you involved in any of this."

He reached up and touched her face, ignoring the painful tug of the IV cannula in the back of his hand. "I'm not sorry. Not about trying to protect you, trying to get to the bottom of what's happening to you. So wipe that guilty look off your pretty face and give me a smile."

She managed a weak smile. "Better?"

"Much. Who else is here?"

"Your mom," she answered. "And Deputy Trask was

here for a while, but he went home to get some sleep. He said he'd be back in the morning."

"Archer Trask? From my class?"

"He was at the bar last night. He was a big help when you passed out."

There was something she wasn't telling him, he thought, but he didn't feel clearheaded enough to call her on it. He'd get it out of her later. "Have you called anyone from my office?"

She shook her head. "Everything's been so crazy here, waiting for you to wake up. Do you want me to call one of them?"

"Call Maddox Heller. Tell him what's happened. And then get him to come pick up you and my mom and take you to my place. Tell him I want someone to stay there with you until I'm released."

He had expected her to argue, but she simply inclined her head and said, "Okay."

Now he knew there was something going on that she wasn't telling him.

"They're going to kick me out of here any minute, so do me a favor and get better, fast. Okay?"

"Count on it."

At that moment, a nurse entered. "Well, look who's awake."

"Hope I haven't been too much trouble," Mike said. "Have I been here long?"

"A few hours. But your vitals have been improving steadily." The nurse looked at Charlie, her expression sympathetic. "I'll need you to skedaddle for a bit. Some-one will let you know when Mr. Strong can have a visitor again. Meanwhile, why don't you try to get some sleep. You don't want to end up in here yourself."

Mike held on to Charlie's hand when she tried to slip

away. "Call Heller. And talk my mother into going home with you."

She bent and kissed his forehead. "Try not to rush this getting-better thing, okay? Do what the nurses and doctors tell you. I'll be in touch soon."

He watched her leave, wanting to ask her to stay with a desperation that caught him by surprise. He wasn't a guy who formed attachments easily. Life as a Marine had been a life constantly on the move, from base to base or battlefront to battlefront. He'd connected to his band of brothers with all the instant camaraderie of war, but romantic entanglements had been short-term affairs, no strings, with women who understood the score. But what was happening between him and Charlie felt different. Long-term and intense.

Permanent? Maybe.

He'd never thought of a relationship outside his family as permanent before. Could what he was feeling for Charlie be different?

He had to get out of this hospital bed, he decided as the nurse finished taking his vitals. He needed to get back to Charlie. It was his job to keep her safe. His job to help her unravel the hidden secrets of her past.

He'd be damned if he was going to hand it off to anyone else.

"WHAT DO YOU THINK?" Archer Trask asked, his voice tense.

Charlie peered at the video on the computer screen, trying to make out the fuzzy images on the security video. "He's the right size, and the hoodie looks right. But the picture's pretty awful."

"It's the best we could do." Trask sighed.

"I know. I'm sorry. I just didn't get a good look at

him. He was basically a silhouette, and I didn't see his facial features at all."

"It was a long shot at best." He took the flash drive out of her computer and put it back in its evidence bag, which he stashed in his jacket pocket. He nodded at the open doorway, where Maddox Heller was standing guard. "What's going on with the muscle?"

Charlie saw Heller's lips quirk in a half smile. "He's keeping an eye on Mrs. Strong and me until Mike comes home."

Trask leaned against the window and cocked his head. "What aren't you telling me, Charlie? You and Strong go to the bar where you and Alice spent her last night on earth, and he ends up in the hospital with a GHB overdose. Then he sends a bodyguard to watch you and his mother until he can get home. Does he think you're a target or something?"

"I think maybe we're both targets now," she admitted.

"When did this start?"

"Well, for me, I started getting the feeling I was being watched or followed a few weeks ago, after I started having the dreams about Alice's death. I tried to contact Craig Bearden, to see if he'd talk to me, but he never returned my call."

"What kind of message did you leave?"

"I told him I thought I was remembering things about that night, and I wanted to talk to him about it."

Trask's gray eyes narrowed. "And he never called back?"

"That's weird, isn't it?" Charlie worried her lower lip between her front teeth. "You'd think if there was anything new about the case, he'd want to know about it. But he never called, never sent an email or anything."

"Maybe he didn't get the message. Did you leave it at home or at his office?"

"His office."

"Maybe someone retrieved the message before he did and forgot to give it to him."

"Or maybe he just thinks I'm a big, fat liar who got his daughter killed," she muttered, looking down at her hands. They had started twisting together of their own volition, a telltale sign that she was feeling anxious and self-conscious. She stilled her hands, clutching them together tightly in her lap. "Anyway, after that, I started getting the weirdest feeling that I was being watched. You know, when you get that creeping sensation down the back of your neck when someone's staring at you? But I never saw anyone."

"Is that why you decided to take the self-defense course?"

"Yes. And then, two days later, someone tampered with the brakes of my car."

Trask pushed away from the window abruptly. "What?"

"My brake line was cut and the fluid drained out while I was at my self-defense class. If Mike hadn't seen the puddle of fluid where my car had been and realized I was in trouble…" She told him about her brakes failing and the way Mike had stopped her car before it crashed. "He saved my life."

"What a stroke of luck. How'd he happen to know whose car the brake fluid came from?"

She frowned at his suspicious tone. "He was watching me leave."

"So, you were being watched by both some unknown person *and* Mike Strong? All in one week?"

"Go to hell, Trask." She stood up and walked toward the door.

Trask caught her arm, his grip gentle. "Sorry. I'm a cop. Suspicious is my middle name. Finish telling me what else happened. Why are you staying here? Because of the brake tampering?"

"No. We sort of blew that off. The guy at the garage couldn't say for sure how the line was cut at the time. So Mike sent it to the security agency for his people to take a closer look. But then I walked into my house a day later after self-defense class and discovered my place had been trashed." She told him about the vandalism and about Mike's decision that she needed a safer place to stay until they could figure out who was messing with her.

"Did you think to call the police?"

"Yes, actually. Officer Bentley of the Campbell Cove Police Department wrote up a report for my insurance company, but he told me that since nothing was stolen, I'd do better to spend my time getting as much insurance reimbursement as my policy would allow."

"He's probably right," Trask admitted. He folded his arms over his chest, looking thoughtful. "What happened to Strong's head? Did that have anything to do with what's going on with you?"

"We think so."

After she finished telling him about the intruder at her house the previous day, he shook his head. "You know, you could have called me if you thought any of this was connected to Alice's death."

She stared up at him with disbelief. "Trask, you treated me as if I was your prime suspect in Alice's death. Why on earth would I go to you with any of this?"

He sighed again. "Fair enough. I hope you realize now that I'll hear you out. We're on the same side, Charlie.

I want to find out what really happened to Alice that night, too."

"Then we need to find whoever trashed my house and tampered with my brakes and drugged Mike."

A small commotion coming from the front of the house drew Trask's attention away from Charlie. He headed out of the room, Charlie on his heels. Maddox Heller, who'd been standing guard outside the office, brought up the rear. They reached the living room to find Amelia Strong engulfing her son in a bear hug.

"Why didn't you call me?" Amelia asked. "I'd have come to pick you up myself."

"I needed Eric's medical degree to talk the doctors into springing me early," Mike answered, gently disentangling himself from his mother's arms. He met Charlie's gaze and smiled, but his expression faded into suspicion when he caught sight of Archer Trask. "Deputy, what a surprise to see you."

"Charlie was catching me up on everything that's been happening to you." Trask crossed to where Mike stood and extended his hand. "I think we all want the same thing. For Charlie to be safe and to find out what really happened to Alice."

Mike hesitated a moment, his gaze slanting toward Charlie once more. She gave a little nod, and he reached out and shook Trask's hand. "Charlie tells me I have you to thank for getting me to the hospital so quickly."

Trask looked at Charlie. "Don't thank me. Charlie was the one who risked her life to help you."

Mike's gaze snapped back to Charlie. "Risked her life?"

Trask looked at her as well, one eyebrow raised.

"I haven't really had a chance to tell Mike everything

that happened that night," Charlie said. "And I wouldn't say I exactly risked my life. I ran for help. That's all."

"What the hell were you running from?" Mike asked.

"Language," Amelia murmured, making everybody in the room chuckle, even Mike.

"Mrs. Strong, why don't we go to the kitchen and fix some sandwiches for everybody," Maddox Heller suggested, gently steering Amelia away from Mike. He looked over at Deputy Trask. "Trask, you can help us by putting ice in glasses."

Within a few seconds, the living room was empty except for Mike and Charlie. She ventured a smile, but he didn't return it. Instead, he crossed to where she stood, took her hand and pulled her with him down the hall to the spare bedroom.

He closed the door behind them and caught her up in his arms, slanting his mouth hard against hers. Caught off guard, she clung to him for balance as the world around her started to spin like a top.

There was nothing gentle about this kiss. It was pure fire, burning her to her core until she felt as if she were nothing but ashes. Then the flames roared again and she rose from the ashes to burn as his mouth traced a path of fire along the curve of her cheek and down the side of her throat.

As if something inside her had snapped, she felt released from shackles, free to be the person she had always wanted to be. Free to take the things she wanted most without fear or shame.

And what she wanted most, she realized, was Mike Strong. His strength. His laughter.

His lips gliding slowly, deliberately toward the curve of her breasts, where they peeked from the collar of her shirt.

When he drew back, it happened so suddenly that her knees started to buckle. He wrapped his arm around her and pulled her over to the bed, where he sat, bringing her down onto his lap.

"Okay," he said in a shaky voice, "before we get too carried away, there's something I need to know. You know, last night, when I woke up, I knew you were keeping something from me. So how about you tell me exactly what you were running from in the alley."

Chapter Fifteen

When Charlie and Mike entered the kitchen, where Trask and Heller waited, Heller pulled Mike aside. "On a hunch, I checked your truck. There had to be some way Charlie's stalker has been tracking y'all without your noticing the tail."

"I would hope so."

"Well, I was right. You picked up a rogue GPS tracker at some point. I've left it there for now."

"Why?"

Heller just nodded for Mike to join him as he crossed to the kitchen table, where Charlie had taken a seat.

"I don't like hiding." Charlie's voice was low and composed, but Mike had begun to understand her well enough to see the barely restrained restlessness lurking behind her eyes as she looked up to meet his gaze. It wasn't just the hiding that was getting to her. She was done with being a target.

"Until we know who's after you, keeping you hidden is the best way to keep you safe." Archer Trask crossed to the empty chair at the table where Charlie sat and leaned toward her. His attitude toward Charlie had changed, Mike noted. On one hand, Mike was glad for Charlie to have a few more people on her side. On the other hand, Trask had just taken the chair Mike had been about to claim for himself. And the warmth in Trask's eyes was really beginning to annoy him.

"So let's figure out who's after me, then," Charlie said, a hint of frustration beginning to seep into her voice. "It has to be connected to whatever happened the night Alice died, doesn't it?"

"I think so," Maddox Heller agreed. "You said the sensation of being watched or followed started shortly after you left a message at the Craig Bearden for Senate campaign office, right?"

"Yes." Charlie looked at Mike, her eyes expressive. She was tired of going over all the details of her story, and he sympathized with her annoyance, but her story was all they had to go on at the moment. And what they knew was limited by how very little she remembered.

"Have you ever considered undergoing hypnosis?" Mike asked.

Trask gave him a sharp side-eye glance.

"You think I'd remember more under hypnosis?" Charlie asked, her tone skeptical. "I don't think drug-related amnesia is something you can counteract with mind games."

"No, but if there weren't any more memories to retrieve, I'm not sure you'd be remembering new details in your dreams."

Charlie pushed to her feet, the chair legs making a loud screeching sound against the floor. She paced the kitchen floor, raking her hair out of her eyes with her fingers. "What if those aren't really memories? What if everything I think I'm remembering is just something I'm making up in my head to fill in all those awful blanks?"

Mike planted himself in front of her and gently closed his hands around her upper arms. "Do you think it's something you're making up?"

She closed her eyes a moment, her brow furrowed. Then her eyes snapped open and she shook her head. "No. I think they're really memories."

"Then that's what we go with." Mike turned to look at the other two men. "Agreed?"

"Agreed," Trask said.

Heller nodded. "It would probably help if we could access more of your memories."

"Do either of you know anyone who uses hypnosis to recover memories?" Mike asked.

"It's not considered a reliable way to remember things," Trask warned. "People tend to remember things that aren't real if the hypnotist leads them at all. Especially people already prone to confabulation."

"Meaning me," Charlie murmured to Mike.

"Lauren Pell is a trained psychiatrist," Heller said. He looked at Mike. "She works in our PSYOPS training division."

"Can we get her here fast?" Mike asked.

"I'll find out." Heller pulled out his phone.

Mike cupped Charlie's elbow and pulled her aside. "You don't have to do this if you don't want to. We can find another way."

Charlie shook her head. "I need to do this. Even if the idea scares me."

He brushed a floppy lock of hair away from her forehead. "Why does it scare you?"

"If there are memories I can retrieve, if it's not drug-related memory loss, why haven't I remembered any of this for ten years? What if I saw something that I don't want to remember?" Tears welled in her eyes, and she blinked hard to keep them from falling. "What if I did something I don't want to remember?"

Mike looked across the room at Trask, who sat with

one foot propped on the opposite knee, watching them curiously. He lowered his voice further. "You were investigated as a person of interest. If there was anything to tie you to what happened to Alice, I have every reason to believe you'd have been charged."

"I didn't kill her," she said. "But what if I did something to put her in that situation?"

"I'll tell you the same thing Craig Bearden told me. The only person to blame is the person who ran over Alice. Nobody else."

"He said that?"

"He did."

That earned him a smile from her. "There was a time when I thought Mr. and Mrs. Bearden actually liked me. They were both always really kind and accepting of my friendship with Alice. But after she died…"

"Death has that effect on people."

"I know." She stepped closer, until her warmth washed over him, and leaned her forehead against his shoulder. "It had a similar effect on me."

Heller's voice interrupted. "Lauren's on her way. She suggests that we all clear out except for Charlie and Mike. She'd like to keep the distractions to a minimum."

Trask stood and stretched. "I'll head back to the station and see if there's anything there that needs my attention. Call if you need me. And be sure to record that session."

He followed Heller down the hallway to the front door. Mike and Charlie trailed after them, Mike locking the door behind the two men before turning back to Charlie. She gazed back at him, worry lines creasing her forehead.

"It's gonna be okay, Charlie. I'm not going to let anything happen to you."

She closed the distance between them, walking into his outstretched arms. "I know. And thank you."

"We have a lot to talk about, you and me," he murmured against her hair. "You know that, don't you?"

She nodded, her hair sliding like silk against his cheek. "I know. But I just can't think about anything like that right now. Do you understand?"

"Yeah," he said, although her reluctance sent a little flutter of anxiety through his chest. What if she didn't want to pursue what they felt for each other? What if she didn't feel the same way he was beginning to feel?

Later, he told himself. *Worry about it later.*

Right now, protecting Charlie was the only thing that mattered.

CHARLIE WASN'T SURE she was really under hypnosis. She felt very aware of her surroundings, of the soft, soothing voice of the hypnotherapist Lauren Pell. She was a tall woman in her thirties, with short dark hair, soft blue eyes and a gentle manner that had made Charlie feel instantly at ease.

"Tell me about the taste of the beer," Lauren suggested. "Was it cold or lukewarm?"

"Lukewarm," Charlie answered, grimacing as she spoke. "And bitter. I remember wishing I'd gotten a drink like Alice's. Hers looked so good, but I was afraid of trying anything with hard liquor in it. Alice teased me about it. Said I was a big chicken."

"Did that make you angry?"

"No." Charlie smiled. "I was a big chicken. But I also wasn't on the way to becoming a sloppy drunk like my uncle Jim. So I didn't feel very sorry about that."

"You must have been a levelheaded young woman."

"I don't think anyone ever accused me of that."

"Think about the beer. You said it tasted bitter. But you drank it anyway?"

"A couple of sips. Three, maybe. I was mostly interested in what Alice was doing."

"Which was what?"

"She was looking out the window beside our table. Just drinking her pretty little cocktail and watching the alley behind the bar."

"What was she watching for?"

"I wasn't sure. And when I asked, she told me she was just bored." Charlie frowned, realizing the strangeness of what she'd just said. "On our big, transgressive night out. That's strange, isn't it?"

"I don't know. I didn't know Alice."

"It *was* strange. The whole night was strange. And then, suddenly, Alice grabbed my arm and said it was time to go."

"Go where?" Lauren asked.

Charlie got up and started walking, her steps a little unsteady. She could feel Alice's hand curled around her wrist, tugging her along as they left the bar and stepped out into the chilly winter night.

Only, she wasn't walking, was she? Not really. She was still seated on the sofa in Mike's living room. Lauren Pell sat in one of the armchairs across the coffee table from her, and Mike was a big warm presence somewhere to her right. But the cold breeze sent a chill skittering through her, and the scent of Alice's favorite perfume wafted toward her as they entered the alley behind the Headhunter Bar.

There's someone out here, Charlie thought. She could hear voices, shaping words that she couldn't quite make out. A man's voice. Maybe a woman's. Charlie couldn't tell for sure.

And it was dark. So dark. The only light came from the dim illumination through the tinted windows inside the bar and one faint light burning inside the cinder block building across the alley from the bar.

There was someone inside the building. Charlie could make out moving shadows through the thin curtains in the building's windows.

But the world was starting to twirl around her. Twirl and twist, growing incrementally darker.

She felt herself falling. Arms wrapped around her, and Alice's perfume filled her lungs. Suddenly, she was on the ground, her face pressed against the damp pavement where the alley intersected with the side street.

"I'm sorry, Charlie," Alice said quietly, her voice almost mournful, "but I have to do the rest of this by myself."

The world seemed so dark. For a long time, there was a universe of nothingness so dense, so vast, that it terrified her. Her breath came in hard gasps as the panic rose inside her, hot and bitter like bile. "The world has disappeared!" she gasped.

"You're okay, Charlie." Lauren's voice was low and soothing. "You can go to your safe place if you need to."

Charlie pictured herself in Mike's arms. Felt them around her, solid and warm. It wasn't the safe place she had originally considered when Lauren had walked her through how they were going to approach the hypnosis session, but it felt right.

Mike was her safe place.

Her breathing settled into a regular cadence, and the panic subsided.

"Do you want to keep going?" Lauren asked.

"Yes."

"You were unconscious, weren't you?"

"I must have been. I think Alice drugged my beer."
Charlie frowned. "She was planning something. I knew
she was. And it had something to do with that building
across the alley from the bar."

"You don't know what that building was?"

She thought about it, tried to picture the place. "The
alley was behind it. I'm not sure I even know what street
the building must have faced. I didn't spend a lot of time
in Mercerville when I was younger. It was sort of the big
city to me then." She laughed at the thought. "Little Mercerville as the big city. Isn't that something?"

"Let's not worry too much about that building. That's
information we can track down later," Lauren said. "I'm
more interested in what happened when the world came
back to you."

Tension built low in her spine. "I don't remember."

"Are you sure? Maybe you just don't want to remember."

Charlie shook her head. "I do want to. It's just a
blank."

"You told me before we started that you had a memory of seeing Alice dead. Can you recall that moment?"

Charlie shivered, but she let her mind return to the
dark alley. She was past the gravel, lying facedown on the
pavement at the edge of the road. Peavine Road, she remembered. That was where Alice's body had been found.

She opened her eyes, bracing herself for what she
knew she'd see.

But Alice wasn't dead.

She stood in the middle of Peavine Road, crying. Her
blouse had been torn at the shoulder, and her wavy blond
hair was tousled and frizzy from the light drizzle falling. The light on the corner seemed to glow underwa-

ter as fog rolled into the streets, washing everything in a dreamy haze.

Charlie tried to call Alice's name, but her tongue was thick. And Alice wasn't listening to anyone. Not even the man who stood nearby, talking to her in fast, tense tones.

When it happened, it was fast and shocking. A large black sedan, moving fast and strangely quiet, the motor hum barely audible over the thudding bass beat coming from inside the nearby bar. It slammed into Alice from behind, hitting her waist high and sending her flying up into the air. She landed on the trunk of the moving car and rolled off, slamming into the pavement with a sickening thud.

"I saw it happen," Charlie rasped, her heart racing with shock. "I saw Alice killed."

"Can you remember anything about the car?"

"It was big and black. A sedan. It looked expensive, but I'm not an expert on cars. I remember the engine was quiet. I think that's why it seems like an expensive car to me. No rattling engine or faulty muffler."

"You said you heard a man's voice talking to Alice. What do you remember about it?"

"It seemed familiar. It still does, but I can't place it."

"You're lying on the side of the road still. You're seeing Alice's body in the road. You must be feeling shocked and traumatized."

Cold crept into her skin. "Yes. I feel as if it's not real, even though I just saw it happen. I think I need to get to Alice, I need to help her. But I can't move. I can only watch the blood spreading across the pavement beneath her head."

"What about the man who was talking to Alice? Can you tell what he's doing?"

"He's walking into the road. I can't see anything but his back."

"What is he wearing?"

"Jeans. A jacket—maybe a rain jacket. It has a hood." Her breath caught. "Like the man I saw in the alley last night."

She watched the man bend close to Alice's body. He reached out one shaking hand as if to touch her, but he pulled it back at the last minute.

But not before his sleeve pulled away from his arm, revealing a half-moon scar on the inside of his wrist. "Oh, my God. He has a scar on his wrist. A half-moon scar."

On instinct, she reached out for Mike. He caught her hand, and the cold, dark alley disappeared. She was in Mike's living room again, seated near a warm fire. Lauren Pell sat across from her, her expression curious.

"I know who the man was," Charlie said. "I remember. He stood up and turned toward me. I saw his face." Even now, the features of the man's face were so clear in her mind, she wondered why she'd never been able to recall them before now. Sandy hair, wisps peeking out from the rain jacket's hood. Cool blue eyes, dark with fear. Straight, sharp features twisted with shock and desperation.

"Who was it?" Mike asked.

"Randall Feeney. Craig Bearden's chief aide."

"ARE YOU SURE he wasn't the person in the car?" Archer Trask asked Charlie. He and Maddox Heller had returned to Mike's house at Mike's request shortly after Lauren Pell departed. She'd left a recording of the hypnosis session with Mike and Charlie, which they'd played for the two men soon after they arrived.

"Pretty sure. I heard him talking to Alice right before she was hit." Sitting next to Mike, Charlie seemed to have recovered from the hypnosis session for the most part, though there was a strained sadness in her hazel eyes that made Mike's heart hurt.

Witnessing the murder of her best friend had clearly traumatized her so much that she'd repressed those memories. She still believed she'd been drugged, but some of the memories she'd thought were gone had, instead, been concealed beneath the trauma.

"But he saw the hit-and-run and never told anyone," Mike added. "So we think he must have some idea who was driving."

"When we went out into the alley, I heard voices. I couldn't make them out. I can't say for sure if they were male or female. But I think they were in that building behind the bar."

"That was the Mercerville branch of Craig Bearden's campaign for state senator," Trask said. "I remember because when we canvassed the area for potential witnesses, it was one of the places we stopped. I remember wondering if Bearden would ever step foot in the place again, knowing his daughter died in the street just a few yards away."

"Did he?" Mike asked, curious.

"Never did. They closed the office and sold the property. Took the proceeds and started a scholarship fund in Alice's name."

"Feeney was never questioned?"

"No. He didn't have any motive, as far as anyone knew. Bearden and his wife both said Alice preferred to stay out of her father's political campaign, so she didn't have much contact with anyone in his office. And we started focusing on the idea that she'd been hit by a driver under the influence, considering how close it had been to the bar."

"But we have a problem going after Feeney, don't we?" Heller said.

"We do," Trask admitted, looking at Charlie. "No offense, but your memories aren't going to give us any kind of legal probable cause to bring him in for questioning. He'll lawyer up and we won't have a leg to stand on."

Charlie looked at Mike, frustration shining in her eyes. He reached over and caught her hand, giving it an encouraging squeeze. She squeezed back and lifted her chin, turning her gaze back to Trask. "So, let's figure out a way to come up with a little probable cause."

Something in the tone of Charlie's voice sent a ripple of tension through Mike's gut. Across from them, Archer Trask frowned, his eyes narrowing.

"Just what do you have in mind?" he asked Charlie.

"If we're right, Feeney intercepted the phone call I made to Craig Bearden, telling him I was starting to remember more about the night Alice died. And after that, he started following me and then tampered with my brakes and broke into my house to scare me off. Maybe twice, if Mike is right about the scar he saw on the intruder's wrist. Then, last night, he apparently drugged Mike so he'd have a clear path to me. I think he was planning to kill me."

"I think you're probably right," Trask agreed.

"So maybe we should offer him what he wants."

"Charlie—" Mike began warningly.

"I think we should set a trap for Randall Feeney. With me as the bait."

Chapter Sixteen

"This is a crazy idea." Mike stopped in the middle of his restless pacing to face Charlie. "You don't need to be there." Ever since Charlie had proposed her plan earlier, all Mike could do was try to come up with reasons why it was a terrible idea.

"Yes. I do. He's tracking us somehow. He needs to see you drop me off at my house alone or he's not going to make his move."

"Oh. I forgot to tell you. We think we know how he's following us." Mike told her about the tracker attached to his truck. "Heller said he left it there, so Feeney knows we're still here."

"He's still going to assume you'll be with me."

Mike started pacing again. "I just don't think you need to put your head in the noose to make this work."

"Well, I do. And Trask and Heller both agree."

Mike grimaced. "They're thinking of the case. Not you."

Charlie crossed until she blocked his path. "I *am* the case."

"Not to me." He cupped her face between his large hands, his touch so gentle it made her chest ache. "You're not just a case to me."

She laid her hands over his. "I know. And you're not just a bodyguard to me, either."

He bent and kissed her forehead, then pulled her into his arms, pressing his face into her hair. When he spoke, his breath was warm against her cheek. "I want this done. I want you to be free and safe. I need that."

She stroked his broad, strong back, marveling at the solid feel of him beneath her fingers. He was a man of steel, inside and out, strong in all the ways she admired.

And he admired her, too. That was the crazy, intoxicating part of their burgeoning relationship. He wanted her, yes. That was evident in the fiery desire she saw in his eyes sometimes when he looked at her. But he also liked her. Respected her choices, even when, like now, they drove him crazy.

She wasn't used to being admired and respected by anyone.

"I can do this," she said, pulling her head back to look into his worried green eyes. "It'll be okay."

"I hope so." He caressed her cheek. "But does it have to be tonight? Can't we have just one more night to ourselves?"

"Just one?"

His eyes narrowed, and he kissed her. Hard and deep, a kiss that sent her head swirling and her heart racing. And he pulled away all too soon, crossing to stand by the fireplace, his gaze directed toward the flickering flames. "Never just one," he growled.

"After tonight, we can have as many nights as we want."

He gave her a look so full of promise she thought her heart would burst, but before she could take a step toward him, the perimeter alarm went off, and Mike instantly went on full alert.

He had added a front door camera connected to a phone app after his mother's unexpected arrival had caught them off guard. He checked his phone and relaxed marginally. "The cavalry," he murmured as he went to the door to greet the new arrivals.

Besides Heller and Trask, a slim redhead about Charlie's size entered, flashing a brief smile at Mike before she turned her attention to Charlie. "Not a perfect match," she murmured. "But it'll work from a distance."

"What's going on?" Charlie asked.

"Mike's right. There's no need to put you in needless danger. This is Meredith Chandler. She works at the agency. Meredith, this is Charlie Winters. And you know Mike."

Charlie looked at Meredith, taking in the short red hair, tall, slim build and pale complexion. They resembled in general, though no one would mistake them up close. Partly because Meredith was drop-dead gorgeous and partly because she walked with the grace of a dancer instead of Charlie's ungainly gait.

But all Meredith would have to do, Charlie presumed, was walk up the flagstone path from the driveway to the front door of Charlie's house and go inside. Feeney would be trying to stay out of sight, which would make it hard to tell one tall, slim redhead from another.

"He's not going to buy that you'd just drop me off at my house by myself," Charlie said to Mike.

"We agree," Trask said, "but we have an idea."

By the time he finished telling Charlie and Mike what they had planned, even Mike agreed it was a pretty good idea.

"I checked with Bill Hardy. He's got your brakes repaired, so your car is ready to go. Mike will drive Meredith there to pick it up. We've warned Bill that someone besides you will be picking it up. Mike will pay. Meredith will drive the car home with Mike bringing up the rear."

"Halfway there, my truck suddenly develops problems and I have to pull over to see what's wrong, while Meredith drives on." Mike nodded slowly. "If Feeney's following us, that'll give him time to catch her alone."

"Only, she won't be alone. We'll be there," Heller said.

"What if he runs the minute he sees Meredith isn't me?"

"I don't think he's going to confront you. He'll sneak, like he's been sneaking this whole time. He may try to break in and catch you unaware. Either way, we'll be there and we'll be ready," Trask assured her.

"I'll get a signal from Heller once things start to go down," Mike said, "and I'll get to the house for backup. Meanwhile, you'll be here behind locked doors, with a perimeter alarm to let you know if there's an intruder. I put the app on your phone, too, so all you have to do is check it and you'll be able to see whoever's approaching. If you feel threatened at all, I'm a phone call away."

"It sounds…very planned out," Charlie said.

Mike crossed to her side and took her hands in his. "You can say no to all of this if you want."

Charlie shook her head. "Why would I say no? I'm the only one who won't be in danger."

Mike squeezed her hands. "I know you don't like sitting on the sidelines, but—"

"I don't like sitting on the sidelines?" She quirked an eyebrow. "I'm a sideline-sitter from way back, Mike. I'm a pro at it."

"I know better," he said softly. "But this time, I need you to be safe, okay? I need you right here where you can't get hurt."

She wanted to argue, not liking the idea of a stranger

she'd just met moments earlier putting her neck on the line so Charlie could be safe. But Meredith Chandler had assured her that she was well trained. Former FBI agent, plus fresh off the new-hire training program Campbell Cove Security had mandated company wide. She would be an asset to the mission.

Charlie would just be in the way.

"Okay," she said finally. "Let's do it. I'll make the call to the campaign office, ask Mr. Bearden to meet me at my house in an hour, and if it goes like we think it will, we can get this show on the road."

What she hadn't anticipated, however, was Randall Feeney answering the phone at the campaign office himself. Charlie's throat closed up for a moment, and he said "Hello?" a second time.

She cleared her throat. "This is Charlie Winters. Is Mr. Bearden in?"

This time, it was Feeney who didn't speak. Finally, he asked, "He's not here this afternoon. May I take a message?"

"I was hoping to talk with him personally. In fact, I really need to see him in person." She glanced at the others, who stood nearby, waiting for word to move.

"I'm not sure what his calendar is like today," Feeney said hesitantly.

"Please try to contact him. It's urgent. I need to talk to him about what happened to Alice. I've remembered more information and I wanted to get his opinion about the things that are coming back to me. I'll be at my house in about an hour, and I should be there for the rest of the afternoon. My address is 425 Sycamore Street in Campbell Cove. Please let him know. It's important."

"I'll see if I can reach him."

"Thank you." Charlie hung up the phone, her hands shaking. "It was Feeney himself."

"Perfect," Trask said.

"If we're right about who attached that tracker to Mike's truck, that's how he'll be following you. He'll be looking for a way to separate you from Mike." Heller picked up the small gym bag he'd brought with him and put it on the coffee table. Unzipped, the bag revealed its contents—four small earpieces. Heller handed them out. "We can communicate through these, in case anything starts to go wrong."

"Don't I get one of those?" Charlie asked.

The other four looked at her blankly.

"Oh, okay. I just sit here and worry. Got it."

Mike crossed to her side. "It'll be over before you know it. I'll be back here, Feeney will be in custody and we'll be on our way to finding out who was behind the wheel of that car."

She sighed, knowing he was right. The wait for word would be interminable, but she'd be a hell of a lot safer here than she would be out there with Mike and the others.

That was the important point, wasn't it?

Trask and Heller left together soon afterward, wanting to be out of sight in case Feeney did a drive-by to see if Mike and Charlie were leaving together. Meredith went to the guest bedroom to find some of Charlie's clothes to wear, leaving Mike and Charlie alone in the living room.

He crossed to where she stood by the fireplace, wrapping his arms around her from behind. "This is going to work."

"You're right," she said, although tension thrummed deep in her chest.

"I'll be back before you miss me."

"Not possible." She turned in his arms to look at him. "You come back to me all in one piece. Understand? This is nonnegotiable."

"Yes, ma'am."

She caught his face between her palms, enjoying the light rasp of his beard stubble against her skin. "Taking your self-defense course was the best decision I ever made in my whole crazy life."

He smiled at her. "I knew the minute you walked into my class that first morning you would be nothing but trouble." He kissed her nose. "And you are. But I have a real soft spot for trouble."

The sound of a clearing throat nearby made him groan, and Charlie pulled out of his arms and turned to face Meredith. She'd donned a pair of Charlie's jeans and a bright green T-shirt that was one of her favorites. Her red hair peeked out from beneath a blue University of Kentucky baseball cap. "Think I'll pass as Charlie?"

"Close enough," Mike said. "You ready to go?"

"Yeah."

Mike turned back to Charlie. "Watch TV. Or read. Just try not to worry. We know what we're doing." He gave her a quick kiss and nodded for Meredith to follow him as he headed for the door to the garage.

Watch TV, Charlie thought. *Read a book. Try not to worry.*

As if she'd be able to do any of those things.

THE FIRST PART of the plan went through without a hitch. Meredith used Charlie's credit card to pay for the repairs, and Bill Hardy, forewarned, put the transaction through without question. He handed over the keys to Charlie's Toyota and waved them off.

Back in the Ford by himself, Mike called in his position. In the Toyota, Meredith did the same.

"Feeney's on the move," Trask said on his end. He and Heller were positioned inside Charlie's house, hidden in case Feeney decided to stage some sort of ambush.

"How do we know?" Mike asked.

"I put one of my deputies on his tail."

"You might have mentioned that before," Mike muttered. "What if he spots the tail?"

"He won't." Trask sounded confident.

Mike was coming up on the intersection of Mill Road and Old Mercerville Highway. As good a place to have a breakdown as any.

Ahead, the Toyota crossed the intersection. But Mike pulled over to the side of the road and parked on the shoulder, turning on his emergency flashers. He waited for a couple of cars to pass, then got out of the truck and walked around to the hood.

He lifted the hood and pulled up the rod to hold it in place. "I'm stopped at Mill Road and Old Mercerville Highway," he murmured into the small mike that protruded from the earpiece. To anyone looking, it would seem as if he was on the phone using a Bluetooth headset.

"Feeney is driving a silver Honda Accord. He looks to be headed directly your way."

While pretending to be checking the water in the radiator, Mike kept one eye on the light traffic passing by him. Sure enough, one of the next cars to pass was a silver Honda. He could barely make out a male driver, who seemed to be the only person in the vehicle.

"I have a visual. Subject is heading down Mill Road. Should be nearing Sycamore Road in two minutes."

"I'm about three minutes ahead," Meredith said. "I'm about to turn into the driveway at Charlie's place."

"Showtime," Trask said. "You know what to do, Strong."

Mike fiddled with the radiator for a few seconds more, until he was sure Feeney's Honda was well out of sight. He double-checked with a glance over his shoulder, then closed the truck's hood and returned to the driver's seat. He turned off the hazard lights, started the truck and pulled back onto the road.

CHARLIE CHECKED THE clock over the fireplace mantel for about the twentieth time in the past half hour. By now, Meredith would be at the house. Trask and Heller would have arrived there a few minutes earlier, setting up for the ambush.

All she had to do was wait and it would all be over.

The trill of her cell phone made her jump. She picked it up off the coffee table and checked the display.

A familiar number jumped out at her. Her heart started to thud faster in her chest.

"Hello?"

"Charlotte. It's been a long time." Diana Bearden's voice hadn't changed in ten years. Still soft and warm. Tinged with a hint of wary friendliness.

"Mrs. Bearden. I…wasn't expecting to hear from you."

"I know. I'm sorry about the distance over these years. I just— It's been hard to be reminded of Alice's death."

"It's been hard for me, too." Charlie blinked back the tears suddenly burning her eyes. "I thought about trying to contact you and Mr. Bearden about a thousand times. I did call Mr. Bearden's office a few weeks back. And today." She paused, remembering the reason for her latest call.

"Craig's out of town. He's in Louisville for a meet and

greet. I was going to go, but…" Her voice trailed off, and for a moment, Charlie thought she'd hung up.

"Mrs. Bearden?"

There were tears in her voice when she spoke again. "I'm sorry, Charlotte. It's just so near the time…you know. And hearing your voice again after so long brings up so many memories."

"I'm sorry." Tears pricked Charlie's eyes.

"I don't suppose you have a few minutes to meet with me today, do you?" Diana asked. "Maybe you could come by the house?"

"I—I don't have my car."

"Then maybe I could come to you?"

"No. That's not good, either." She thought about Mike and the others, probably neck-deep in danger as they spoke. He'd told her to stay put. Her safety was on the line.

"I just— I'm feeling so alone right now. Craig doesn't understand. He's poured all his grief into his campaign. It's like he thinks he can make everything right by winning and changing laws that might have saved Alice all those years ago. But it won't bring her back." Diana was crying helplessly now. "Nothing will ever bring her back. And I just— I need to talk to someone who understands. I think you understand, don't you, Charlotte?"

Charlie bit back a sob. "Okay. You can come here." She gave Diana the address. "I'll be waiting."

"Thank you," Diana said quietly. "You just may be saving my life. I'll be there in a few minutes." She hung up the phone.

Charlie put her phone back on the coffee table and sat on the sofa, gripping her hands tightly together. Now that she'd agreed to see Diana, she was already second-guessing her decision. Mike would probably be furious at her for agreeing to have Diana Bearden come here. And maybe it had been a stupid decision.

But how could she say no to Alice's mother after all this time?

She checked her phone, in case Mike had left a message while she was talking to Diana. But her voice mail was empty.

The clock over the mantel showed only seven minutes had passed since the last time she checked.

What was happening at her house now?

"FEENEY'S PARKED HIS CAR. The GPS signal hasn't moved for two minutes." Trask's voice sounded tinny through the earpiece.

"Do you have a location?" Mike asked.

"Somewhere between here and Mill Road. What's your position?"

"I've just pulled onto Sycamore. I'll keep an eye out for the Honda."

He spotted the vehicle about two blocks farther down Sycamore Road, parked at the curb about a half mile from Charlie's house.

"Found it," he said into the mike. "Half mile up Sycamore. Unoccupied. Feeney must be on foot."

He pulled the truck up behind the Honda and got out, reaching down to unsheathe his boot knife as he walked. He looked into the car's interior to be sure Feeney wasn't hiding, then he shoved the blade of the knife into the front and back tires on the street-facing side of the Honda.

"Vehicle's incapacitated," he said into the mike. "Got a visual on Feeney yet?"

"Nothing yet." It was Heller who answered. "Be careful. Don't want him to spot you."

"Got it covered." Mike cut through a side yard and

headed into the thick woods that stood behind the homes on this part of Sycamore Road. Once hidden within the trees, he pulled the pot of camouflage paint from his backpack and covered his face to match the camo jacket and pants he wore.

The afternoon had waned quickly since Charlie had made the call, twilight already drifting over the afternoon on gathering dark clouds, bringing with them the threat of rain. It also provided better cover for Mike as he tried to make up the time he'd already lost, but it also made him a little wary about Charlie stuck at his house alone with darkness falling.

"We have a visual." Trask's voice buzzed in his ear as he crept through the trees behind the house next door to Charlie's. He paused in place, peering through the thicket in hopes of catching sight of Randall Feeney.

There. He was dressed in dark colors, moving through the woods about forty yards east of Mike's position.

"Showtime," he whispered.

Chapter Seventeen

The wind picked up, swirling dead leaves around Mike's feet as he crept closer to where Randall Feeney crouched near the edge of the woods directly behind Charlie's house. For one heart-stopping moment, Feeney turned his head toward Mike, who froze in place, holding his breath.

Then, as rain started to fall in fat drops from the gunmetal sky, Feeney dashed through the backyard and up to the side of the house. He looked around him, checking for any sign that he was being watched, then he pulled open a small window built into the house's foundation.

It was a tiny space, but Feeney was a slim man. He squeezed through the opening and slipped inside.

Mike muttered a curse. He should have checked the house for just that sort of point of entry. He'd made sure that all the windows on the upper floor were locked, but he hadn't even thought about there being a cellar in the small house. He should have asked Charlie.

He should have done a lot of things differently.

"Feeney's entered through a cellar window. I didn't even think to check if it was locked. He'll probably be coming up through an interior door." Mike followed Feeney's path to the window and crouched to one side, listening through the opening for any sounds the man might be making.

Taking a chance, he peered through the narrow window into the cellar. The small, musty space was utterly dark, the gloom alleviated only by the faint gray light from the window and the narrow beam of a small flashlight several yards inside the space.

Feeney was crouching near the back of the cellar, next to what looked like a furnace unit. His body blocked whatever it was he was doing, but based on where he was crouching, he seemed to be near the pipes.

What was he doing?

Suddenly, Feeney stood and started to turn back to the window.

Mike pulled back quickly, heart racing, and flattened himself against the wall.

Something came flying out of the window and hit the ground, sliding across the wet grass. It looked like a coil of green twine.

But it wasn't. And suddenly, Mike knew exactly what Randall Feeney had been doing in the cellar.

He scrambled toward the green coil, growling into the headset's mouthpiece, "He's cut the gas line in the furnace room beneath the house. He's going to try to blow it up. Get the hell out now!"

Several things happened at once. Feeney's head and shoulders appeared in the window as he started to haul himself out. Mike grabbed the green coil of cannon fuse and pulled out his knife, slicing the leading piece of fuse trailing from the window. He flung the coil toward the tree line with one hand and leveled the knife toward Feeney, who had stopped half in and half out of the house.

"Very careful, Mr. Feeney," he warned as the man stared back at him with wide, scared eyes. "You've just armed a very nasty bomb, and I wouldn't want to see you blown up with it."

Heller came around the side of the house, half-crouched, ready to spring. "Trask just turned off the master gas switch. If nobody does anything stupid, we can end this thing with everybody still alive."

Trask appeared then, Meredith Chandler right behind him. He eased over to the basement window and nodded for Heller to join him. The two men pulled Feeney out of the window and jerked him to his feet.

"I want a lawyer," Feeney said.

"That can be arranged," Trask said, pushing Feeney toward the wall of the house. "Spread your legs and put your hands against the wall."

Feeney complied.

"Anything in your pockets I need to know about? Needles, weapons?"

"A lighter in my front pocket. A phone in the back."

Trask pulled the lighter and the phone from Feeney's pockets and handed them to Mike to hold while he patted his prisoner down.

The phone vibrated suddenly against Mike's palm. He looked at the display and saw a message from someone called D. The girl isn't there. I'll take it from here.

His heart plummeting, he crossed to Feeney and shoved the phone in front of his face. "Who is D?"

Feeney just looked at him, a faint smile curving his lips.

Mike showed Trask the message. "We knew he probably had an accomplice, whoever was driving the car that hit Alice."

Mike sent a text back. Where are you now?

There was no response.

"Damn it, Feeney, who is D?"

Feeney continued smiling.

THE PERIMETER ALARM sounded in the hallway just as Charlie was finishing a quick application of lipstick. It was silly, she knew, to worry about how she looked after all these years, but maybe that was why it seemed so important to her. It was her first face-to-face meeting with Alice's mother in almost ten years. She wanted to show a little respect for the occasion.

She was halfway to the door when she remembered the camera app on her phone. Pulling it up, she checked the camera feed.

Diana Bearden stood in front of the door, her image slightly distorted by the camera lens. Charlie knew from her press photos that she hadn't aged much in the past ten years, but she was struck anew by how much Diana looked like her daughter might have looked if she had grown into middle age.

Giving her hair a quick finger combing, she shoved her phone in the pocket of her jeans and unlocked the door.

For a moment, Diana just stared back at her through the screen door, her blue eyes sharp and probing, as if she were trying to read past Charlie's exterior to see what existed at the core of her soul. It was a disconcerting sensation, forcing Charlie to paste on a smile and open the screen door. "I'm so glad you're here," she said as she stepped back to let Diana inside.

After locking the door behind them, she turned around to look at Alice's mother, mentally rehearsing what she wanted to say. *I'm sorry* came to mind, along with *I miss Alice like crazy.*

She was so caught up in what she thought she should say that it took a couple of seconds to register what she was seeing in front of her.

Diana held a pistol in one perfectly manicured hand, the barrel pointed straight at Charlie's heart.

"You just couldn't let it go, could you?" Diana said.

Her heart sinking, Charlie slowly shook her head. "No. I couldn't."

A VIBRATION AGAINST his hip drew Mike's attention briefly away from Randall Feeney's smiling face. It was his phone, sending him a notice that the perimeter alarm at his house had been breached.

"Someone's breached the perimeter at my house," he told Heller, already moving toward the front of the house. He pulled up the camera app and checked the feed, stumbling to a halt in surprise as he recognized the tawny-haired woman in a dark blue suit who stood at his door.

What was Diana Bearden doing at his house?

He punched in Charlie's cell phone number. The call went directly to voice mail.

Heller had caught up, grabbing Mike by the shoulder. "What the hell is going on?"

"Diana Bearden is at my house. Charlie just let her in." The tail end of the motion-activated camera shot showed Charlie letting Diana inside. The door closed, and a few seconds later, the shot went dormant.

"Diana," Heller said, his voice dropping in pitch.

D, Mike thought, his heart suddenly stuttering. He turned to look at Heller. "It was Diana Bearden. She was Feeney's accomplice."

"And now she's at your house with Charlie."

Mike started running before Heller finished his sentence.

"I DON'T REMEMBER EVERYTHING, you know." Charlie tried to control the tremors running through her as she stared down the barrel of Diana's pistol. It couldn't be very large, she realized—it fit rather snugly in Diana's small hand. But the big black hole at the end of the barrel still appeared to be enormous, and it never wavered from the center of her chest.

Center mass, she thought. Wasn't that what shooting instructors called it? The center of the body, where most of the body's vital organs lay. One or two shots there, and nobody would be walking away.

"You remember enough," Diana said. "That's why you called my husband again today, isn't it?"

"Feeney told you?"

"He tells me everything." Diana twitched the barrel of the pistol toward the center of the living room. "Where's the bathroom?"

The question caught Charlie off guard. "You want to go to the bathroom? Now?"

Diana laughed. "No, I want you to go there. Now."

Charlie walked slowly down the hallway toward the bathroom door on the right. As they passed the open door of the office, she spotted His Highness sitting in the doorway, his blue eyes glaring hate at Diana Bearden. He bared his teeth and hissed.

Diana swung the pistol toward the cat. Hizzy stood his ground, growling.

It was the distraction Charlie needed. She pitched her shoulder into Diana's chest, slamming hard against her sternum. A grunt of pain erupted from the woman's throat, and she tumbled into the wall, her head cracking against the door frame.

As her gun hand hit the ground, Charlie stomped on her wrist with her full weight, feeling the bones beneath her feet crack. The gun fell loose from Diana's fingers as she howled in pain. Charlie kicked it away and straddled Diana's waist, pinning her to the floor with both hands.

"You were in the car!" she cried, adrenaline pumping through her like venom. "You hit Alice with your car, on purpose! You let her die. You let me think it was all my fault! How could you do that to your daughter?"

Diana tried to fight free of Charlie's grasp, but her broken wrist was useless, and Charlie was bigger and stronger, now that there wasn't a pistol to equalize things between them.

"Why?" Charlie wailed, tears burning a path down her cheeks. "Why did you do that to Alice?"

"Because she knew!" Diana screamed. "She knew and she was going to tell Craig what we were doing."

The light in the cinder block building behind the Headhunter Bar, Charlie realized. The voices she'd heard when she entered the alley had been coming from there. From the old Bearden campaign headquarters.

"Alice was looking for you that night. That's why she'd talked me into going to that bar. She knew it was the best place to watch the old campaign office. Because she knew you were meeting someone there when Mr. Bearden was out of town. Didn't she?"

Diana just stared at her a moment, then bucked her hips, trying to knock Charlie off her.

Charlie pressed hard on Diana's broken wrist, and she screamed.

"You were afraid she'd tell Craig. It would ruin everything. Craig's political career would fall apart. Your dreams of being a senator's wife would be down the toilet. And Feeney would lose his cushy little job as a toady if Craig knew. You couldn't let that happen. Alice—" Her voice faltered, but she gritted her teeth and forced the words out of her aching throat. "Your daughter, your only child, was acceptable collateral damage. Was that it?"

The sound of a key in the lock drew her attention away

from Diana's baleful glare. The older woman made one last attempt at escape, shoving the heel of her hand into Charlie's chin, snapping her head back.

Charlie's grip on Diana faltered, and Diana shoved her off, sending her reeling into the wall. Charlie scrambled after the other woman as she bolted for the end of the hall, where the gun had landed in the middle of the kitchen floor.

She tackled Diana by the legs and scrambled forward over her back, jerking Diana's left hand away as her fingers brushed against the butt of the pistol.

She heard heavy footfalls coming up behind her. "I've got her, Charlie." Mike's voice, low and reassuring, sent a little shudder darting down her spine.

She leaned forward and shoved the gun sideways. It skittered farther into the kitchen, landing under the kitchen table. Then she scrambled forward, off Diana, and turned to look at Mike.

He spared her a quick, intense look that made her stomach turn inside out before he holstered his gun, reached down and hauled Diana Bearden to her feet.

Maddox Heller entered the hall behind Mike and Diana, pistol in hand. He skidded to a stop, taking in the whole tableau. His shoulders relaxed, and he dropped the pistol to his side. "You good here?"

"We're good," Mike said, his gaze locking with Charlie's again. "And you can take Charlie off my self-defense course roster when you get back to the academy."

Heller put his pistol back in the holster under his jacket. "Yeah? Why's that?"

Mike shot Charlie a lopsided grin. "Because she already passed."

"FEENEY PUT MOST of it on Diana Bearden," Trask told Mike and Charlie a few hours later. "But we caught him red-handed trying to blow up Charlie's house, so he's not getting away with anything."

"Did he admit to drugging Mike?" Charlie asked.

"He said Diana blackmailed him into it. Apparently he's been skimming money from Bearden's campaign coffers, and he thought Diana was covering it up for him. But apparently she was smart enough to make sure all the stink would fall on him once it came to light."

"Do you believe him?" Mike asked.

"Yeah, I think he's realized the truth is about the only defense he has."

"Did he say why he drugged me? What was he going to do?" Mike asked.

Trask glanced at Charlie. "I think we both know what he was going to do."

Next to Mike, Charlie shivered. He put his arm around her, pulling her closer.

"How did Diana know Charlie was at my house? She'd already sent Feeney to blow up her house."

"She's not talking, but Feeney told us Diana was beginning to suspect we were onto Feeney. So we think when Charlie called out of the blue and left that message about remembering things, Diana thought it might be a setup." Trask's smile looked like a grimace. "She called you, learned quickly that you weren't where you were supposed to be and figured out you were alone."

"So she made her move." Charlie sighed. "I used to wish my mother was just like Mrs. Bearden."

Mike tightened his arm around her. "I'm glad she's not."

Charlie looked up at Archer Trask. "Are we done here?"

"For now. We'll probably have more questions soon, but I think we're good for today."

Outside, a cold, misty rain had begun to fall. Mike hurried Charlie to his truck and helped her into the passenger seat. Once he took his place behind the wheel, he turned the heat up. "Better?"

She flashed him a sheepish smile. "I'm not that cold, but I can't seem to stop shaking."

"That's delayed reaction. But I have a prescription for that." He shot her a quick smile.

"Oh?" She turned to look at him. "What's that, Dr. Strong?"

"Well, it starts with a big cup of hot chocolate with whipped cream. Then there's a roaring fire and a blanket big enough for two—"

"I'm sold," she said with a big grin that made his insides sizzle. "How fast can we get there?"

By THE TIME the local news moved on to another story besides the scandalous tale of adultery, betrayal and murder among the rich and famous, a week had passed. Hizzy's stitches had been removed and the cone of shame relegated to the trash bin, Charlie's insurance money had paid for new furniture and a state-of-the-art security system, and Mike's mother had reluctantly returned home to Black Rock, North Carolina, with a promise from Mike and Charlie to visit for Christmas.

Mike finished pushing Charlie's sofa into place near the fireplace and dusted his hands on his jeans. "Happy now?"

She walked over to where he stood near the hearth, wrapping her arms around his waist. "Delirious."

He grinned down at her, enfolding her in a tight embrace. "Good. I intend to keep you that way. Delirious Charlie is my favorite flavor." He bent to kiss her, his tongue sliding over her lips as if sampling her taste. "Yup, definitely my favorite."

"Let's not get ahead of ourselves," she warned, gently extricating herself from his embrace. "We have one more thing to add before the room will be complete."

Mike groaned. "Don't tell me you bought a second sofa."

She gave his arm a light tug. "No, just something that would make that corner look absolutely perfect." She led him into the mudroom, where she'd stashed her newest purchase.

Mike stared at the little fir tree leaning against the window in the small room. "A tree."

"A *Christmas* tree," she corrected, picking up the new plastic bin she'd bought earlier that day for all the ornaments she'd purchased during her buying spree. She carried the box into the living room, leaving Mike to haul the tree and its stand.

Together, they set up the tree in the corner and arranged the red velvet tree skirt at the bottom. "It already looks lovely," she said with a happy sigh.

"So, a Christmas fan," Mike said, smiling at her. "I'll add that to my list of important things to know about Charlie."

Unexpected tears pricked her eyes. She blinked them back as she opened the plastic bin and pulled out a new packet of silver garland. "I wasn't, you know. Not for a long time." She ran the strands of silver tinsel through her fingers. "Not after Alice died. It was so close to Christmas, I could never seem to muster up the mood."

Mike took the garland from her hands and pulled her into his arms. "I'm sorry. I know this can't be easy for you, especially now."

She leaned her head against his chest, taking comfort

from the strong, steady beat of his heart beneath her ear. She thought about the pages she'd written about Alice, about her own memories of that night. She had hoped by writing everything down, she could make sense of what had happened.

But there was no sense in what happened. Only sadness and bittersweet release. It was time to close that file and write something new. Something brighter. Something full of hope and meaning.

"I know now," she said. "I know what happened to her and why. It makes me so sad for her. And grateful that she never knew how her mother betrayed her. But knowing means I can finally let it go. Alice wouldn't have wanted me to mourn her forever."

"No, from the way you've described her, I don't think she'd have been happy about that at all."

She drew her head back to look at him. "She'd have liked you. Big, strong, badass. She might have fought me for you. Might have even won."

He bent his head and kissed her nose. "Not a chance, Charlie. Not a chance in this world."

"Are we finally having that talk about us we kept threatening to have?" she asked, cuddling closer.

"I guess we are. So I'll go first. I'm all in, Charlie. You're it for me. I think I knew it from the first time you stepped into my class that day, all spitfire and trouble."

She grinned. "You make me sound so interesting."

"You are. The most interesting woman I've ever known."

"And that," she said with a light pat on his backside, "is why you're it for me, Mike Strong. Because you're apparently blind and a little on the dim side, so I can always keep you believing I'm fabulous."

He laughed, the sound rumbling through her like distant thunder on a warm summer night.

"And because you're the best man I know," she added, letting the truth shine in her eyes for the first time in as long as she could remember. "A man who, for some strange reason, really does believe in me."

He bent for another kiss. "Always, Charlie. Always."

* * * * *

Look for more books in
Paula Graves's new series,
CAMPBELL COVE ACADEMY, *in 2017.*

You'll find them wherever
Mills & Boon Intrigue books are sold!

With shaking hands, she unzipped her bag and reached inside for Cole's wallet.

Cole stared back at her from a California driver's license. He hadn't lied about being a California boy. Ignoring the cash in the billfold, she jammed her fingers into the slot behind his license and pulled out a stack of cards.

The gold-embossed letters on the top card blurred before her eyes and she slid down the length of the door until she was crouching against it.

Cole Pierson was a DEA agent, and he must be looking for the woman he believed murdered Johnny Diamond and stole his drug money.

He was looking for her.

IN THE ARMS OF
THE ENEMY

BY
CAROL ERICSON

First Published in Great Britain 2016
By Mills & Boon, an imprint of HarperCollins*Publishers*
1 London Bridge Street, London, SE1 9GF

© 2016 Carol Ericson

ISBN: 978-0-263-91922-6

46-1116

Our policy is to use papers that are natural, renewable and recyclable products and made from wood grown in sustainable forests. The logging and manufacturing processes conform to the legal environmental regulations of the country of origin.

Printed and bound in Spain
by CPI, Barcelona

Carol Ericson is a bestselling, award-winning author of more than forty books. She has an eerie fascination for true-crime stories, a love of film noir and a weakness for reality TV, all of which fuel her imagination to create her own tales of murder, mayhem and mystery. To find out more about Carol and her current projects, please visit her website at www.carolericson.com, "where romance flirts with danger."

For all my SHS friends

Chapter One

Her head throbbed as she stared at the dead guy. He had to be dead. She zeroed in on his chest, watching for the rise and fall of his breathing. Nothing.

Dried foam clung to his parted lips and chin in silvery trails, clinging to his beard like gossamer spiderwebs. His open, bloodshot eyes bugged out from their sockets like those of a surprised cartoon character.

She checked the carpet around his body—no blood, no weapon, just a plastic water bottle on its side with a quarter of its contents still inside.

She sat back on her heels and massaged her temples, which now throbbed as much as the back of her head. What had happened in this cheap motel room? Who was he?

Who was she?

A sob bubbled in her throat. That terror had slammed into her head-on before she even saw the body on the floor, when she'd come to, lying diagonally across the bed, fully clothed. She'd put that problem on the back burner when she noticed the dead guy, but a complete memory loss couldn't be ignored forever.

There had to be a clue to her identity somewhere. She rose to her feet, her gaze sweeping the room, with its up-ended lamp, disheveled double bed and cracked picture frame above that bed.

The dead man hadn't gone down without a fight. With her? Had she killed this man in a fight?

She took in his large frame sprawled on the threadbare carpet and shook her head. Hard to believe. But then maybe—she glanced at her toes, painted with pale pink polish—she was some ninja amazon woman.

A hysterical laugh crackled through the room and she clapped a hand over her mouth. She didn't like the sound of that laugh. Wrapping her arms around her midsection, she tiptoed toward the open door of the bathroom. She held her breath and flicked the light switch with her knuckle.

At least no more dead bodies greeted her. She shuffled toward the chipped vanity and slowly raised her head to face the mirror.

She gasped. Leaning forward, she traced the outline of a red spot forming high on her cheekbone, beneath her right eye. Then she rubbed the painful area on the back of her head, her fingers circling a huge lump. Had she and the man gotten into a brawl?

She stepped back, studying the fine-boned face in the mirror, a slim column of a neck and a pair of narrow shoulders encased in a flimsy T-shirt. That slip of a thing that stared back at her with wide eyes couldn't have taken down a kitten, never mind a full-grown man.

She bit her bottom lip and winced. She hunched forward and dabbed at the lip she now saw was swollen. The dead guy had done a number on her before…succumbing. But what had he succumbed from?

Maybe someone had attacked them both and left her for dead. Maybe that someone would return. She backed away from the mirror and stumbled out of the small bathroom.

The walls of the dumpy motel room closed in on her all at once and she listed to the side like a drunken sailor on the deck of a ship. Reaching out a hand to clutch the faded bedspread, she sank to the edge of the bed. She should call the police, 911.

Her gaze traveled to the inert form on the floor and she shivered. Unless she'd killed him.

She crept to the window, where she hooked a finger between two slats of the blinds and peeked outside. She squinted into the gray light. The green numbers on the digital clock by the bed had already told her it was just after six thirty in the morning.

A small, dark car huddled in a parking space in front of the room. Could it be theirs? His? Hers?

She patted the pockets of her jeans—no keys, no ID, no money. She gulped back her rising panic and lunged for the closet. She swung open the door and jumped back as a small wheeled suitcase fell over on its side, just missing her bare toes.

Dropping to her knees, she scrabbled for the zipper with trembling hands. When she flipped open the suitcase, she plunged her hands into a pile of clothes—her clothes. She'd packed in a hurry.

She pushed the bag away from her and crawled on her hands and knees to peer under the bed. Nothing but dust occupied the space and she sneezed as it tickled her nose.

What woman didn't carry a purse with her?

She searched the rest of the room, giving the body on the floor a wide berth. She ended in the middle of the room, hands on her hips.

One place left she hadn't searched. She slid a sideways glance at the dead man, and then pivoted toward the bathroom. She yanked a hand towel from the rack. She returned to the man and crouched beside him. With the towel covering her hand, she tugged at his jacket, which fell open, exposing his neck and an intricate tattoo curling around it and down his chest. Vines, barbwire, a skull and the letters *L* and *C* intertwined. LC. Larry?

She rifled Larry's front pockets and heard the jingle of the keys before she saw them. She closed her fingers, still wrapped in the towel, around a key chain and pulled it free of Larry's pocket. She cupped the keys in her palm, frowning at the yellow daisy key chain—didn't seem like Larry's style at all. Maybe the car belonged to her.

A pair of boots, socks stuffed inside, was lined up near the door of the motel room, and she put them on—a perfect fit, kind of like Cinderella in an alternate universe. She eased open the door and pressed her eye to the crack.

Luckily for her, the motel didn't seem to be a hotspot of tourist activity or any other kind of activity—except for in this room. She swung the door wide and stepped into a cool, damp blast of air. Tucking her chin to her chest, she scurried to the compact car and jabbed at the key fob hooked to the key chain.

The lights of the little car flashed once in greeting, and she blew out a breath. She dropped onto the front seat and slid down. Then she pulled open the glove compartment, and a stack of napkins tumbled out.

Leaving them where they fell, she plunged her hand into the glove box and started pulling papers out, glancing at each one before tossing it to the floor.

When she found the car's registration, she ran a finger across the printed words and read aloud, her voice filling the car, startling her. "Hazel McTavish."

The dead man in the hotel room didn't look like a Hazel. Could she be Hazel? Hazel lived in Seattle, Washington. Was that where she was now? No bells of recognition rang in her head. Seattle meant about as much to her at this point as Timbuktu.

Peering into the back of the car, she scanned the seat and floor. She plucked a black leather jacket from the floor and shook it out. It had to be hers.

With her blood racing, she jammed her hands in the

pockets. Her trembling fingers curled around a slip of paper, which she pulled free.

Timberline, WA.

At least there was a common denominator here—Washington. Could she be in Timberline now?

She scooted from the car and locked it with the key fob. She reached into the motel room and yanked the Do Not Disturb sign from the inside door handle, hooking it on the outside before slipping back into the room.

Larry hadn't moved.

Tapping her toe, she assessed the big man on the floor. Did he have a wallet? A phone? He'd landed on his back, and if he kept his wallet in his back pocket, she doubted she could turn him over to do a search.

Her stomach churned. She didn't want to try. Didn't want to touch him.

She had to make some kind of move. She couldn't hang out here until someone came looking for Larry—or her. And where was *here*?

She scurried to the other side of the bed and the telephone on the nightstand. She grabbed a cheap notepad printed with the words *Stardust Motel, Seattle, Washington*, and dropped it.

She returned to the closet and pulled out the suitcase. The clothes in there obviously belonged to her. She wasn't stealing. Her gaze shifted to the dead guy. Theft was the least of her moral concerns right now.

As she slid the door closed, she noticed two bags stacked on the far side of the closet. She parked the suitcase by the front door and dragged open the other closet door.

She unzipped the first duffel bag and peeled back the top, releasing a stream of air between her teeth. Stacks of bills were nestled neatly in the bag, and she clawed through them all the way to the bottom.

Hugging a few thousand dollars to her chest, she stumbled backward until the back of her legs hit the bed. She sat.

What did it all mean? Were she and Larry bank robbers who'd had a disagreement? Lottery winners who couldn't decide how to split their windfall?

She dropped the cash on the floor and returned to the closet. With both hands, she pulled the money duffel off the other one and unzipped the bag on the bottom. This time she swayed and grabbed the closet door to steady herself.

She ran her fingertips along the plastic baggies in the duffel, which looked like they were stuffed with ice chips—but this ice didn't melt. She snatched her hand back from the drugs packaged neatly in the bags.

With her heart hammering in her chest, she swept up the hand towel she'd dropped next to Larry's body and darted around the room, wiping down surfaces from the bathroom to the TV remote to the duffel bags and all the doorknobs and handles in between.

Maybe the dead man had keeled over from a heart attack or a stroke or an aneurysm, but she had no intention of being here when the cops showed up.

She zipped up the drug bag and hoisted the money bag back on top. She gathered the stacks of bills from the floor where she'd dropped them and froze.

She had no purse, no ID, no memory. How could she make her getaway, find herself with no money?

The cash in her hands felt solid, sort of like a crutch, something to hold on to. She needed this money now. If it turned out she was a drug dealer, she'd return it to…someone. She'd pay it back once she discovered her identity.

She stuffed the money into the suitcase by the door and added a few more stacks for good measure. She'd count it later. She'd use just what she needed to get by.

All the excuses she reeled out for herself couldn't quell the sick feeling in her stomach. She'd make this right, but she couldn't leave her fate to strangers when she didn't even know her own story.

Larry's body emitted a tinny classical tune, and she dropped the money on the floor. She tiptoed toward him and crouched down, clutching the towel in her hand.

A light glowed from the front pocket of his shirt, and she plucked the phone out, using the hand towel. The cell slid off of his body and landed beside his arm.

Squinting, she leaned forward. The display flashed a call from an unknown number, and then went dark. Drug dealers and bank robbers probably didn't store contact names and numbers of their associates in their phones.

Since she was hovering over the body anyway, she swiped at the man's pockets where she'd touched him. She would wipe down the car, take her suitcase and hit the road—first stop Timberline, the name of the town on the slip of paper in her pocket. She was about to rise when a dinging sound stopped her.

The phone lit up again, but this time a text message flashed on the display.

She hunched forward and read the text aloud to the dead man. "'Did you get the girl? Rocky's...'"

In place of an adjective for Rocky's emotion, the texter had inserted a little devil face with smoke coming out his ears. Rocky must be very, very angry.

Was she the girl who had to be gotten? Would've been nice if the texter had used her name to give her a head start on reclaiming her identity.

Cell phones could be tracked. She pushed to her feet and finished wiping down every possible surface in the room. When she was done, she tucked a corner of the towel in the waistband of her jeans and peeked out the door.

She'd leave the car here—those could be traced, too.

She might be Hazel McTavish from Seattle, but she needed to do a little research before stepping into Hazel's life.

But before she left without the car, she wanted to check the trunk first. She'd found a bag of money, a bag of drugs, what next? A bag of weapons?

Poking her head out the door, she cranked it from side to side. The people at this motel didn't seem to be early risers—probably because they were sleeping off the night's activities or had used the room for just a few hours.

She kept her head down and scurried to the compact, unlocking the trunk with the key fob. It sprang open and she used the towel to ease it up.

Chills raced up her spine and her mouth dropped open in a silent scream as her eyes locked on to the vacant stare of her second dead body this morning.

Chapter Two

DEA Agent Cole Pierson turned away from the dead woman's stare. Money, drugs, dead bodies—and he hadn't even officially clocked in yet.

He returned to the motel room, where the odor of decomposing flesh had started to drift through the air. He swiped the back of his hand across his nose. Someone had left the heat blasting in here, which had accelerated the process of the body's breakdown.

Cole still had no problem identifying the deceased—Johnny Diamond. Whatever had happened in this seedy motel room, it couldn't have happened to a more deserving dirtbag.

The King's County Sheriff's Department had descended on the room like a pack of ants at a picnic. One of those ants, Deputy Brookhurst, approached him with a wide grin.

"Quite a haul for you DEA boys, huh? Crank, cash and Johnny Diamond."

"Now we just have to piece together the rest of the puzzle. Where'd he get it, where was he going with it and who were his contacts? Oh yeah, and who offed him?"

With the toe of his boot, Cole prodded the black duffel bag on the floor, containing hundreds of thousands of dollars of methamphetamine, bagged and ready for the street.

Then he wedged his hands on his hips and surveyed the room. What had Diamond been doing in this flea trap?

Why risk stealing a car, murdering the owner and stuffing her body in the trunk with this much cash and product on hand? Diamond had been a slick adversary from the day he'd burst onto the drug scene four years ago. He'd managed to keep out of their clutches precisely because he'd avoided missteps like this.

Maybe Diamond had been planning to cash out and head for a tropical island somewhere. Cole smoothed his gloved hands over the pile of money stashed in the other duffel bag and frowned.

"Brookhurst, are you sure your guys didn't touch the cash?"

"Hold on." Brookhurst widened his stance and hooked his thumbs in his pockets like some movie star cowboy. "Are you accusing my boys of something?"

"Stealing? No. Did they move it around? Reposition it? Run their hands through it?" Cole held up his own hands. "Hey, I wouldn't blame 'em."

Brookhurst's puffed-up chest deflated. "I don't think so. Why do you ask?"

Cole traced the uneven grid of the money stacks with his fingertip. "The bills are stuffed into the bag in tight rows, but those rows are messed up at the top—as if someone thumbed through the money. You checked Diamond's pockets?"

"I told you—a set of keys with a flower key chain in the front pocket, wallet in the back pocket. Had maybe a hundred bucks in his wallet."

The county coroners parked a gurney next to Diamond's body. "We're ready to take him if you're done with him."

"Copy us on the autopsy and toxicology reports. You still think it looks like poison?"

One of the coroners held up a plastic bag containing the bottle of water that had been on the floor, and shook it. "Smells like bitter almonds."

Cole whistled. "Cyanide."

"Along with the foaming at the mouth and his reddish skin color, that's my guess. But it's just a guess and we have a lot of tests to run."

"Poison." Cole drummed his fingers against his chin. "The murder weapon of choice for women, but the motel clerk said Diamond checked in as a single."

Brookhurst nudged him and chuckled. "Maybe his old lady mixed up a little something special for him when she caught him cheating, or maybe she was cheating and wanted to bypass the divorce. I should start sniffing the drinks my wife mixes for me."

Cole's jaw tightened and he nodded once. Cheating-spouse jokes didn't hold much humor for him anymore.

Hearing a commotion outside, Cole strode to the door of the motel room. A deputy had stopped two women outside the yellow tape. One of them, speaking Spanish, kept pointing at the car with the dead body in the trunk.

Cole joined the knot of people. "What's going on, Deputy?"

The officer jerked his thumb between the two women. "This one's saying the other one saw a woman here this morning."

They'd already questioned one of the women, who was a maid at the motel, but hadn't seen the second woman yet.

"Espera." Cole sliced his hand through the air. "Wait. *Habla inglés, señora?"*

"Sí, yes, I speak English."

"What were you doing at the motel this morning?"

"Trabajo. I work here as a maid. I have the overnight shift."

"What time was this?"

"After seven o'clock, *señor*. I was almost done with work."

"Where did you see this woman? What did she look like?"

"By this car. I thought maybe she came out of the room. She walked past the car and she was pulling a suitcase." She twirled her finger in the air. "One with wheels."

"Did you see what she looked like?"

The maid put her hands about six inches apart. "*Flaca.* Skinny. Not tall, not short. She was wearing dark pants, maybe jeans, and a dark jacket."

The woman was observant. "Hair?"

"No, *señor*." She shook her head.

His brows shot up. "No hair?"

"Under a hat." She put her hands on top of her head. "Like *una...gorra*."

The other maid spoke up. "Like a knit beanie, pulled over her head."

Cole's pulse ratcheted up a notch. Like she was trying to disguise herself. "Did you get a good look at her face?"

"No, sorry. I notice because there was nobody else outside. I don't think she saw me. She walked past the car, fast, and then turned the corner up there." The maid pointed to the front of the motel.

"Toward the road." They'd already questioned the motel clerk and he hadn't seen or heard a thing. Had this mysterious woman poisoned Johnny Diamond, taken some of his cash and hightailed it out to the road to hitch a ride?

Cole got the contact information for the two women, thanked them and returned to the motel room, where the coroner had already loaded Diamond onto the gurney. The DEA and Cole personally had been trying to nail Diamond for four years. It figured that Diamond's death would provide even more questions than answers. Nothing had been easy with that guy.

What had Diamond been doing back in his old stomping grounds instead of plying his trade in Arizona, where he'd been wheeling and dealing for four years? Had that woman lured him this way?

Cole turned to Deputy Brookhurst. "Did you find any other fingerprints besides Diamond's in this room?"

"We barely found any of Diamond's."

Cole narrowed his eyes. "Wiped clean?"

"Looks like it."

"How about his phone? Did your guys search the Dumpsters and bushes for Diamond's phone? There's no way a man in Diamond's business would be without a cell."

"We looked. We'll try to track his number through the different providers and see if we can locate his phone by pinging." Brookhurst slapped Cole on the back. "Don't worry, Agent Pierson. We'll keep you guys in the loop. We called you as soon as we found out you had a flag on Johnny Diamond, didn't we?"

"You sure did, and I appreciate it. I've been after this SOB for a long time." Cole snapped his fingers. "Did any of the deputies do a search on the GPS in the stolen car? I noticed it had a built-in one."

"Damn, I don't think we've done that yet—a little distracted by what we found in the trunk."

"Yeah, poor Hazel McTavish. I wonder how she had the bad luck to run across Diamond." Cole flipped up the collar of his jacket. Seattle days could be cold enough, but Seattle nights could chill you down to your bones. "I'm going to check the GPS and see if I can find out where Diamond and his mysterious lady friend were headed."

He shouldered his way through the deputies and EMTs gathered around Hazel's trunk, and slid into the front seat of the car. He sniffed the air and got a whiff of some flowery scent—probably belonged to Hazel, but he'd have the King County boys dust for prints in here, too.

He poked his head out the door and yelled back, "I'm going to start the engine to look at the GPS."

The GPS beeped to life as he cranked on the ignition. With a gloved finger, he tapped the screen. He swiped his finger across Recent Destinations and blew out a breath—next stop Timberline, Washington.

HER HEART STUTTERED when the bell above the door of the tourist shop, Timberline Treasures, jingled. She turned from the bin she'd been filling with little stuffed frogs, and released a sigh.

She smiled at the family with two young kids. "Welcome. Let me know if you need anything."

The parents smiled back and started to browse through the key chains and magnets.

She wiped her sweaty palms on the seat of her jeans. She'd have to stop freaking out every time someone came into the store—or find another job. There was no way anyone could trace her to Timberline from that motel room. She'd wiped down all her prints and had even taken Larry's phone just in case he'd had any more information about her, or pictures, or any references to Timberline.

Not Larry, Johnny—Johnny Diamond. When she got to Timberline four days ago, one of her first stops had been the public library to use a computer. It hadn't taken her long to discover the dead man at the Stardust Motel was Johnny Diamond—drug dealer, thief and all-around bad guy.

What she'd been doing with him and how he'd wound up dead, she still didn't have a clue. The online article she read didn't give a cause of death, but the authorities suspected homicide—no witnesses and no suspects.

She brushed a wisp of hair from her face. Diamond's

phone didn't contain any incriminating evidence, and she'd destroyed and dumped it soon after.

Linda, her new boss, new best friend and owner of the store, came from the storage area in the back and plunked a box on the counter. "Can you help me sort through these items, Caroline?"

She'd adopted the name from the North Carolina plates of the semi that had picked her up a mile from that motel outside of Seattle. The choice of a last name had been trickier.

"Of course." She turned to the family. "Do you need any help?"

The mom swung a key chain around her finger. "We'll take one of these—just a little something with the town's name on it."

Caroline plunged her hand into a bin filled with furry frogs. Holding one up, she shook it. "How about one of these? It's a Pacific chorus frog and this particular toy is unique to Timberline."

The little girl's eyes widened as she tugged on her mom's sleeve. "Mom, can I have it?"

"Okay." She rolled her eyes at her husband, who shrugged.

Caroline brought the stuffed frog to the counter and winked at Linda. Linda rang up the family's purchases and when they left the store, she patted Caroline on the back. "You're a born salesperson."

Scooping the trinkets from the box, Caroline said, "I want to do my best to repay you for your kindness, Linda."

"When that haunted, hunted look leaves your eyes that will be repayment enough for me. It took my sister, Louise, years to recover from the abuse dished out by her boyfriend. When you told me your story of domestic violence and I saw that bruise under your eye—" she patted Caroline's hand "—I knew I had to help you."

Caroline blinked back tears as a pang of guilt twisted in her belly. She'd told Linda Gunderson a little lie to explain why she had no ID and why she was using a fake name, Caroline Johnson. She didn't want her abusive ex tracking her down.

Linda had gone above and beyond by introducing Caroline as her cousin's daughter, who'd moved out West for a fresh start. Linda extended her kindness even further by offering her the duplex next to her own, which she and her sister owned, and giving her a job at her shop so she could start earning some money with very few questions asked by the others in this small town.

But that haunted, hunted look in her eyes? That wouldn't go away until she knew her identity and what had happened at the Stardust Motel.

"I appreciate everything you've done for me, Linda."

"I needed help in the store, anyway, with Louise off on her cruise for a month." Linda sniffled and dabbed her nose. Then she shoved a handful of magnets at her. "Can you stock these and the pencils before you leave?"

"Of course." Caroline gathered the items and deposited them in their proper places around the store. When she was done, she took the empty box from the counter and left it by the back door of the storage room.

She lifted her black leather jacket and her new purse from the hook and returned to the store, where Linda was helping someone select a sweatshirt. Caroline waved on her way out.

If she hurried, she could make it to the library before it closed. She'd just scratched the surface of Johnny Diamond—enough to discover his talents for all forms of criminality, but not enough to find out about his personal life or any women in it. Had she been one of those women?

Once outside, she glanced at the moody sky, threatening rain, and then hurried across the street toward the civic center at the end of the block that boasted the sheriff's station, city hall and a cozy library.

She pushed through the glass doors and rounded the corner to the reference section. Two of the three public computers were occupied, but the third glowed in welcome and she strode toward it.

She was two steps away from pulling out the chair when a man slipped in front of her and plopped into it.

"Excuse me." She put her hands on her hips and hovered over his very broad shoulder. "I was just about to use this computer."

The man cranked his head over his shoulder and raised his eyebrows over a pair of greenish eyes. "I'm sorry. I was already seated here, but the log-in I got from the reference librarian didn't work and I went back for another."

"Oh." Caroline shifted her gaze to the pad of paper on the table next to the computer, which had been there before he grabbed the chair from under her nose. "I guess I'll wait."

"I really am sorry. I won't be long. The internet went out at my hotel. Otherwise, I'd be there on my laptop."

She waved her hand. "That's okay. Maybe one of the others will free up."

He turned his head to the side to take in the other two users, and his lips twisted into a smile. "Looks like they're here for the duration. I'll just be a few minutes."

"I'll be over by the magazines. Don't let anyone sneak in ahead of me."

"Wouldn't dream of it."

"Thanks." She pivoted toward a collection of love seats scattered in front of the magazine rack. He must have thought she was a real pain—or worse, that she'd been trying to come on to him. Attractive man like that probably had women making up all kinds of excuses to get close to him and exchange a few words.

She snatched a celebrity magazine encased in plastic from the rack and sat on the edge of one of the love seats, facing the computers.

True to his word, about five minutes later, the man stood up from the computer and stretched. He tapped on the keyboard and tucked his notebook under his arm.

She jumped to her feet. On her way back to the computer tables, she replaced the magazine. "That was fast."

"It's all yours. Have a nice evening."

"You, too." She settled in the chair, warm from his presence. She still had a password from the previous time she'd used the computers here, so she clicked a few keys and swore. The computer was locked and asking her for a password. The guy hadn't logged off.

She shrugged off her jacket and hung it on the back of the chair and tromped off to find the reference librarian.

The librarian looked up from her own computer behind the reference desk. "Can I help you?"

"I'm trying to use computer number one, but the person before me didn't log off and now I'm being prompted for a password that I don't have."

"That keeps happening. He probably did log off, but we've been having issues with that computer. If you don't mind, you can access with the same user log-in so we don't have to shut it down and restart it. The password is *timberline4,* the number, not the word. And it's all lowercase with no spaces."

"Thanks." Caroline returned to the computer and entered the password. As the computer digested her entry, she scooted her chair closer. She'd do another search on Johnny Diamond and try to dig a little deeper this time—beyond the article about his murder.

The computer monitor woke up, and she didn't even

have to launch the search engine since the previous user hadn't closed out, thinking he'd logged off.

As the window filled the screen, an icy fear gripped her heart. She didn't have to search for Johnny Diamond—the man sitting here before had already done so.

Chapter Three

With her hands shaking and her belly in knots, Caroline scrolled through the display. Specifically, the man before her had done a search of Diamond's social media sites.

Did drug dealers really post pictures of their meals and funny cat videos? She clicked on the same links he'd accessed, but found nothing. No wonder he hadn't spent much time at the computer. Diamond didn't seem to have a social media footprint.

But why was that guy even checking? What was Diamond to him? She slumped in her chair and closed her eyes. He didn't look like an associate or fellow drug dealer. Too clean-cut for that, but what did she know?

Too clean-cut. She gripped the arms of the chair. A cop?

She forced herself to breathe. There was no way the cops could've traced her here. She'd hitched different rides to get to Timberline, avoiding bus stations and cameras.

Her fingers dug into the fabric on the arms of the chair. Unless the cops knew something about Diamond's destination. Her search of his background hadn't turned up anything on Timberline, so what connection could he have to this town except through her?

What connection did she have to this town? Why had she scrawled its name on a piece of paper and slipped it into the pocket of her jacket?

Her nose stung with tears as she pushed away from the table. She'd been a fool to come here. Nobody had recognized her yet or provided her with an identity, and she might've walked right into a trap set by Johnny Diamond and his cronies. The man using the computer could be one of those cronies. There must be plenty of clean-cut, attractive drug dealers out there. She'd have to leave this town.

Then what? She had no place else to go. Maybe she should just turn herself in. Could she really be charged with murder if she had no memory of the act? If she had no memory of her life?

She hadn't discovered much more about herself other than she knew Spanish. She'd come across a Spanish-language TV show and could understand every word they were saying. With her pale skin and light brown hair she didn't look Latina, but she could be half or have spent time in a foreign country. The possibilities were endless.

Blowing out a breath, she did a hard shutdown of the computer, just in case it didn't log her out, either. She didn't need anyone snooping into her browsing history, and Mr. Clean-cut would probably be none too happy if he found out someone had been snooping into his.

Maybe he was just interested in the murder. He didn't seem to recognize or have any interest in her.

She looped her purse across her body and squared her shoulders. She wasn't going to run. She had some digging to do first.

Ten minutes later she was seated at the bar of Sutter's, a local restaurant, flipping open a menu. She'd used the money from Diamond's bag—the drug money—to buy a few clothes, a purse, and pay first month's rent to Linda for the duplex. Once she got her life back, she'd return all the money she'd used to the police…anonymously.

The bartender tossed a cocktail napkin on the bar in front of her. "Are you ordering dinner?"

"I'll have the Sutter's burger and a root beer."

He took the menu from her and tapped it on the edge of the bar. "Caroline, right?"

"Good memory." *Unlike some people.*

"Part of my job. I'm Bud."

"I'll take that menu, Bud."

Caroline jerked her head to the side and almost slid off the bar stool.

The man from the library straddled his stool and took the menu from the bartender. He nodded at Caroline. "Were you able to get your work done on that computer? I think the library needs to upgrade."

"I—I was just—" she zeroed in on the menu "—looking up restaurants."

His green eyes flickered. "And you found this one."

He must've heard Bud say her name. She twisted the napkin in her lap. "Oh, I've been here before. I was checking out a few other places."

"Are you new to Timberline?"

"Sort of. My mother's cousin lives here and invited me out." She said a silent prayer for Linda Gunderson.

"Working at Evergreen Software like everyone else?"

Bud delivered her root beer with a wink, and she plunged her straw into the foam while he took the man's order, giving her time to think.

If she refused to answer his questions, it might seem suspicious, but she didn't want to tell him her life story— especially since she didn't have one, outside of waking up with a dead Johnny Diamond on a hotel room floor.

And she didn't want anyone to know *that* story.

He handed the menu to Bud and turned his rather sharp green eyes back to her. "Evergreen?"

"No. I'm working at my cousin's shop right now." She toyed with her straw. Two could play at this game. "I guess you're not a local, either, since you mentioned the internet connection in your hotel going down."

"That's right." He thanked Bud for his beer and took a sip through the foamy head. "I'm here doing some research for a book."

She released the breath she'd been holding in one slow exhale from parted lips. "What kind of book?"

"Sort of a travel book that also touches on the history of the area and local legends and customs." He held out his hand. "I'm Cole Pierson, by the way."

"Caroline Johnson." She wiped her fingers on her cocktail napkin and squeezed and released his hand quickly.

If Johnny Diamond was from this area, the book might explain why Cole was snooping around his social media. Maybe she could even get some info out of Cole about Diamond without arousing his suspicion.

The bartender delivered her food, and she hesitated.

Cole said, "Go ahead. You don't need to wait for me."

As she sawed her burger in half, Cole watched her with his head to one side. "Who's your cousin?"

Biting her lip, she placed her knife across the edge of her plate. Did his research make him naturally nosy, or did he sense her secrets?

"Linda Gunderson. She owns—"

"Timberline Treasures." His cell phone buzzed in his front shirt pocket, but he ignored it. "I heard about the store that Linda and her sister own. Maybe you can put in a good word for me so I can interview them."

"Louise is out of town, but I'm sure Linda would be happy to talk to you about Timberline's history, and you won't need an introduction from me."

"Is that a no?"

Bud placed a plate overflowing with mashed potatoes and several slices of meat loaf in front of Cole, and Cole whistled. "Looks good."

Caroline took a big bite of her burger. Did he expect her to respond? He really didn't need an introduction to Linda, since she loved talking about Timberline. Was he trying to extend their contact with each other?

Not that she minded, since he was a sweet piece of eye candy, but she had other priorities here.

He wiped his mouth with a napkin. "So how about it? You'll tell your cousin she can trust me?"

Caroline's heart skipped a beat. Trust him? How had they jumped from exchanging a few words over dinner to trust?

"Trust you?" She gave a nervous giggle. "I barely know you. Like I said, you don't need an introduction from me. Linda will talk to you about Timberline."

He took another sip of beer and then picked up his knife and fork, holding them poised above his plate. "Do you know anything about Timberline? Did you visit your aunt much?"

"Cousin, and no. This is my first time out here."

He raised his brows as he cut into his meat loaf. "What brings you out here now?"

"Fresh start." She shrugged.

His glance shifted to her right cheek and the bruise she'd been masking with makeup. Or had she imagined that glance?

The man made her nervous. He asked too many questions. Everyone else had accepted her story without blinking an eye.

Time to deflect and go on the offensive.

"Is that what you were doing in the library? Research?"

"Looking into some local stories, local personalities."

She pushed away her half-eaten burger. Was Johnny Diamond a Timberline local? Maybe they'd been headed here together? If so, nobody seemed to recognize her yet.

"Why this town? What's so special about Timberline?"

She needed an answer to that question herself. Why was the name of this town scribbled on a piece of paper and stuffed in her jacket pocket?

Cole cocked his head. "The Timberline Trio case for starters, and all the recent fall-out from that old case."

She nodded. She'd heard the Timberline Trio case mentioned a few times since she'd arrived, but didn't know much about it—something about some kidnappings that happened twenty-five years ago.

"You really haven't been around much, have you?"

"Well, I guess I won't be a good person for you to interview, then." She grabbed her check from the bar and plucked a ten and a five from her wallet. "Good luck with your research."

She slapped the check and the cash on the bar and spun around on the stool and hopped off. She couldn't get out of here fast enough.

"Nice meeting you, Caroline Johnson." His voice trailed behind her, but she didn't turn around.

Just because a stranger asked questions didn't mean you had to answer them—no matter how attractive the stranger was.

When she hit the sidewalk, she blew out a breath, which turned frosty in the night air.

Linda's duplex sat at the end of the main street in town, so Caroline was able to walk everywhere—at least to work and back. She had enough money from Johnny Diamond's loot to pay cash for a used car, but she didn't have a driver's license or any other ID. Walking would have to do for now.

She reached into her jacket pocket for her hat and tripped to a stop on the sidewalk. It must've fallen out. She scanned the ground around her, and then kicked at the curb with the toe of her boot.

She'd left it, along with her umbrella, on the bar, and

the last thing she wanted to do was go back in there and have another exchange with the nosy, if hunky, writer.

She could leave them at Sutter's and pick them up tomorrow. Nobody would steal a hat or umbrella. Bud had probably already put her things behind the bar.

Hugging her jacket around her body, she took a step, and a drop of rain pelted her cheek. She looked up at the dark sky and shivered. A ten-minute walk in the cold rain without a hat or umbrella would turn to misery after about one minute.

She had every right to march back into Sutter's and grab her hat and umbrella. She peeked through the window at Cole chatting with Bud. He was probably giving him the third degree, too.

She could always swing through the back entrance and maybe get one of the waitresses to get them for her. She took off at a swift pace and slipped into the alley between two businesses a few doors down from Sutter's.

Trailing her hand along one wall, she strode to the back of the buildings and turned right.

A low light illuminated the red awning above Sutter's back door. She tugged at the handle and stepped into the warmth. Moving toward the buzz of the restaurant, she had a clear view of the bar, and it looked like Cole had left.

The door to the men's room swung open, almost hitting her, and she jumped back.

"Nothing yet."

The low timbre of Cole's voice stunned her, and she flattened herself against the wall and ducked behind a cigarette machine.

The bathroom door slammed shut, but Cole stayed put in the hallway and continued his conversation, his back toward her.

"I met a woman tonight who sort of fit the profile—slim, new to town, had a dark cap, too."

He paused, while Caroline's heart thumped in her chest so loudly she couldn't believe he didn't hear it.

"Naw, she's related to someone here in town and isn't Diamond's type—too pretty, too normal."

Caroline closed her eyes and ground her teeth as her stomach lurched. If she got sick here and now, it would be all over, and Cole would know she wasn't normal—not at all.

"I'll keep looking around—and not a word to the boss, Craig."

He ended the call and went back to the bar.

Caroline crept to the back door and stumbled outside.

She might not be who she claimed to be…but neither was Cole Pierson.

Chapter Four

Cole pocketed his phone and perched on the edge of the bar stool. "How much do I owe you, Bud?"

"Do you want another beer?"

"I'm good. Just the check." Cole fingered the soft, black stocking cap on the bar beside him. Caroline had left in such a hurry she'd forgotten her hat and umbrella.

Her attitude had set off alarm bells in his head. She'd been skittish, nervous. Hadn't liked his questions. Didn't seem to know much about the town where she had relatives. Why would a young, attractive woman come to a small town like Timberline to relocate when she'd never been here before?

She didn't seem too concerned about his possible interview with Linda Gunderson. He'd make sure to follow through on that.

When Bud dropped the check, he pointed to the cap. "Caroline leave her hat?"

"Her umbrella, too." Cole ducked beneath the bar and hooked a finger around the umbrella's wrist strap.

"I can put it back here for her."

"You know what?" Cole balled the hat in his fist and shoved it into the pocket of his down jacket. "I'm stopping by her cousin's shop tomorrow, anyway. I'll return them to her."

"It's on you, then." Bud swept up the check and cash. "Change?"

"Keep it." Cole shoved his money clip into his front pocket. "What do you know about Caroline?"

Bud winked. "Pretty gal, huh?"

Bud had just given Cole the angle to play. "Does she have a husband or boyfriend lurking around?"

"She's single. Came here to stay with Linda Gunderson, her cousin, but then you know that, since you're going to Timberline Treasures to return Caroline's stuff."

"You've never seen her out here before?"

"Nope, but I don't know Linda that well. She rarely comes in to Sutter's and never sits at the bar, although she's no stranger to a little vino now and then." Bud hunched forward. "I heard Caroline was running from some trouble."

"Oh yeah?" Cole's pulse ticked up along with his interest. "What kind of trouble."

"Man trouble." Bud tapped his temple. "Came to town sporting a shiner. The word is she's running from a bad relationship, so you might want to think twice before heading down that road with her. Jealous boyfriends and husbands just might get you killed."

"You got that right." Cole rapped on the bar. "Thanks for the tip."

When he stepped outside, Cole zipped up his jacket against the cold. Was Caroline's jealous boyfriend Johnny Diamond? And had she taken care of the problem herself?

THE NEXT MORNING after breakfast at his hotel, Cole drove his rental into town. The internet connection had been back up, and he'd done a search of Caroline Johnson—perfect name to reveal nothing and everything. He'd run her name through the DEA database, too, but nothing clicked.

He pulled his car into one of the two public lots on Main

Street. The small town of Timberline had done a good job preparing for the increased population and traffic from Evergreen Software, the company that had revitalized this former mining and lumber town.

He tucked Caroline's hat and umbrella under one arm as he made his way to Timberline Treasures. Taking a deep breath, he flung open the door and a little bell jingled his arrival.

He didn't know if Caroline would be working today or not. If not, he could always grill Linda Gunderson about her cousin. But he hoped Caroline would be here…because he wanted to see her again.

An older woman looked up from behind the counter. "Good morning. Let me know if you need any help."

"I do need some help, but I don't need a Timberline frog."

"Oh? What do you need?"

Caroline stepped out from the back of the shop. "Information."

"I'm glad I found you here." Cole held up the cap and umbrella. "You left these at Sutter's last night."

Caroline's eyes widened. "And—and you took them?"

"I knew I'd be dropping by Timberline Treasures today to talk to Ms. Gunderson, so I told Bud I'd bring them to you."

"Thanks." She didn't make a move toward the counter, so he weaved his way through the bins and shelves on the store's floor and placed them on top of the glass counter. Then he thrust out his hand toward Linda. "Ms. Gunderson? I'm Cole Pierson. I'm writing a book about Timberline."

Linda's pale skin flushed as she shook his hand. "Oh dear, not a book on the Timberline Trio case, I hope."

"Not at all. This is a travel book that includes some of

the town's lore. The Timberline Trio will probably make a brief appearance, but the crime is not the focus."

"Good, because we had some problems when a TV show came here to film. Nothing but trouble." She pursed her lips.

"I met your cousin Caroline last night at Sutter's and she said you might be willing to talk to me about the old Timberline."

"I think I can do that." She fluffed her permed gray hair. "Is this going to be on camera?"

He held up his cell. "Just recorded on my phone, if that's okay."

"That's fine. I'd be happy to talk with you. Are you also interviewing some of the real old-timers and the Quileute out on the reservation?"

Cole smiled over gritted teeth and nodded. This pretense could turn into a full-time job. "On my list."

The door tinkled behind him, and he glanced over his shoulder at an elderly couple struggling to push a stroller through the door. Cole maneuvered through the shop's displays to grab the door for them and hold it open.

The woman said, "Thank you so much. Our daughter has us bring so many items for the baby it's like pushing a truck instead of a stroller."

Cole hunched forward and chucked the baby beneath his chubby chin. "Is this your grandson?"

"Our first." Grandpa beamed.

The baby grabbed Cole's finger and gurgled. "You're a strong little guy, aren't you? Little bruiser."

He straightened up and met Caroline's wide eyes. Her eyebrows were raised and her mouth was slightly open. Heat rushed to his cheeks and he cleared his throat. "Cute kid."

"You're back." Linda bustled toward the couple and cooed over the baby.

As she chattered with the grandparents, Cole returned to the counter. "I was hoping to chat with Linda in the store today, but if she's too busy maybe I can buy her lunch."

"We're not going to be that busy today—not with the rain gusting through." Caroline tapped her fingers on the glass top. "Do you have kids?"

"Me? No. That?" He jerked his thumb toward the baby Linda now had in her arms. "Just making the grandparents feel good."

Actually, that had been one of many disappointments from his failed marriage. The fact that he and Wendy didn't have children. Although, given how the marriage ended—badly—that was probably a good thing.

"Do you?"

"Do I what?" Her blue eyes narrowed in her usual suspicious manner.

"Have kids?"

"Oh, no."

"Did your husband come out here with you for that fresh start?"

"I'm not…married." Her brows collided over her nose.

"Sorry." He held up his hands. "You started it…the personal questions."

"Then I apologize. You just seemed like a natural with that baby."

The couple at the door called out, "Goodbye. Have a nice day."

Cole waved.

"Friends of yours?" he asked as Linda returned to the register.

"Their daughter and son-in-law moved to Timberline when she took a job with Evergreen. They're retired and have been coming for visits since little Aaron was born."

Linda rubbed her hands together. "Now, where were we? Do you have questions about Timberline?"

"Is it okay if we do this now? I don't want to interrupt business for you."

She flicked her fingers in the air. "We won't be busy, and now I have Caroline to watch the store for me."

"Can I buy you coffee across the street at Uncommon Grounds?"

"I told him he could talk to you in the back, Linda."

Linda knitted her brows and her gaze darted between the two of them. "Are you worried about being in the store by yourself, Caroline? You've done it before. I think you can handle it."

Did Caroline have a problem with him talking to Linda alone? Cole pasted a smile on his face. "It's up to you. Thought I'd buy you a coffee for your trouble."

"It does sound nice and I haven't had mine yet this morning." She patted Caroline's arm. "We'll just be across the street. If something comes up, give me a holler."

"Of course, of course." Caroline's shoulders dropped. "I know how much you enjoy talking about Timberline's history."

Some weird undercurrent passed between the two women, like a force field excluding him, and a muscle ticked in his jaw as his senses picked up on it.

Linda gave Caroline's arm another pat and then smacked the counter with the flat of her hand, which broke the tension. "It's settled. Coffee it is."

"Enjoy yourselves." Caroline brushed her light brown hair from her face. "I'll hold down the fort."

Cole stopped at the door. "Do you want us to bring you back anything?"

"No, thanks. I'm good."

The door shut behind them and Caroline waited for the bells to fade before covering her face with her hands.

She'd be a lot better once Cole Pierson, or whatever his name was, left Timberline. That pat on the arm from Linda reassured her that her so-called cousin wouldn't be spilling the beans about her to Cole.

Maybe this interview was just what she needed to get Cole off her back. If he couldn't shake Linda's story that she was a cousin from back East who was escaping a bad relationship, maybe he'd move on.

And she could get back to the business of finding out who she was and what she was doing with a lowlife like Johnny Diamond.

She had discovered that the body in the trunk of the car outside the motel room was Hazel McTavish, and most likely Diamond had murdered Hazel when he stole her car at the airport in Seattle. So how far-fetched was it to assume that Caroline was also one of Diamond's victims?

Except she'd had a packed bag with her in the motel room. If he'd carjacked Hazel at the airport, maybe she'd been at the airport, too.

She rubbed the back of her head, where a hard knot had formed in place of the bump. She needed to regain her memory. How did people do that without going to a hospital and getting involved with law enforcement and psychiatrists?

The door to the shop swung open, and Caroline jumped. Her grip on the edge of the counter tightened as she watched a single man stroll through the door, shaking out his umbrella.

She had an idea of what one of Johnny Diamond's cronies might look like, and it wasn't this guy, with his crisp khakis and belted raincoat. But that's what she'd thought about Cole Pierson, too, and he obviously had some involvement with Diamond if he was looking for her.

She forced a smile to her face. "Can I help you find

something? All the wood carvings in the front are 50 percent off."

The man tilted his head, a puzzled look in his eyes. "I'm just looking around. It's been a long time since I've been to Timberline."

Either she was paranoid or she was giving off a weird vibe, because this guy was checking her out. Probably a little of both. She coughed. "Feel free to browse."

She dusted behind the counter while keeping an eye on the shopper. He picked up and discarded many items after studying them intently.

He finally picked up one of the stuffed frogs and shook it.

"That's unique to Timberline. A local artist makes those."

"I think I used to have one of these frogs." He tossed it in the air and caught it by one leg. "I'll take it."

"Do you have children?"

"A daughter." He brought the frog to the counter.

"I'm sure she'll like it." Caroline's blood thrummed in her veins as she rang up the man's purchase under his scrutiny. He was studying her like he'd been studying the trinkets in the shop. Maybe he was just an intense guy.

"Is she with you? Your daughter?"

"No, I'm on a...business trip."

She counted his change into the palm of his hand and shoved the plastic bag toward him. "Hope she likes it."

He walked toward the door slowly and then stopped with his hand on the knob. "Are you a local?"

Did she just have one of those faces that invited questions, or was this a small-town thing?

"No. I'm staying with my cousin, who owns this shop."

His shoulders drooped. "Ahh, well, thank you."

"Enjoy your stay."

When the door closed, she collapsed against the counter. Would she suspect every person who walked in here of having ulterior motives? Of course, as the saying went, sometimes they really *were* out to get you.

She'd been right to suspect Cole. He'd lied to her about being a writer. He was searching for Johnny Diamond's companion. He was searching for her.

Crossing her arms, she strolled to the front door and leaned her forehead against the cool glass. She couldn't see into Uncommon Grounds, the coffee shop where Cole had taken Linda to grill her. Caroline had to trust that Linda would keep her secrets—even the ones she didn't know about. If Linda told Cole that she didn't have a second cousin named Caroline and had never laid eyes on her before she'd discovered her crying in the alley behind her store, he'd have every reason to believe she was the mystery woman with Diamond. And she had to be a mystery to Cole or he would've recognized her.

But who was *he*? If he was Diamond's associate, he might be wondering about some missing drug money. Did the police mention how much money was found in the hotel room? Surely not. How would Diamond's cohorts know whether or not she'd stolen any money?

They might want to find her for other reasons. Revenge? Information? Could Cole be a cop?

The door to the Uncommon Grounds opened, and Caroline jerked back as Linda appeared on the sidewalk with Cole behind her. They were both laughing. That didn't mean anything, though. Cole Pierson was a charmer. He had the good looks to beguile a woman of any age.

Hadn't he cast a spell on her? Caroline should've taken her burger to go last night and gotten the heck out of Sutter's. If she had, she wouldn't have overheard his conversation. Better to know your enemies and keep them close.

She could keep Cole close—no problem.

His question about children had troubled her. She'd

never considered that she might have a husband and children somewhere. Didn't she owe it to them to turn herself in to the police? If she were missing, they'd be looking for her. Even if she didn't come from this area, she might be able to find out if they were.

Maybe she should start looking at missing persons reports from other states.

As Linda and Cole approached the shop, Caroline backed away from the door and grabbed her duster.

They were still laughing when they entered on a wet gust of wind that sent the bells into a frenzy.

"Looks cold out there."

"It's freezing." Linda held out a coffee cup. "Which is why we got you a latte."

"Thanks, Linda." Caroline took the cup from her.

"Thank Cole. It was his idea."

"Thanks, Cole." She raised the cup in his direction. "Did you get what you wanted?"

"I think so. Enough to settle a few questions and raise a few more, which is always a good start to, ah...research."

She took a sip of coffee, eyeing him over the rim of her cup. The man drove her crazy. Was he toying with her?

The pressure of Linda's hand against the small of her back nudged her toward the counter. "I gave Cole a long, boring history of this shop and a more interesting account of the local artists, including Scarlett Easton, who's quite famous for her modern art, although I prefer her landscapes."

Caroline released a few short breaths. Linda had kept mum about her sudden appearance in Timberline.

"I sold a Libby Love frog while you were out living it up at Uncommon Grounds."

"Wonderful. I was wondering if we'd do any business today with the rain coming down."

Caroline jerked her thumb over her shoulder. "Might be a good day to continue with that inventory."

"I am taking the hint." Cole grabbed a frog. "And to show my appreciation for your time, I'll buy a frog, too."

"I thought you didn't have children."

"I don't have any, but that doesn't mean there's not a kid or two in my life."

Linda rang him up and tucked the frog into a plastic bag. "Let me know if you need anything else, Cole, and do go talk to Evelyn Foster out on the reservation. She can tell you about all the Quileute legends and myths."

"I'll do that." He held up his hand. "Stay dry."

Linda went to the window and watched him walk away. "Nice man. Good-looking, isn't he?"

"Cut to the chase, Linda. Did he ask about me?"

"Nothing to worry about, Caroline. He didn't ask anything a man attracted to a woman wouldn't ask."

Her nostrils flared. "Attracted? What does that mean?"

"Don't worry. I told him a little about your past." She held her thumb and index finger about an inch apart. "Just so he knows you're not ready to jump into anything right now."

"What did you tell him?" Caroline pressed two fingers to her temple. "Y-you didn't reveal that I really wasn't your cousin and had just arrived in town, did you? I'm not sure I trust him. M-my ex could've sent him. He could be looking for me right now."

Linda cinched both her wrists with a surprisingly strong grip. "I promised to keep your secrets, Caroline, and I'm not going back on that just for a pair of twinkling green eyes and a set of broad shoulders."

"What exactly did you tell him?"

"I stuck to the story. My cousin's daughter contacted me a few weeks ago, was in a bad relationship, wanted a fresh start and asked to visit for a while—and you are that cousin." She cocked her head. "Besides, if your ex really did send Cole looking for you, wouldn't he already know what you looked like? You have nothing to fear from Cole—except his devastating charm."

Biting her lip, Caroline folded her hands around her coffee cup. Had his conversation with Linda convinced Cole that Caroline Johnson was not the woman he was looking for, despite the black beanie?

If not, she had a lot more than Cole's devastating charm to fear.

SINCE LINDA HAD a bridge game with friends that evening that entailed her to concoct some complicated dessert to outdo the other ladies, Caroline had convinced her to leave early and let her close up.

Only a handful of customers had come into the store, and no more suspicious characters. Cole Pierson was the only suspicious character she'd actually met. She doubted more were on the way. She could either leave Timberline and abandon any hope of ever discovering why she'd been headed here originally, or stick it out and convince Cole she really was Linda Gunderson's cousin, who had no connection to Johnny Diamond, his drugs or his money.

She traced the edge of the piece of paper in her pocket on which she'd written the name and number of a therapist in Port Angeles. She'd asked Linda for a recommendation with the excuse that she wanted to work through her issues associated with the domestic violence. Linda was more than happy to oblige.

A therapist would have that confidentiality thing. The therapist probably couldn't keep a confession of murder confidential, but Caroline didn't believe she'd murdered Johnny Diamond. Maybe she'd killed him in self-defense, but she had no intention of admitting that to... She took the slip of paper out of her pocket and read aloud, "Dr. Jules Shipman."

Caroline locked the front door and flipped Open to Closed. Then she dipped her hand in her other pocket and called Dr. Shipman on the prepaid phone she'd purchased a few days ago.

She left a message after the beep, giving as little information as possible. Time enough to get into all the gory details of her life once she was lying on Dr. Shipman's couch.

She transferred the money from the register to the safe and dropped the accounting slip on top of the bills. She flicked off the lights and reached for her beanie and umbrella.

She smoothed her fingers across the soft material of the knit cap. She'd been foolish to keep this hat. How had Cole known the woman with Diamond had a hat like this? Had Johnny told him? Had someone seen her at the Stardust?

She pulled it on her head and shoved out the back door. She could stop playing this cat-and-mouse game and ask him. As she yanked the door shut, she shivered.

What then? Would he kill her? Interrogate her? Arrest her? She didn't know which of those options would be the worst.

As she marched along the alleyway running behind the Main Street shops, a noise caught her attention. She glanced over her shoulder at a man unfurling an umbrella.

He looked up and she could make out the pale oval of his face, but not much more. As he turned, the wind caught the edge of his trench coat and Caroline gasped.

Was he the man from the store who'd bought the Libby Love frog? Had he been watching her? Waiting for her?

She splashed through a puddle as she turned the corner and made a beeline for the more populated Main Street. Nobody was walking on the rain-soaked sidewalks, but people were going in and out of the restaurants and hopping into their cars.

She headed for the lights and warmth of Sutter's. She'd pick up some dinner to take back to her duplex, and mull over what she planned to say to Dr. Shipman.

She ducked into Sutter's and pointed to the bar as the hostess approached her. "I'm getting it to go."

She walked up to the bar and her stomach sank as a tall, good-looking man flashed a grin at her.

"We gotta stop meeting like this."

She tipped her chin at his almost empty plate. "Meat loaf again?"

"What can I say?" He spread his hands. "I'm a sucker for a home-cooked meal, even when it's not at home."

She waved down Bud. "Can I get a grilled chicken sandwich to go, with a side of sweet potato fries?"

"Coming right up." He jerked his thumb at Cole. "Did this guy give you your hat and umbrella?"

"He did."

"I was going to hold them behind the bar for you, but he said he'd be seeing you today."

"Did you think I was trying to steal them?" Cole crumpled his napkin and dropped it in his plate. "I don't think the hat would've fit."

"Just keeping you honest, man." Bud winked at Caroline and she gave him a weak smile.

Everyone seemed to think Cole Pierson was the greatest guy ever. What would they think if they knew what she knew? That he was a lying SOB and possible drug dealer...or undercover cop.

A burst of rain pelted the window next to the bar and Cole whistled. "I think it's going to get worse before it gets better."

"It's bad out there." She dug for some cash in her purse,

so she could pay and be on her way as soon as Bud came up with her order.

"Linda told me you didn't have a car here yet and you walk all over town."

"It's not bad."

"Except on a night like this. Can I give you a lift to your place? Even though it's not far, you'll get drenched walking that half mile."

Her jaw tightened. "Linda told you where I live?"

"She mentioned it was lucky the other side of the duplex she and her sister own was empty when you came to town." He leaned in close, his lips brushing the wet strands of her hair. "I'm not trying to move in on you or anything. I know you've had a rough time of it."

She blinked against the tears pricking her eyes. Was he referring to the brawl she'd apparently had with Johnny Diamond in the hotel room, or her manufactured past with the abusive ex? Cole's soothing tone almost made her want to confess everything to him. Almost.

She squared her shoulders. "Linda gossips too much. I dumped a jerk—nothing I can't handle."

"Thatta girl." A wide grin claimed his face. "Don't let the bastards bring you down."

"Here's your change, Cole." Bud swept up Cole's plate. "Your food will be up in a minute, Caroline."

Cole pocketed his cash. "So, how about it? I'm parked right out front."

She wanted to tell him to take a hike, keep his questions to himself and mind his own business. But that would make him even more suspicious, and maybe Linda had convinced him that she was really her cousin in need of a fresh start.

"I'd love a ride, thanks. If it's not too inconvenient."

"No problem at all."

Bud returned with a bag hanging from his fingers, and

then twisted his head around to look at the TV mounted above the bar. He called to the other bartender. "Denny, turn up the volume. It's a story on the Johnny Diamond murder."

A chill raced down Caroline's spine, but she kept motionless.

Cole tipped his head back to take in the TV monitor. "I heard about that—found the guy with drugs and a car with a dead body in the trunk."

Her dinner still dangled from Bud's fingertips and she wanted to scream at him.

Cole asked, "Was he a local boy?"

"Diamond? No, but he ran with a local motorcycle gang, the Lords of Chaos."

The sounds around Caroline receded and she felt like she was spinning through a vacuum. Larry. LC, the tattoo on Johnny Diamond's neck, stood for Lords of Chaos. Timberline had been Johnny Diamond's destination, not hers. Or maybe it had been hers, too. Nobody seemed to recognize her here, nobody except Cole Pierson, and for him her identity was all speculation.

"Do you think he was on his way here when he was killed?"

Bud hunched his shoulders. "I don't know. I hope not. Timberline has had enough trouble with the Lords."

The story ended. Denny turned down the sound and Caroline could breathe again—almost. "My food?"

"Sorry." He placed the bag on the counter. "Napkins and utensils inside."

She handed him a twenty. "Thanks, keep it."

Cole rose from his stool before she did. "Ready?"

"Uh-huh." She looked at Bud's curious expression and said, "Cole's giving me a ride home in the rain."

"Good idea. Have a good night."

Caroline turned, hugging the bag to her chest. So now

if Cole murdered her and dumped her body in the woods, someone would connect him to her disappearance—and she was only half kidding.

She preceded Cole through the restaurant in thoughtful silence. Was the revelation of Johnny Diamond's connection to a motorcycle gang news to Cole or was he a member, too? She could always check his body for tattoos—and she was only half kidding about that, too.

As he opened the door for her, she slid a glance at his hand and the wrist revealed when his sleeve rode up. No tattoos there and she hadn't noticed any on his neck.

He opened his umbrella. "Here, get under. I'm just one door down."

A small sedan flashed its lights and beeped once, and Cole held the umbrella over her head while she climbed into the car. When he slammed the door, she did a quick survey of the console and the backseat.

No weapons and no dead bodies. Things were looking up.

He opened the driver's side door and collapsed his umbrella. As he slid onto the seat, he tossed the soggy umbrella in the rear. "Whew. This is a deluge. Even with your umbrella, you would've been soaked to the bone."

"Yeah, thanks."

He started the car and then turned to look at her, studying her profile. "Glad to do it."

"Straight ahead." She pinned her hands between her bouncing knees.

"All the way at the end where the businesses stop?"

"Yes."

The car crawled through the flooded streets, and Cole hunched forward. "You'd think a town in Washington would do a better job of drainage."

"Timberline's old."

"The influx of money from Evergreen Software should start going toward the town's infrastructure."

"Linda says it's helped a lot." Caroline tapped on the window. "Up ahead on the right where the two yellow lights are."

Cole pulled into the driveway she didn't use. "I'll get the door for you."

He pulled his umbrella from the backseat and unfurled it before getting out of the car. Two seconds later, he was opening her door, holding the umbrella over her head at great expense to his own well-being.

As she groped for the keys in her purse, he stayed right by her side, keeping her dry. When she made it to the covered porch, she pulled him up next to her. "You're drenched."

"You're not."

She released his sleeve. Was this his strategy? Cozy up to her so she'd spill her guts?

"Well, now it's all yours." She inserted her key into the lock and turned. "Thanks again and good luck with your book."

"Good luck to you, too, Caroline Johnson."

His voice trailed to a whisper as he melted back into the rain.

She blew out a breath and pushed open her door. That sounded like a goodbye. Linda must've been convincing.

She stepped into the small living room and the hair on the back of her neck quivered. Her gaze darted from the bookshelves to the pillows on the couch to the magazines stacked on the coffee table.

Someone had been in her house. A primal fear seized her and she turned and fled back into the driving rain.

Chapter Five

Cole dumped his umbrella in the backseat and slicked back his wet hair. He'd have to look elsewhere for Johnny Diamond's killer. One of the Realtors in town had mentioned a new single female renter at one of the cabins.

He took one last look at Caroline's door. He was relieved she wasn't connected to Diamond, but disappointed that he didn't need to spend any more time with her.

She sure as hell didn't want to spend any more time with him. After her experience with her husband, she must hate all men. He could understand that, but hell, he didn't hate all women after his own experience. But then his wife had just cheated on him, not given him a shiner.

A yellow oblong appeared on the porch and it took him a minute to realize that Caroline had opened the door. Had she changed her mind about him and wanted to invite him in for a drink? A guy could hope for the best.

As he squinted into the darkness, she flew off the porch and disappeared. Had she fallen?

He opened his door and peered through the sheets of rain at Caroline scrambling in the mud on the side of the short walkway to the porch, which she'd obviously missed.

"Caroline?" He slammed the car door and jogged toward her, leaving the umbrella behind in the car.

She looked up at him, her face pale, her eyes huge.

"What happened? What's wrong?" He crouched beside her and hooked his hands beneath her arms, pulling her up.

She stuttered through chattering teeth. "Someone... s-someone was in my h-house."

A shot of adrenaline coursed through Cole's body. "Someone's there now?"

"I—I don't know."

He pulled her onto the porch. "Stay here."

His hand hovering over the gun in his jacket pocket, he crept into the house. He blinked. It didn't look like there was a thing out of place. He'd expected chaos.

He moved silently across the wood floor, leaving a trail of puddles in his wake. He poked his head into the kitchen in case someone was crouched behind the counter that separated kitchen from living room. He couldn't detect any disturbance in this room, either.

He edged down the hallway and checked both bedrooms, including beneath the beds and in the closets, and even swept aside the shower curtain.

What had given Caroline the idea that someone had broken into her place? All the doors and windows were intact.

He zipped his pocket over his gun and returned to the porch, where Caroline was hugging the wall. "It's okay. There's nobody here."

He put his arm across her shoulders and felt the vibrations from her trembling body. He nudged her into the house and shut the door behind them.

"Can I get you something? Hot tea? A shot of whiskey? Both? You're wet and muddy."

She stared at him with wide eyes, her arms folded across her stomach. Her voice came out as a harsh whisper. "Was it you?"

Her soft words punched him in the gut. "Me? What?"

"Did you break in here to search through my things? To

frighten me? To…to—" she waved her arm up and down his body "—to do this?"

"I don't understand." He stepped back. "Do you think I'm working for your husband or something?"

"I don't know."

"I'm not. I'm…not." He couldn't tell her about his mission here. He was doing this investigation on his own dime, anyway. He just wanted to reassure her. He wanted to snap his fingers and dissolve the fear that rimmed her eyes.

"I swear I don't know your husband, but from what Linda told me he sounds like a jerk. Look…" Cole ran a hand through his damp hair. "My stepdad used to knock my mom around. I'd never help out anyone who hurt women or children. Never."

Caroline's mouth softened and her lashes fluttered. "I'm sorry."

"You don't have to be. Just know I'm not on your husband's side. I don't even know your husband and wouldn't want to, except to plant one on his face."

She pulled her shoulders back. "Okay. It wasn't you."

"Of course not." Cranking his head from one side to the other, Cole asked, "How'd you know someone had been in here? Looks neat to me."

"I'm very particular. I can tell."

"Maybe Linda came over. She lives in the duplex next door, right? Maybe she had to get something or was going to leave something for you?"

Caroline shook her head and the droplets from her hair rained down on the floor. "Linda wouldn't do that. Someone was in here."

"And you think it was your ex or someone he sent?"

Her gaze dropped to her fingers, twisting in front of her. "Maybe. I suppose it could be a thief."

"A very neat thief."

"A thief who didn't want to be discovered."

"But one totally unaware of your super detection abilities." Cole smiled like an idiot, wanting to touch her, but afraid he'd send her over the edge. "You need to get out of those wet clothes. And the mud. You should see the mud."

"I dropped my dinner just inside the front door. I'm going to take a hot shower and curl up with my sweet potato fries."

"Do you want to call the police?"

"No!" A red tide washed over her cheeks beneath the mud smears. "I have no proof anyone was here. The sheriff's department would put me down as a lunatic."

"Are you sure you're going to be okay here by yourself?"

"I'll be fine. Linda should be home soon. I'll ask her if she was here. Maybe you're right."

"I can stay while you shower. I mean, wait in here."

"Really, I'm okay. I've been on edge." She breezed past him and picked up the bag of food on the floor, and then opened the front door. "Thanks for coming back and helping me. I feel like a fool."

"I wasn't going to leave you flailing around in the mud."

She rolled her eyes. "That bad, huh?"

"You were scared and had a fall." He put his finger to his lips. "I won't tell a soul."

"Good night, Cole."

"Good night, Caroline." He left the house and waited on the porch as he listened for the click of the dead bolt.

Jamming his hands in his pockets, he put his head down and walked briskly to his car, keeping to the paved walkway.

He started the engine and cranked on the heat and defroster full blast. Blowing on his hands and rubbing them together, he eyed Caroline's duplex over the steering wheel.

Had he miscalculated? Would her ex really travel across the country to stalk her, or more unbelievably, send someone else to do it? How had she been so sure someone had broken in? Was it paranoia or was she really expecting trouble? And from what quarter? An abusive ex-husband, or from someone equally as dangerous? A drug trafficker looking for his money?

Cole felt a stab of guilt that he'd circled back to his original suspicions. He'd put those to rest after talking to Linda Gunderson, and what earthly reason would Linda have to lie for a complete stranger? To fabricate a whole life for this stranger?

Money? Timberline Treasures hardly looked like a bustling, profitable enterprise.

He threw the rental into gear and backed out of the driveway. Maybe Caroline had paid Linda to claim her as a cousin. Linda told a mighty convincing story.

As he watched Caroline's porchlight fade into the darkness in his rearview mirror, he set his jaw. There were too many puzzle pieces that didn't fit. Caroline Johnson hadn't quite convinced him that she wasn't the woman with Johnny Diamond.

Which meant…he wasn't done with her yet.

THE FOLLOWING MORNING, Caroline hunched over her coffee cup, trying to wake up. She'd waylaid Linda last night on her way in from her bridge party, but Linda insisted she hadn't let herself into Caroline's duplex.

Could she have imagined it? She shifted her gaze to the magazines stacked on the coffee table and the throw pillows set at a precise angle on the sofa. Ever alert, Caroline had set up the room so that any disruption could be detected—and she'd detected several. The edges of the magazines hadn't been lined up. One of the pillows had been positioned so that the tree on the front was upright, when she'd left it on its side.

If someone had broken in, at least he hadn't discovered her stash of money hidden under a loose floorboard in the bedroom closet. Was that what he'd been after?

She sipped her coffee and smacked the counter. How could she have been so stupid to display her fear in front of Cole?

At first he'd been solicitous, worried, had even revealed a piece of his own history, but she could see the doubt creeping back in his eyes the more she blabbed on about the break-in.

How ridiculous of her to admit that she was primed to recognize an intruder by the slightest hair out of place. And while she was sure there were a few exes who stalked their spouses after they'd moved from one coast to the other, how likely would it be for an abusive lover to sneak into his ex's house for a careful search? He'd be more apt to lie in wait and attack her, not rearrange her magazines.

Cole had to believe she was either crazy or lying, and she had her money on lying. He'd already suspected her of being the woman in the motel room with Diamond, and she'd just handed him further reason to investigate that suspicion.

And who the hell was Cole Pierson, anyway? She'd had no time to do an internet search on him, but she doubted she'd find any more on him than he'd found on her.

Her phone buzzed and she recognized the number as Dr. Shipman's. This could be the solution to all her problems—or just the beginning.

"Hello?"

"Is this Caroline Johnson?"

"It is."

"Hi, Caroline, this is Dr. Shipman returning your call."

"Yes, hello. Thank you." She moved to the sofa and sank against the cushions. "I was wondering if you could take on another patient. I'm interested in starting this week if you can fit me in."

"I am accepting new patients. You're in Timberline?"

"Yes."

"I had a cancellation this afternoon if you can manage to get here by two o'clock?"

She was working only until noon today and Linda had already told her she could borrow her car for appointments. "I can be there by two."

"Do you have medical-insurance coverage?"

"I—I'm paying cash. How much do you charge?"

"Seventy-five an hour, but we can work out a plan if that's too steep."

"I can manage that, thanks. I'll see you at two o'clock."

She collapsed against the tree cushion that had caused her such panic last night. Maybe Dr. Shipman could do hypnosis or something. She had to get her life back—whatever that life was.

Then she could stand tall before Cole and tell him the truth—or run and hide forever.

When she heard Linda's familiar tap at the door, Caroline pushed up from the sofa and stuffed her stocking feet in her ankle boots. She drew back the curtain and waved at Linda on the porch. Then she retrieved her purse from the kitchen counter and answered the door.

"Looks like we have a reprieve from the rain today." Caroline held out her hand, palm up, and caught a drop of water from the rain gutter.

"Would be nice to have a day to dry out." Linda tipped her head to the side. "Are you okay this morning?"

"I'm fine. I think I overreacted. Larry has no way of knowing I'm in Timberline or even Washington." She'd given her abusive ex-husband the first name she could think of.

"Totally understandable. My sister thought every bald guy she saw was her ex." Linda jingled her car keys. "Time to open the shop."

A feather of uneasiness tickled the back of Caroline's neck as she followed Linda to the car. "Speaking of bald guys, the man who bought the stuffed frog yesterday had a shaved head, said he used to live here and was back on business. Ring a bell with you?"

"Haven't heard about any returnees. Why do you ask?"

"I don't know. He seemed..." She shook her head. "I really don't know, Linda. I'm letting my imagination run wild."

As Linda settled into the driver's seat, she said, "You don't have to worry about that nice and very good-looking Cole Pierson. He's definitely here to write that book and his only interest in you is romantic."

Linda had no idea who Cole was...and neither did Caroline, but she doubted he had romance on his mind when he looked at her—especially now that she'd revealed her hand.

"Well, I'm not ready for romance. Even so, I appreciate that you kept our little secret. If he found out I was a stranger to town, others would find out, and I'm still nervous about Larry tracking me down."

Backing out of the driveway, Linda traced the seam of her lips with a finger. "He won't get any more out of me."

Caroline had a feeling all Cole had to do was crook his little finger at Linda and she'd tell him everything.

As they worked side by side in the shop, Caroline told Linda about her appointment with Dr. Shipman that afternoon. "So, is it okay if I borrow your car? I should have it back by five o'clock."

"Of course. I think you're doing the right thing by talking to someone, and Dr. Jules Shipman comes highly recommended."

The phone rang and Linda answered it. While she was talking, the door swung open and Cole strode into the shop.

Caroline swallowed. She had some backtracking to do with him to regain his trust.

"I thought you'd never dry off after that soaking you got last night." She flashed a big smile.

His eyebrows jumped to his hairline. Had she poured it on too thick?

"I took a hot shower and then went down to the hotel bar for a whiskey. Warmed me right up. How about you? Feeling better?"

"Yes." She covered her face with both hands. "I am so sorry I went cray cray on you. I've been so stressed and on edge."

"So you don't think anyone broke into your place and searched it, including me?"

"Did I really accuse you?" She peeked through her fingers. "I'm an idiot. Nobody broke in. If my ex really wanted to contact me, he'd come here himself and confront me. That's more his style, anyway, but he's not going to do that. I never talked to him about my mother's family and he's never heard of Timberline."

"Glad to hear it and glad you're feeling better. I just came by to check on you."

Linda ended her call. "Good morning, Cole."

"As long as that rain stays away for a few more hours, it will be."

"Caroline." Linda turned to her. "I don't think I can loan you my car to go to Port Angeles, after all."

"Oh?" Caroline curled her hands into fists. Why did Linda have to talk about her personal business in front of Cole? Of course, Linda still believed he was a mild-mannered writer and didn't know he was some imposter looking for Johnny Diamond's last companion.

"That was my mechanic, Louie. He finally got a part for my car that's taken over a week to get here, and he wants to do the work this afternoon."

"Port Angeles?" Cole shoved a hand in the pocket of his jeans. "I was planning to go out there this morning."

Of course you were.

Caroline tucked her hair behind one ear. "My appointment isn't until this afternoon, but I appreciate the offer. And don't worry about the car, Linda. I'll reschedule the appointment."

Cole interrupted. "I can wait until this afternoon. I was just going to go to the library, since it's bigger than Timberline's and it has a couple of articles on microfiche that haven't been transferred online yet. It's no problem at all."

"Perfect." Linda clapped her hands together. "I don't want you to cancel your appointment, Caroline. Maybe you two can even stop for some lunch. You can leave before noon."

Linda was playing matchmaker. Cole had done such a number on her.

Caroline didn't want to be in Cole's presence any longer than she had to, especially trapped in a car with him. But if she refused, would that make her look suspicious again?

"I—I don't need lunch. I brought half of my sandwich from last night's dinner."

"We can skip lunch, but I'd be more than happy to drive you to Port Angeles. How long is your appointment?"

"About an hour."

"That works for me…unless you still think I'm the one who broke into your place last night."

"Caroline, did you really think that?" Linda's eyes grew round.

Great, now she seemed like the crazy one, and she'd

seem even crazier if she refused a perfectly good ride from a perfectly respectable man like Cole. What possible excuse did she have?

"That was just me freaking out a little. I'd be happy to hitch a ride as long as I'm not putting you out."

"Then it's settled. I'll swing back around at twelve."

She waved as he left the store and then rounded on Linda. "Are you trying to set us up or something?"

"Was I that obvious?"

"Linda, I meant it. I'm really not interested in any romantic entanglements right now. I—I need to figure out why I put up with Larry's abuse in the first place before I can move on."

With tears in her eyes, Linda patted her back. "I know, dear. It would be nice to see you with a good man, and Cole Pierson is a good man."

A good liar.

Caroline hugged the older woman. "I appreciate your concern. I'm sure Cole has a million women vying for his attention back home—wherever that is. Did he ever tell you where he was from?"

"He lives in San Diego with a dog named Thor, and his sister watches the dog when he's on his travels."

Seemed Cole had concocted a more thorough backstory than she had.

The rest of the morning flew by and twelve o'clock arrived sooner than she wanted. Cole walked in on the dot.

"Are you ready?"

"In a minute. You're sure it's no trouble?"

"I need to get to Port Angeles myself. No trouble at all." He winked at Linda. "How about it, boss lady? Can your minion escape?"

"Of course. You two have fun."

Caroline rolled her eyes at Cole just so he'd know she wasn't hatching this plan with Linda, but maybe it wasn't such a bad idea for him to think she had the hots for him. That would really mess with his mind and distract him from whatever suspicions he already had about her.

"She means well." Cole opened the sedan door for her and shut it before she could respond. He slid onto the driver's seat. "Do you have an address in Port Angeles I can punch into the GPS?"

She plunged her hand into her purse and pulled out the slip of paper with Dr. Shipman's address. She read it off to Cole as he entered it into the car's GPS.

"Linda told me you're from San Diego. How long have you lived there?"

"All my life. Have you ever been there?"

"I…" She had no idea. "Visited once when I was a kid. How long have you been writing travel books?"

"This is my first try."

At least he wasn't going to try to lie his way through this part of his life. The rest was probably all fabricated, too. She'd keep peppering him with questions so he wouldn't have a chance to pin her down.

By the time they reached Port Angeles, she was exhausted from the effort. She'd kept him from needling beneath her exterior, though. He'd enjoyed talking about his big, slobbery dog so much she had to believe that part.

The voice on the GPS began directing them down streets, and he turned on the last one. "I'll just drop you off in front and pick you up in an hour?" He pulled up next to the curb in front of a two-story office building. "Do you want to take my cell number in case you're earlier or later?"

"Write it down." She shoved the piece of paper at him, not wanting him to see her prepaid phone and make any assumptions about it or her.

"Pen." He leaned across her lap to reach the glove compartment, and her hands hovered over his thick, sandy-colored hair. She had the strongest urge to run her fingers through it, but restrained herself.

He scribbled a number on the slip of paper and handed it back to her. "I'll be back in an hour, right here."

"Okay, thanks."

She waited until he drove away before heading toward the therapist's office. Cole hadn't asked her about the appointment and she hadn't volunteered.

Like everything she said to him, she had to consider the effect and consequences. She'd be relieved when he moved on—mostly. She'd miss seeing his familiar face around town. She'd either have to familiarize herself with a few more people in Timberline or get her memory back.

She walked beneath the stairs to Dr. Shipman's first-floor office, took a deep breath and opened the door, poking her head inside the reception area.

A potted plant waved in the corner and two chairs bracketed a small table sporting an open magazine.

Caroline crossed the room and pressed a red button with her thumb, following the instructions on the wall.

Then she turned and perched on the edge of one of the chairs, clasping its arms. What would she discover about herself? It might be better to remain in blissful ignorance.

The door to the inner office opened, and Caroline jumped—her usual reaction to any sudden movement.

A woman stepped into the room with a slight curve to her lips and a soft twinkle in her dark eyes. "Caroline?"

"That's me." She bounded forward, her hand outstretched. "Thanks for seeing me on such short notice, Dr. Shipman."

"Call me Jules, and you did me a big favor by filling in for a cancellation today." She swung the door wide. "Come on in."

Caroline practically tiptoed into the room, with its

muted light and comfortable furniture. She glanced from the chair to the sofa. "Where should I sit?"

"Wherever you like."

She took the sofa just in case she had to stretch out and have a good breakdown.

Jules sat in the armchair across from her. "Would you like some water? Coffee? Tea?"

"No, thank you."

Jules folded her hands in her lap with the same little smile on her face. "You can start. Tell me anything you have on your mind or why you're here today."

"Can I ask you a question first?"

"Of course."

"What I say in here—" Caroline circled her finger in the air "—to you, is confidential, isn't it? You won't tell anyone else. You won't tell the police."

The woman's expression didn't waver. "That's correct, unless you pose a danger to yourself or others."

She slumped against the back of the sofa. "I don't."

Jules settled into her own chair and took a sip of a fragrant tea…and waited.

Caroline rubbed her eyes. "I don't know who I am. I have amnesia."

Jules blinked. "How long have you been in this state?"

"Almost a week."

"Why don't you want to go to the police?"

Caroline sucked in her lower lip. If she told Dr. Shipman the truth, would she believe Caroline had killed Johnny Diamond? If so, that confidentiality thing would go right out the window. She'd have to play this by ear.

Leaning forward, she plucked a tissue from a box on the table next to the sofa. She dragged the tissue across her right cheekbone and pointed to the bruise healing there. "I have reason to believe I'm a victim of domestic violence."

"Do you also have a head injury? Something to explain the memory loss?"

"Yes." Caroline rubbed the bump on the back of her skull. "I'm afraid my spouse or partner will come after me. I—I think I'm on the run."

Jules steepled her fingertips together. "Is that why you asked about hypnosis in your message?"

"I'm hoping, through hypnosis, I can regain my memories."

"You didn't have a purse? ID?"

"Nothing. I've even checked a few missing-persons websites. I just want to recover my identity and then I can figure out where I need to be."

"Why Timberline? Is that where you...woke up?"

"I regained consciousness in a park in Seattle. I had some cash in my jacket pocket and a scrap of paper with Timberline written on it, so I made my way there, thinking I had family or a lifeline there."

"Nothing?"

"I met a very kind stranger and she's been helping me, but I thought it was time to be proactive, since my memory doesn't seem to be returning on its own. I—I thought it might."

"It could, either in bits and pieces or prompted by trauma, but hopefully you won't have to experience any trauma to regain your memory." Dr. Shipman rose from her chair and stepped behind her desk. "Can we try something right now? I just want to see how susceptible you are."

Caroline's heart somersaulted in her chest. "Absolutely."

"I have a form for you to sign." Dr. Shipman pulled open a drawer and then looked up. "Is Caroline Johnson a made-up name?"

"Yes."

"Well, it's the only name you have, so you can sign as Caroline Johnson." She waved a piece of white paper at her.

When Dr. Shipman put the form in her hands, Caroline reviewed it quickly and scratched out the unfamiliar signature at the bottom. No warning listed on that piece of paper could be any worse than her current limbo hell.

"What now?" She settled back on the sofa, folding her hands in her lap.

"I have a pendant I use." Dr. Shipman opened her fist to reveal a silver disc on a chain. "It can be any object, but I like this one. Keep your eye on the disc. Relax, clear your mind, breathe deeply and don't concentrate on anything."

"If I can relax, it'll be a first time since this whole nightmare began."

"Which is perhaps why the memories haven't been forthcoming. When I snap my fingers and tell you to wake up, that will end the session." Dr. Shipman held up the pendant. "Open your mind. Let go. Shrug off the barriers."

Listening to Jules's soothing voice, Caroline focused on the disc shining in the dim room and tried to release every muscle group from head to toe. Her breathing deepened and her lashes fluttered as she fought to maintain a view of the gleaming circle that now represented a kind of lifeline.

The pendant faded. The room faded. Her body floated into the air.

A desert landscape, stark and rugged, invaded her head. People crowded against her, suffocating her, holding her in. She railed against them—her family. She had to get away from her family.

A woman's voice, soft and gentle, asked her questions, and she answered, because the woman wasn't one of her family members. She could talk to her even though she couldn't hear her questions, and couldn't hear her own answers to those questions.

Would the woman help her get away? She had to escape. She had to survive and return home. The desert? It was her home...and wasn't.

The sleepiness descended on her and her tongue felt too thick to form any more words. Would the nice lady leave her? Would she have to fight her way out on her own?

"Caroline."

The strange name floated into her consciousness. She didn't know a Caroline.

"Caroline? Wake up."

The voice sounded comforting, but it was meant for Caroline, not her.

"Caroline. Wake up."

A snapping sound jerked her out of her lethargy and into awareness. *Snap. Wake up.*

She passed a hand across her face and ran her tongue along her teeth. Caroline. *She* was Caroline. Her eyes flew open and she met Dr. Shipman's clear gaze. She floated back to the surface.

"How do you feel?"

"That depends. What happened?" Caroline clasped her hair into a ponytail. "I remember a desert, so different from the Washington landscape, and I'm pretty sure my real name isn't Caroline."

"When I asked where you were, you responded that you were home, but you didn't tell me where that was. You had family there, but you were trying to get away from them."

"Maybe—" Caroline touched her cheek "—this happened at home with my family. Maybe my spouse lives with my family and everyone wanted me to stay with him. I got the sense that I have a big family."

"Does that scenario feel right to you?" Dr. Shipman clenched her fist over her heart. "Here?"

"I knew the group of people in the desert. They had to be family. Maybe that's why they're not looking for me." Could Johnny Diamond have been a family member?

"Do you want to continue next week?"

"Absolutely." She smoothed her hands down the denim covering her thighs. "So, I'm susceptible to hypnosis and you think I can recover my memories?"

"I believe you can. In the meantime, do you feel safe?" Dr. Shipman rose from her chair as she pocketed the pendant. "That blank slate you face every day must be terrifying."

Caroline's mind flitted to the man coming to pick her up. She *did* feel safe with Cole, as long as she kept her identity a secret from him. He exuded a confidence and power that gave her a sense of security. Could you feel secure with someone who put you on edge all the time?

"Caroline? You *are* safe, aren't you?"

She pushed herself out of the comfy sofa. "I am—for now."

After paying Dr. Shipman in cash and setting up her next appointment, Caroline returned to the reception area. The outside door opened and she tripped to a stop.

A dark-skinned man with shaggy brown hair edged into the office, keeping his head down.

Caroline averted her gaze and strode past him and out the door. Everyone deserved their privacy.

She pulled the door shut behind her and peered down the street, looking both ways. She didn't want Cole to see her coming out of a therapist's office, although it would bolster her story. Why would Johnny Diamond's accomplice or murderer want to see a shrink?

In fact, her appointment with Dr. Shipman might be just the thing to get her off Cole's radar again.

Caroline blew out a breath and headed toward the sidewalk just as he pulled up to the curb across the street.

Waving, she strode to the car and yanked open the passenger-side door.

She dropped onto the seat and swung her purse into the back. "How'd your research go?"

He nodded once. "Good. Everything okay with your... appointment?"

"You're very discreet, but I don't have any secrets." She smoothed her hair back from her face. "In case you haven't guessed, I just saw a therapist."

His head jerked up. "Really?"

"Linda thought it was a good idea, and after speaking with Dr. Shipman, I have to agree." Caroline's openness extended only so far. She didn't have to tell him about the hypnosis or what she'd discovered from it.

"That's great." He jerked his thumb over his shoulder as he pulled away. "Dr. Shipman's the therapist? I saw her name on the directory when I dropped you off."

"Yeah. I like her."

"Good. Have you ever been in an abusive relationship before?" He held up one hand. "And you can tell me to mind my own business."

She'd wanted to tell him to mind his own business on several occasions, but this wasn't one of them. "That was my first and my last."

"Good to hear that. My mom didn't stay long with her abuser, either."

Caroline let him talk, sealing her lips, not wanting to get into any details about her relationship with Larry—details she might have to recall later.

Cole hit the steering wheel with the heel of his hand. "Let's celebrate your new resolve."

"Celebrate?"

"I know you ate lunch before we left, but I didn't. Do you want to get something to eat, or just a coffee, before we head back to Timberline?"

"Sure. I'd like that." And for a change with Cole, she was telling the truth. The therapy seemed to allay his suspicions again, and with Dr. Shipman's help she was on the road to recovering her memories. For the first time since she'd regained consciousness at the Stardust, Caroline had some hope.

As they drove toward the wharf, Cole turned his head to glance at her. "Restaurant or coffeehouse?"

"You're the one eating. You choose. I can have a coffee anywhere."

He pulled into a small parking lot of a café that sported a blue-and-white-striped awning over the front door. "Looks like I can get a sandwich here."

He stepped out of the car and slammed the door. As he came around to the passenger side, she cracked open the door.

Pointing into the car, he said, "I left my jacket in the backseat. Can you grab it for me when you get your purse?"

"Okay." She twisted around and poked her head into the back. As she tugged his jacket from the seat, his wallet fell to the floor. Her fingertips tingled, and then she snatched the wallet and shoved it into her purse.

Curling her fingers around the strap of her bag, she straightened up and slid from the car. She pressed Cole's jacket into his arms. "Here you go."

"Thanks."

She held her breath. Would he notice his missing wallet right away?

He didn't even put on the jacket as he guided her into the restaurant, with his hand on her arm.

The waitress waved toward the back of the room. "Anywhere is fine."

They took a booth in the corner, and Cole plucked two menus from a holder on the edge of the table.

Caroline hugged her purse to her chest. "I'm going to use the ladies' room first. Order me a cappuccino if the waitress comes around."

With her heart pounding, she made a beeline for the restroom. She stepped into the single bathroom and locked the door behind her. Leaning against it, she closed her eyes and took a deep breath.

This was the second time in a week that she'd stolen from someone—not that she planned to steal anything from Cole. But she didn't want to let down her guard now that he seemed to trust her. She still had to pin down his true identity, as he'd tried to do with her.

With shaking hands, she unzipped her bag and reached inside for Cole's wallet. She wedged her shoulder against the door and flipped open the leather.

Cole stared back at her from a California driver's license. Hadn't lied about being a California boy. Ignoring the cash in the billfold, she jammed her fingers into the slot behind his license and pulled out a stack of cards.

The gold-embossed letters on the top card blurred before her eyes and she slid down the length of the door until she was crouching against it.

Cole Pierson was a DEA agent, and he must be looking for the woman he believed had murdered Johnny Diamond and stolen his drug money.

Cole was looking for her.

Chapter Six

Cole ordered Caroline's coffee, and a sandwich and soda for himself. His cell phone rang from his jacket pocket and he grabbed the folds of leather, feeling for it. Then he reached for his other pocket and pulled his phone out.

He released a breath when he saw his sister's number pop up instead of the agency's. He didn't need his boss tracking him down right now. Only his partner, Craig Delgado, knew he was using his vacation time to follow up on Diamond's murder. Cole had worked too long and hard on the Diamond case to drop it now—even though his quarry was dead.

"Hey, Kristi. I can't talk right now. What's up?"

She snorted over the line. "Why are you asking me what's up in the same breath as telling me you can't talk?"

"Just being polite. I'm working right now."

"Okay. Just called to shoot the breeze. Give me a call back when you're not busy with important DEA stuff."

"Everything good?"

"I have a husband to worry about me now, big brother. Relax. Everything's fine."

"Then I'll call you later." He ended the call and dropped the phone back into his jacket pocket. Then he frowned and patted the other pocket.

Had he left his wallet at the sheriff's station? He picked

up the jacket and looked at the seat. He even checked the inside breast pocket, which he never used.

He'd tossed his jacket into the backseat of his rental when he'd left the station, and he was positive his wallet had been in the pocket. It must've fallen out.

He glanced toward the restrooms and then flagged down the waitress. "I'm going back to my car for a minute. Can you let my friend know in case she gets back before I do?"

"Sure."

He stuffed his arms in his jacket sleeves and jogged out to the rental. He opened the back door and ducked inside the car, running his hands along the seat and peering beneath it.

Caroline's purse had been back here, too. She'd grabbed his jacket for him. What else had she grabbed? Did she still suspect him of being some crony of her husband's?

He slammed the door and leaned against the car with his arms crossed. What would she discover from his wallet? He'd left his badge in the hotel safe, but he had business cards in case he needed them for the various police agencies.

She'd find out he was a DEA agent...and that he'd been lying about it. So what?

The fact that Caroline would see him as a liar and an untrustworthy person burned a hole in his gut. She'd had enough people in her life she couldn't trust. He'd wanted to be different.

Cole shook his head. It didn't matter, did it? He'd exhaust his investigation in Timberline and then return to work—with or without Diamond's hotel companion—and Caroline would continue to pick up the pieces of her shattered life with her cousin in the small-town embrace of Timberline.

If they could enjoy each other's company for a week or

so, maybe he could do a little to restore her faith in men. She would understand why he'd withheld the truth of his identity from her, just as he understood she'd felt compelled to lift his wallet to check him out.

With these noble thoughts, he pushed himself off the car and returned to the restaurant. As he walked through the door, Caroline's light-colored eyes watched him over the rim of her oversize coffee cup.

"Everything okay?"

He slid into the booth across from her. "I thought I forgot my wallet in the car."

"Oh." Her cheeks reddened as she reached for her purse. "I have it here."

His eyes narrowed as he watched her toss the wallet on the table between them and then slurp from her coffee cup.

"I—I didn't take your money." Glancing up, she covered her mouth with her hand and giggled.

He recognized that as a nervous response. "How did you happen to have it in your purse?"

"It fell from your pocket when I got your jacket out of the back, and I dropped it in my purse. It was easier than trying to stuff it back in your jacket." She blinked. "Sorry."

"Caroline." He took her hand in his and played with her fingers, warm from her coffee mug. "It's okay. You still suspected me of having some connection with... Larry, right? I can understand that you saw my wallet and decided to check things out for yourself."

"I... I—"

He put a finger to her plump lips to stop any more lies from escaping. "I'm not mad. I get it."

"I just... I'm sorry."

"And now you know I work for the Drug Enforcement Agency, and I'm not really writing a book." He squeezed and released her fingers before dragging a napkin into his lap.

"I did see that. I'm really sorry." Her mouth stretched into a tight grin. "Are you gonna have to kill me now?"

"Funny. Actually, I'm doing a little legwork on my own time."

"What does that mean? If you can tell me."

"Technically, I'm on vacation." He pulled some lettuce from his sandwich and dropped it on the plate.

"You have an interesting way of spending your time off."

"It's just that I've been tracking this one guy for a while. Lucky me, he wound up dead, but I still have unanswered questions about him and...his last days." Cole took a big bite of his sandwich to keep himself from divulging any more details to Caroline.

He'd come clean about his identity. He didn't have to reveal his whole case file on Johnny Diamond. She probably didn't care, anyway. Wendy had hated hearing about his work—had found it boring. Turned out she had more fun on the other side of the law.

Cole swallowed and took a long drink of soda.

"Drug dealers in Timberline?" Caroline widened her eyes. "Somehow I never expected that from this place."

"Really? You haven't been following the Timberline Trio case very closely, have you?"

"N-no."

"Turns out those three kids were kidnapped in exchange for some drugs."

"That's terrible. What happened to them—the kids, I mean?"

Cole cocked his head and squinted at her. "You really are out of the loop. Nobody knows. The kids vanished without a trace. The FBI with the help of some locals finally nailed down the who, but not the why or where."

"Who kidnapped them?"

"Some local biker gang kidnapped the kids for some

sick dude who was part Quileute, the Native American tribe out here. That didn't sit well with the tribe members. If they ever got their hands on him, he'd be a goner, nothing left for the FBI to arrest."

"So, they don't know where he is?"

"He disappeared shortly after the kidnappings, but was never tied to the crimes until the Lords of Chaos became part of the picture. Nobody knows what he did with those kids, and their bodies were never found."

Caroline hunched her shoulders and took another sip of her cappuccino.

Way to win over and impress women. Wendy hadn't appreciated his talk about work; why would Caroline? Especially since she'd so recently experienced violence in her own life.

"Sorry, too much information." Cole took another bite of his sandwich. Seemed to be the only way to shut himself up.

"It's sad and tragic, but it doesn't bother me to hear about it. No wonder Linda doesn't talk about the case."

"How's your cappuccino?"

"It's nice. How's your sandwich?"

He raised his eyes to the ceiling as she caught him in midbite.

"How long are you going to be investigating in Timberline and what exactly are you looking for?"

He chewed a little longer, searching for an answer. If he admitted that the possibility of finding Johnny Diamond's female companion and probable killer had drawn him here to Timberline, she'd figure out that's why he'd been stalking her. He might owe her the truth, but he didn't owe her an answer. He was still on DEA business even though the agency, outside of his partner, didn't have a clue he was here.

Cole wiped his mouth with his napkin. "Turns out my

dead drug dealer was from around this area, or at least hung out with the local biker gang."

"I figured that." Caroline traced the edge of her cup with her fingertip. "And how much time are you going to give it?"

"Maybe a week. I have to return to my real job sometime." He drew a circle in the air above the remaining half of his sandwich. "Sure you're not hungry? Do you want this?"

"No, thanks, but does the sandwich offer mean you forgive me for lifting your wallet?" She covered her eyes with one hand. "I don't know what came over me."

"I get it, but I hope this conversation and my business cards put to rest the idea that I came out here to look for you."

A rush of pink washed across her cheeks. "That whole notion was silly."

"Don't worry about it. Looks like you're getting on the right track with the therapy and everything."

"I think she'll really help."

The waitress hovered at their table, waving the check. "Can I get you anything else?"

"I'm good." Cole raised his brows at Caroline, and she shook her head. "Just the check."

The woman set it on the table with a flourish.

"Let me get this." Caroline dragged her purse into her lap. "I still feel so guilty about snatching your wallet and violating your privacy."

"All you had was coffee."

Cole reached for his wallet, but she put her hand over his. "Let me get it."

"Okay, but it's not necessary to make it up to me."

"I insist." She plucked a twenty from her wallet and placed a saltshaker on top of it and the check.

They left the restaurant and Cole slung his jacket over

his arm. Any trace of the sun had ducked behind some rolling gray clouds. He tipped his head back to look at the sky. "Rain again?"

"Seems to be a perpetual state of affairs up here. I prefer the dry heat of the desert."

Caroline tripped over a crack in the pavement, and Cole caught her arm. "Whoa."

She tucked her chin against her chest as she hunched into her jacket and broke away from him, rushing to the car as if she thought the skies would open up on them then and there.

As he opened the car door for her, Caroline's words sunk into his consciousness. "The desert? I thought you were from back East somewhere. And don't worry, I'm not going to ask you from where."

"I am, but that doesn't mean I don't like the desert climate. I'm sick of snow, and I'm getting pretty tired of the rain already."

"You and me both." He shut the door and made his way to the driver's side. He thought they'd gotten over the distrust, but she was still skittish. Must be habit. She'd probably walked on eggshells with that scumbag husband of hers.

Caroline was quiet, thoughtful, on the ride back to Timberline. Cole didn't want to disturb her train of thought. In fact, he didn't want to disturb her anymore.

She pushed all his buttons and he was attracted to her beyond belief, but her actions screamed of complications he didn't want or need right now. He could see pursuing a relationship with her once he'd wrapped up here if she'd been a Timberline local, someone with a life and a plan.

But Caroline seemed lost, rootless and afraid. He wanted to rescue her in the worst way, but he had other priorities right now. And it wasn't like she was crying out to be saved.

She had him at arm's length and wanted to keep him there.

As they drove into Timberline, he said, "I hope Linda got her car fixed."

"So do I. Thanks again for taking me into Port Angeles for my appointment."

He rolled up to the curb in front of Timberline Treasures. "No problem. I'm just going to stick my head in and say hello to Linda."

Caroline didn't tell him to stay in the car, but she didn't exactly encourage him, either. He thought they'd made some progress over lunch, but she'd done a one-eighty once they got to the car, and the ride home couldn't have been chillier if they'd been riding in a convertible in the rain.

He yanked the door of the shop open for her, feeling irritated with himself. He didn't need any more complicated women in his life—no matter how good she looked in her skinny jeans.

Linda glanced up from helping a customer and smiled.

She probably thought her little matchmaking scheme had come off famously. Cole would let Caroline break the bad news to her and tell her what had gone wrong, because he sure as hell didn't know.

NOT WANTING TO get into any small talk with Cole, Caroline wandered around the shop, picking up and replacing items she saw a hundred times a day.

Where had her preference for the desert come from? The fact that she'd blurted it out to Cole had to mean her memory was coming back, unless she'd been influenced by the hypnosis. She'd have to watch what she said around the DEA agent.

DEA agent looking for a suspect in Johnny's murder was better than drug dealer looking for his missing cash, but only marginally. If he had any idea that she'd been the last person to see Diamond alive, even if she couldn't remember it, he'd haul her into custody so fast her head would spin.

The customer finally left the shop and Caroline asked, "Did you get your car fixed?"

"I did. Did you get to your appointment okay?" Linda glanced quickly at Cole.

"It's okay. Cole knows I was seeing a therapist."

"And I wholeheartedly approve—" he held up his hand "—not that Caroline needs approval from me."

"And you?" Linda hunched forward, folding her arms on the counter. "Did you find what you needed at the Port Angeles library?"

He slid a sideways glance at Caroline before answering. "Yep."

Cole hadn't asked her to keep quiet about his real purpose in Timberline, but who was she to spill anyone else's secrets?

"We even had a bite to eat before we hit the road back to Timberline," she said.

Linda's eyes sparkled. "Sounds like a nice day. I'm glad Cole could step in and give you a lift."

"It worked out." Caroline pressed her lips together. She didn't want to give Linda any ideas about her and Cole. Even if she were in a position to start a relationship, it wouldn't be with a DEA agent.

"It's always nice getting to know someone." Linda beamed.

"We did get to know a little more about each other." Cole crossed his arms. "What I learned about Caroline is that she doesn't know much about her adopted home."

"Timberline?" Linda's smile froze on her face. "She never visited before, but she's learning something new every day."

Caroline nodded as her stomach sank. Linda needed to stop talking before she revealed too much information, and maybe she needed to leave town so she wouldn't be putting Linda in any more awkward situations where Linda had to lie—especially to DEA agents.

Dr. Shipman had indicated that hypnosis could work for her, so it could probably work for her anywhere and with anyone. She should try to recover her identity far, far away from Timberline—and Cole Pierson.

"She didn't even know that the biggest mystery out of Timberline, the kidnapping of those three children, had been partially solved. But I guess you had your own issues to deal with, didn't you, Caroline?"

Caroline ground her back teeth together. Did he suspect her again? He kept swinging back and forth between believing she was Linda's cousin looking for a fresh start and suspecting she might be the woman in Diamond's motel room at the time of his death.

"Yeah, I haven't been paying much attention to the local news."

Linda sighed. "I'm glad the authorities finally identified who took those kids. Now if someone could only figure out what Rocky did with them."

"Rocky?" Caroline stopped swinging the key chain around her finger as her heart skipped a beat. Rocky was the name on the text Johnny had gotten on his phone.

So she was connected not only to a drug dealer, but to a kidnapper. What kind of madness had she escaped?

Chapter Seven

"R-Rocky?" Caroline swayed on her feet and dropped the key chain back in the bin.

Linda responded in a hard voice. "Rocky Whitecotton. He was Quileute, although they've all but disowned him. One of their own, Scarlett Easton, made the connection between Rocky and the Timberline Trio, along with a former member of the Lords of Chaos."

Cole had moved closer to Caroline, almost hovering, but she didn't turn his way. What would he see in her face?

"Lords of Chaos?" She sounded like a parrot, but she couldn't form a coherent thought in her head.

"That motorcycle gang. I think I mentioned it to you before." Cole's voice sounded close, almost like a whisper in her ear, almost accusing.

She swallowed and scooped her hair back from her face. "Wow, Timberline does have quite a sordid history. Are you going to put all of this in your *book*, Cole?"

He jerked back sharply and sucked in a breath. "Not really the kind of thing my books focus on. I want to show the charm of a place, not unearth all of its dirty little secrets."

"Your *books*? I thought this was your first one."

"This one and the ones I plan to write in the future."

Linda had been glancing between the two of them with a crease between her brows. "Anyway, the FBI knows that Rocky was responsible for the kidnappings, that he gave the Lords of Chaos drugs to do the dirty work, but they don't know why he did it, or what he did with the children."

"I've heard all this before." Cole jerked his thumb over his shoulder. "I'm going to hit the road, but I think you left your phone in my car, Caroline. Do you want to come out with me to get it? Or I could drive you home."

"I'll do a little work here and go home with Linda, but I'll come get my phone." She patted her throwaway phone in the pocket of her jacket just to make sure it was there, and then followed Cole through the door.

Before he could open his mouth, she spun around on him. "Don't worry. I'm not going to tell Linda or anyone else that you're DEA. Did you think I would?"

"I didn't think so." He scratched the sexy stubble on his chin. "But for a minute in there, I thought you were going to blow my cover. I'm sorry I'm asking you to lie for me. I don't like that, but you did go snooping through my wallet. I just don't want the locals to know that I'm looking into Johnny Diamond's past."

"Maybe the good folks of Timberline would be able to help you. I doubt anyone here has any loyalty to some scumbag drug dealer who's connected to an outlaw biker gang."

"You never know about these small towns. I'm sure there are still a lot of people here who have connections to the Lords. A few of them were just in town last month, causing trouble, as usual."

"They were here? In Timberline?" Caroline crossed her arms over her stomach.

What did she think she'd find here? She'd discovered nothing about her identity, but had plenty of reason to regret her decision to come to Timberline. She should've stayed in Seattle, a big city where she could get lost. She could've found a hypnotherapist there, worked things out in relative safety and anonymity.

Of course, if she hadn't come to Timberline she never would've heard Rocky's name or found out that a DEA agent was hot on her heels.

She never would've met Cole at all.

He squeezed her shoulder. "Are you okay? It's not like the Lords are going to come after you or wreak havoc through Timberline."

No, just wreak havoc with her mind—like Cole was doing now with his comforting hand on her shoulder. Maybe she should confess everything to him. He'd want to know that Diamond had received a text mentioning Rocky. It couldn't be a coincidence. Rocky was not a common name. Did that mean that Diamond also had something to do with the Timberline Trio? Maybe his connection to Rocky could help the FBI find out what had happened to those kids twenty-five years ago. Didn't she owe it to them to speak up?

"I just hate the thought of violence. I really do. I couldn't harm a spider—and I hate spiders. I don't understand people who commit violent acts."

Cole tilted his head to one side, studying her face. "Just keep seeing Dr. Shipman. I'm sure you'll work things out, Caroline."

She stiffened. That sounded like a goodbye. Maybe he didn't want anyone around him who knew his true business in Timberline. She bit the inside of her cheek to bring herself back to reality. This was what she wanted—get rid of Cole and his questioning eyes, his hovering presence, his suspicions.

"You're right. Once I get sorted out, I probably won't even stay here in Timberline. I'll most likely get lost in some big city."

"In the desert."

"What?" Her gaze flew to his face.

"You said you liked the desert. You could head to Phoenix or Albuquerque. Hell, even L.A.'s a desert."

"I might do that." She plucked her phone from her pocket. "I know I don't need my phone from your car, so thanks for the ride and…and say goodbye before you leave town."

"I will." His fingers brushed her cheek and he turned toward his car.

She didn't wait for him to drive off. She pivoted toward the store and shoved the door hard, setting off the tinkling of the bells.

"What happened? Didn't you two hit it off?" Linda screwed up her mouth. "I sensed a lot of tension between you."

"I appreciate your efforts, Linda, but I'm not ready for any romantic entanglements right now."

"But if you were—" Linda winked "—Cole would be just the man to start with. He's so…safe. A girl would feel protected with him."

Linda must be picking up on Cole's law enforcement vibe, just as Caroline had. As a DEA agent, he was accustomed to being large and in charge. He was even here in Timberline on his own time. He was obviously dedicated to his job and justice—and that would mean moving heaven and earth to find Diamond's accomplice.

Caroline could never tell him about her role in Johnny Diamond's life. He wouldn't understand. For all his smiling helpfulness, the man had a hard edge. She saw it in his eyes when he talked about the drug dealers and the kidnappers and the outlaw biker gang. He had little patience for people like that—people like her.

The lawman and the criminal—ha, that would never work in a million years.

"I'm sure he'll make some woman a great husband. He even likes babies."

"Just not you." Linda came from behind the counter and gave Caroline a hug. "How did your therapy go? Do you think it's going to help you? I really think it saved my sister."

"I think it will help." Deserts, large families and escape—it was a start.

LATER THAT EVENING, Linda was feeling social and invited Caroline out to dinner. Caroline wanted to stay away from Sutter's, since that seemed to be Cole's dining choice most evenings, but when Linda went out for dinner that's where she went.

A quick survey of the dining room assured Caroline that Cole had either chosen another place tonight or hadn't made it over here yet. She and Linda took a table in the middle of the room—another of Linda's conditions. She liked to see and be seen when she went out. She missed her sister more than she let on.

Caroline pulled out her chair and then paused, her gaze following the bald man who was making his way to the bar. She nudged Linda. "Do you know that guy? The one with the shaved head and green scarf?"

Linda leaned to the left and squinted. "Never saw him before in my life. Could be a new Evergreen employee. Why?"

"He came into the store the other day. Bought a frog."

"You don't still think Larry is sending spies out here, do you?"

Linda raised her brows in a way that made Caroline flush three different heat levels. She had to suffer through those looks if she wanted to keep up the pretense of the abusive husband. Neither Linda nor Cole would think she was so silly and paranoid if they knew her real reason for being in Timberline and jumping at every loud noise.

"He just seemed suspicious." Caroline flicked open the menu and sniffed. "I know it's ridiculous. I just can't help it."

Linda's face softened. "I know, dear. You have every right to be on edge. I don't know the man, but I can find out who he is. Even with Evergreen setting up shop, Timberline is still a small town and I have my sources."

That inconvenient guilt niggled in her belly. It had never occurred to Linda that Caroline might be lying about everything and that Cole could be, as well. The man with the shaved head could be lying to the bartender right now.

Chloe, their waitress, came up to the table, tapping her pencil against her notebook. "Hi, ladies. What can I get you tonight? Start you off with a glass of wine?"

"That sounds perfect." Linda nudged Caroline's arm. "Let's indulge, just one and I'm driving."

Caroline hadn't had any alcohol since she'd been born in that motel room, but surely she could stop at one and not fall into an alcohol-induced conversation with Linda.

"I'm in. I'll have the house white, whatever that is."

Chloe raised her pencil in the air. "It's a chardonnay from the Willamette Valley. Is that okay?"

"That's fine."

"And you'll have the same, Linda?"

"Yes, thank you, Chloe."

"Do you want me to bring a carafe?"

"Oh no, just a glass for each of us is fine."

As Chloe turned from the table, a twentysomething man with long black hair caught in a ponytail nudged her back. "I need to talk to you. Now."

She brushed him off. "I'm working here, Jason."

"Hello, Jason." Linda gave the young man a smile.

"Hi, Ms. Gunderson. Sorry to interrupt." He nudged Chloe in the back again.

"We can wait for our wine. Have you met my cousin Caroline Johnson?"

Jason held up one hand. "Nice to meet you, ma'am."

"Go see what Jason wants, Chloe."

As Jason and Chloe wandered away, heads together, Linda took a sip of water. "Those two are such a nice couple. Jason's Quileute, from the reservation. Hardworking young man."

Caroline covered a smile with one hand. Linda obviously enjoyed seeing love flourish.

When Chloe came back with their wine, her smooth brow was creased with worry.

Linda didn't seem to notice and Caroline didn't know Chloe well enough to inquire, so they ordered their food.

Caroline kept up the conversation with Linda while glancing toward the bar every once in a while. The bald guy hadn't spoken to anyone except the bartender, Denny, and didn't seem to be meeting anyone, since he'd already started eating his burger.

Linda had drained her wineglass, and when Chloe returned to deliver their food, she ordered a second glass.

"I'm eating a big meal." Linda waved her fork over her plate, which was overflowing with a thick pork chop and mashed potatoes and gravy. "I should be okay to drive."

"If you say so." Caroline took a sip of water and tossed her napkin on the table. "I'm going to use the restroom. I'll be right back."

She scooted back from the table and veered toward the perimeter of the room. She glanced over her shoulder before entering the short hallway to the bathrooms and the exit.

The man at the bar was still eating and hadn't noticed her. She washed her hands at the sink and took a deep breath before stepping into the hallway. She flattened herself against the wall and hunched forward a little until she could see the bar.

She didn't know what she hoped to discover about the man from here. She'd gotten lucky the night she'd overheard Cole on his cell phone. Luck like that wouldn't strike twice.

Nothing about the man screamed biker, drug trafficker or even cop.

So why had he made her senses spike? Because he'd been watching her from the end of the alley the night she'd suspected someone had broken into her place? The night of the pouring rain, when Cole had rescued her from the mud and had made everything okay?

She huffed softly through her nostrils. He was in law enforcement. That's what those guys did—set everything right again. Could he set her right again?

No. Once he discovered her identity, or at least what she knew of her identity, that hard, cold look would come into his eyes and they'd turn to green chips of ice.

A pretty blonde stopped next to the man with the shaved head and perched on the stool next to him, facing him. They chatted, heads together, and then she handed him some papers.

Maybe Linda could ID the blonde, Caroline thought. Before she could peel herself from the wall, Chloe and her boyfriend stumbled into the hallway, their voices harsh whispers as they argued about something.

Caroline cleared her throat. Two sets of eyes pinned her, so she gave a weak smile, eased out of the hall and scurried back to her table. She didn't want them to think she was eavesdropping. She had enough of her own problems.

Caroline widened her eyes when she saw a half carafe of wine in front of Linda, who was chatting with one of her card-playing friends.

"Here she is, my sweet cousin Caroline."

Caroline smiled at the other woman. "Irene, right?"

"You have a good memory."

Caroline coughed to mask the laugh bubbling from her throat. "Linda talks about her good friends all the time."

"Linda's lucky to have you here while her sister is gone. When is Louise coming back, Linda?"

"About two weeks."

"And while the cat's away the mouse will play." Irene tapped a fingernail against Linda's wineglass. Then leaned close to Caroline. "Louise doesn't like it when Linda has more than a glass of wine."

"Oh, stop it. Louise isn't my keeper." Linda waved her hand. "Stop causing trouble. I'll see you next week."

Irene winked at Caroline and left the restaurant.

"I can drive, Linda. Finish your wine and don't worry about it."

"If you think you can."

Caroline held up her water glass. "I just had the one glass, but you can do me a favor."

"Anything for my little cousin." Linda hiccupped and pressed her fingers against her lips.

The blonde had finished speaking to the man at the bar and had started making her way to the front door, stopping here and there along the way.

"Who's that attractive blonde in the skirt and heels?" Caroline tipped her head toward the woman.

"Where?" Linda twisted her head from side to side.

Nudging Linda's toe beneath the table, Caroline hissed, "Shh." She held up her hand and jabbed her palm with her index finger. "Right there, talking to that couple two tables over."

Linda hunched forward, slurring her speech. "That's Rebecca Geist. She's a Realtor, but she probably won't be here much longer. She's engaged to a very rich man. Besides..." Linda glanced both ways. "She was beaten up pretty badly a few months ago."

Caroline recoiled from the tinny odor of Linda's alcohol-infused breath. "Here in Timberline?"

"She was helping some woman, a TV reporter, who was doing a story on the Timberline Trio case. You know that show *Cold Case Chronicles*?"

Caroline nodded as if she did, although she'd never heard of it.

"Well, the host of that show only pretended to be doing a story on the Timberline Trio." Linda's voice was a harsh whisper, but the couple at the next table glanced over. "But she really thought she was one of kidnapped kids. She wasn't, but her snooping around got her into other trouble, and since Rebecca had been helping her, it got Rebecca in trouble, too."

A sharp pain lanced Caroline's left temple, and she massaged her head. "It seems as if that case never ended for this town."

"That's for sure, and I don't think it ever will, since the children were never found. That kind of thing haunts a town." With a shaky hand, Linda tipped more wine from the carafe into her glass. "We're cursed."

Caroline tapped the edge of Linda's plate with her fork. "Finish your pork chop. Do you want some of my fries from my fish and chips?"

"I think I have enough food here. I'll finish." She took another sip of wine.

Caroline toyed with the fries on her plate as she watched the Realtor leave the restaurant. The man with the shaved head was probably here to buy property or something. Maybe he was making the move to Timberline for a job at Evergreen. He'd told her he was here on business.

Caroline finished her dinner and five minutes later followed the progress of the man from the bar as he skirted the dining area on his way out of the restaurant. When he reached the hostess stand, he looked over his shoulder, meeting Caroline's gaze, a slight smile playing about his lips.

He turned and left before she could break eye contact. What did it mean? What interest could he possibly have in her? Unless—she gripped her fork so tightly her knuckles turned white—he was the one she was supposed to meet in Timberline.

That scrap of paper in her pocket with Timberline written on it in her own handwriting had to have been there for a reason.

Maybe she should approach him. Maybe he had the answers she'd been seeking. He didn't seem menacing. She hadn't gotten that kind of vibe from him—except when he'd been watching her in the rain.

She dug a pen from her purse and scribbled down Rebecca Geist's name on a napkin. Perhaps she'd look into some Timberline real estate.

"Can we leave, Caroline? I'm so tired."

She looked across the table at Linda's drooping eyelids and mottled cheeks. "Of course, and don't even think about driving. You're downright tipsy."

"Am I?" Linda giggled.

Caroline couldn't get her out of there fast enough. Was Linda a blabbermouth drunk? Would she spill all her secrets?

A tall man came through the front door of the restaurant and the stakes just got higher.

"Look, there's Cole." Linda waved and called his name.

Caroline touched Chloe's arm as she passed their table. "We'd like the check, Chloe. Right away."

The waitress nodded absently. "I'll be right with you."

Cole made his way to their table and pulled out a chair.

He lifted the carafe and swirled the sip of wine left in the bottom. "Looks like I missed the party."

"Party of one." Caroline rolled her eyes.

"I hope you don't plan to drive home, Linda."

"Caroline has offered, although I'm fine. I ate a lot."

Cole raised his brows at her half-eaten pork chop and pile of potatoes. "Yeah, I think you'd better give Caroline the keys."

Linda murmured, "My sweet cousin."

Caroline's stomach bunched into knots. "Excuse us if we don't hang around, Cole."

"That's okay. I'm just here for a pickup."

Since Chloe didn't seem to be returning anytime soon, Caroline pulled some cash from her wallet and dropped three twenties on the table as she scooted back her chair.

"You're not going to wait for the check?" Cole stood up when she did, and placed a hand on Linda's shoulder.

Snatching her jacket from the back of the empty chair, Caroline said, "That should cover it. Are you ready, Linda?"

"I think so." Linda had dropped her chin to her chest and closed her eyes.

Cole mouthed the words, *Do you need help?*

She shook her head. She didn't want to embarrass Linda and cause a scene.

She gripped Linda's upper arm. "Ready? One, two, three."

Linda rose to her feet unsteadily and bumped her shoulder against Caroline's.

"I'm just going to hang on to your arm through the restaurant. You'll feel better when you get some fresh air."

"Oh, do stop nagging me, Louise."

Caroline shrugged her shoulders at Cole. She had to get Linda out of here fast.

With just a few shuffled steps and a little bit of a stagger from Linda, Caroline managed to get her safely out of the restaurant without setting off too many wagging tongues.

If Chloe knew about Linda's fondness for chardonnay, chances were the rest of Timberline did, as well.

Caroline took Linda's keys from her purse and poured Linda into the passenger seat, snapping her seat belt in place. Then she did the same for herself.

As she pulled away from the curb, a motorcycle roared out of the alley and fishtailed on the wet asphalt before zooming off. Looked like Chloe's hotheaded boyfriend. Caroline tightened her hands on the steering wheel. She couldn't account for other drivers, but she always took care to drive safely, since she had no driver's license. At least she had only a mile to go and crazy Jason on the bike was long gone.

As her passenger snored softly beside her, Caroline pulled the car into Linda's side of the driveway. She nudged her shoulder. "Linda? We're home."

She parked and helped her from the car. The older woman leaned heavily against her and Caroline staggered up the two steps to the front door. She led Linda to her bedroom, where she kicked off both shoes after about five tries and then crawled under the covers fully clothed.

Caroline tucked the covers around her shoulders, then tiptoed to the bathroom, found a bottle of aspirin and shook a couple into her palm. After filling a glass with water from the tap in the kitchen, she put it and the two aspirin on Linda's nightstand.

If the woman woke up in the middle of the night, she might be able to stave off an even worse hangover by taking the aspirin.

Caroline grabbed her purse and hitched it over her shoulder. She studied Linda's key chain in the palm of her hand. Maybe she should keep the house key so she could lock the dead bolt from the outside.

She penned a note to Linda and then placed her set of keys on the piece of paper on a table by the front door.

Caroline pulled the door closed behind her, locked the dead bolt and pocketed Linda's house key. It was the least she could do for the woman who'd taken her in and lied for her.

A soft patter of rain caressed her cheek when she stepped off the porch. For a moment she lifted her face to the drops. The rain wasn't so bad, after all.

She began to cross the driveway to her own side of the duplex when a gruff voice behind her stopped her cold.

"Where's the money, bitch?"

Chapter Eight

Cole cracked open his car door as Caroline walked across the driveway to her own place. Looked like he'd come too late to help her with Linda. Caroline must be stronger than she looked or Linda had recovered some of her mobility.

He put his boot down on the gravel and heard voices. Had Linda followed Caroline outside? Then a man's voice carried into the street. "I said, where's the money, bitch?"

A surge of adrenaline rushed through Cole's body and he yelled, "Hey!"

As he rounded the front of his car, rushing toward the driveway, Caroline screamed. Cole slipped on some wet leaves and recovered his balance in time to see Caroline lurch forward onto her hands and knees in the middle of the driveway—alone.

He rushed to her side, his fingers curled around the butt of his gun in his pocket. "Are you injured? Did he hurt you?"

She shook her head. "No."

"Where is he? Where'd he go?"

With glassy eyes she pointed into the copse of trees, shrouded in darkness, on the other side of Linda's duplex.

"Get inside and lock the door. Call 911." He pulled her to her feet. Once the local cops got here, he'd have to reveal his true identity, but it would be worth it to nail the man who'd attacked Caroline.

She grabbed handfuls of his jacket. "H-he has a knife."

"I have a gun." He patted his pocket and then grabbed her hands and kissed them. "Go."

He watched her until she disappeared inside, then took off at a jog toward the blackest spot in his vision. He might have a gun but he didn't have a flashlight.

He pulled out his cell phone and swiped on the flashlight, holding the phone in front of him to light a small, pathetic path into the dense woods.

When he got to the edge of the tree line, he stopped, head to one side, and listened for any movement. Either the guy was hiding, concealed and silent, or he was long gone. Cole thrashed through the bushes and branches, stopping periodically to listen, but only a few birds twittered an answer.

He'd never find anyone out here and he risked getting knifed before he would ever be able to see the threat coming at him.

With his phone in one hand and his gun in the other, he made his way out of the forest and back to Caroline's front door. No sirens yet.

Could the man threatening her be connected to her husband? Maybe she had good reason to be paranoid, but why would he be asking her for money, unless she'd taken money from her husband when she escaped from him? So many things didn't add up about her—the woman of mystery.

He pocketed his gun and knocked on her door. "Caroline? It's me, Cole."

A chain scraped across its metal track and a dead bolt clicked before she inched the door open. Her face had yet to regain its color.

"Are you okay? Can I come in?"

The door widened and she stepped back. "I'm okay. Shaken, but okay. Did you find anything out there?"

"Too damned dark and I don't have a flashlight other than the one on my phone." He crossed the threshold. "What happened? I heard him ask for money. Was he trying to rob you?"

"I guess so." She shut the door and put both locks into place again. "I had just come out of Linda's house after putting her to bed and locking her door."

"He accosted you in the driveway? Because I saw you through the passenger window first, and I didn't see anyone else on the driveway."

"He came up behind me. Maybe he'd been hiding in the woods."

"Did you see him?"

"He told me not to turn around—and I didn't. He said he had a knife and then put it to my throat." She placed one hand around the column of her throat as if to protect it.

"What else did he say? When I got out of my car, I heard voices and then he shouted."

"The shout? That's pretty much what he said to me. He said 'Give me the money, bitch.' I started to turn, instinct I guess, and that's when he said he had a knife and he didn't want me to move. He put the blade to my flesh and then shouted again, and that's what you heard." She twisted her fingers in front of her. "When you yelled, he pushed me and I turned around, but only saw him plunging into the trees."

"How did he expect you to give him any money when he didn't want you to move?"

"I don't know." She hunched her shoulders. "Maybe he was going to grab my purse or something."

Cole rubbed both her arms from her shoulders to her elbows and back up again. "Your body is trembling. Sit down. Do you want some water? Tea?"

She moved like a zombie to the sofa against the wall

and sank down on the end, clasping her hands between her knees. "Water maybe, thanks."

He strode into the kitchen and opened a few mostly empty cupboards before finding one with a single row of drinking glasses lined up. He lifted one from the shelf and filled it with water from the tap.

When he returned to the living room, he handed her the glass and then paced away from her. "Do you think this had anything to do with Larry?"

"Wh-why would it?"

He studied her face. Every other thing that had happened to her she'd put at the feet of Larry. Why back off from that stance now?

"You can tell me the truth, Caroline. Did you take some money from him? Is that why you've been so worried that he'd come after you?" Cole spread his hands. "I wouldn't blame you. The guy sounds like he had it coming."

Her doe eyes darted from the door to his face and back again, like she was an animal caught in a snare.

He took two steps toward the couch and sat on the cushion next to her. His weight on the soft sofa had her tilting toward him, her shoulder bouncing against his.

"It's okay." He put his arm around her, taking care not to draw her nearer—even though he wanted to. "You can tell me anything. I won't judge you. I told you, my mom got out of an abusive relationship, and if she'd stolen money from the SOB, my stepfather, our lives would've gone much more smoothly. Hell, it was probably just as much your money as his, so you didn't really steal it."

Her body stiffened. "I—I did take money out of our accounts, but it was mine, too. I guess he tracked me here to Timberline. He must've been paying closer attention to my chatter about relatives than I thought he was. He remembered the Gundersons from Timberline and sent someone out here to find me. It probably wasn't hard. Everyone here knows I'm Linda's second cousin. Everyone knows I'm Caroline Johnson. Larry's cohort probably got Linda's address, and waited for us to come home. He got me alone and jumped on the opportunity. I'm going to have to leave Timberline."

Cole dropped his arm from her shoulders and rubbed his jaw. That rapid-fire response was the most he'd gotten out of Caroline since the day he'd met her.

"That was my first thought—that this had something to do with your husband. But why would this guy, this friend of Larry's, approach you this way? Why wouldn't he just knock on your door and tell you that Larry expected his money back or he'd see you in court? Technically, when you initiate divorce proceedings, neither party is supposed to touch any of the common funds. Believe me, I speak from experience. Of course, each state is different, but what are the rules in…? Where are you from, exactly?"

"Now you think this is some random attack? Just some thug holding me up for cash?"

Cole pressed his thumbs against either side of his head. "I don't know. It just doesn't make sense that Larry would send someone else out here to get his money. If he knew where you were, wouldn't Larry come to Timberline himself to confront you?"

"That's not Larry. He'd send someone else to do his dirty work."

"Is that why you didn't call the police?" With his shoulder still pressed against hers, he felt her body jerk. "You didn't call, right? They would've been here by now. Most people I know rush to call 911 when something like this happens."

Closing her eyes, she leaned against the back of the sofa. A pulse beat wildly in her throat. "Please don't call them. I'll call Larry myself and tell him I'll return the money. I don't want the police involved. I don't want to cause any trouble in Timberline."

Cole scanned her face, the parted lips, lashes fluttering against the smooth skin of her cheeks. A tear slid from the corner of one of her eyes, traveled to her hairline and meandered toward her ear.

Was that tear even real? Did anything she'd told him since the day he'd met her at the library have one kernel of truth in it?

She sniffled and rubbed her eyes as she sat forward. "Please. I'd rather handle this my own way."

"Which is what? Leave Timberline for parts unknown?" His voice sounded harsh to his own ears and Caroline flinched at the tone.

He didn't know if he was angry at her for lying or angry at himself for getting taken in by a pretty face and a sad story—again. Or even worse, was he angry because she was leaving?

He was *not* telling his sister about this one. She'd start to have doubts about whether he could date without supervision—not that Caroline had ever been dating material, though he'd wanted her to be. He could be a man and admit that, even admit he'd been a fool.

"I think that's best, don't you?" She grabbed his arm and turned those big, baby blue eyes on him.

He shook her off. "Do what you want, Caroline. I think you've been lying to me from the get-go."

Her face drained of all color and she jerked back from him.

"I don't know what your game is with your husband and his so-called friend. I don't know if he's abusive or if you told that story to your cousin so she'd take you in. Who knows?" Cole jumped up from the sofa to get away from the scent of her flowery perfume. "Maybe it's all a scam you two are running to get money out of Linda and Louise."

Caroline emitted a strangled cry and covered her mouth with both hands.

He turned away and walked toward the window. "All I do know is not calling the sheriff's department after someone pulls a knife on you is a huge red flag. You didn't realize that a DEA agent, of all people, wouldn't be suspicious about that?"

She gulped down the water he'd brought her and wiped her mouth with the back of her hand. "Actually, I thought you'd be relieved to keep the cops out of it, since you'd have to come clean about who you are and what you're doing in Timberline."

"Is that a threat? 'Cuz bring it on." He spread his arms out to his sides. "You can go ahead and tell everyone in town that I'm DEA. You know the funniest thing about it? I'd realized my cover would be blown, but I figured it would be worth it to keep you safe. Pretty funny, huh?"

She dropped her gaze from his and another tear slid from the same eye. She must've perfected the art of crying from one eye only. She'd have to work on the tear ducts for that other eye.

"That's not funny at all. I'm grateful and humbled you'd feel that way."

His heart lurched—just a little—and then he widened his stance and crossed his arms. "Yeah, another sucker."

Rolling the glass between her hands, she rose from the sofa and sauntered to the kitchen to place it on the counter. He tried like hell to keep his eyes off her rounded hips as they swung from side to side, and her long, tangled, toffee-brown hair tumbling down her back.

She turned suddenly and his gaze jumped to her face. "I'm not going to do it."

"Do what? Scam Linda? Leave town? Give your husband his money back?"

"Blow your cover."

"Whatever. Do what you have to do. I'm not hanging around much longer, anyway. This was a wild-goose chase for me."

Except for meeting Caroline, this investigation had been a bust. The single female in the cabin hadn't fit the description of the woman at the Stardust at all. Only Caroline had come close in appearance and general arrival time to Timberline, and her cousin Linda had vouched for her already.

Caroline's visit to the therapist had also thrown him for a loop. There would be no reason for Johnny's murderer or girlfriend or accomplice to head to Timberline and see a therapist.

"I'm not a bad person, Cole. I mean, I don't *feel* like I'm a bad person." She folded her hands in front of her. "I'm not trying to...scam Linda."

"Whatever is going on between family members is their business. I'm out. I don't need to be involved anymore. I'm not going to rat you out to the police, or Linda or Larry or Larry's many friends, real or imagined."

"I appreciate that...and everything you've done for me." Caroline tipped her chin toward the window. "You saved me out there. You comforted me the other night when I thought someone had broken in. You're a good guy, Cole Pierson."

"That's me." He thumped his chest twice with his fist. "The good guy."

Caroline's cell phone rang.

"Better get that. It's probably your accomplice." He stalked toward the front door and whipped off the chain.

Caroline's voice, high-pitched and breathy, stopped

him. "Linda? What's wrong? Oh, my God. Hang on. I'll be right over."

He'd turned at the door and watched Caroline as she swiped a key from the countertop and grabbed her jacket.

"What's the matter with Linda?"

"I'm not sure. She's sick, vomiting, and she collapsed on the floor when she tried to get out of bed. I'm going over to help her. C-can you call 911?"

"I will, but I'm coming over with you. I have some first-aid training as part of my job."

She nodded and flew out the front door.

He followed, phone in hand, calling 911.

And just like that, he'd been swept back into the helter-skelter world of Caroline Johnson—or whatever the hell her name was.

Chapter Nine

Caroline paced back and forth across the hospital's emergency waiting room. "I didn't think she was that drunk. Maybe it's been a while and it hit her wrong."

"She's getting up there in age, and it looked like she drank a lot on an empty stomach. Bad combination." Cole patted the plastic chair next to him. "Have a seat."

Caroline glanced over her shoulder at his worried face. Just when she thought he was going to walk out of her life for good, he'd been a steady rock when they'd found Linda semiconscious on the floor of her bedroom, choking on her vomit. He'd taken control of the situation. He'd known just what to do and had probably saved Linda's life.

While Caroline had been a babbling idiot, he'd explained everything to the EMTs as they worked on Linda and loaded her into the ambulance.

Then, instead of abandoning her, he'd driven Caroline to the emergency room, following the ambulance and getting her settled in the waiting room. He did all that and he hated her. Imagine what a man like that would do for someone he loved.

She plopped onto the chair next to him, stretching her legs in front of her. The only silver lining from that entire episode in the driveway was that Cole clearly still believed she was Linda's cousin and had nothing to do with Johnny Diamond. That was the *only* good that came out of it.

Of course she couldn't call the Timberline Sheriff's Department. They'd have wanted her name, driver's license, information about her mythical husband, Larry. It was one thing telling a few lies here and there around town, but she couldn't put herself in the hands of the police—not now. She needed a few more sessions with Dr. Shipman.

Cole put a steadying hand on her bouncing knee. "Linda's going to be okay. She overindulged, got…snockered, got sick and didn't have enough fluids in her body. They'll hook her up to an IV and she'll be fine."

"I'm so glad she was able to get to her phone and call me. She could've died."

"She knew she could count on you."

"Really?" Caroline slid a glance at him from the corner of her eye. "I thought I was trying to scam her."

His jaw formed a hard line, as if she'd just reminded him he couldn't trust her.

She bit her lip. She should just shut up about all that instead of trying to prove something to Cole. In a sense, he was right. She'd been lying to Linda since the day she met her behind the shop. She'd taken advantage of her good and sympathetic nature, all the while hiding her true intentions.

Cole lifted one shoulder. "Okay, maybe I was harsh earlier. You're here now, and I'm not going to say another word about it."

She rubbed her eyes. "You said a few things back there. You're divorced?"

"Another statistic."

"But you don't have children. You mentioned that in the store the other day."

"One of my regrets, but since the marriage ended I suppose it's a good thing we didn't bring kids into the mix."

"How'd it end?" He'd left his hand on her knee and she

traced a finger across his knuckles. "I'm sorry. You don't owe me any explanations."

He flexed his fingers. "I don't mind. In some ways it's easier opening up to the woman of mystery. You know nothing about her, so you won't read any judgment in her eyes or tone."

Caroline snatched her hand away and stuffed it in her jacket pocket. "Like I said, you don't have to tell me anything."

"She cheated on me."

"That's awful. I'm sorry." Was his wife crazy? Hot, sexy, steady. What more could you ask for in a man?

"With a drug dealer."

This time Caroline couldn't contain her surprise. Her mouth dropped open. "You're kidding."

"I wish I was."

"Did she pick him on purpose? I mean, what are the odds that she'd fall into the arms of one of her husband's natural enemies?"

"Natural enemy. I like that." Cole stretched and yawned, obviously no longer bothered by the incident... or hiding it well. "It's complicated."

"Is it someone she knew before you?"

"Exactly. Wendy ran with a wild crowd. I met her at a club while I was working undercover. I just didn't realize she was in so deep with the bunch we were investigating. Bust went down and I ran into her about six months later, getting her life together, she said."

"So, she fell hard for the straight-arrow DEA agent. She liked the domesticated lifestyle for a while and then started to get the itch," Caroline murmured.

Cole leveled a finger at her. "You're good. One session with that therapist and you've got it all figured out."

"Is that what happened?"

"Yeah. I discovered what was going on pretty fast.

She'd been with the dude once, and I knew it right away." Cole hit his forehead with the heel of his hand. "God, she could've ruined my career."

"It's a good thing you got out of that marriage when you did."

"Uh-huh." He tipped back his head and stared at the ceiling.

As Cole got lost in thoughts of the past, Caroline twirled a strand of hair around her finger. No wonder he'd gone ballistic on her when she refused to call the police. She thought she'd had him fooled, but he never really trusted her.

He couldn't nab her for Johnny's accomplice, but he'd known something wasn't right about her. He didn't want to get tricked by another wild woman, and she didn't blame him.

God, she must've come across exactly like his ex—troubled, needy, looking for a white knight. Cole Pierson could totally deliver in the white knight category, but he'd want to know his damsel really needed rescuing and wasn't running a con.

Caroline wasn't, but she'd have to tell him the truth to explain everything—and she wasn't ready to do that. So he'd go his way and she'd go hers, whatever that way turned out to be.

She'd have to leave Timberline unless she wanted another experience like tonight's. She didn't think for one minute the encounter in her driveway was a random incident.

Give me the money, bitch.

That could mean only one thing. Johnny Diamond's business partners somehow knew she'd lifted some cash from the duffel bag. But how? The police had those bags—the cash and the drugs. How would Johnny's associates know about the missing money? That wasn't the type of information the authorities would release. Had the accounts of Johnny's murder mentioned drugs or money at all? Must've mentioned drugs, because everyone knew he was a drug dealer.

She sucked in her bottom lip and chewed it. Maybe Johnny's cohorts believed she'd taken all the money. That could be bad—really bad.

And how did these guys even know who she was or what she looked like? *Rocky.* Rocky, the kidnapper of little children, somehow knew who she was.

Her stomach rolled with nausea. She had to get out of here.

The emergency room doors swung open and Chloe from Sutter's and her boyfriend, Jason, came into the waiting room. Jason was holding up a bloodied and broken hand.

Caroline clutched the arms of the chair. Had he done that on Chloe's face? Caroline shifted her gaze to Chloe, who gave her a half smile and a shrug. "Boys being boys."

Whatever that meant, but at least Chloe didn't show any signs of abuse. Maybe Jason had hit the wall in anger—better than hitting Chloe.

The doors to the examination rooms swung open and the doc on duty strode across the waiting room, never looking up from his clipboard. "Ms. Johnson?"

She shot out of the plastic chair and Cole jumped up beside her. "I'm Caroline Johnson."

"You're—" he flipped a page over on his clipboard "—the cousin. Ms. Gunderson is going to be fine. She was dehydrated, weak and extremely intoxicated. We're getting some fluids into her right now and she's resting. Because of her age, we're keeping her overnight."

Caroline sighed and caught Cole's arm. "She's going to be okay?"

"She'll be fine, but I've warned her to lay off the booze

in the future. Her body can't handle it. She wants to see you, but don't tire her out. She'll be released tomorrow."

"Thank you, Dr...?"

He nodded once, dropped the clipboard at the front desk and shouted out a few orders before disappearing behind the swinging doors.

The nurse at reception rolled her eyes. "That's Dr. Nesbitt—busy man. Stella will take you back to see Linda."

"Thanks." Caroline tugged on the hem of Cole's jacket. "Do you want to go back with me?"

"I'm sure Linda doesn't want me there when she's not feeling well. Give her my best, and I'll be waiting here for you."

"Thanks, Cole. I won't be long. The charming Dr. Nesbitt said she needed her rest."

One corner of his mouth lifted. "I never got to eat my dinner tonight. I'm going to get a candy bar from the vending machine. Take your time."

Caroline pushed open one of the doors and a nurse in a pink lab coat met her with a big smile. "I'm Stella. Follow me."

Caroline followed Stella's comforting pink form down a hallway past a few curtained off areas until she stopped at an open door. She tapped. "Linda, Caroline's here to see you."

Linda was so white, she practically blended in with the sheets, and Caroline rushed to her bedside. "Are you feeling better? I was scared to death, but Dr. Nesbitt said you're going to be okay."

Linda looked at her with a pair of watery eyes and a deep furrow between her eyebrows. "I felt like I was going to die."

"I'm so sorry." Caroline took her clammy hand in hers. "I should've never left you in that condition."

"How could you know I'd react that way?" She covered her eyes with her free hand, which was trembling. "It was so foolish. I'm glad Louise wasn't here to witness it."

"We all do foolish things." Caroline smoothed the crisp sheet over Linda's thigh. "Are you comfortable here? They're keeping you overnight. Do you want me to bring you anything?"

"N-no. I'll try to get some sleep." Linda glanced over Caroline's shoulder at the open door and dropped her voice to a whisper. "Did that young doctor say anything about what caused my illness?"

Caroline began to organize the items on the small tray next to the bed. "You drank too much wine, Linda, became ill and then got dehydrated."

"Oh." Linda sank back against her pillow. "Would you believe me if I told you that's never happened to me before, Caroline?"

"Of course. Sometimes things hit us funny." She drew her eyebrows together. "What are you driving at?"

"I felt ill, really, really ill. It hit me before I even left the restaurant." Linda put her hand over her mouth and murmured, "I don't even remember leaving the restaurant. I didn't make a scene, did I?"

"Not at all." She patted the older woman's hand. "I guided you out of there and nobody noticed a thing."

"I'm not trying to make excuses, but I wonder if I had a touch of food poisoning."

"Really? Maybe that's why you didn't finish your meal. But doesn't it usually take a few hours before the symptoms of food poisoning appear? It doesn't happen immediately, does it?"

"I don't know, but something didn't feel right."

"I can check with Sutter's tomorrow to find out if there were any other complaints."

"Would you?" Linda clutched her hand in a weak grip. "I'm so glad I had you to call on, Caroline. You more than paid me back for any assistance I've given you since you came to Timberline. You'll stay for a while, won't you? You've truly become like a daughter to me."

Tears stung Caroline's nose. How could she tell her she was ready to hightail it out of town? "I'll stay until Louise comes back, at least."

"Is that all?" The corners of Linda's mouth drooped. "You're welcome to start over here. We'd love to have you."

"You know what?" Caroline pulled the sheets up to Linda's chin. "You're tired. Get some rest, and I'll be back to pick you up tomorrow when they spring you from this joint."

Linda gave her a weak smile. "And Cole?"

Caroline snapped her fingers. "I almost forgot. Here I am, basking in your gratitude, and you owe your life to Cole. He was with me when you called, and he came over to help out. He cleared your air passages while we were waiting for the EMTs."

A hot red blush flooded Linda's pale cheeks. "Oh, for Cole to see me like that. I'm mortified."

Caroline laughed. "You have such a crush on that man. He was so relieved he could be there to help, and he sends his best wishes."

A small smile settled on Linda's lips and her eyes fluttered closed.

Caroline squeezed her hands and whispered, "Sweet dreams."

She tiptoed from the room and thanked Stella in the hallway. Blowing out a breath, she pushed through the double doors to the waiting room. "You're right. She would've been *mortified*, her words, if you'd gone back there and seen her bedridden."

"She's doing okay?"

"She's fine, embarrassed and…"

"And what?" Cole steered her toward his rental car and hit the key fob.

Caroline leaned against the passenger door, crossing her arms. "She said her reaction to the wine was uncharacteristic for her."

"I'd hope so."

"Said she'd never felt that way before and thought it might even have been food poisoning."

"Really?" Cole tossed his keys in the air and caught them in his palm. "Did Dr. Speedy in there run any kind of tests on her?"

"I—I don't know. What kind of tests?" Caroline dug her fingers into her biceps.

"Toxicology."

"Toxicology?" A chill had crept across her flesh, and she hunched her shoulders. Didn't toxicology tests reveal poisons in the system? She didn't want to have that discussion with Cole.

"I don't think so." She yanked open the car door and practically dived inside. "It's cold out here."

By the time Cole got around to the driver's side and cranked on the engine and the heat, he seemed to have forgotten about toxicology tests.

"Are you still heading out of town?"

"I want to, but I can't leave Linda to fend for herself right now. Maybe once she recovers, I'll think about it."

"You should. If your assailant in the driveway was here on your husband's behalf and wasn't a random robber, then your hiding place has been compromised." Cole held one hand out to the side. "And that's all I'm going to say on that subject."

For a brief time she'd forgotten about the man demanding money. Her previous questions lingered. How did they know about the missing money? How did they know where to find her? How did they know who she was?

Could the man have been someone who followed her and Linda from Sutter's, thinking they were both drunk and easy targets?

What about the man with the shaved head? Caroline braced her forehead against the cold glass of the window and went cross-eyed watching the dribbles of water on the pane.

Cross-eyed—that's how she felt right now. She didn't know what direction was up.

"You've had quite a day. Are you going to be okay?"

"Do you care?" She sealed her lips. Why did she feel compelled to goad him? It bugged her that he thought poorly of her, but she couldn't control that as long as she continued to lie to him about her situation. She had to pay that price, but it was getting to be an awfully high price to pay.

He let her question hang in the air between them until he pulled into the driveway of the duplex next to Linda's car.

As she reached for the door handle, he said, "I want you to be okay, Caroline, despite everything…even though I might be a damned fool." He leaned across the console, slipped his hand behind her head and kissed her hard on the mouth.

When he released her, breathless, lips throbbing, he said, "Just call me a damned fool."

She scrambled from his car and hurried to her front door, one hand pressed against her hot cheek.

If he was a damned fool for kissing her, what did that make her for liking it?

THE FOLLOWING MORNING, Caroline called the hospital to find out how Linda was doing and what time she'd be released. They wanted to hold her for the morning, so Caroline decided to pay a visit to Rebecca Geist, the Realtor the bald guy had talked to at the bar.

She drove Linda's car to Rebecca's office with the memory of Cole's kiss on her lips. They seemed drawn to each other even though they both sensed the danger that such an attraction presented. Caroline understood the danger from him and he only sensed it from her, but it didn't seem to matter. If she could spar with and play cat and mouse with Cole all day, she'd be one happy cat… or mouse. She never knew who was who and which was which. They were both a little bit cat and a little bit mouse.

And she was a little bit crazy to even go near the DEA agent investigating the murder of Johnny Diamond.

She parked in front of the Realtor's office and wandered inside as if she were actually interested in buying a place in Timberline.

Rebecca was chattering away on the phone a mile a minute and waved as Caroline walked through the door.

As the conversation continued, Caroline thumbed through some listings and got herself a cup of water from the dispenser.

Rebecca finally ended the call and stood up, straightening her slim skirt. "Sorry about that. I'm Rebecca Geist."

Caroline crossed the room and shook the woman's hand, fighting off a grimace at her firm grip. "Caroline Johnson."

Rebecca leveled a long, coral-tipped fingernail at her. "Linda Gunderson's niece, right?"

"Cousin, second cousin."

"That's right. Are you looking to stay here in Timberline? Get your own place? That's a sweet little piece of property the Gunderson sisters own, that duplex at the end of Main Street. It's a great location. I know neither of those ladies has children. Is that going to be yours one day?"

Caroline swallowed. So Cole wasn't the only one who

thought she'd come to town to wiggle her way into an inheritance. Did everyone else believe that? She rolled her shoulders. Would she rather they believe she'd come here straight from a motel room containing the dead body of a drug dealer?

She shrugged. "Not that I know of. That's why I'm here. I'd like to get an idea of available properties and the pricing."

"There aren't a whole lot of residential properties on the market right now." Rebecca tapped her long fingernails against the blotter. "There's that one cabin with the dead body."

The pen Caroline had been toying with flipped out of her fingers. "A dead body?"

"Turns out one of the town hotshots murdered his mistress years ago and stuffed her body in the chimney of a cabin he owned."

"I wouldn't be interested in that." Caroline crouched down to pick up the pen and press her hand against her galloping heart for a second or two.

"I think that's the only cabin available right now. The Kennedy cabin is vacant and will be going on the market soon, but the owner left town for a while."

Rebecca pulled a binder from the bookshelf next to her desk and shuffled through a few plastic-coated pages. "There are some big houses for sale, close to Evergreen Software, but those are more for families and Evergreen employees. Would you be interested in looking at one of those? Three thousand square feet minimum with at least four bedrooms and two bathrooms."

"That's huge. No, I was more interested in one of the cabins." Caroline ran her fingertip along one of the flyers for the big Evergreen Development homes. Maybe the guy with the shaved head was looking at one of these. He did mention a daughter. Or was that a lie?

She closed the binder. "Do you have many people looking at those right now?"

"Not many. Evergreen's still doing well, but they're currently in a hiring freeze."

This trip had been a bust. She was no closer to learning the identity of the bald man than when she'd walked through the door. "Well, thanks for your time."

"My pleasure." Rebecca held out her business card between two fingers. "Let me know if you have any more questions."

Caroline took the card and slipped it into her purse. She turned toward the door and took a few steps before stopping and taking a deep breath. "I think I saw you at Sutter's last night."

"That was me, picking up some food. My fiancé lives in New York, so I do that a lot. Work late, eat at my desk."

"You were talking to a man at the bar." Caroline turned slightly to the side. "Shaved head, thirtyish. He looked familiar."

"Oh?" Rebecca's eyebrows snapped together. "You didn't grow up here, did you? Your cousins aren't true locals."

Did Rebecca look annoyed? "No. This is actually my first visit to Timberline."

"He's just an out-of-town client. Unless you're from Connecticut, I doubt you know him."

"I guess not." Caroline waved. "Thanks again."

When she got to Linda's car, she sat in the driver's seat, hands on the wheel, staring straight ahead. There had been something odd about Rebecca's response. Caroline could understand wanting to protect the confidentiality of a client, but buying real estate wasn't the same as getting cosmetic surgery.

And why had Rebecca asked her about being a local?

Had she been implying her client was a local? Couldn't be a local from Connecticut.

Leaning forward, Caroline bumped her forehead against the steering wheel. This man had just become a distraction from all her other problems.

A man had pulled a knife on her last night, demanding money, and she didn't know if the encounter was related to Diamond or not. Linda had fallen ill and needed her, even though she wanted to leave. And Cole had kissed her—after admitting he didn't trust her any more than he'd trusted his cheating wife.

She'd better watch her back while she stayed in Timberline caring for Linda, and she'd better watch her heart around Cole Pierson.

Her phone buzzed and she grabbed it from the console, checking the display. "Hello, Dr. Shipman."

"Hi, Caroline. Have any more memories come to you since our previous session?"

"I did sort of spontaneously say I liked the dry heat of the desert. I'm not sure if that was just the power of suggestion from the hypnosis or a true memory from my past."

"Interesting. Did it feel real?"

"It did, yes."

"The reason I'm calling is because I need to go out of town the day after tomorrow, and I didn't want to cancel our appointment without giving you a chance to reschedule earlier. Tomorrow is usually a day off for me, but I'm trying to schedule some make-up appointments. Can you make it tomorrow in the morning or later in the afternoon around five o'clock?"

Linda's friends had already told her they were swooping in tomorrow to bring Linda some dinner and play some cards. "Five o'clock would work."

"Great. I'll see you then."

Caroline dropped the phone in the cup holder and started the engine. She couldn't wait to dig into her past once again with Dr. Shipman, but first she needed to take care of some business in the present, and that meant collecting Linda from the hospital and putting her crazy investigation of the man with the shaved head on hold.

By the time she arrived at the hospital, she'd convinced herself that the attack last night was a random act, the guy with the shaved head was really just here on business and that she'd have her life back after just one more session with Dr. Shipman.

And that she'd allow Cole to kiss her once more before he left town.

Linda didn't seem to share her optimistic outlook this morning, as she was sitting on the edge of the bed with her head down and her hands clasped between her knees.

"Ready to blow this joint? Had enough of Jell-O and daytime TV?"

"Yes, get me out of here."

Caroline crouched in front of Linda. "Are you okay? You seem…down."

"I'm fine, Caroline. Let's go."

"Do I need to talk to Dr. Nesbitt?"

"He's not even here. I've signed all their forms and turned over all my insurance information." She held out a handful of papers to Caroline. "I'm supposed to stay hydrated and rest."

"Then let's get you hydrated and resting."

The nurses insisted Linda leave in a wheelchair, so Caroline pushed her into the waiting room. When they got through the doors, Stella, the nurse from last night, called after them. "Caroline? I have a prescription for Linda at the desk."

"Okay." She squeezed Linda's shoulder. "I'll be right back."

When she got to the front desk, Stella hunched forward, sliding the prescription across the counter. "Just a heads-up. Linda's feeling a little out of sorts. Maybe it's just embarrassment."

"Thanks." Caroline shoved the prescription in her back pocket and returned to Linda. "I parked close. Do you want to walk or wheelchair it all the way?"

"I can walk."

She pushed the wheelchair outside and tried to help Linda to her feet, although the older woman brushed off her helping hand.

Stella wasn't kidding. Caroline had never seen Linda in a bad mood or even mildly upset before.

She opened the car door for her, settled her and then hopped into the driver's seat. When she'd shut her own door, she asked, "Do you want to tell me what's wrong?"

"You'll just think I'm crazy, like all the rest of them in there."

"I swear I won't."

"I think I was poisoned last night."

Chapter Ten

A rash of goose bumps raced across Caroline's arms. "What?"

"Last night. I don't think I had that much wine. I was ill, sick. I was poisoned."

"You mean like food poisoning? Did you ask Dr. Nesbitt how long that would take to hit you?"

"Dr. Nesbitt, that young fool."

"What does that even mean, Linda? Are you talking about food poisoning?"

"I'm talking about poisoning poisoning. I think someone poisoned my food or wine last night."

Caroline hung on to the steering wheel as her mind spun out of control. Poison. More poison? Was someone out there trying to frame her? What were the odds that two people she'd been hanging out with had both ingested poison?

Could she be some kind of whacked-out person who poisoned other people and then blacked out? Caroline pinched the bridge of her nose, squeezing her eyes shut. She hadn't blacked out last night.

Could someone have poisoned the wine, thinking she'd be the one drinking it? Had the poison been meant for her and not Linda?

Wait. What poison? This was all speculation on Linda's part.

"Did the hospital run any tests for that? Any toxicology tests?" Cole had suggested that last night. If he found out about Linda's suspicions, would he tie Caroline to Johnny Diamond again?

"The hospital and that quack doctor didn't believe me. I saw them snickering behind their hands. The old broad couldn't handle her booze and is making excuses."

"I'm sure they weren't thinking that."

"And I'm sure they were." Linda adjusted her seat belt and closed her eyes. "Just take me home."

Wrinkling her nose and checking the rearview mirror, Caroline started the car and pulled out of the hospital parking lot. "Linda?"

"Yes?"

"Why would someone try to poison you?"

"Why would someone break into your house?"

The steering wheel slipped out of her hands. "I—I don't think anyone did. I was overreacting that night. Do you think the poison was meant for me? Is that what you're trying to say?"

"Is he after you, Caroline? Is your husband stalking you?"

She hunched over the steering wheel and squinted at the road. How should she respond to that? As far as she knew, she had no husband. But someone could very well be stalking her, chasing after her for the money she stole from Johnny.

Maybe the cops had put out the word that empty bags were found with Johnny's body and they suspected that the bags had contained drugs and money. Maybe the cops, the DEA, wanted Johnny's associates to come after her and do their work for them. Maybe Cole was here to sweep up the refuse.

Caroline dragged in a shuddering breath and blew it out. "I don't think so, Linda, but you're right. My presence here is putting you in danger. Once I get you settled, I'll be on my way."

Linda sniffled and dabbed her nose with a tissue. "I didn't mean it like that, dear. I'm worried about you."

"And I'm worried about you. Do you want to take your suspicions to the sheriff's department? I can't believe the hospital just ignored you."

"Oh, you know doctors. They always think they know best, and I'm not setting myself up for the same type of ridicule from those fresh-faced sheriffs, either."

"Should I talk to the bartenders last night, or Chloe, to see if they noticed anyone suspicious hanging around?" Rebecca's mysterious client had been at the bar last night. Did he have an opportunity to put something in the wine?

Caroline's head throbbed with all the possibilities and scenarios—none of them good. She wished her appointment with Dr. Shipman was this afternoon. She couldn't stand to be in the dark one more night.

"I've gone and worried you, haven't I? I should've kept my mouth shut. I didn't mean to say anything to you at all, but those doctors made me so mad."

"I'm sorry if you've been swept up in any of my craziness. You've been nothing but kind to me, but I really think I've worn out my welcome." Caroline held up her hand as Linda started to interrupt. "I have an appointment with Dr. Shipman tomorrow. I'm going to ask her for a referral to a therapist in a big city somewhere, and I'm going to take myself and my problems out of your hair."

"Caroline, I never meant to drive you off with my silliness."

"Poisoning isn't silliness."

"I'm not even sure that's what happened. I'm probably just an old fool who drank too much wine."

"I've been thinking about leaving, anyway. I can't stay here. It was always a temporary solution."

"And Cole?"

Heat surged to her cheeks. "What about Cole? I told you I wasn't ready for a romantic relationship."

"I know. It's such a shame you two couldn't have met at another time, in another place. He's a catch."

Another time and place? She had no other time and no other place. She had no past, no family, no life. The truth of it all punched her in the gut, and she could dissolve into a flood of tears right now if she weren't driving Linda home.

She'd never allowed herself a good cry. Maybe she just wasn't the crying type, but then what type was she? She didn't have a clue.

What had happened to all the hope and optimism she'd felt on her way to the hospital? If someone had really tried to poison her and mistakenly poisoned Linda instead, she was in big trouble. Maybe the man in the driveway was expecting an easier time of it with a drugged-out victim. She had to get away.

When they got to the duplex, Caroline helped Linda wash up and change clothes. Then she led her to her favorite chair. "Tea, water, glass of wine?"

Linda chuckled. "If you're here when Louise gets back, and I hope you are, please don't tell her about this. She can be insufferably self-righteous."

"Not a word from me." Caroline ran her fingertip over the seam of her lips. "How about that tea?"

"I'd love some if you'll join me. What did you do this morning before you picked me up?"

Caroline called over her shoulder as she filled the tea kettle with water. "I cleaned up my place and went to the library."

The lie came easily to her lips, but she didn't want to worry Linda about her obsession with the man from Connecticut.

"You didn't see Cole?"

"Not this morning." She ran her tongue along her bottom lip. Not that she hadn't been thinking about him and that kiss all day.

"Well, he's here now."

She dropped the kettle onto the burner. "Here?"

"He just drove up."

He tapped on Linda's door seconds later, and Caroline wiped her hands on a dish towel and answered the door.

"Linda home safely?"

"She is." She swung open the door. "See for yourself."

"Feeling better, beautiful?" Cole swept a bouquet of flowers from behind his back, and Linda clapped her hands together.

"They're lovely."

Cole knelt before her and held out the flowers for her to smell. "You look much better. How'd they treat you?"

Caroline hovered over Cole's back, holding her breath. If Linda told him about her suspicions, he might start looking at her again. She couldn't afford to have Cole prying into her past.

"Just fine. I feel better." Linda touched the petal of a pink rose. "Caroline, could you please put these in a vase for me? There's one in the cabinet beside the dining table."

"Of course." She held out a hand that was not altogether steady to take the flowers from Cole. "Do you want a cup of tea?"

Shaking his head, he perched on the arm of Linda's chair.

As she arranged the flowers in a vase, Linda and Cole exchanged small talk, but she didn't once hear the word *poison.*

Then Linda raised her voice. "Did Caroline tell you she's thinking of leaving town?"

The teakettle's piercing whistle interrupted Cole's response. Why did Linda have to keep up her matchmaking efforts? Caroline poured the boiling water over tea bags in the cups and carried them into the other room.

"I mentioned it to Cole last night," she said.

"I'm not sure small-town life suits Caroline." Cole raised his eyebrows at her, and she felt like sinking into bed and pulling the covers over her head.

There were so many lies swirling among the three of them right now, she couldn't keep them straight.

She sat down, cupping her warm mug. "Visiting family in Timberline has been a welcome respite, but I really need to start thinking about my future."

"And what does the future look like for Caroline... Johnson?"

Swallowing, she rolled her lips inward. Did he doubt her name now?

"One thing it includes is continued therapy, which I think is a wonderful plan." Linda blew on the surface of her tea and took a sip.

"I think it's a good plan, too. I saw a therapist a few times after my divorce, and it helped me," Cole admitted.

"Caroline has one more appointment with Dr. Shipman tomorrow before she leaves." Linda's gaze slid from Caroline's face to his. "In fact, I was wondering if you could take her to the appointment."

Caroline rolled her eyes at Cole and shook her head. "I thought I was going to borrow your car, Linda. You'll be having dinner with your girlfriends, right?"

"Yes, but your appointment is late and by the time you finish and drive back here, it'll be dark. I just don't think it's a wise idea for you to be on your own right now, Caroline, especially after a therapy appointment."

"It's therapy, not surgery. Besides, Cole probably doesn't want to drive me. I'll be fine."

"I have no problem driving you, and I happen to agree

with Linda. Consider it a date." He leaned over and kissed Linda's cheek. "Now I have to get going. I have some research to do this afternoon."

"I'll walk you out to your car," Caroline said.

"Thank you for the flowers, Cole."

Caroline walked with him to the front door, her hand on his back, her knuckle drilling into his spine.

When they stepped onto the porch, he broke away. "Ouch. Why are you hustling me out of the house?"

Grabbing his hand, she dragged him into the driveway. "I thought you were going to say something about the man with the knife. I don't want Linda to know about that. She's had enough upset."

"Oh, is that why you don't want to tell her? You haven't reported it to the cops yet, either, have you?"

"No, and I'm not going to, which is a good thing for you, Mr. Rogue DEA Agent. What are you even doing here? What are you looking for?"

"You have your secrets, I have mine. I'm not going to tell you my business, but I will give you a ride tomorrow. You have someone running around town pulling knives on you, you haven't reported him to the police and you're going to drive off to Port Angeles by yourself? You're either brave, a martial arts expert or you know more about the knife attack than you're saying, which is no surprise. You know a lot more about a lot of things than you're saying."

She tossed her head, shaking her hair out of her face. "I will accept your ride, but I will not be cross-examined. Linda is still hoping for some kind of happily-ever-after for us."

"Ain't gonna happen." He snorted.

"You got that right." Somehow Caroline's gaze had dropped from his incredible green eyes to his incredible lips, and the sneer she'd planned for her own lips had softened into a pout.

He moved a step closer to her and she leaned in like a magnet. Cupping her face with one large hand, he possessed her mouth with a kiss so hot the drops of rain that had started falling sizzled on her skin.

He deepened his kiss and they stood locked together as the heavens opened above them. Without missing a beat, Cole flipped up the hood of his jacket and pulled it over both their heads.

She pulled away first, only because she'd lost feeling in the hands that had been gripping the sides of his jacket.

Resting his forehead against hers, nose to nose, he whispered, "No happily-ever-after here."

She tipped her head back, letting the rain course down her face, mingling with her tears. "Not for us."

As he reached for her again, she spun around and ran back to Linda's house. She slammed the front door behind her and leaned against it, panting.

"What took you so long? What were you doing out in the rain?"

"Saying goodbye."

CAROLINE STAYED INDOORS the following day. She spent most of her time at Linda's, watching TV, making sure Linda was drinking lots of fluids, and trying not to think about Cole. She'd offered to open the store today, but Linda preferred her company here.

The afternoon rolled around quickly, and she went home to get ready for her appointment. She returned to Linda's with a coupon for the local pizza place. She waved it in the air. "You ladies are ordering pizza tonight, right? This coupon will get you a discount. It was with an advertisement on my doorknob."

"Leave it by the telephone." Linda sat up from where

she'd been reclining on the sofa. "I'm feeling so much better now, and I want you to forget about what I said about being poisoned. I drank too much and got sick. End of story."

"That still doesn't change the fact that I need to be on my way. I need to start making some plans."

"You could do that here in Timberline."

"I don't think so." She sat next to Linda and took her hand. "While this place has felt like home, due mostly to your hospitality, there's something about it that's hostile. I feel the undercurrent."

"I understand. It's beautiful country, but the rain and the brooding forest aren't for everyone." The older woman squeezed Caroline's fingers. "Just take care of yourself wherever you land. Do not go back to Larry no matter what he promises, and drop me a line to let me know you're okay."

"You're wonderful." She blinked back a few tears. If her family had been anything like Linda Gunderson, she probably wouldn't be in this mess right now. What had she been running from? What brought her into Johnny Diamond's sphere?

She heard tires in the driveway and jumped up. "I'm going to run out there so Cole doesn't have to go into the rain, because you know he'll come right up to the door to get me."

"That's because he's a gentleman. And I know it won't be Cole you wind up with, but next time it should be someone like him."

"It will. I promise." She blew Linda a kiss before dashing down the driveway as Cole opened the car door.

She burst in the passenger side and shut the door on the rain. "You don't need to go out in that stuff."

"I think the storm is finally moving through. It might actually clear up by the time we get to Port Angeles."

"Are you going to do more *research* there, or what?"

"I have a few sources to check, but I'm getting to the end of the line. I didn't discover what I'd hoped to discover, and I actually want to take a real vacation for a week or so before I get back to work."

"Hawaii? Caribbean?"

"Nothing that exotic. I'm going to visit my sister and her family. They live in San Diego, too, but I'm not always in town."

"I'm sure it will be more relaxing than this."

"Yeah, I'm not one for relaxing."

"Since you're working on your time off, I guess not."

"Do you know where you're headed?" He held up one finger. "I'm not giving you the third degree."

"I think I'm going to get lost in a big city. I don't think small-town life is for me."

"Probably not. Everyone wants to know your business."

They switched to less loaded topics on the rest of the drive, and she discovered Cole played bass in an oldies cover band and had gone to college on a swimming scholarship.

His face lit up as he told her his stories, and she ached to tell him stories of her own, but she had nothing. Just a blank slate.

Laughing at Cole's account of a drunk at a bar trying to sing onstage with his band, she turned her head to look out the window. As they passed the Quileute reservation, an electric jolt seemed to pass through her body and she grabbed the edges of her seat.

"Something wrong?"

"I don't know." She massaged her temples. "It's like I just had a rush of adrenaline."

"Probably stress, that whole fight-or-flight thing. You probably need to release some steam, exercise. When I get that way, I need to hit the pool and do some laps. What do you like to do, run? You look like a runner."

"I am—long distances." Her heart tripped over itself. Where had that come from? It was the truth. She felt it. She was a runner. Maybe that had just come from seeing running clothes—shoes and shorts—in the suitcase from her former life. But it felt right. Just like the desert had felt right.

She repeated with a firm voice, "Yes, I'm a runner."

"I hate running, unless I'm chasing a suspect. Then I can get into it."

She liked to run, she preferred the desert and the Quileute reservation had given her a shock. She tapped on the glass of the window. "Did you mention that the man who kidnapped those children all those years ago was from the Quileute tribe?"

"Rocky Whitecotton? Yeah, although the tribe had pretty much disowned him even before they discovered he was behind the kidnappings. He didn't actually kidnap those kids himself. He had members of the Lords of Chaos do his dirty work." Cole shot her a sideways glance. "Why do you ask?"

"I saw the sign for the reservation back there. It reminded me of that guy."

"A real weirdo from what I've read."

"Do you think he killed those kids?"

Cole's jaw tightened and she remembered he liked kids. "Probably. No trace of them has ever been found."

She nodded and then started humming to the song on the radio. Why would Rocky Whitecotton be upset with Johnny Diamond for not finding her? What did she have to do with this whole drug trade?

Caroline felt primed for her session with Dr. Shipman and couldn't wait to get into that office.

She and Cole exchanged more small talk until they reached the coast and Port Angeles.

He pulled up to the curb in front of the office building. "An hour?"

"That should do it. I'll be out front at six."

"I'll be here. Have a good session."

As she opened the car door, a gust of wind snatched it from her grasp, flinging it open. "Sorry. I guess we have the wind to thank for blowing the clouds away, though."

Ducking her head against the strong breeze, she ran toward the low-slung stucco building. She grabbed the handle of Dr. Shipman's door and pulled it open, careful to keep a grip on it as the wind blasted through the open spaces of the office building.

She clicked it behind her and smoothed her hair back. The door to Dr. Shipman's office remained firmly closed, so Caroline pushed the button on the wall to indicate her presence.

She picked up a magazine and thumbed through it while bracing her shoulder against one wall. A few pages later, when Dr. Shipman still hadn't opened her door, Caroline checked the time on her phone—five after five.

She was probably with another patient. Caroline dropped the magazine and glanced at her phone again. Should she text Cole and let him know she'd be running late?

She doubted he even had business in Port Angeles. He seemed ready to wrap up his fruitless investigation—fruitless because he'd located his quarry but hadn't realized it.

She tapped her toe as another ten minutes passed. Should she knock? Maybe another patient was having a breakthrough—or a breakdown. She took out her phone again and called Dr. Shipman.

Her phone rang twice and rolled over to voice mail. Jules must've turned it off for a session.

Caroline crept up to the inner-office door and pressed her ear against the solid wood, her hand falling to the doorknob. No voices murmured in the space beyond.

Had Dr. Shipman forgotten about the session? Caroline rapped lightly on the door and held her breath. She tried again. "Dr. Shipman? Jules?"

She flattened her palms against the door and licked her lips as a puff of fear lifted the hair on the back of her neck. It came out of nowhere, perhaps originating with the dead silence from the office.

Her fingers curled around the door handle again. This time she twisted—and it turned.

She bumped the door with her hip, opening it a crack. "Jules?"

The low light of the office indicated Dr. Shipman had been in session. Caroline eased the door open farther. The hushed atmosphere of the empty room repelled her and she recoiled.

Then a piece of paper caught her attention—and the single white square on the floor sent her pulse racing. She'd been in this office only once, but that had been enough to tell her that Dr. Shipman was precise and orderly. Why would she leave a piece of paper on the floor unless she'd departed in a hurry?

Caroline squared her shoulders and strode into the room. The air closed in around her, heavy and dank. She choked on a metallic odor that filled her nose and mouth.

She couldn't stop herself. She wanted to, but her legs wouldn't listen to her screaming brain. Crossing to the desk, her feet sank into the carpet with a slow, methodical pace.

She peered around the edge of the solid piece of furniture, her gaze tracking from the single low-heeled pump on its side to the dark, wet stain on the carpet, to Dr. Shipman's blank stare.

And then the memories hit her.

Chapter Eleven

The wind picked up the leaves on the walkway and stirred them into a mini tornado. Digging his elbows into his knees, Cole balanced his chin on his clasped hands.

If Caroline wasn't running some kind of scam, why didn't she trust him enough to tell him what was going on with her? Maybe he could even help.

For everything he'd learned from his sister about letting his sensitive side show with women, he must be failing miserably. Caroline was as secretive now as the day he'd met her in the library. Of course, that had been only a few days ago, even though it seemed as if he'd known her a lot longer.

He sat back and took a sip of his coffee. He didn't have any investigating to do in Port Angeles, and Caroline had probably already figured that out. So, after he picked up a coffee, he decided to wait for her on a bench outside the office, even though he'd be sitting here for another forty minutes.

A low wail started somewhere in the building before he heard a door crash open. He jumped up from the cement bench in time to see Caroline flying out one of the offices, her mouth open as she struggled with a scream.

The scream finally won, and the high-pitched sound sent a river of chills down his spine. He rushed toward her, and she blindly fought him off, scratching and kicking, until her wide blue eyes locked on to his and she collapsed against his chest.

"My God. What happened? What happened in there?" He started to move toward the open door, becoming aware of a few people poking their heads outside, but Caroline hung on to him, dragging him away.

"Caroline, what's wrong?"

"She's dead. Dr. Shipman is dead. Someone slit her throat."

A spike of adrenaline shot through him. "Are you sure?"

"I don't know. I don't know. Don't make me go back."

A man hung over the iron railing on the second floor of the building and called down, "Should I phone 911?"

"Yes." Cole glanced at Caroline. "Possible dead body."

Caroline sobbed and sagged against his chest. He stroked her soft hair. "Can you wait here? I want to take a look myself."

She grabbed his shirt. "Do you think I don't know what a dead body looks like? I know."

A few other tenants from the building gathered outside, and a woman spoke up. "Is it Dr. Shipman?"

"Yes, did you see anything? Hear anything?" Cole asked.

The woman called back, "I didn't see or hear a thing. I didn't hear any gunfire. Was there gunfire?"

Cole led Caroline to the bench he'd just vacated in a hurry and urged her to sit. Crouching in front of her and taking her hands, he said, "Can you wait here while I have a look?"

"I'll stay with her." The woman who had spoken before turned and locked her office door. "The police should be here any minute."

"Is that okay with you?" He touched Caroline's pale

cheek and she nodded, her eyes still seeing something far, far away.

Cole lunged to his feet and walked up to the yawning door of Dr. Shipman's office. He crept into the outer office, where nothing seemed out of place, and proceeded to the open door of the inner office.

He poked his head in first and sniffed, detecting the odor of blood. She must've lost a lot to have the smell permeate the air.

Keeping his hands to himself, he crept farther into the office, noting a piece of paper on the floor, but nothing else amiss. When he got to the heavy oak desk, he peered over the top.

A woman, presumably Dr. Shipman, lay sprawled on the floor, one arm out to her side, the other flung across her waist. She'd probably been dead or well on her way by the time she hit the floor.

A gash marred the slim column of her throat, and blood soaked the gray carpet beneath her head and neck. Cole scanned the floor for the murder weapon, but just that single piece of paper stood out.

The items on her desk were well-ordered and upright. Dr. Shipman had been caught off guard, with no time to put up a fight. His gaze swept the area and he detected small specks of blood on the door behind the desk. It must be spray from the initial cut, when the knife sliced through her artery.

The killer hadn't escaped that shower of blood, even standing behind Dr. Shipman, which he must've been doing. He never would've been able to stroll out the front of the office.

Cole pinned his gaze on the back door, which must lead to a parking lot or alley. The perp had probably sneaked out through there.

The sirens rolling up outside disturbed Cole's concentration, and he closed his eyes and took a deep breath. Why would someone want to kill Caroline's therapist? He had no doubt in his mind that Dr. Shipman's death was related to the craziness swirling around Caroline.

He heard voices at the office door. "Hello? This is the police. Come out with your hands up."

He turned away from the body and walked into the waiting room with his hands held clearly in front of him. "I'm Cole Pierson, a friend of the woman who found the body. I'm also a DEA agent."

The Port Angeles police officer leading the charge kept his weapon aloft. "Anyone else in there?"

"Just the dead body—Dr. Shipman, throat slashed."

The other officer stepped around his partner. "Do you have some ID?"

Cole spread apart his fingers. "In the right inside pocket of my jacket. My weapon's in my left jacket pocket."

The cop responded, "Let's see your identification."

Cole carefully pulled out his DEA badge and handed it over.

The officer glanced at it and holstered his gun. "Were you with Ms. Johnson when she found the body?"

"No, I was waiting outside to pick her up, when she left the office, screaming."

"Why'd you come inside?"

The other police officer had started moving toward the inner office.

"I just wanted to see if Dr. Shipman needed assistance."

"Did she?"

"Already dead, throat slit." Cole slid his badge back into his pocket. "I didn't touch anything in here, but my friend may have."

"We have two homicide detectives from Clallam County on the way, so we'll let them do the heavy lifting. We're here to secure the crime scene."

Cole backed out of the office. "I'll let you get to work. There's a back door in that office. The killer probably made his way out through that door."

When he stepped outside, Cole gulped in buckets of fresh air and headed toward Caroline, still on the bench with an officer talking to her.

She glanced up at his approach, her eyes glassy and vacant.

He caught the tail end of their conversation. "I—I don't have any ID. I lost my wallet on the way to Timberline. I haven't had time to replace my driver's license…or anything else."

Cole flipped his badge open for the officer. "Is there a problem?"

Eyeing Cole's badge, the cop said, "I asked Ms. Johnson for her driver's license or ID, and she doesn't have any."

"Yeah, she lost her wallet last week." Cole avoided the wide-eyed stare Caroline turned on him.

The officer frowned and tapped his pencil. "Can you vouch for her?"

"Sure."

"I'll need your cell phone number, Ms. Johnson. We're going to have to verify your identity."

She gave him the number and he wrote it down. "Do not leave the area. You're a witness, and like I said, we're going to have to verify your identity. Thanks to Agent Pierson, I'm not taking you in now to fingerprint you, but you'll have to come to the station tomorrow for an interview and we'll do it then."

"Okay, thank you. I'll be there."

"That's all I have, but the homicide detectives from county will want to question you when they arrive."

"All right, but I told you everything I know. I had an appointment with Dr. Shipman, buzzed her when I walked in, called her and then listened at her door. When I didn't

hear any voices, I opened the door and…found her body."
Caroline rubbed her nose. "I didn't know her well. I had
seen her only once before."

"Okay, well, you can repeat all of that to the detectives.
Please wait here for a few more minutes."

The officer talked briefly to Cole and then started
clearing curious looky-loos away from the office door.

Cole sat down next to her and stretched his legs in front
of him. "What's going on, Caroline?"

She jerked her head toward him. "I don't know. Why
are you asking me that?"

He lowered his voice. "You know why Dr. Shipman
was murdered."

"Why would you say that? I barely knew her. One session—that's all we had."

"What did you tell her in that one session that someone
didn't want her to know?"

"I don't know what you're talking about." Her face
crumpled and she covered it with both hands—hiding her
lying lips, her lying eyes.

A man in a black suit and dark red tie approached them.
"Ms. Johnson? I'm Detective Rowan with the Clallam
County Homicide Department. I understand you found
Dr. Shipman's body."

She dropped her hands. "I did."

"Can you tell me the circumstances of your visit and
what happened?"

Caroline repeated her story, never veering from what
she'd told the Port Angeles police officer.

Detective Rowan had a few questions for Cole, too, and
then took their phone numbers before heading for the cops
clustered around the doorway of Dr. Shipman's office.

"That's your story and you're sticking to it? You're a
one-time patient of Dr. Shipman's in the wrong place at
the wrong time?" Cole murmured.

"What do you want from me?"

"How about the truth?"

She gripped his arm, her fingernails digging into him through the sleeve of his jacket. "I didn't kill anyone."

He blinked. "I never accused you of killing Dr. Shipman or anyone else. I doubt you have the strength to come up behind someone and slit their throat, although Dr. Shipman looked petite, like you. That's why a lot of women choose poison as their murder weapon of choice."

Caroline's face drained of all color and her eye twitched.

All the noise and activity around Cole ceased, replaced by a roaring in his ears. It had been right in front of him all along—a petite woman with a black cap heading to Timberline. His first instincts had been correct, but her relationship to Linda Gunderson had thrown him off. Had a sweet lady like Linda been lying all this time? Why would she lie for a complete stranger? Unless they really were cousins and that's why Caroline was on her way to Timberline.

Caroline half rose from the bench and Cole grabbed her arm and pulled her back down. "Poison. What do you know about poison?"

Her jaw hardened. "Nothing. I don't know what you're talking about. I didn't kill anyone. I know that now."

"Now? You know that *now*?"

She glanced at the huddle of cops. "Shh."

"You're going to tell me what's going on, Caroline Johnson, and you're going to tell me now." His fingers still encircled her wrist in a vise and he became aware of the delicacy of her bones. He loosened his hold. "You can't go on like this."

"I know." She rubbed her palms against the denim covering her thighs. "But not here."

She stood up and swayed, and he jumped up next to her and caught her arm. "Drink?"

She nodded.

Taking her arm lightly, he checked in with the detective and then led her across the street to his rental car, which it seemed he'd parked there days ago.

When Caroline had snapped her seat belt, she turned to him. "What were you doing at the office so early?"

He cranked on the ignition. Were they both telling the truth now? "I didn't have any research to do. What I'd been looking for had been right under my nose all along, and I didn't see it because…"

"Because?"

"I didn't want to." He threw the car into Drive and squealed away from the curb.

He found a restaurant overlooking the harbor, and they bypassed the dining area and headed straight for the bar. As one couple rose to leave a table in the corner by the window, Cole claimed it.

A busboy scurried over and collected the glasses and wiped the table. "A waitress will be right with you, or you can order at the bar and bring it back to the table."

"We'll wait." Cole pulled out a chair and sat down like he was ready to conduct an interrogation. He was.

Before he could start with his first question, the waitress was taking their drink order.

When she left, Cole hunched forward. "Who the hell are you?"

"Let me tell this my way. I'm not going to be bullied."

"Me? A bully? I think I'm handling you with kid gloves considering you've been lying to me from day one and playing me for a fool."

"Playing you for a fool? I hardly think that's the case."

"Really?" His hands curled into fists. "The longing looks. The gentle touches. The kisses."

She made a cross with her two index fingers. "Whoa. *You* kissed *me*."

The waitress cleared her throat. "One chardonnay and an Angeles IPA on tap."

She left them to their private conversation, and Cole straightened the edge of the cocktail napkin beneath his beer mug. He had to get a grip, put his bruised ego aside and focus on the important issues at hand. "Go for it."

Caroline splayed her hands on the table and her chest rose and fell quickly. "I'm the person you're looking for. I was in that room with Johnny Diamond when he died."

A muscle twitched at the corner of Cole's mouth. She'd been right under his nose all this time. Once again he'd allowed his attraction to someone to derail his instincts and common sense.

He gulped back some beer and wrapped his hands around the mug, squeezing until his knuckles were white. He returned to the one piece of information that had thrown him off. "Are you related to Linda Gunderson?"

"No. I'd never seen her before in my life, or at least not that I know of." Caroline's lips tilted up on one side in a half smile.

"I'm glad you think this is amusing. How'd you con her? How'd you get her to lie for you—and so convincingly?"

"When she first saw me in Timberline, she thought I was a battered woman." Caroline touched the fading, yellow bruise on her right cheekbone. "Her sister had been abused by a boyfriend, and she was very sensitive to that. I'm ashamed to admit it, but I did play on that. I told her a story about Larry and how I'd escaped from him and wanted to remain undercover. She's the one who suggested the family connection."

"Wow. So, how close did you stay to the truth? Were you Diamond's woman?" Cole had to take another sip of beer to wash the bitterness of that statement from his mouth. "Did he knock you around…before you poisoned him?"

A splash of wine hit the table as her hand jerked. "I told you. I didn't kill anyone, and that includes Johnny Diamond. After I discovered Dr. Shipman's body, I remembered everything that happened in that room at the Stardust Motel."

Cole's nostrils flared as he narrowed his eyes. "You remember what happened? I would hope so."

She licked a drop of wine from her lips. "But that's all I remember. I don't remember what happened before that."

"What are you talking about?" The antennae that had been suppressed by his feelings for Caroline began to wake up and get ready for another snow job. "Who the hell are you and what's your connection to Diamond?"

"I—I don't know."

"Is that why you were seeing Dr. Shipman, to find yourself? That's all very new age, but—" he drilled his finger into the tabletop "—I want answers right now. Who are you?"

"I told you. I don't know." She smacked the table with her palm. "I have amnesia. I don't know who I am."

Cole opened his mouth. Closed it. Ran a hand through his hair. Took a long pull from his glass.

What the hell could you say to that?

Chapter Twelve

Cole's jaw tightened and then he ground out, "You're lying."

She grabbed his hand. "I'm not lying, Cole. I don't know who I am."

He left his hand beneath hers, cold and unresponsive— just like his hard green eyes.

Once she knew for sure she hadn't killed Diamond, she'd wanted to confess everything to Cole, or at least everything she remembered. She couldn't carry this burden by herself anymore, but she hoped she hadn't made a mistake trusting Cole.

"Why didn't you go straight to the police? They could fingerprint you, just like they're going to do tomorrow. They could tell you like *that*—" he snapped his fingers "—who you are. Even if you're not a criminal, you might have a thumbprint on file for a driver's license or any kind of background check."

"I was afraid. I woke up in a seedy motel room with a dead man. There had obviously been a struggle. I found cash and drugs in the room and the body of a dead woman in the trunk of the car. I had no memory of what I was doing there, who I was." Caroline's bottom lip trembled and she sucked it between her teeth. She wanted Cole to believe her because she told a convincing story, not because he felt sorry for her.

"I didn't know if I had murdered someone, was involved in the drug trade or had pissed off someone in the drug trade. I was afraid if I'd gone to the cops, they'd arrest me."

"You said you remembered what happened at the Stardust. So, what happened?" Cole folded his arms across his chest, which looked huge and implacable right now.

"Johnny was going to kill me or at least incapacitate me with some drug. He thought I was in the bathroom, taking a shower, but I was looking for an opportunity to escape. I cracked open the bathroom door and saw him mixing up some powder in a bottle of water. I knew he was going to suggest I drink the water, so when I came out of the bathroom I swapped the poisoned bottle with another one in the mini fridge. He had no idea I'd seen him put the poison in the water bottle, so when he went out to the car I switched the bottles. When he returned to the room, I made sure he saw me drink the water he thought was poisoned."

"He drank the poisoned water from the fridge later?"

"Yes. He kept watching me for signs of the poison. If I had been smart I would've pretended to feel the effects, but then *he* started to feel the effects. He knew right away what I'd done, but it was too late. That's when I got the bruise on my face and the head injury that would cause my amnesia."

"He attacked you?"

"When he realized what I had done, he punched me and threw me across the room. I think he would've killed me with his bare hands if the poison hadn't started doing a number on his system. I never saw the end of him, since I'd lost consciousness by the time he died."

Cole blew out a breath. "That's quite a story, but a lot of questions remain. What were you doing with him in the first place and why was he trying to kill you?"

"That I can't tell you." She took a sip of wine and relaxed into the warmth that spread through her body. Cole might not believe her yet, but she felt as if she'd just shrugged a hundred pounds of weight off her shoulders.

"When I discovered Dr. Shipman's body, all those memories from the motel room flooded my mind. The whole scene played out in my head like a movie."

He rubbed his chin. "Why would Diamond use poison to kill you? Why not strangle you like he did Hazel McTavish?"

"The woman in the trunk."

"Maybe he was just trying to incapacitate you and not kill you." Cole drew a pattern on the tabletop with his finger as if he were connecting dots. "But the dose he was planning for you killed him, and he was a big man. Unless…"

"What?" She leaned forward, lips parted.

"Unless he didn't plan to allow you to drink all the water. If a few sips had knocked you out, he could've taken the bottle or knocked it over."

She nodded. "That could be. Anyway, when I woke up in that condition, I couldn't remember any of that. When I found Hazel's body in the trunk of her car, I knew I had to get away. I took the suitcase that was obviously mine and a little cash from the bag in the room, which I swear I'll pay back, and took off for Timberline."

"Why Timberline?"

She reached into her purse, hanging from the back of her chair, and withdrew the slip of paper. She smoothed it out on the table in front of Cole. "This was in my jacket pocket. I figured maybe I had people here, friends, someone who could help me out."

He pinched a corner of the paper between two fingers. "Probably not the smartest move, as Diamond's associates could trace you to Timberline…and probably did."

"Why would they?" She pressed a hand against her pounding heart. "This paper was in *my* pocket, in *my* handwriting. I tested that. I always figured Johnny way-laid me on my way to Timberline."

"Caroline, didn't you ever wonder how I tracked you to Timberline?"

Heat splashed her cheeks. "I—I thought maybe be-cause Johnny had connections to the area. I searched for the story of his murder when I got to town. That's how I discovered his name. I thought that's maybe why you were looking here first, and of course, I didn't know you were DEA when we first met. How did you know to come to Timberline? And how did you know to look for a woman?"

"Someone had entered Timberline in the GPS of Ha-zel's car, and someone saw you leave the motel room that morning."

She sucked in a quick breath. "Who?"

"A maid at the motel. But you disguised yourself well. All she could tell me was a petite woman with a dark beanie had been near the car that morning."

Caroline massaged the back of her neck. "I feel pretty stupid. I don't know how I thought I could outwit the po-lice or a bunch of drug dealers."

"You've done a good job of it so far. Linda was the key. When she spoke so glowingly of her cousin, it made me doubt I'd found my woman."

Heat crept up Caroline's throat at his phrasing and she dropped her gaze to the table. "I'm glad you did find me, Cole. C-can you help me now? I'm afraid I've endangered Linda's life, too. When she got sick the other night, she thought she might've been poisoned. I think I was the in-tended target, but I'm afraid for her,"

She put her hand over her heart. "I swear to you, I didn't kill Johnny. It happened just the way I told you. I'm afraid the man in the driveway the other night is one of Johnny's guys, although I don't know how they know I'm here or why they suspect I have any money."

Cole cleared his throat. "We let that slip out, Caroline. We have informants, moles in the drug community, and we let it be known that copious amounts of cash had been stolen from Diamond's stash."

She covered her mouth. "They think I have it, but who am I? Why was I traveling with Johnny?"

"Maybe once we confirm your identity, we'll have the answer to that."

"I read in an online news story that Johnny carjacked and murdered Hazel McTavish from a parking lot at the Sea-Tac Airport to get her car. Who's to say he didn't do the same to me? Maybe I was just at that hotel or maybe I was riding in Hazel's car."

Caroline raised her brows at Cole, hoping for confirmation, reassurance.

Scratching his stubble, he said, "You had a piece of paper with Timberline written on it. Also, why would Johnny want to poison a complete stranger? As much as I want you and Johnny Diamond to be strangers, I just can't see it."

She collapsed against the back of her chair. "I know we weren't strangers."

"Did you remember something else?"

"It's not something I just remembered. It's something I knew all along." She smoothed her hands across her face. "Did you wonder why Johnny didn't have a cell phone with him?"

"You took it?"

"I was afraid he might have my name, number or picture on it. Since I didn't know my name, I wouldn't have been able to tell."

"What did you do with the phone?"

"Took out the battery and the SIM card, destroyed the

phone and dumped it on the side of the highway—but not before I read an incoming text."

"What did it say?"

"It said 'Did you get the girl? Rocky's...' and then it had a little devil emoticon."

Cole's eyebrows collided over his nose. "Rocky?"

"Rocky. Timberline. What are the odds?" She tossed back the rest of her wine. "Not only am I connected to Johnny Diamond in some way, I'm also connected to Rocky Whitecotton, a man who kidnapped and probably murdered three children."

"This is a great clue, Caroline. I'm gonna phone it in to my partner, see if he can look up some connection between Johnny Diamond and Rocky Whitecotton."

"I'm glad I could do something to help, since all I've been doing is putting up roadblocks for you and the DEA."

Cole ran a hand across his mouth. "I know I'm stating the obvious here, but you need to find out who you are."

Her pulse quickened and a flash of joy shot through her body. "Does that mean you believe me?"

"I may be crazy or just blinded by...my feelings, but that's a wild story for anyone to concoct. Not to mention, if you were working with Johnny Diamond and Rocky Whitecotton, you wouldn't be in Timberline fraternizing with the DEA."

"Is that what this is?" She picked up her wineglass and swirled the drop of golden liquid in the bottom. "Fraternizing?"

Cole grunted and signaled to the waitress for another round. "Of course, there's always the possibility that you *are* in league with those two and you just don't remember. Have you remembered anything since coming to Timberline?"

"It's not exactly a memory, but I can understand and

speak Spanish. I discovered that while stumbling across a Spanish language TV show."

"God, it's so strange how the mind works. What did you recall during that first session with Dr. Shipman?"

Caroline raised a hand to her throat as memories of Dr. Shipman's body and the lurid gash leaking her blood onto the floor slammed into her full force. "She hypnotized me. I remembered being part of a large family somewhere in the desert, but I was desperate to leave."

"Maybe you did leave and Diamond was sent to bring you back."

"To whom? To what? What kind of family sends drug traffickers to retrieve their family members?"

"A crazy one—plenty of those out there." Cole smiled at the waitress as she brought their drinks, and as soon as she turned her back, his face resumed its serious expression. "You started to remember with Dr. Shipman and you may have continued your progress today, but someone made sure that didn't happen by taking out Shipman."

"I thought of that." Caroline curled up the edge of her cocktail napkin with fidgeting fingers.

"That means whoever is watching you, whether it's the guy with the knife or someone else, suspects you've lost your memory and knows you've been seeing Dr. Shipman to get it back."

"How could he know I was seeing Dr. Shipman? How would he know I had an appointment today? Because I don't think it's a coincidence I'm the one who found her."

Cole froze. Then he closed his eyes and cursed. "If they're watching you, they know you've been with me. I'm the one with the car."

"You mean they've been following you? Following us?"

"Worse. I probably would've picked up a tail…but not a bug."

"A bug, like a tracking device?"

He jerked his thumb over his shoulder. "They probably know we're sitting in this restaurant right now."

A sudden chill claimed her body and she dropped her hand from her wineglass to her lap. "They've been tracking our movements?"

"My guess is Linda's car also has a bug."

"I think I might know who it is."

"But you didn't even see the man with the knife in the driveway."

"Not him, although he's probably part of the team. A man came into Timberline Treasures the other day, and I got a weird vibe from him. I've seen him a few times since." Caroline lifted her shoulders. "I even did a little sleuthing myself."

"You followed him?"

"I saw him talking to a local Realtor in Sutter's, and I paid a visit to her—Rebecca Geist. I couldn't get much out of her. I pretended he looked familiar to me, but she was closemouthed about him."

"What does he look like?"

"Medium height, shaved head, around thirty. Nice-looking guy. Looks more like a software engineer for Evergreen than a drug dealer."

"You never know. I've seen all kinds. I'll have a look at him. First—" he rapped his knuckles on the table, making the wine in her glass dance "—we need to find out who you are. The fastest way is to bring you by the Port Angeles Police Station tomorrow and get you fingerprinted."

"I'm scared." She stuffed her hands beneath her thighs. "What if I'm someone...bad?"

"We'll deal with it, Caroline. Whatever happens, we'll deal with it. You need to be protected one way or the other."

One side of her mouth quirked up. "I thought that's what you were doing."

"I can do it a lot better if I know who you are and what your role is in all this."

Her gaze dropped to the full glass of wine the waitress had put before her. "And if it turns out I'm one of the bad guys? Will you arrest me?"

"We're a long way from that right now." Cole wedged a finger beneath her chin and tilted up her head. "Do you trust me?"

"I have to. You're all I have."

He pulled some cash from his pocket. "Are you going to finish that wine?"

"No."

"Then let's get out of here and take care of that bug."

When they got to the parking lot, she stood aside and watched as Cole slid beneath his rental car with his legs sticking out.

Several minutes later, he emerged with a broad smile on his face and a black object in his greasy palm. "Got the little son of a bitch."

Seeing the bug in his hand gave her a shock, even though Cole had been confident it was there. Despite what the man with the knife and Dr. Shipman's murder indicated, the tracking device was solid proof someone in Timberline had her in his sights.

Could she put her faith in Cole or would it better to run? She could put everyone and everything behind her and continue with her plan of melting into a big city until she knew for sure who she was and if she'd committed any crimes.

Of course, she was a day away from the fingerprints that would tell her all she needed to know.

Cole obliterated the bug beneath the heel of his boot and then swept the pieces into the water. "I'll do the same to the one on Linda's car. Let's get out of here."

Caroline took a step away from the vehicle, twisting

her fingers in front of her. "Where are we going? A-are you going to turn me in?"

"Turn you in? You don't trust me, do you?" He opened the passenger door and made a sweeping motion with his hand. "I'm not going to turn you in, Caroline. I'm not even officially on duty. We'll see what happens with the fingerprints tomorrow, but you have to promise me you won't bolt."

Had he read her mind? "What happens if the fingerprints tell you I'm a wanted criminal? A drug dealer?"

"I doubt that's going to happen. If it does, I can at least remand you to psychiatric care. Nobody's going to toss you into prison."

Psychiatric care? She didn't much like the sound of that, either, but what choice did she have unless she planned to make a run for it tonight?

And that was not out of the realm of possibility.

Chapter Thirteen

Neither of them had been able to eat a thing at the restaurant in Port Angeles, so by the time they reached Timberline, they were both starving.

As Cole drove up to the duplex, Caroline asked, "Should I tell Linda what happened?"

"She probably heard it on the news by now, anyway."

"But the police won't release my name, will they?"

"They're not releasing your name. I asked them not to, and the press wasn't there yet when we left."

"Thank you." She touched his forearm, tense and corded. "Thanks for protecting me. I know if you hadn't been there or hadn't vouched for me, the cops would've taken me in."

He rolled into the driveway and parked. "Don't be too grateful. I didn't want to turn you over to the system just yet. We'll want first crack at you."

"Well, thanks, anyway." She popped open the door. "I'll deal with Linda. Should I tell her the jig is up?"

"Tell her what you like, but you're not doing it alone." He turned off the engine. "I'm not letting you out of my sight."

Her stomach knotted and she tried to swallow against her tight throat. Even if she wanted to bolt, Cole wouldn't let her.

She shrugged. "Suit yourself."

She slammed the car door and stalked up to Linda's porch with Cole literally on her tail.

He grabbed her arm. "Hold on. Shine your phone light beneath Linda's car for me, so I can search for that bug."

She obliged, and just like in the parking lot of the restaurant in Port Angeles, Cole emerged with the same type of device he'd found on his car. He destroyed it and pocketed the evidence.

"We're not telling Linda about that." She stepped onto the porch and knocked once. "Linda? It's Caroline…and Cole."

There was no answer above the murmur of the TV, and Caroline's already frazzled nerves unraveled a little more. "Linda?"

"I'll be right there."

Relief flooded Caroline's body, so fast and strong she had to brace a hand against the doorjamb to steady herself.

A minute later, Linda opened the door. "Are you all right? I heard about the murder of Dr. Shipman, and I've been worried sick about you."

"It was terrible." Caroline gave the older woman a quick hug. "The police were at her office when we got there."

"Oh, such a shame, and when you were late coming back…" Linda pressed a hand over her heart.

"Caroline needed a drink after the news—we both did."

"I'm glad Cole was with you." Linda clung to Caroline's arm. "Do the police have any idea who did it? A current patient?"

"They didn't tell us anything, and of course, I'd seen her only once."

Linda clicked her tongue. "Such horrible news and too close for comfort."

"Are you feeling better, Linda?" Caroline glanced around the tidy living room. "Did your friends drop by?"

"I'm fine. Everyone made such a fuss, but they did

bring goodies and they cleaned up everything before they left. I'm going to get into bed early and read."

"That sounds like a good idea. We'll be right next door if you need anything."

"You and Cole?" Linda's eyes kindled with that match-making light.

"Neither one of us had dinner, so we'll probably order in some pizza."

"I wish I had some leftovers to give you, but we ate all our pizza. Would you like to take some brownies for dessert?" Linda bustled to the kitchen with that familiar spring to her step. "Karen made a double batch of her famous brownies and then had the nerve to leave them all here."

"Homemade brownies sound like the cure for everything right now." Cole joined her in the kitchen, and she handed him an oblong plastic container. "Are you sure you're going to be okay, Linda?"

"I'll be fine, especially knowing the two of you are next door." When she opened the door, she touched Caroline's cheek. "I'm so sorry about Dr. Shipman and that you had to be exposed to more violence. You need a nice, long vacation."

"I just might take one."

Cole's body stiffened beside her and she pushed past him on her way out the door.

He kept pace with her, balancing the plastic container full of brownies on one hand. "Pizza sounds good. How about a movie to go with it? I'm not tired. I can stay awake all night if I have to."

On her porch, she rounded on him. "Am I your prisoner now?"

"Better mine than the Clallam County Sheriff's Department."

She threw open her front door and dropped her purse

on the kitchen table. She thrust her phone and the pizza advertisement that had been hanging on her doorknob earlier at him. "Anything but anchovies."

"And pineapple. I hate pineapple on my pizza."

He phoned in the order, while she pulled off her boots and turned up the thermostat. Maybe she could lull him to sleep with food, beer and heat.

"Do you want a beer?"

His eyes narrowed. "I'm good."

"Wine?"

"Don't drink the stuff, but you knock yourself out."

She stood at her open refrigerator door. "I think I'll have a diet soda instead."

"Caffeinated?"

"Yes."

"I'll have the same."

She stuffed down her irritation as she grabbed the sodas from the fridge. She didn't want him to think she resented the babysitting. Because if she let that show, he'd suspect that she had plans of running, not that she didn't. But the less she revealed her emotions to him, the better.

She rinsed the tops of the soda cans and wiped them with a paper towel. "Can okay?"

"Always tastes better from the can." He'd pulled off his own boots and now sat on her small sofa with his stocking feet propped up on the coffee table.

"Make yourself at home." She handed him the can and sat on the chair across from him—the only other place to sit in the living room.

"I will, thanks." He snapped the lid and slurped the foam from the top. "Did you shake this first so it would explode all over my shirt and I'd be forced to go back to my hotel and change?"

"Oh, stop. I'm not going anywhere. It's time I learn the truth—good or bad."

He hunched forward, resting his forearms on his knees, clasping his hands lightly. "Seriously, Caroline. It's for the best and for your own safety. The people after you killed Dr. Shipman. They're capable of anything."

"You're right. I think the only reason I've lasted this long is they probably figured out there's something wrong with me. I haven't done what they expected me to do. I haven't told anyone about Johnny. I've been pretending to be Linda's cousin." She massaged her temples. "Honestly, I don't know what they think. I didn't even take that much money from Johnny's bag. I just needed a little seed money, a head start."

"Do you want to give me that money now?"

She scooted forward in the chair. "Will that look good for me? If I hand over the money I took?"

"Anything will help."

She didn't want it, anyway. She launched herself out of the chair and headed for her bedroom, where she pulled up the rug in the closet. She felt for the uneven floorboard and pushed on one edge until the other side tipped up. She lifted the slat, ran her fingers along the stacks of bills and then collected them all. She replaced the board and the rug and returned to the living room.

"Here you go." She dumped the cash on the sofa cushion next to Cole.

Raising one eyebrow, he thumbed through the neat stacks. "This is not a small amount."

"I didn't know how much I'd need to get started somewhere else. I—I haven't used that much of it."

"Do you have a bag or something? I'd hate to stuff this much cash in my pockets—and I'd need some big pockets."

She pivoted toward the kitchen and pulled a cloth grocery bag from a drawer. "You can have this."

He took the sack dangling from her fingers and proceeded to tuck the stacks inside. "This will go over well."

The doorbell rang and they both twitched as if they expected someone had come for the money.

She crept to the window and peered out. "It's the pizza."

"I'll get it." Cole wedged the bag of money between the sofa and the end table and rose to his feet, reaching for his wallet.

After he paid for the pizza, he took it into the kitchen. "How many pieces?"

"I'll start with two and work my way up." Caroline peeled apart two paper plates that had come with the pizza and slapped them down on the counter.

Cole placed two pieces on one plate and three on another. They resumed their positions across from each other and ate for a while in silence.

Cole waved a piece of crust at her. "Have you ever tried to remember on your own?"

"All the time, until my brain hurt."

"Have you tried self-hypnosis or meditation?"

"Like swinging something in front of my own face and telling myself I'm getting sleepy?"

"A darkened room, a fixed object, silence, relaxation."

"Yeah, because I've had so much silence and time to relax since I've been on the run."

"It's coming back to you in flashes, though. The trauma of discovering Dr. Shipman's body prompted a break, didn't it?"

Caroline covered her mouth and closed her eyes, the horror of that moment creeping back into her psyche after she'd been pushing it aside all night. Dr. Shipman had mentioned in their first session that a trauma might start the flow of memories—she just hadn't known the trauma would be her own murder.

"What a terrible way to die. There was no struggle in that room. She must've known him—or thought she did."

"He could've been posing as a patient."

"I never saw any of her patients. Well, just one, a dark-skinned man with longish hair. I'm sure the police have tracked down all her clients." Caroline lunged for the remote. "Could we just watch a movie? Something mindless?"

"I'm all for mindless entertainment. What's on?"

"Linda and Louise have premium cable in here, so we should have lots of choices."

Caroline paused at a raunchy comedy about drug dealers, and Cole shook his head. "I don't think so."

She flipped through a few more shows and gestured to a romantic comedy. "Is this better?"

"This is one of my sister's favorite movies. I could really impress her and score points if I actually watched it. Do you want to watch it?"

"Romance *and* comedy? Just what I need." Caroline curled her feet beneath her in the straight-back chair.

"More pizza?" Cole held up his empty plate.

"Maybe later."

He pushed out of the sofa, took their paper plates and napkins to the kitchen and returned with one glass of wine. He patted the cushion next to him. "Why don't you come over here and get comfortable. You could use a glass of wine, too. You're still suffering from the shock of Dr. Shipman. I can see it in your eyes."

Her gaze darted from the sofa to the wine to his face. Caroline wanted all three more than anything right now. She uncurled her body from the chair and joined him.

Hell, she might be in jail by tomorrow night. Might as well live it up.

She cupped the wineglass in her hands. "Are you sure you don't want a glass or a beer?"

"After everything that's gone on today? I'd rather stay alert."

She eased back against the cushion, taking a sip of wine. It warmed her chest and belly and made her fingertips tingle. "Ahh."

"I thought so." Cole squeezed her knee. "Take it easy and enjoy the movie."

They laughed in the right places and she even sniffled once or twice—must be the wine. When the story slowed down, she found her heavy eyelids drooping over her eyes. Her head dipped to the side and hit Cole's shoulder. She jerked it upright.

"Are you falling asleep?"

"No." She put the wineglass on the table beside the sofa—right next to the bag of money. She focused on the movie again and the foolish woman who couldn't see that the hometown boy from her childhood loved her so much more than the rich fiancé from New York.

Did she have a man in her life somewhere who loved her like that? Impossible. A man like that would've moved heaven and earth to find her. A man like that would've never allowed Johnny Diamond to take her. A man like that would be there for her, regardless of what she did or who she was.

Cole's arm crept around her shoulders and he wrapped a lock of her hair around his finger. "That fiancé guy's an idiot. He needs an ass-kicking."

She giggled, and the act must've been too much effort because she yawned at the end of it. Her head dropped to Cole's shoulder again and it felt too heavy to lift this time, so she left it there.

His arm around her tightened, and his chin rested on top of her head.

The swell of the violins indicated that the girl with the

big-city job must've finally realized that the hometown boy was the one for her.

Caroline must've drifted off, because the next thing she knew, Cole had swept her up in his arms and was carrying her to the bedroom. As he placed her on the bed, she grasped his shirt, terrified of being alone, terrified of finding out who she was tomorrow.

"Don't leave me, Cole. I couldn't stand it if you left me."

The mattress dipped as he stretched out beside her on the bed, cradling her head against his chest.

"I'm not going to leave you, Caroline Johnson, or whoever the hell you are. I know you didn't kill anyone. As crazy as your story sounds, I believe it. I believe you. And whatever you did to get mixed up with Diamond, I'm going to be right by your side to see you through it."

"What if I've done something terrible? How will you be able to stand beside me?"

"If you did do something terrible, you're going to need a friend even more. Can you trust me? If not, then this between us, right now, means nothing. But if you can, then God, I want you."

Chapter Fourteen

Oh, God. She wanted him, too. She couldn't possibly have another man waiting for her somewhere when she felt so strongly about this one. Wouldn't a husband or boyfriend be the first thing she would've remembered from her session with Dr. Shipman?

She rolled onto her side to face Cole. "I do trust you."

He brushed his warm lips across hers, while curling an arm around her waist to draw her closer. His green eyes held a question, and she wanted to answer that question with a resounding yes.

Opening her mouth against his, she slipped her hands beneath his shirt and smoothed them across the hard, flat planes of his back.

He deepened their kiss, his tongue probing her mouth before tangling with her own tongue. His hands wandered over her body, stroking, brushing, but never grabbing, as if giving her every opportunity to halt his exploration.

She didn't. She wouldn't.

She ran her fingernails along his back and trailed them onto his belly, outlining the six-pack she'd known would be there.

He tightened his abs even more and sucked in a breath. "That tickles."

"Mmm, that's useful information." She pinched his side before grabbing the hem of his shirt. "May I?"

He raised his arms and she pulled the long-sleeved knit shirt over his head and dropped it to the floor. She skimmed her hands across his chest and along his chiseled pecs. "You're a work of art, Cole Pierson."

"And you're a tease. Why do I have my shirt off and you still have yours on?" He yanked off the sweatshirt she'd been wearing and the T-shirt beneath.

He wasted no time flicking the bra straps from her shoulders and cupping her breasts with both hands. Ducking his head, he sucked one nipple into his mouth. The pleasure of it ached between her legs, and she threw her head back in ecstasy.

As his tongue toyed with her other nipple, his hand slid to the waistband of her pants. With sure fingers, he undid her fly and peeled her jeans away from her hips.

He gave her jeans a tug. "Do you wanna help out here, or are you going to make me work for it?"

Arching her back, she lifted her hips from the mattress and he pulled down her jeans and kicked them off the foot of the bed.

His gaze hungrily devoured her body, and she tingled in all the right places. She hoped that if and when she regained her memory, she wouldn't lose Caroline's, because this was a moment she never wanted to forget.

As if in a hurry to see the rest of her, Cole unclasped her bra and rolled her panties over her hips and down her thighs. He rolled back to his side, propping his head up with his hand, his elbow digging into the pillow.

He didn't touch her, but the way his eyes flicked over her naked body made her breasts feel heavy with desire and her pulse throb with need. She squirmed beneath his gaze, pinning her thighs together, suddenly shy.

Then, with one finger, he traced the line of her jaw and circled her throbbing lips. He pressed the pad of his thumb against her bottom lip, then dragged his finger over her chin to the base of her throat, where her pulse was fluttering wildly.

She released a small moan as his gentle, slow touch ignited a fire in her belly. When his finger skimmed over her mound and nudged between her thighs to feel her wetness, the moan turned into a gasp and she grabbed his wrist.

"Do you want me to stop?"

His voice, rough around the edges, gave her a thrill, since it revealed she wasn't the only one being tortured by unspent passion.

She hooked her fingers in the belt loops of his jeans and pulled herself closer to him. "If you stop now, I'm going to be a quivering mess, but why am I the only one who's naked here?"

"I just wanted a minute or two to…commit your body to my memory."

She blinked and gave him a shaky smile. She knew what he meant, but didn't want to acknowledge it. If there was ever a time for forgetting, it was now. She wanted only to lose herself in this moment.

"Well, now it's my turn." She unbuttoned his fly and pressed her palm against the bulge that was barely contained by his briefs. "D-do I turn you on that much?"

"You have no idea." He swung his legs over the side of the bed and pulled off his jeans, underwear and socks all at once. He reached into a pocket of his pants and pulled out his wallet. He withdrew something from the billfold and held up a condom between two fingers.

She had no idea if he'd bought that here or if he always carried a spare, but it didn't matter. It was a nod to the truth that they hardly knew each other. In fact, knew each other less than if this were a one-night stand from a bar pickup.

It didn't matter. She knew all she needed to know about Cole Pierson, and she had to have this night with him before she went to the police station tomorrow, because she may never have this chance again.

Batting her eyelashes, she whispered in a husky voice, "I like a man who's prepared."

He got back on the bed, and she nudged him onto his back. "Didn't I tell you I wanted my turn?"

She pressed the front of her body against his side, hooked her leg over his thigh and trailed her fingernails along the tight skin of his erection. She leaned over and took his brown nipple gently between her teeth as she slid her hand up and down his shaft.

Cole shivered and closed his eyes. "That feels out of this world."

She sculpted his body with her hands, kneading and stroking his warm flesh. Her lips and tongue soon followed, but she couldn't concentrate as he began to touch her—everywhere.

With a groan, he pulled her into his arms, on top of him, and scattered kisses across her face. His lips locked on to hers as he buried his hands in her hair, driving his erection between her moist thighs.

He smoothed one hand over her derriere, and their hips rocked together. Then he flipped her on her back and straddled her body, with a knee on either side of her hips. He ripped open the condom, and she took it from him.

She plucked it out of its foil packet and ran her tongue along his tip before fitting the condom over it and rolling it down the length of him.

Scooping his hands beneath her bottom, he tilted up her hips and eased into her inch by delicious inch. Once he'd entered her fully, he drew out again and drove home.

She winced and grabbed on to his shoulders. Clearly, she was no virgin, but maybe it had been a while since she'd had a man. Making love with Cole wasn't bringing back any memories—only making them.

He pulled out and nuzzled her neck. "Are you okay?"

She grasped his buttocks, digging her nails into his muscled flesh. "I will be as soon as you're back inside me."

The man didn't need an engraved invitation. He took up where he'd left off without missing a beat. As he drove into her over and over, he showered her with kisses and nipped at her breasts. He tickled her with his tongue and explored her with his fingers.

She didn't know what direction was up, and as he took her to the edge, all she could do was hold on to him.

Because she'd been riding high, his assault on her body and senses complete and unwavering, her orgasm hit her like a sledgehammer. It took her breath away and she felt like she was in a freefall from an awesome height.

When the first wave of pleasure subsided, another clawed through her belly. But before she even had time to process it, Cole's body stiffened and a sheen of sweat broke out across his smooth chest.

He raised his head and looked at her through heavy-lidded eyes. His body shook as he spent himself, and at the end, he kissed her again, like he meant it, like she would be his forever…even though she was his for this moment and this moment only.

Later, she curled up against his body, his heartbeat strong and sure beneath her cheek, his breathing deep and heavy.

Her eyelids flew open. This was the chance she'd been waiting for. With Cole sound asleep, she could slip out of this bed, grab the bag of cash and never have to show up at the police station tomorrow.

Her leg jerked and Cole murmured in his sleep. She leaned in close and peered at his strong face in the darkness.

Leave Cole? Betray him?

She snuggled in close to his body and draped her arm

around his waist. Even if it turned out she was a drug trafficker and was facing twenty-five years in prison, she could never abandon Cole.

He'd given her this one night…and that's all she had to hold on to.

COLE BLINKED AGAINST the morning light leaking through the blinds. He bolted upright, a shot of adrenaline spiking through his system. He flung his arm to the side and swept it across the cool…empty sheet.

He rolled off the bed, scrambling for his jeans. Barefoot and buttoning his fly, he crashed into the living room and made a beeline for the bag of cash next to the sofa. He plunged his hand into the canvas bag and pulled out the stacks of money. Was it all there?

"Caroline?" He cranked his head around the small room, which gave him a view of the empty kitchen. He'd passed the bathroom on the way to the living room, and she wasn't in there, either.

How could he have allowed himself to be duped that way? It had been what she'd wanted all along—the food, the offers of booze, the sex.

She'd wanted an escape—and he'd handed it to her because he couldn't keep it in his pants.

As he shoveled the money back into the bag, the front door swung open and Caroline stepped across the threshold with a paper bag clutched against her chest with one arm.

She froze, her gaze tracking from the money bag to his face. "What are you doing?"

"Just checking on the money."

She kicked the door closed behind her. "Just checking on me, you mean. You thought I skipped out."

"I did have a second of panic. I'm sorry."

She walked past him, swinging the bag. "I could act

aggrieved and insulted, but I'm all about the truth today and the truth is, I woke up in the middle of the night and the thought crossed my mind."

"What stopped you?"

"You." She plopped the bag on the kitchen counter. "So, I don't blame you for thinking the worst when you woke up alone this morning."

"I still feel guilty." He joined her in the kitchen, where she was pulling eggs, milk and bacon out of the bag.

"That makes two of us." She held up the package of bacon. "But I'm going to atone for my guilt by cooking you breakfast—all ingredients courtesy of Linda."

"And I'll atone for mine by helping you, but I don't want to cook shirtless." He returned to the bedroom to put on his shirt from last night, visited the bathroom briefly, then sidled up next to her at the counter. "Put me to work."

She handed him a pan for the bacon and started cracking eggs in a bowl. "Is the Port Angeles Police Department going to call me today or do they expect me to call them? Or is it the sheriff's department that's going to call?"

"It's the Port Angeles Police. They'll call you with a time to come in. They've probably dusted the office for prints and will want to compare yours to any they found. And will share whatever they have with the homicide detectives." Cole peeled off several slices of bacon and lined them up in the skillet.

"That may be a surprise for all of us."

"I'll protect you, Caroline. If something turns up on your prints, I can tell them you're with us, with the DEA."

"And then you'll take me in yourself?" She beat the eggs with a fork, the tines clinking against the glass bowl in a furious rhythm.

"If you're involved with Johnny Diamond in any way, we'll have to deal with it. You know that, right? I can't just let you walk away."

"I know that you have to do your job, Cole." She gave him a watery smile. "Can we just enjoy breakfast until that time comes?"

He came up behind her and wrapped his arms around her waist. "Absolutely. And while you're waiting for the call, I'm going to check out the mysterious stranger from the shop and Sutter's—the one supposedly buying real estate. Do you have any idea where he's staying?"

"None, but maybe we can tail Rebecca Geist, the Realtor. She's the only one I know for sure who's been in contact with him." Caroline waved a fork at the TV. "Do you think the local news will have anything new on Dr. Shipman?"

"We? Did you just say we can tail her?"

"I sort of figured you wouldn't want to leave my side, because I just admitted I had thoughts of fleeing last night."

He kissed her neck. "That's not the only reason I don't want to leave your side."

Turning to face him, she curled her arms around his waist. "Whatever happens, I'm glad it was you in Timberline looking for me."

A sizzle and pop from the frying bacon interrupted the kiss he was about to plant on her mouth. He pulled away from her and prodded the bacon with a fork. "When we finish breakfast, let's go back to my hotel so I can shower and change. Is Linda opening the shop today?"

"She is, but I already talked to her this morning when I picked up the food and told her that I'd be waiting for a call from the police, so she told me to take the day off." Caroline poured the egg mixture in the pan next to his. "Of course, once I get arrested, I'll be taking a lot of days off."

"It won't go down like that, Caroline." *At least not at first.*

She bumped her hip against his. "However it goes down, I'm ready to face it."

She might be ready to face it, but was he?

An hour later, after they'd finished breakfast and Caroline had showered and changed into a pair of black jeans and a blue sweater that matched her eyes, they drove into the parking lot of his hotel, a newer one located away from the town center and closer to Evergreen Software.

He wanted to stop by the hotel gift shop, buy more condoms and bed her again in his hotel room, but she had a nervous, faraway look in her eyes after listening to a news report on the radio about Dr. Shipman's murder.

The trauma of what she'd experienced yesterday seemed to hit her out of the blue, and she'd stop talking and start twisting her fingers into knots. Cole had dealt with enough crime scenes and enough people not accustomed to the gore to recognize the symptoms.

He gave the gift shop a sideways glance as they passed it on their way to the bank of elevators. He punched the call button with more force than necessary and Caroline gave him a sharp glance.

When they got up to the room, he turned on the TV, but selected a movie channel. She didn't need to watch any more news. "You can help yourself to the mini bar while I'm in the shower."

"Do I look like I need a drink at ten o'clock in the morning?"

"There's other stuff in there."

"I don't need any distractions, Cole. I'm not going to watch the news, if that's what you're worried about."

"Just try to relax."

To his disappointment, she didn't come in to check on him once during his shower, so he wrapped a towel around his waist and checked on her instead.

She was sitting on the edge of the bed, watching a

crime show, her jaw set and her hands clutching the folds of the bedspread.

He sat next to her and took one of her hands in his. "It's going to be okay."

"It's my fault Dr. Shipman was murdered. If I had never gone to see her, the people after me never would've targeted her." Caroline looked at him, her blue eyes filling with tears. "And you know the worst part? I lied to her. I never even gave her a chance to refuse me as a patient because of the danger."

"Do you think she would've refused to see you? I don't. She probably suspected more than you were telling her. Don't blame yourself, Caroline."

"Stop calling me Caroline." She jumped up from the bed. "It's not even my name. Do you know where I got that name? The trucker who picked me up down the road from the Stardust had Carolina plates. That's how real I am."

Cole rose from the bed and wrapped his arms around her trembling body. "You're real to me. Whatever's in your past is just that—past. And if it happens to be something bad, you're not that person anymore. Knowing you like I do now, I can't believe you've done anything criminal in your past, and I know criminals."

A tear ran down her face and she buried her head against his chest. "I don't want to disappoint you. I don't want to see that look fade from your eyes when you look at me and realize…"

"Not going to happen." He pulled away before his desire for her became too obvious. "I'm going to put some clothes on, and then let's have a look around Timberline together. Now that I know everything, maybe I can help you remember why you're here, why you had that scrap of paper in your pocket."

"Are you going to hypnotize me?" Her gaze dropped to the towel slipping down his hips.

He grabbed the towel before it slipped any farther. "I would if I could, but I don't know jack about hypnosis. You went through a session already. Do you think you could practice some self-hypnosis?"

"I could give it a try."

"I know you've been afraid to remember, but maybe now that you're open to the truth, you can force your memories to come back."

"Maybe you're right, but now—" she pressed her hand against her forehead "—nothing is there."

"You've had a lot to deal with. Stop stressing over things you can't change." He picked up the remote and aimed it at the TV. "And stop watching these crime shows. Find a comedy."

He tossed the remote on the bed and headed back to the bathroom after sweeping up some clothes. Several minutes later, when he entered the other room fully dressed, the TV was silent and Caroline was reclining on the bed against a stack of pillows with her eyes closed.

He crept toward his boots in the corner of the room, and she opened one eye. "I'm trying."

"Good. Now let's go take Timberline by storm and see if you can remember anything."

As they walked down the hallway toward the elevator, Caroline peered over the railing down to the lobby. She choked and grabbed his arm. "Cole, that man. He must've followed us. He's down there, in the foyer."

"What?" Cole crowded next to her and looked down four floors to the spacious area. "Where?"

"He just crossed in front of the reception desk. He might be going out that side door to the parking lot."

Cole took off for the stairwell and banged through the fire door, with Caroline trailing behind him. He wanted to tell her to stay back, but he didn't know what the man looked like.

Cole ran down four flights of stairs, and she kept up with him all the way. When he reached the bottom, he burst through the final door into the lobby. "Which way?"

Panting, she pointed to the right of the check-in desk.

As he headed for the side door leading to a parking lot, she grabbed on to his belt loop to keep up. "What are you going to do?"

"I'm going to find out who the hell he is." Cole pushed through the glass door. "Do you see him?"

Caroline tugged on his sleeve. "Over there, at the trunk of that white car."

With clenched fists and a heart beating out of his chest, Cole strode toward the man as he closed the trunk. "Hey! You!"

The man turned with a scowl on his face, and then he saw Caroline and his eyes bugged out of their sockets. He reached into the pocket of his raincoat, and Cole charged him, knocking him against the car and pinning his arms under his body.

"What the hell is wrong with you?" The man bucked and loosened one of his arms. He took a swing and Cole blocked the punch.

"I'm a DEA agent. I'd think twice before assaulting me."

The man slumped. "What do you want? I haven't done anything wrong. You can check my trunk. Do you think I have drugs or something?"

Cole plunged his hand in the man's coat pocket and pulled out a glove. "Do you have any weapons on you?"

"Weapons? No. I told you, I haven't done anything wrong. I'm just getting into my rental car, for goodness sake."

Cole released him and fished for his badge. He flipped it open so the man could get a good look at it. "Open your trunk for me."

The man seemed unsure of Cole's authority, but complied, anyway.

The lid popped and Cole lifted it, his gaze scanning the cargo space, empty except for a gift basket filled with sweets.

He backed up and slammed it shut. "What's your name and why are you bothering Ms. Johnson?"

Caroline made a sudden movement beside him and sucked in a breath.

"I'm sorry." The man tugged at the lapels of his trench coat as he turned toward Caroline. "I didn't know I was bothering you. You're the woman from the tourist shop, right?"

"Yes. He's… I'm… We're just overreacting."

Cole raised his eyebrows. She'd been worrying about this guy for a few days and *now* they were overreacting. "Wait a minute. You felt threatened by him. Let's at least see who he is."

"You felt I was threatening you?" The man slicked a hand over his shaved head. "I'm so sorry. I never meant to make you feel that way."

"Who are you? Can we start there? As you saw, I'm Cole Pierson with the DEA, and this is Caroline Johnson."

"I'm James Brice, and I'm going to reach for my wallet in my back pocket." He did so and showed Cole his New York driver's license. "I'm in town for business. I bought a stuffed frog from Caroline a few days ago. I had no idea I had made her uneasy."

"I'm sorry." Caroline crossed her hands over her chest. "I have some other things going on in my life right now, and I think I just projected onto you."

Brice held up his palms. "No harm done."

Cole stuck out his hand. "Sorry, man. We've both been on edge."

Brice shook his hand and opened the car door.

As Cole took a few steps back to the hotel, his hand on Caroline's back, he furrowed his brow. *Brice.*

He stopped and pivoted. "Are you any relation to Heather Brice, one of the children kidnapped as part of the Timberline Trio?"

Brice didn't turn from his car, but his shoulders slumped. "Heather was my little sister. I'm in town to sell my parents' property here, but was trying to keep a low profile."

Caroline covered her mouth. "I am so sorry."

Brice faced them, his back against the car. "In fact, that's why I may have shown a little more interest in you than appeared normal, Caroline."

She tilted her head. "Why?"

"Because when I first saw you in that shop—I thought you were my kidnapped sister."

Chapter Fifteen

All the blood drained from her head and she felt like she was going to pitch forward, face-first.

Cole must've sensed her shock, or maybe she'd already started her free fall, because he put an arm around her shoulders.

"Me?" Her voice squeaked and she cleared her throat. "Why would you think that?"

"Just something about the look of you. I learned later that you were new to town and related to Linda Gunderson, the owner of Timberline Treasures." James shrugged. "It happens now and then. I'll see a woman about the age my sister would have been, and do a double take. Wishful thinking, I guess."

Cole asked, "Does anyone in Timberline know you're here?"

"Only Rebecca Geist. She's helping me list the properties. They're mostly commercial or vacant lots. After the kidnapping, my parents didn't have the heart to stay here."

"Did the FBI notify your parents that they ID'd Rocky Whitecotton for the crimes?"

"They did. That's why I'm here. Maybe they felt a sense of closure after that news."

At the mention of Rocky's name, Caroline almost doubled over as her stomach churned. Somehow this was all connected, and she might even be connected to the kidnapping of this man's sister. Maybe she even had information about the kidnappings buried in her brain.

Cole asked, "Did your parents ever suspect Rocky?"

"Not that I know of, but they don't speak of it—ever." James spread his hands. "Look, I'm sorry for the misunderstanding, but I'm asking you to keep this to yourselves. I want to fly under the radar while I'm here taking care of my family's business."

"No problem."

As they turned away, Caroline twisted her head over her shoulder and said, "Sorry. Sorry…for your loss."

James nodded and slammed the car door, peeling out of the parking lot seconds later.

Caroline chewed on her bottom lip as they returned to the hotel.

Cole opened the door for her. "I feel stupid. Poor guy."

"Yeah, that's my fault. I'm sorry for dragging you into it, but at least I wasn't totally imagining things. He *was* interested in me—just not how I thought he was."

"At least I don't have to track him down now."

"What if I know something about his sister? About all the kidnapped kids?"

"I thought about that, but the kidnappings occurred twenty-five years ago. I doubt Rocky Whitecotton is still talking about his past crimes. If he's connected to Johnny Diamond, I'm sure he has new crimes to talk about." Cole snapped his fingers. "That reminds me. I contacted my partner about looking into any connections Diamond could've had with Whitecotton."

"I thought Rocky Whitecotton had fallen off the face of the earth?"

"That's my understanding, but he's not someone we ever had on our radar—at least not recently. The FBI may have moved him back up their list based on the new information regarding the kidnappings, but we've never searched for him."

"Are we still going to explore Timberline to see if anything jogs my memory?"

"Yeah, give me a minute in the room to call my partner, Craig."

As Cole talked to his partner, Caroline called Linda to check up on her.

"Have you gone to the sheriff's station yet?"

Caroline corrected her. "Police station. Not yet. I'm still leaving Timberline, Linda, even though I'm so grateful for everything you did."

"I know you are." The bells on the shop door jingled. "Customer just walked in. We'll talk later."

Caroline ended the call with a tear trembling on her eyelash. She might not have another opportunity to talk to Linda again.

A few minutes later, Cole ended his own call. "That's interesting. Still no leads on Whitecotton. Unless he changed his name and went into some kind of criminals' witness protection program, he really has disappeared. Maybe he was smuggled out of the country."

Caroline dropped her phone. "Spanish."

"What?"

"I told you I knew Spanish."

"You told me you could understand some Spanish on a TV show."

"It's more than that, Cole. I can speak Spanish fluently." She tried it out, the words and phrases coming to her lips naturally.

Cole spoke Spanish, too, and kept up the conversation for another minute. He switched back to English. "As far as I can tell, you have a dialect from Mexico."

"Really? You can hear that?"

"I'm not great at it. My partner's better." He held out his

phone. "Would you be willing to talk to him? His name's Craig Delgado."

"Of course."

He placed a call to his partner again and gave him some background on her that left out all the bad parts. Then he put the phone on speaker and handed it to her.

She and Craig spoke for a few minutes—about the weather, about the Timberline landscape and about Cole—until he snatched the phone from her.

"What do you think, Craig?"

"I think I'd better continue giving her the lowdown on you."

Cole rolled his eyes at Caroline. "I mean about the accent."

"Yeah, that's definitely Mexico. I'd go even further and say northern interior, maybe around Chihuahua."

Caroline leaned toward the phone in Cole's hand. "Is that a desert climate, Craig?"

"It can be. The Chihuahua Desert extends from New Mexico all the way down south into Mexico."

"Craig, does the FBI have any leads on Whitecotton going to Mexico?"

"I can check on it, and you know our boy Johnny Diamond made several trips down there—illegal ones."

"Check out Whitecotton for me."

"When are you coming back from your so-called vacation?"

"Dude, I think that vacation just ended."

His conversation with Craig over, Cole tapped the phone against his chin. "You may have been down in Mexico with these guys."

Caroline folded her arms over the knots forming in her belly. "I'm scared, Cole. What was I doing with them? What was I doing in Mexico?"

"Your fingerprints might tell us everything we need to know."

She uncrossed her arms and studied the tips of her fingers as if she could read her past there. She saw nothing.

Cole took both her hands and pressed her palms against his chest. "It's going to be okay, Car…"

He stopped when she flashed him a look. She wasn't going to lash out at him for calling her Caroline again. He was just trying to help, but he was dreaming. He wanted to rescue her because he hadn't been able to rescue his wife from her demons.

"It's not going to be all right, is it? I know you're trying to make me feel better, but my situation keeps getting worse and worse."

"You know what might make you feel better?" He pressed a kiss against the inside of her left wrist. "Let's get out of this hotel room and explore Timberline. It's better than waiting around for the police to call."

"You're right." She flipped her hair over her shoulder. "I'm going to face everything head-on today."

As Caroline buckled her seat belt in his car, she said, "Where to first?"

"How about Evergreen Software? Have you been there yet?"

"You think I came here for Evergreen Software?"

"Let's take a drive to the facility. You never know. We're close by, anyway."

About five minutes later, Caroline took in the modern white buildings that comprised the Evergreen campus, but she felt no twinges of recognition or familiarity. "I don't think I came back for this, Cole."

"It's impressive though, isn't it? I thought I read somewhere that the Brice family had some property out here, too, that they sold to Evergreen."

"I felt sorry for James Brice."

"Yeah, I slammed him against that car pretty hard."

Caroline punched Cole's arm. "Not that. He seemed sad to be here wrapping up everything for his parents."

"I don't blame the parents for taking off. I can't imagine what they went through—to lose a child like that."

"And the guilt."

"Guilt?" He swung through the Evergreen parking lot once more before exiting the facility. "Why would they feel guilty?"

"I think there would always be that element of what you could've done differently as a parent. Just those three were taken. Why those three? Did the bikers who were involved in the kidnappings ever say why?"

"Those bikers were all dead by the time the truth came out. Only Dax Kennedy is still around, and he was a younger member of the motorcycle gang at the time and wasn't directly involved in the kidnapping."

"Well, I'm sure those parents drove themselves crazy wondering why. The siblings, too. Poor James."

"It was hard on the siblings. In fact, the kidnapped boy's brother duplicated the kidnappings just a few months ago."

"Oh, my God. This town has been through a lot. Was Johnny Diamond involved in the kidnappings? Maybe that's how he knows Rocky."

"He wasn't around then, too young, but there's no doubt that his membership in the Lords of Chaos connects him to Whitecotton." Cole pulled up to a fork in the road and idled the engine. "Do you want to head to the forest? There are a couple of nice trails out there. The peace and tranquility might do you good."

She checked the time on her phone. "Especially since the police department should be calling anytime now. They did say afternoon, right?"

"They might be waiting for all the fingerprints to come

in, but I'm guessing there were a lot in Dr. Shipman's office."

"Speaking of guilt." Caroline squeezed her eyes shut. "She would be off on her trip right now if I hadn't become her patient."

"I know it's hard, Caroline, but you need to put the blame on her killer."

She sat forward suddenly. "Can we stop by Linda's shop on our way through town? I want to check up on her."

"Did she sound okay on the phone?"

"She did, but she had a rough time of it the other night and maybe she's trying to get back on her feet too quickly."

"Especially if it was poison." Cole jerked the steering wheel to the right to go into downtown Timberline. "She's a fighter, that one."

As Cole's car traveled down Main Street, Caroline spotted flashing emergency lights ahead, and butterflies swirled in her stomach. "Look at that."

"Excitement in downtown Timberline. I hope nobody's hurt."

"Cole." She grabbed his thigh, digging her fingernails into the denim of his jeans. "Is that ambulance in front of Timberline Treasures?"

He swore. "It looks like it is."

"Hurry, hurry." She sat up, straining against the seat belt, her heart thundering in her chest.

"I can't get any closer. I'm pulling up here."

When he parked the car, Caroline tumbled from the passenger side and ran down the sidewalk. She pushed through the clutch of people gathered near the door of Linda's shop. "Let me by."

Quentin Stevens, one of the Timberline Sheriff's Department deputies, held up his hand as she charged toward the door. "Hold on, please."

"Is it Linda Gunderson? I'm her...cousin."

Deputy Stevens's eyes widened. "Are you Caroline?"

"Yes, yes."

Cole had caught up with her and placed a steadying hand on her back. "What happened, Deputy?"

"Aggravated assault and robbery."

Caroline covered her mouth. "Assault? Someone assaulted Linda?"

"I'm afraid so."

"Is—is she…alive?"

"She's alive, sustained some injuries."

"I need to see her."

"She's been asking for you, so go on in, but she's being treated so don't get in the way of the EMTs doing their job."

Caroline grabbed Cole's hand, dragging him along with her in case Stevens tried to stop him.

She bolted toward Linda, who was bloodied and stretched out on a gurney, with two EMTs cleaning her wounds and taking her vitals.

Caroline cried out and dropped to the side of the gurney, clutching Linda's hand. "Oh, my God. What happened?"

Linda parted swollen lips, but no sound came out.

Another deputy tapped Caroline on the shoulder. "You're Ms. Gunderson's cousin?"

She rose to face him. "Yes, can you tell me what happened? Is Linda going to be okay?"

"You'll have to ask the EMTs about that." He shook Cole's hand. "I'm Deputy Unger."

"Cole Pierson. This is Caroline Johnson. Do you know what went down in here?"

"Ms. Gunderson's having a hard time communicating, but it sounds like a man entered the shop, threatened her with a knife and took all the money from the register. Why he felt he had to beat her up is a mystery to me. Must be some kind of sadist or hard-core criminal."

Caroline leaned against Cole for support. "It—it was a robbery? He stole her money?"

"Yeah, in broad daylight, too." The officer shook his head. "Sometimes I wonder what Evergreen Software is bringing in, with all the jobs and revitalization."

One of the EMTs spoke up. "Ma'am, we're taking her to emergency if you want to come by the hospital later."

"Was she injured badly?"

"She has a nasty cut on her head and she lost a lot of blood. I'm surprised she's still conscious, but she's hanging in there."

Caroline felt a soft tap against her calf and crouched beside the gurney.

Linda grabbed on to Caroline's sleeve and pulled.

Caroline moved closer as Linda mouthed some words. "What is it?"

Linda shifted her eyes to the deputy and then whispered in Caroline's ear. "The man wanted information about you. I told him the story you made up."

Chapter Sixteen

Linda's head fell to the side as her eyes closed and her mouth gaped open.

Caroline choked. "What's wrong? What's wrong with her?"

"She lost consciousness. We're moving her now. Back up, please."

As Cole helped Caroline to her feet, the EMTs expanded the legs of the gurney and wheeled Linda out of the store to the waiting ambulance.

The deputies asked Caroline a few more questions, and while they continued collecting evidence from the store and dusting for prints, she sat in the corner with her hands pinned between her knees, Linda's whisper echoing in her head.

Someone had roughed up her friend trying to get information about *her*, and it seemed that Linda had known she'd been lying all along.

When Deputy Stevens stopped by to tell her they'd wrapped things up for now, she said, "Did Linda give a description of the man? Did anyone on the street see him leaving the store?"

"White guy, but dark complexion, wore his hair in a ponytail."

Caroline furrowed her brow. "D-did she tell you what he said to her?"

"Told her to hand over the money in the register and to be quick about it. After he stuffed the money in his pockets, he came around the counter and hit her. Knocked her to the ground and kicked her."

Caroline gasped and nausea claimed her stomach. "Anything else? Did he say anything else?"

"Nope. Headed out the back door to the alley." Stevens waved his hand in the air. "You can stay here if you'd like to clean up. We have what we need and it's no longer a crime scene, but you may want to close up shop for the day."

So, Linda had lied for her again.

"I will, thanks."

When all the deputies had left the store and only a few people remained on the sidewalk out front, Caroline locked the door and flipped over the sign to read Closed.

She sank back in the chair while Cole paced through the racks.

"This is too much of a coincidence. This has to be connected to Johnny Diamond and...you," he finally muttered.

"It is."

"I don't know why this guy came in here and robbed Linda and then knocked her around, but he was probably hoping to find you here, and then covered his tracks."

"He didn't even cover his tracks."

Cole stopped pacing like a caged animal and stationed himself in front of her. "How do you know?"

"Linda told me."

"Linda told you what?" His green eyes narrowed to slits, making him look like a dangerous jungle cat. "She could barely speak and then passed out."

"She whispered to me, Cole. She told me the man was trying to get information about me. She told me she stuck with my story."

"Oh, God." He spanned his forehead with one hand

and massaged his temples. "He must've demanded answers and then punched her when he didn't get the ones he wanted. Miserable coward."

"This has to end. Everything and everyone I touch is getting destroyed."

"Wait. So Linda knew you weren't telling the truth all this time?"

"I guess she must've suspected something was off. Maybe it was when I thought someone had searched my place."

. "She turned out to be a loyal friend."

"Too loyal." Caroline's cell phone buzzed and she pulled it from her pocket. The number on the display didn't even send terror into her heart like she'd thought it would. "Hello."

"Ms. Johnson, this is Detective Rowan with Clallam County Homicide. We're ready to take your prints now at the Port Angeles Police Department. Can you come in this afternoon?"

"I'll be there."

COLE GLANCED SIDEWAYS at Caroline. She'd been so quiet since leaving Timberline Treasures, blaming herself for everything, no doubt.

She'd called the hospital before they left for Port Angeles, and the nurse on duty told her Linda had some swelling on the brain and they were keeping her in a coma for now, but that she was out of immediate danger.

At least the thug who'd beat up Linda must know by now that Caroline wouldn't or couldn't spill the beans about whatever they were afraid of. If they wanted Diamond's money back from Caroline, they were out of luck. The DEA had it now.

"We're almost there. Are you ready?" Cole squeezed her knee and it bounced under his touch.

"I am ready. What's the plan?"

"We'll walk in and get you fingerprinted. Then they'll run them to verify your identity, which can take about thirty minutes."

"They're not going to come back to a Caroline Johnson, so then what?"

"If you have a criminal record, I'll step in at that point and tell them that you're working with the DEA. Then we'll research everything there is to know about your real identity before I...bring you in."

Her lips puckered for a soft whistle. "And what happens if the prints come back for someone who *doesn't* have a criminal record—but the name isn't Caroline Johnson?"

"Again, I'll step in and make up some plausible story. Even if you weren't a criminal in your other life, technically it's illegal to give a false name to the police, but I can smooth that over for you."

She traced the knuckles of his hand, still on her knee. "You've done that a lot, Cole. Thanks."

"And once we find out you don't have a criminal past, I'm going to get you the best psychiatrist in the world and you're going to get better."

"Then I'll help you figure out the connection between Johnny Diamond, Rocky Whitecotton and the Timberline Trio."

The police station came into view. Caroline's posture stiffened and she licked her lips.

She jumped out of the car and made a beeline for the station, staring straight ahead, placing one foot in front of the other as if afraid to veer off course.

Cole took a few long strides to catch up with her and opened the door of the facility, placing a steadying hand on Caroline's back. The Port Angeles station was small, as befitted a small town. Detective Rowan from the county wasn't going to be here, but the Port Angeles cops were under orders to email the results to him immediately.

Cole might have to make his case for Caroline to Rowan instead of the small-town cops.

The officer at the front counter looked up. "Can I help you?"

Caroline shook off Cole's hand and stepped up to the window. "I'm Caroline Johnson. I found Dr. Jules Shipman's body and I'm here to get fingerprinted, since I didn't have any ID on me—and still don't."

"Oh, right. Officer Farella is expecting you." He left the front desk and ducked into the back, with another officer trailing him.

Another man opened the door on the side. "Come on back, Ms. Johnson. I'm Officer Farella. I'll be doing the honors today." He extended his hand and Caroline shook it.

Farella reached past Caroline, hand outstretched. "You must be Agent Pierson with the DEA, right?"

"Good to meet you." Cole shook the other man's hand, sizing him up. Didn't seem like a hard-ass that would play hardball, but you never knew.

"Dr. Shipman's murder isn't something the DEA is interested in, is it?"

"Can't say right now. You understand."

"Sure, sure." Farella swept his arm to the side, indicating a cubicle with a table, scanner and computer inside. "Ms. Johnson, after you. Have a seat in front of the scanner."

Cole pulled out the chair for her and she perched on the edge of it, eyeing the machine.

"You've probably never had this done before, ma'am, but it works just like a scanner. We'll do one finger at a time and then your palms."

Caroline followed Farella's instructions, the muscles

in her face strained and tight, her cheekbones protruding sharply.

When he finished, he entered a code and pressed some buttons. "This computer will send your prints automatically to the Washington State Department of Justice, which is connected to the national database. It takes about half an hour. We have some coffee here, but the stuff next door at the Coffee Grinder is a lot better, and I have Ms. Johnson's cell phone number so I can call when we have a match."

"Thanks, we'll wait next door." Cole helped Caroline, who seemed incapable of moving, to her feet and led her out of the station.

Once on the sidewalk, she collapsed against him. "I'm so nervous."

"Then you probably don't need any caffeine. Do you want some decaf tea instead or something else?"

"Tea is fine." She reached for her phone. "I'm going to call the hospital to check on Linda's condition."

While he ordered a tea for her and a coffee for himself, Caroline found a table and got on her phone. She'd ended the call before he made it to the table, a cup in each hand.

"How's she doing? Out of the coma yet?"

"Not yet, but it's just a precaution at this point due to her age. They think she's going to pull out of it just fine."

"That's a relief. We're almost at the end of the line. We're going to have answers."

"*I'm* almost at the end of the line."

He drew a circle on the inside of her wrist with the tip of his finger. "I'll do whatever I can for you."

She dredged her tea bag through the steaming water. "And I'll do whatever I can for you, to make up for everything—the secrets, the lies."

"You have amnesia. I think that excuses a lot."

"You know one thing I do remember?"

He hunched forward and she held up her finger. "About the immediate past, not my past life."

"Yeah?"

"The description that Linda gave of her attacker sort of matches the description of a man I saw in Dr. Shipman's office—the only person I saw in Dr. Shipman's office. He was coming in as I was leaving my first appointment."

"Dark-complected Caucasian with long hair?"

"Yes, only his hair wasn't in a ponytail. It was loose and kind of scraggly. He kept his head down, so I didn't get a look at his face."

"You should report that to the deputies in Timberline."

"I think I have a lot to report to a lot of deputies and detectives and DEA agents."

Cole checked his phone with a frown. "It's been thirty-five minutes."

Her blue eyes brightened. "That's encouraging. If I were on the FBI's most-wanted list, you'd think the Port Angeles police would be storming this place with guns blazing."

"Farella probably got busy and hasn't checked the computer lately." Cole stood up and held out his hand. "Are you ready to meet your fate?"

"As long as you're by my side." She put her palm in his. "Bring it on."

He kept hold of her hand as they walked back to the station. His next hold on her might be completely different. As they got to the door, he dropped it—didn't want Farella to think there was anything more between them.

They walked up to the window and Farella came from the back, a piece of paper clutched in his hand and creases lining his face.

"Ma'am, we have a problem."

Cole swore under his breath as Caroline laced her fingers in front of her.

She cleared her throat. "What's the problem, Officer Farella?"

"There are no fingerprint records for you in the state of Washington—or anywhere else in the nation. It's like you don't even exist."

Chapter Seventeen

Caroline sagged against Cole's side as relief flooded her senses. She wasn't a criminal. She wouldn't be going to jail or some psychiatric facility today.

"Th-that's odd, I guess."

"That *is* unusual." Cole rubbed his chin as if this were some great mystery.

"Would I have fingerprints on file if I never committed a crime or held some job where I needed to be fingerprinted?"

Farella spread his hands. "Never had anything notarized? Never bought property? Some states even require fingerprints on the application for driver's licenses. It's just very unusual today for someone to have no fingerprints on file. Are you sure you're not in a witness-protection program?"

His words punched her in the gut, and Caroline grabbed Cole's sleeve and sucked in a quick breath.

Farella chuckled, glancing from her face to Cole's. "I was just kidding…I think."

"What next?" Cole asked. "You'll need to report this to Detective Rowan."

"Yeah, I'll send him the results and he can check your prints against the ones we took in the office to rule them out. We may have a lead on the killer, anyway."

"Can you reveal anything?"

"Not much. A witness saw a man in the alley behind Dr. Shipman's office around the time of the murder. We're working with that person now."

"Is that it for me?" Caroline shoved her nervous hands in her pockets.

"That's it for now—at least we know you're not some criminal on the run." Farella chuckled again and Caroline laughed along with him with giddy abandon.

She held up her cell phone. "Well, you and Detective Rowan have my number if you need anything else."

"We probably will. When we catch this guy we'll have a trial, if he doesn't plead out, and you'll most likely be called as a witness." Farella shook his finger in her face. "Let's just hope you have your ID by then."

"God, I hope so."

She and Cole left the station silently and she kept her lips sealed until they got to his rental car. Once she closed the door, she let out a scream that bounced off the windows.

Cole covered his ears. "You really are a mystery woman."

"But I'm not a criminal, right?" She grabbed his arm, her fingers sinking into the slick material of his jacket. "If I were, my fingerprints would've been in the system."

Chewing on his bottom lip, Cole adjusted the rearview mirror, checking for tails like he always did. "I don't want to rain on your parade, but it just means you were never *arrested* for a crime. It doesn't mean you never committed one."

She slumped in her seat. "You still believe I was involved in some criminal activity with Johnny Diamond?"

"No, just doing a reality check."

"Well, in my reality, as slim as that is, I'm clear. Now I just have to discover who I am and what I was doing with Diamond." She took his hand. "Can you help me?

I'm officially turning myself in to the DEA. I'll make a statement and everything. I'll repeat for the record all I know about my time with Johnny at the Stardust Motel, and you can get someone to pick my brain apart, hypnotize me or whatever it takes to bring back my memories."

He brought her hand to his lips and kissed it. "Sounds like a plan."

"I want to visit Linda in the hospital. Can you take me there? When she's better, I'm going to tell her everything. Once I'm officially in your custody, Diamond's associates will figure any drug money I took is in the hands of the DEA. They won't be able to get to me and it'll be worthless for them to hurt anyone else close to me."

"I'll take you to the hospital, but I'll wait there with you."

"Do you still think I'm going to make a run for it? I'd just be putting myself in further danger if I did."

"I'm not worried about that, but until you're safely in our custody, Diamond's cohorts will be out to get you."

They drove back to Timberline and Caroline peppered him with questions about the fingerprints. "Is it really that unusual for someone not to have prints in the national database?"

"These days, it is. For adults, anyway." He drummed his thumbs on the steering wheel. "Caroline, do you think it's possible that you lived in Mexico? The Chihuahua Desert, the Spanish speaking?"

A spike of fear pounded her poor, addled brain. "If I had been living in Mexico, would that explain why I have no fingerprints on file in the US?"

"It could."

She turned to stare out at the green, watery landscape flying by.

It seemed that all roads led to Mexico.

LINDA'S DOCTORS HAD moved her to a room in the hospital next to the emergency facility. Cole drove to the main hospital and left the car in the parking structure.

As they stood in front of the elevator, he said, "I'm going to walk you up to Linda's floor, and then I'm going to make a few calls. I'll notify the DEA office in San Diego about you. They'll want you to come in right away."

"As soon as I get Linda's friends on board to take care of her while I'm gone. But how am I going to get on an airplane without a driver's license?"

"The DEA will handle everything."

They rode the elevator up to Linda's floor and Caroline approached the nurses' station. "I'm Caroline Johnson. I'm here to see Linda Gunderson. The doctors okayed it over the phone."

The nurse clicked her keyboard, and Caroline looked over her shoulder at Cole, who was against the wall by the stairwell, on his phone.

"You can go right ahead, Ms. Johnson. She's in room 528. She's sharing, so please don't disturb the other occupant."

"Thanks." Caroline waved to Cole to get his attention, and then pointed down the hallway. He nodded.

Her low-heeled boots clicked on the linoleum as she passed every room, checking the number. She found Linda's room at the end of the hall and pushed open the door.

Her heart skipped a beat when she saw the monitors and tubes hooked up to her friend. She eased into the plastic chair next to the bed and took Linda's hand. "Hang in there, Linda. I'm going to tell you everything when you come out of this."

The patient on the other side of the curtain coughed.

As Caroline held Linda's hand, the cell phone in her

pocket buzzed. She hoped the police hadn't suddenly discovered something about her fingerprints.

She pulled the phone out and screwed up her mouth as she glanced at Linda's number coming through. How was Linda calling from her phone when she was lying in a coma in this bed? Maybe one of her friends had gotten hold of Linda's cell.

"Hello?"

"You listen and you listen good. Your little game is over…*Caroline*. You're coming back with us right now and you're handing over all of Johnny's money—*our* money."

The harsh voice grated against her ear and the phone almost slipped from her grip.

"I don't know who you are. I don't know who any of you are. I lost my memory when Johnny threw me across the room. Don't you get it?"

"But you remember that Johnny threw you across the room?"

"That and that he tried to kill me."

"He wasn't trying to kill you, just bring you back. That's all we want. Nobody's going to hurt you. Don't you want to be with your family again?"

A sob rose in her throat. She wanted a family more than anything. She wanted an identity more than anything— just not her real one. "It's too late. I'm turning myself in to the DEA."

The man swore. "Is that who that cop is? He's DEA?"

"Yes, and he knows everything that I know, and I'm going to get my memory back and he's going to know even more. H-he's standing right here listening to everything I say."

The man laughed, which ended in a cough. "You're in a hospital room alone with a comatose patient right now."

Caroline jumped from the chair and glanced over her shoulder. "You're watching me?"

"How's your friend, the shop owner?"

A chill dripped down her spine. "She's hurt, thanks to you."

"She's gonna be hurting a lot more if you don't do what I tell you to do. Got it? That one, the DEA agent once we figure out who he is—and we will—and your sister. You remember your sister, don't you? Or maybe you don't. She's still in Mexico with her family, but we can get to all of them if you don't come with me now."

A sister? She had a sister? Her head began to throb and she massaged the base of her skull. "What do you want?"

"Told you. We want you to come home. Once you regain your memory, you'll want to come home, too."

"Apparently not. Why was I on the run in the first place? Because that's why I was with Johnny, wasn't it. You or Rocky sent him."

Silence stretched on the other end of the line and then the man said, "So you remember Rocky?"

"N-no. I just saw his text to Johnny, after Johnny was dead."

"Does that DEA agent know about Rocky?"

"No."

"I thought you told him everything?"

"Not everything, just that I'd been with Johnny Diamond when he died and that I had amnesia."

"Give him the slip and meet me here."

"I—I can't do that."

"Do it, or everyone you care about is going to pay the price. We just attached another tracker to his car, so if you tell him and he follows you, we'll know. We're also checking your phone when you get here, so don't even think about texting or calling him, or we'll start with your sister's kid."

Caroline clutched a hand to her throat. "How do I know

you're telling the truth? How do I know I even have a sister?"

"I guess you'll find out when you get your memory back—but it'll be too late then."

Closing her eyes, she said, "Okay, I'll meet you, but I don't have a car. Where am I going and how will I get there?"

"Get down to the loading dock of the hospital. You can get there by taking the elevator to the basement level and exiting the door to the right. You don't have to go past the nurses' station to do it. There will be a car waiting for you. Do *not* try to get a message to the DEA agent. We'll be watching and you'll be sorry."

"I'll be there."

"Now." He ended the call.

She glanced at the curtain dividing the beds. How could she get a message to Cole? And what message would she leave? She didn't know who the caller was or where she was going. Had no description of the car, either.

She took two steps to the curtain and yanked it aside, meeting the wide-eyed gaze of the elderly man in the bed. "When a guy comes in here looking for me—and he will come looking for me—tell him I went back to Mexico."

COLE STOPPED TOSSING his phone from hand to hand and checked the time. How much time did Caroline need with a woman in a coma?

He pushed himself off the wall and sauntered to the nurses' station. "My friend's been in with Linda Gunderson for a long time. Is it okay if I go back and get her?"

"Room 528."

"Thanks."

He checked the room numbers as he walked down the hall. When he reached 528, he opened the door and poked his head inside. The machines connected to Linda hissed and beeped, but Caroline wasn't at her bedside.

He stepped inside, his heart thumping uncomfortably in his chest. She couldn't have left already. He'd been at the nurses' station the whole time. Calling her name, he headed toward the open door of the bathroom and leaned into the small, empty room.

She'd bolted.

"Excuse me." A faint voice floated from the other side of the curtain, and Cole spun around and pulled it back.

An elderly gentleman raised his hand. "She left and she told me to tell you something."

A pulse thudded in Cole's temple. "The woman visiting next door? What did she say?"

"She went back to Mexico."

Cole collapsed in the chair next to the man's bed, pinching the bridge of his nose. "What else did she say?"

"Just that. She came on my side of the room and told me a man would be looking for her and to tell him that she was going to Mexico."

Cole punched his fist into his palm. He'd allowed her to scam him. Had she remembered everything and decided she liked that life better than this one? Did she ever really have amnesia? She couldn't have faked all those emotions...could she?

"That was after her phone call."

Cole's head jerked up. "Phone call?"

The old man pointed a crooked finger at Linda's bed. "She was talking on the phone before she came over here. Crazy talk."

"What kind of crazy talk?"

"Someone trying to kill her. Diamonds. The DEA. Crazy stuff. When she whipped back the curtain and told me to tell you she was going to Mexico, that confirmed it. Crazy."

They'd gotten to her. Cole dragged his hands through his hair. But how had they convinced her to go with them? And where had they taken her?

"Did you hear anything else from the phone call? A place? A name?"

"The only name I remember is Johnny. That's all I got out of it. I didn't hear her mention the name of any place except Mexico, which she said to me after the phone call."

Cole gripped the man's frail hand. "Thanks. You don't know how much you just helped me."

"I hope she's okay. Real pretty gal, but sad eyes."

"She'll be okay."

And he'd go to hell and back to make sure of it.

He left the room and looked up and down the hallway. An exit sign glowed green next to a heavy door. He strode toward it and pushed against the metal bar. It opened onto a stairwell.

He should've checked out the floor before allowing her to go to Linda's room herself. Cole jogged down the stairs until he reached the bottom floor and burst through the final door.

He found himself on a loading dock, and he approached a guy with a clipboard, doing inventory of some boxes.

"Did you see a woman come out this way recently?" As the man's face began to close down, Cole pulled out his badge.

"I didn't, but I just stepped out here." He jerked his thumb to his right. "Try down there. Those two trucks are almost done unloading."

"Thanks." Cole moved to the next truck and flashed his badge at the man signing for a delivery. "Did you see a woman come out of that door in the past fifteen minutes? Average height, long brown hair, slim, black leather jacket and boots?"

The man eyed the badge, ripped off a copy of the form he was signing and handed it to the truck driver. "Yeah, I saw her."

"What did she do? Where'd she go?"

"When she walked down the steps, a car flashed its lights at her and she got in."

"What kind of car? Did you see who was in it?" Cole tipped his head back and scanned the overhang of the loading dock.

"Small, black compact. I didn't see who was in it. Just noticed because usually people don't come out of the hospital this way to get picked up."

"Are there cameras out here?"

"Not yet, but the hospital's working on it."

"Did you see what direction the car went?"

"Can't see from here which way he turned. Just went up to the alley that leads to the side street."

"Thanks." How was he going to track a small, black compact? No license plate. No description of the driver. Cole felt like punching something, or someone.

He made a turn to go back to the front of the hospital and the parking structure when someone yelled behind him. "Hey!"

He pivoted toward the voice, and a guy standing next to the first man he'd talked to waved his arms at him. Cole backtracked.

"Yeah?"

"You're a cop or something?"

"DEA. Why?"

"Joey here told me you were asking about a woman down here in the last half hour."

"That's right. Did you see her get into the car? Do you have any information about the car?"

"I saw her come out of the hospital but I didn't see no car."

"Oh, okay, thanks." Cole's stomach sank. *Back to square one.*

"But you aren't the only one looking for her."

"Oh? Who else?"

"Some local boy, Jason Foster."

"Jason Foster? Quileute? Dating that waitress at Sutter's?"

"That's the one. He was all agro down here, asking me if I saw some chick, where she went. Man, I told that dude if he was getting rid of Chloe to let me know 'cuz I always had a thing for her, you know?"

"What did he do after that?"

"Took off on his Harley."

"Thanks. I appreciate the heads-up."

What did Jason have to do with all this? He'd shown up at the emergency room with a broken hand the night Linda got sick. Cole had seen Jason earlier that same night hightailing it out of Sutter's back entrance, worried and preoccupied.

Cole raced to his car and drove into town. He pulled across the street from Sutter's and went into the restaurant, which was just getting ready for the dinner crowd.

He spied Chloe talking to Bud at the bar and wiping down menus, but better yet, he saw Jason nursing a beer at the end of the bar. As Cole walked toward him, Jason glanced up.

Then he left his half-full beer glass and headed for the back door.

"Jason!" Cole started moving faster, but the younger man took off at a sprint, bursting from the restaurant.

Cole caught him before he got to his bike, and tackled him. Panting heavily, he jerked Jason's arm behind his back. "What do you know about Caroline Johnson? Why were you looking for her?"

"Oww." Jason twisted in Cole's grasp. "I was trying to save her, man."

"Save her from whom? Where is she?"

"From Rocky Whitecotton. They have her at the Kennedy cabin. I—I think they're gonna kill her, man."

THE MAN WITH the tan, leathery skin prodded her in the back with his gun. "We don't go through the front door."

She tripped as she walked around the side of the rustic cabin set practically in the middle of the woods. Did she know this place? Images rushed at her from all sides. Different images from before—lush greenery replaced the arid desert. She didn't have her family with her, but she wanted them.

The man, Vic, knocked on the door in some kind of code, and a lock clicked from inside.

A terrible fear descended on her and she stumbled backward. She didn't want to go inside. She didn't want to see the person on the other side of that door. It was happening again. He would take her, take her away from all her happiness.

The door opened and a dark eye appeared at the crack.

She covered her mouth. "No, no."

Then the door swung open and Vic pushed her inside and she fell on her hands and knees at the feet of another man. She tipped her head back and stared into the lined face of Rocky Whitecotton.

The man who'd kidnapped her twenty-five years ago.

Chapter Eighteen

Rocky smirked. "You remember, don't you? You even remember what you'd forgotten until last year, when you went snooping around and discovered the truth about your real identity."

She got to her feet and faced him, squaring her shoulders. "That my real name is Heather Brice, and you kidnapped me and Kayla Rush and Stevie Carson…and others."

"The three of you were young enough, especially you, that you forgot all about your old lives and old names. You were happy enough at the commune, weren't you?"

"Until we found out about the drug dealing, the crime, the murders."

"We only murdered our enemies, and I was happy to let you all leave when you discovered our…business and disapproved. Your sister has a happy life in Mexico City with her husband and children."

"Because she doesn't know she's really Kayla Rush, has a twin and was snatched from her real family when she was five years old."

"And you wouldn't know that either if you hadn't gone poking around. You were studying to be a nurse. You gave up your lifelong dream to make some crazy journey to Timberline to find yourself. I couldn't let you do it, Meadow."

"My name's Heather."

"You've been Meadow Castillo longer than you've been Heather, and definitely longer than you've been Caroline Johnson."

"Did you send Johnny Diamond to kill me?"

"Just to bring you back home. He was an idiot. He wasn't supposed to use cyanide, just a little something to knock you out, and he ended up killing himself—and losing our drugs and money." Rocky snapped his fingers. "Where's the money?"

"I don't have any money. The DEA played you when they released the information about all of Johnny's money being missing. I took a small amount to make a start somewhere, and I don't even have that."

His dark eyes narrowed and glittered dangerously. "You're quite cozy with the DEA now, aren't you?"

She shrugged. "They don't know anything because I didn't know anything. They certainly don't know you're here."

"That's supposed to make me feel better? I gathered children from five different states and the kidnappings were never linked. Escaped to Mexico with my new family to start my own tribe of people, and supported my family through my enterprises. I dropped off the radar. The FBI never had a clue where I went and neither did those idiot Quileute who'd banished me from the reservation." He leveled a finger at her. "And you made me come back, put my commune in danger, just to search for a family who's forgotten all about you."

James Brice's sad face flashed across her mind, and his comment that his parents never spoke of the kidnapping and couldn't bring themselves to return to Timberline to sell the last of their property here echoed in her brain.

He was her brother. His instincts had been right. She had a family, and she wanted to get back to them.

She shrugged. "Then let's just go. I suppose you snuck across the border, undetected, and we'll have to return to Mexico the same way. I have no ID, no passport."

"What happened to it? When reports first started coming back from Vic here that you had amnesia, I couldn't figure out why you just didn't look at your passport."

"Johnny must've done something with my purse and everything in it. It was nowhere to be found. I had nothing."

Rocky slapped Vic on the back. "I should've sent you to find Meadow. You did a better job than Johnny."

She stepped back. "He murdered my therapist. He assaulted my friend."

"Outsiders, Meadow. Come back with us now and forget this life. You have your brothers and sisters, your nursing studies."

"Not River…or Stevie." Her nose tingled and she swiped at it.

"River died in that motorcycle accident. Nothing we could do about it."

"Is that really what happened, or did he discover that he was really Stevie Carson and had been ripped from his real family?"

"There you go again." Rocky stroked his beard. "Are you going to come home to Mexico and forget all this, or…?"

"Or what? You're going to kill me like you killed Stevie? How many of us are you going to kill? River and I won't be the last to question and figure out how we came to be part of your isolated commune at the edge of Copper Canyon in Mexico."

"I'm hoping the rest will turn out like Summer. She's content with her little family."

"That's because you've always intimidated her, and she

was lucky enough to get away from you when she fell in love with Gerardo.".

"I'll forgive you everything, Meadow—our drugs and money that we lost, cozying up to the DEA and even dragging me back here from my compound. Come home now and don't breathe a word of any of this to anyone again."

A pounding at the back door made all of them jump, and her heart did a somersault. Had Cole found her somehow? She knew she could never return to Mexico with Rocky. Those children at the compound, her brothers and sisters, all had blood brothers and sisters and parents who were devastated by their loss.

She had to make everyone whole again, had to make herself whole.

Rocky gestured for Vic to investigate the knock, and Vic crawled across the floor and peeked up through the blinds. "It's Jason."

She folded her arms across her midsection. Why was Chloe's boyfriend here?

Rocky was wondering the same thing. "What is that loser doing here?" He nodded. "Get the door."

During her entire conversation with Rocky, Vic had kept his gun pointed at her. Now he held it in front of him as he opened the door for Jason, and she shuffled a few steps toward the front door. Maybe she could make a run for it while he was occupied with him.

Vic growled. "What the hell do you want? We don't need no more supplies. We're heading out tomorrow."

"Jason?" She hugged herself. "What are you doing here?"

"I—I've been helping Rocky. I'm the one who tried to poison you in Sutter's that night. Sorry, but Rocky's like family to me." Jason pulled the door closed behind him and walked across the room toward Rocky. "My uncle Danny worked with him."

Rocky snorted. "Danny turned out to be worthless, just like you. Sent him here to do a job and he ended up blowing the whole cover off my connection with the Lords of Chaos. It's Danny's fault the FBI fingered me as the catalyst behind the Timberline Trio. Now, what do you want?"

"I'm here to warn you. I heard the FBI knows you're here. You'd better make a move tonight." He reached for the front doorknob, and Vic lunged for him.

"What are you doing?"

The back door crashed open and Cole filled the frame, pointing his weapon right at Rocky's head. "Drop the gun, Vic, or your boss dies."

Vic grabbed Jason around the neck. "I'll shoot this little weasel right here and now."

"Get down, Caroline."

She dropped to the floor and scooted out of the way of the two weapons at cross purposes.

"It's over. I called the FBI and the sheriff's department on my way here. You're going to be surrounded in a matter of minutes."

Rocky reached for his waistband and she screamed. "He has a gun."

Before Cole could get a shot off, Rocky thrust the gun beneath his chin and blew his brains out.

He fell to the floor in front of her, and it all ended the way it had begun.

She was staring into the eyes of another dead man.

Epilogue

The press conference ended, and Heather retreated to the hotel banquet room that had served as a refuge for the families. Her eyes misted over as she surveyed the room filled with joyous children and their parents.

Her own parents, Patty and Charlie, and her brother, James, hovered around her as if they thought she'd suddenly disappear again.

Her mother hugged her for the thousandth time since they'd reunited. "I just can't believe how this all worked out. It's an incredible story."

"What's incredible is how James recognized me after all these years."

"I can't tell you how shocked I was when I found out you were Linda Gunderson's cousin and not my sister. I was so sure."

"And you were right. Now I really feel guilty for slamming you against the car." Cole slapped James on the back as he shook his hand.

Her father gripped Cole's shoulder. "In the end, you're the one who rescued Heather, so we can forgive anything that came before."

Linda, fully recovered from the beating, squeezed Heather's arm. "You should've told me the whole story, Heather. Maybe I could've helped you figure out who you were sooner."

"You did enough, Linda. Covering for me resulted in a beating and a poisoning. You need to go away with Louise the next time she takes a cruise."

The host of the TV show *Cold Case Chronicles* joined their group with her FBI boyfriend, Duke Harper, in tow. "Mr. and Mrs. Brice? I'm Beth St. Regis."

Mom smiled and nodded. "I watch your show."

"Did your daughter tell you that I'm going to be doing a special on the Timberline Trio? Happily, it won't be a cold case anymore."

Dad put his arm around Mom. "She told us, Ms. St. Regis, but we're not interested in the spotlight."

"I understand completely. You don't even have to appear on camera, but could I get some contact information for you?"

"Beth." Agent Harper rolled his eyes. "You need to respect their privacy."

"What do you think, Heather?" Her father hugged her close.

"I think it's an important story, and I'm sure Beth will do a great job. I've already been talking to her."

Beth mouthed a thank-you.

"I don't see the harm, Dad." James smiled at Beth. "Are you at that table over there?"

Her family wandered away with Beth, and Heather grinned at Cole. "She can get anyone talking."

A man with black hair and an intense stare limped across the room toward them, a beautiful Native American woman hanging on to his arm.

"Heather? I'm Jim Kennedy, and this is Scarlett Easton. I just wanted to personally apologize to you for the role my father played in the kidnappings."

"Oh, please. No apology is necessary." She gestured to Cole. "This is Cole Pierson with the DEA."

Cole shook Jim's hand. "I heard the story about how

you and Scarlett dug into the case and made the connection between Rocky and the Lords of Chaos. You're the ones who put the FBI on Rocky's trail and got him on our radar."

Cole turned to Scarlett. "And your cousin Jason helped me stop Rocky."

Heather said, "I don't know if I would've been able to put the final pieces of the puzzle together if I hadn't read an online article about the two of you and the work you did."

Scarlett hugged her in a warm embrace. "I'm so glad you found your way back home, and look at all these people you've been able to reunite with their families."

"You know, Jim, we all lived with Rocky for years and looked at him as a father figure," Heather murmured. "I knew even as a child that he was a bad person, but as children we're trapped. We don't have many choices, but it sounds like you made the right ones."

"Yeah, and some of us are lucky enough to find our real families." He put his arm around Scarlett and kissed the side of her head. "If any of those kids, your commune brothers and sisters, need help coping, give me a call. I work with vets who have PTSD and I have a lot of referrals."

"I'll keep that in mind."

When they left, Cole cranked his head from side to side. "This is turning into quite a party. Even the Timberline sheriffs and the FBI are having a good time."

Heather tugged on his sleeve. "You haven't met Summer—I mean Kayla—yet. Here she comes with her twin."

Kendall Rush wrapped Heather in a bear hug. "I am so grateful to you for bringing my sister back to me."

Kayla smiled shyly. "Now I have two sisters, because you'll always be my sister, Meadow. I'm sorry—Heather."

She smiled. "Cole, this is my sister, Kayla, and her husband, Gerardo."

Everyone shook hands, and remembering all the different names was getting to be a challenge.

Kendall introduced her fiancé, Cooper Sloane.

As Cole shook his hand, he said, "The Timberline Sheriff's Department still talks about you—best sheriff the town ever had. Any chance you'll come back?"

"Not a chance. Neither my fiancée nor my daughter can take the rain. We'll be staying in Phoenix."

Kendall looked around the room. "This is such a happy occasion, except we're missing someone. Did Stevie have a good life?"

"Rocky, as much as he tore apart other families, did it all to establish his own tribe, as he called us," Heather answered. "Despite his criminal activities, he treated us all with kindness. It was a commune—we were isolated and didn't have a lot of modern conveniences, but we learned to depend on each other and we all had our jobs. River, as we knew him, loved working with machinery. He loved dirt bikes and motorcycles. I'd say he was happy, wouldn't you, Summer?"

"I think he was, as much as any of us were."

Kendall put her arm around her twin's waist. "I know you and Gerardo have a life in Mexico, but we're going to visit as soon as we can and you have to come up for our wedding."

As the crowd began to thin and her parents retired to their hotel room with James, Heather turned to Cole.

"For one terrifying week, I didn't have a name or a family or an identity. Now I have three names, more family than I can visit in twenty Christmases and I know who I am."

"Quite a turnaround."

"But through all the darkness, I had one shining light—you."

"I was your shining light, really? Because I was pretty sure you couldn't wait for me to leave Timberline."

She grabbed the lapels of his jacket. "That's just because I didn't know if you were a drug dealer out to kill me or a cop out to arrest me, and you turned into my white knight out to save me."

Cupping her face with his hand, he whispered, "Now you just have too much damned family around. How am I ever going to get you alone again, Caroline, Meadow, Heather?"

"I'll tell you what, *señor*. I have to go down to Mexico to take care of some business. I'm sure you can make up some reason why you need to be down there. We could sneak away, drink tequila, take long siestas.

He nuzzled her ear. "Do we really have to take a nap during the siesta, or can we do…other things?"

"Oh, we can do other things, but will all the excitement go out of it for you now that I'm no longer a woman of mystery?"

"I don't want a woman of mystery. I plan to find out every little detail about you, but don't leave me if I happen to call out Caroline in the throes of passion."

"Leave you, Cole Pierson? Never going to happen."

Then he kissed her and she knew exactly who she was.

* * * * *

Give a 12 month subscription to a friend today!

Call Customer Services
0844 844 1358*

or visit
millsandboon.co.uk/subscriptions